ALSO BY BEN SCHOTT

Jeeves & The King of Clubs

Schott's Original Miscellany
Schott's Food & Drink Miscellany
Schott's Sporting, Gaming, & Idling Miscellany
Schott's Quintessential Miscellany

Schott's Almanac (2006–2011)

Schottenfreude: German Words for the Human Condition

To write one homage to P. G. Wodehouse may be regarded as staggering good fortune – to write a sequel is surely fortune leafed in gold.

I am again indebted to Sir Edward Cazalet and the Wodehouse Estate for their gracious permission to take a second bite at the plum of comic fiction.

Jeeves & The Leap of Faith picks up from where *Jeeves & The King of Clubs* left off, but both books merely bask in the sunlit uplands of The Master's genius, and it is to his timeless oeuvre that I direct any and all new readers.

Sean O'Casey once attempted to dismiss P. G. Wodehouse as 'literature's performing flea' – to which our hero replied: 'I believe he meant to be complimentary, for all the performing fleas I have met have impressed me with their sterling artistry and that indefinable something which makes the good trouper.'

Plum was certainly a trouper, and undoubtedly an artist of sterling brilliance – if he was also a performing flea then I am truly honoured to be a lesser flea upon his back.

Pip pip!

BEN SCHOTT

x 2020

Jeeves & The Leap of Faith

MIDNIGHT

'Is it safe?'

    'No, sir.'

    'How far do you think it is, across?'

    'Just under seven feet, sir.'

    'And down?'

    'Eighty-five feet, sir.'

    'That pavement looks dashed unforgiving.'

    'Indeed, sir.'

    'And even from here those railings seem fearfully pointed.'

    'They do conclude at a penetrating apex, sir.'

    'So, all in all, you wouldn't risk it?'

    'Well, sir, not being in your shoes, literally or metaphorically—'

    'Is this really the time for metaphors?'

Dash it all – it's no good.

    I realise that any Modern Novel worth its salt should be fizzing with innovation – plunging *in medias whatsit* with dramatic flashbacks, artful foreshadowing, and agile leaps of narrative pep. But it's long been the firm belief of Bertram W. Wooster that if a tale's worth telling, it's worth telling well: with a zippy beginning, a comical middle, and a cliff-hanging end – in that order, mind – lingering only when strictly necessary to essay such poetic asides as the echoing tick of a grandfather clock, or an enchanting moonlit vista.

So, to begin at the beginning.

In the beginning was the word, and the word was with . . .

I.

MONDAY

'Jeeves!' I hollered, springing through the timber of 3A Berkeley Mansions.

'Good evening, sir,' my man replied, emerging, as is his habit, from out of the jungle mists.

'We've cracked it!'

'Sir?'

'The crossword!'

'Very good, sir.'

'The *Times* crossword!'

'I was not aware the *Sporting Times* carried a crossword, sir.'

'*The Times*, Jeeves.'

'I see, sir.' He paused. 'When you say "we", sir?'

'We means me – plus the massed ranks of the membership committee. I don't think I've seen that rabble so intently focused since we disguised Bingo Little as a postman to steal Graydon Hogg's mail.'

'I recall that episode keenly, sir.'

We both stared down at the carpet in sombre reflection.

'*Anyway*, I've spent a long and arduous luncheon deciphering this.' I lifted the paper aloft.

He looked surprised. 'The entire crossword, sir?'

'Heavens no! Just Fourteen Down.'

'LOOT, sir?'

'You've done it?'

'Yes, sir.'

'The whole bally box?'

'Naturally, sir. I find it an engaging way to pass the time while your eggs are boiling, or your bath is running. Whichever is the shorter.'

'And you *memorise* them?'

'That would imply too active an effort, sir, though I tend to recall them for a week or so.'

This all seemed highly unlikely, even for one with so capacious a hat size, and so I unfolded the paper and put him to the test.

'Seven Down: *Death before a hundred is dry enough.*'

'DEMI-SEC, sir.'

'DEMISECSIR? Doesn't fit – doesn't even make sense.'

'Forgive me, sir. DEMI ... SEC ... sir.'

'Eh?'

'DEMISE – meaning *death* – before C – the Roman numeral for *a hundred* – giving DEMI-SEC – which is *dry enough.*'

'Like the champagne! Clever. All right, let's see. Twenty-three Across: *Exhaling very, very loudly during exercise.*'

'PFFFT, sir.'

'It's no use *pfft*ing, Jeeves, that's what it says here!'

'Forgive me, sir, you misapprehend. The answer is P-F-F-F-T.'

'How on earth do you fathom that?'

It was, according to Jeeves, embarrassingly simple: the musical term for *very, very loudly* is *fortississimo* – the abbreviation of which is *fff* – and this occurs *during* – that is to say, in the middle of – *exercise* – as represented by the abbreviation for physical training – *P.T.*

'Is P-F-F-F-T even a word?'

'A degree of latitude is commonly permitted with onomato-poeia, sir.'

'Is it now? What about Thirty-one Down: *Short dash to attempt admission*. Five letters.'

'Well, sir—'

'Hold your ponies! I'm determined to unriddle this Sphinx alone. But can you ensure they start delivering a second copy of *The Times*?'

'Very good, sir.' He brushed an invisible mote of dust from his sleeve. 'Incidentally, sir, the decorators are here.'

I groaned.

For several months Jeeves had been vexing me to upspiff my bed-room as part of an elaborate scheme of improvements to the rooms I call home. He is firmly of the opinion that the smell of fresh paint should never be far from one's nostrils, that carpeting should be as lush as forest moss, and that sofas should be chucked away after each and every sitting. I have, in more jaundiced moods, wondered if he's taking backhanders from the furniture department of Harrods.

'Is this vital, Jeeves? Might we not let sleeping rooms lie?'

'I could not recommend further delay, sir. The paintwork has seen better days, and the brocade is pilling most distressingly.'

He handed me the card of an outfit called Dicks & Rudge, and I followed him to my boudoir where two overalled painters were busy with measuring tapes, discordantly whistling 'Sonny Boy' like kettles competing to boil.

'Permit me to introduce, sir, Mr Fred Dicks and Mr Charles Rudge.'

Charlie wiped and extended his hand. 'Afternoon, chief. Nice gaff you've got 'ere.'

'I should coco,' nodded Fred. 'Very choice.'

'How long is this all going to take?' I said a little stiffly, irked that my inner sanctum was so densely populated.

'That depends, chief. Were you wanting paper or paint?'

'Paper.'

Charlie in-drew his breath with practised concern. 'Room this size?' He turned to Fred, and together they launched into the effortless cross-talk of Palladium patter acts.

'Furniture out ... '

   'Dust sheets up ... '

'Strip back ... '

   'Rub down ... '

'Sugar water ... '

   'Lining paper ... '

'Cornice and skirting ... '

   'Sockets and switches ... '

'Make good ... '

   'Furniture back ... '

Charlie shook his head. 'The thing is, guv, how long is your proverbial piece of string?'

Jeeves was having none of this transparently mercenary flim-flam. 'I estimate four days, sir. At the very limit.'

'Yeah,' conceded Fred, folding like a cheap tent, 'sounds doable.'

Calculating I could easily decamp to the Drones for such a spell with only minimal hardship, I nodded my grudging consent. 'Do you have any samples I might see?'

They did: six large pattern-books, ordered by colour and design, which had been carefully arranged on my bed.

Jeeves stepped forward. 'I have taken the liberty, sir, of inserting bookmarks at several suitable choices. All are appropriate for a room of this size and luminosity, and all would happily complement the existing furnishings.'

I flicked through Jeeves's suggestions without much joy:

Sarcoline Cartouche

Zinnober Diaper

Malachite Spandril

Jessamy Half-drop

'Is it just me, or do these all sound like unfortunate medical conditions?'

Fred and Charlie sniggered.

'Of those marked,' said Jeeves crisply, 'I especially commend the *Periwinkle Chevron*, which, if you will permit me, sir, combines delicacy with elegance.'

I studied said pattern.

'It's a little ... *dull*.'

'Should a bedroom be the locus of tumult, sir?'

Fred and Charlie laughed out loud.

'Furthermore, sir,' Jeeves rose above the cheap seats, 'the *Periwinkle Chevron* is really most soothing.'

There are chaps who defer to their domestics in every respect – from soft furnishings to selection of spouse – and while I usually resist such timid submission, I have, on rare occasions, yielded to Jeeves's whim on certain sartorial matters. Readers may recall footling contretemps concerning Etonian spats, Alpine hats, plus fours, a white mess-jacket with brass buttons, a cheerful pink necktie, a sprightly check suit, some soft-fronted evening shirts, and a pair of jazzy slippers in the tartan of Clan Wallace.

But if a line is to be drawn between master and servant, it is surely to be drawn at the threshold of one's personal, private bedroom.

'Are there any *other* patterns?' I enquired.

Charlie and Fred looked first at Jeeves, then at each other, and finally at me, before shrewdly concluding that I was the one with the chequebook and pen.

'Funny you should ask, boss.' Charlie withdrew from his satchel the sample book he'd clearly been instructed to conceal. 'There is this.'

Flicking through its pages, it was obvious why Jeeves had disapproved: pattern after pattern of sporting glory and Corinthian prowess – from schoolboy rugby and village cricket to country-house tennis and college croquet.

And then my eye fell on a gold-plated fizzer.

'This is more like it!' I held up a hunting scene replete with foxes, hounds, and horsemen in pink. 'What think you, Jeeves?'

'I think, sir, it would suit the saloon bar of a rural public house.'

'*Au Cointreau*. It is spirited and chipper, and will cheer me every morn.'

'If I might be permitted to disagree, sir, the *Periwinkle*—'

I'm afraid to say I rather gave Jeeves the squelch.

'No! My mind is made up. I should like to order,' I glanced down at the title of my hunting design, '*Jorrocks's Jaunts and Jollities.*'

'Okey-doke.' Charlie flipped open his notebook. 'But it's going to nudge up the price. Whole lot of extra sweat getting them 'orses, dogs, and foxes straight – 'specially round the wainscot.'

'So be it: worth every penny.'

There was an uneasy silence.

'Right,' said Fred, 'let's have a cuppa tea.'

To say you could have cut the domestic atmos. with a knife is putting it a touch strong, but the air was certainly thick with the fog of grievance. Jeeves is accustomed to getting his way in matters of taste and propriety, and is inclined to sulk like a thwarted dachshund on the rare occasions he's vetoed. But this was my bedroom, dammit, and mine were the eyes that would close each night and open each dawn to the godawful banality of his *Periwinkle Chevron.*

To put it another way: I decided to dine at the Drones.

*   *   *

'Can't keep away, Mr Wooster?' Bashford grinned as I drifted back into the lobby and flicked the old Homburg onto a moose horn.

'So it would seem, Bashers. What news on the Rialto?'

'Actually, sir, Mr Fink-Nottle was asking after you. He's gone up to the bar.'

'Gussie, Gussie, Gussie,' I sang to myself while striding to the oasis, 'a guinea to a gooseberry the booby's in a pickle.'

'Bertie, I'm in a pickle.'

'What-ho, Gussie. I had a sort of feeling you might be.'

'Let me tell you about it—'

'Might a man before the firing squad be granted a final swig?'

'Of course, sorry. Have what I'm having.'

'Barley-water? I don't think so!'

Gussie Fink-Nottle's aversion to alcohol was so notorious that many Dronesmen had taken to calling him, with affection, Drink-Nottle. And, frankly, this was no bad thing, for even a sniff of the barmaid's apron, as they say in the lower sort of taverns, rendered the man comprehensively doolally. Devotees of my reminiscences may recall the shockingly inebriate prize-day speech he unleashed on the unsuspecting scholars of Market Snodsbury Grammar School – where *many* unfortunate things were said, including a number of criminal slanders against your present correspondent.

'Barley-water!' Gussie scoffed. 'How little you know me. This is a Parisian Blonde – and she's *tremendously* rich in vitamins.'

'Since when do you imbibe?'

'Since Emerald gave me the elbow.'

I leaned across the mahogany to summon from McGarry his swiftest dry Martini – for *this* was newsflash stuff.

The last time I'd seen Augustus Fink-Nottle he was sailing off into the purple vapours with a spirited lass by the name of Emerald Stoker. Despite more than a passing resemblance to a befreckled Pekinese, there was much to commend Miss Stoker as a permanent romantic fixture, not least her dab-handed skill in the culinary dept. I was a spectator when she and Gussie had clicked over one of her ambrosial steak-and-kidney puds, and, within the drop of a fork, there had been talk of elopement, talk of America, and talk of special licences from the Archbish. of C.

But now there was talk of elbows, and I was entirely agog.

'What transpired, Gussie? Don't tell me Emerald caught vegetarianism?'

'Worse: she caught *Taricha* anaphylaxis.'

This, as he explained at wearisome length, is a perilous allergy to the toxins exuded by certain species of newt. But to know Gussie for more than a second is to know that even the mildest aversion to the family *Salamandridae* would render any potential suitor utterly out of bounds. So crazed is Gussie for these semi-aquatic blisters, I've long suspected his loathing of liquor was more truly a loyalty to water. And just as dog owners grow to resemble their pets, it pains me to report that the same holds true for obsessive fanciers of newts.

'No wife of mine will have *Taricha* anaphylaxis!' Gussie declared, taking delivery of his second, or possibly third, Parisian Blonde.

'So, in point of fact, Gussie, *you* gave *her* the elbow?'

'Not at all! I didn't *ask* her to become anaphylactic.'

I was musing on how much zippier was Gussie off the wagon, rather than at its reins, when a cry of strangulated anguish rang out.

'What's the hullabaloo, McGarry? Don't tell me we're missing Boot-Finding?'

'No, sir, that's this Sunday. I think what you heard is the investment committee.'

I turned to Gussie in stupefaction. 'We have an *investment* committee?'

'Oh, yes. It's chaired by Fittleworth.'

Every so often, life presents a dilemma upon which the manuals of etiquette are woefully silent, and this was a snorter: whether it demonstrates better breeding to choke oneself into a frothy stupor or to expectorate one's dry Martini across four foot of well-polished bar, and six-foot-two of well-regarded barman.

Being in semi-polite company, and having nothing but esteem for McGarry, I opted for the former, and thus it was some time before I'd amassed sufficient O_2 to gasp out the word: '*Boko?*'

The committee was meeting (drinking) in an alcove around the corner. Boko Fittleworth was indeed in the chair, flanked by Barmy Fotheringay-Phipps, Stilton Cheesewright, and Bimbash Kidd.

They were clearly drunk – drunker than even the pre-prandial hour might suggest – and they displayed the waterlogged demeanour of gamblers drowning their sorrows.

'Is this the investment committee I see before me?' I gave a formal bow.

'It is,' said Stilton, with whom relations have often been a tinge unpasteurised.

'I'd no idea you existed.'

'That's because we run the club's finances with the silent efficiency of a Silver Ghost.'

'It didn't sound very silent just now.'

Boko wagged his finger in my approximate direction. 'Our mandate, Bertie, is long-term capital growth underpinned by portfolio diversification.' (The fiscal probity of this statement was enfeebled somewhat by hiccoughs punctuating each word.)

Further interrogation revealed that Boko's idea of 'portfolio diversification' involved hedging a number of hefty equine bets with wagers on Wimbledon, Henley, the Eton–Harrow match, and Freddie Bullivant's performance in the inter-club snooker.

To be fair, this was not as recklessly madcap a plan as it might seem – for although in day-to-day life Boko is essentially innumerate, freezing like a startled fawn when asked to split a cab fare, he has an inexplicable ability to judge form and calculate the most complex of odds.

'So how are we doing?' I asked.

'Fair to middling. Cambridge won the Boat Race, no surprise there, but we made a killing on the length. Goodwood was bad-wood, on account of the mud, but we had a lucky Trooping the Colour, and a fabulous Crufts, so I'd say we're up to par.'

'Sorry, *how* does one bet on Trooping the Colour?'

'How many soldiers faint, and when.'

'But,' interrupted Stilton, waving an official piece of paper awash with red ink, 'we have a more pressing problem.'

The letter in Stilton's paw was from the Commissioners of His Majesty's Inland Revenue, who'd adjudicated, most unsportingly, that the investment committee had erred in declaring gambling losses as a deductible business expense. Since this had been club policy for generations, more than half a century of back tax and compounded fines were now due.

'How deep is the hole?' I asked.

'A hundred grand,' said Boko, morosely.

'Ye gods and little fishes! So much for plucking the goose.'

Between you and me, though, I was less surprised than I let on. The Drones is a noble institution, of course, but as any nerve specialist will tell you: institutions should seldom be run by their inmates. That the club's financial cogs were being oiled by spanners like Boko and Stilton helped explain the recent spate of bureaucratic incompetences. Only a fortnight earlier, for example, every member (and member of staff) had been given a gratis case of absinthe after the wine committee 'came over funny' during a buying spree in Paris.

'When do we have to cough up?' I asked.

'A week today.'

'They shall not pass,' roared Gussie, fuelled by the Dutch courage of his Parisian Blondes. 'We must appeal!'

Boko sighed. 'This *is* the appeal.'

'And what if we can't raise the splosh?'

'They seize the clubhouse. And with no clubhouse ... ' Boko dropped his hands in despair.

'So what's the plan?'

'I'm glad you ask. I've just put it to a formal committee vote, and the next order of business is to get seriously – and when I say seriously, I mean *truly* and *comprehensively* – pontooned.'

Knowing there'd soon be no further sense to be had from this mob, Gussie and I retreated to the dining-room and sat at the Cowards' Table – so called because two wide columns shield it from prying eyes and flying rolls.

'Listen, Gussie, I'm sorry to hear about Emerald.'

'Who?'

'Emerald Stoker? Your until-very-recently betrothed. The one with whom you're pickled?'

'Oh, don't mind about her,' he said, casting a thirsty eye down the wine list. 'She's ancient history. The pickle I'm in concerns Vonka.'

'Vonka?'

'Vonka the *peacherino*. We're engaged!'

'Of course you are,' I sighed. 'Let's hear the tale of the tape.'

Gussie's new belle went by the unlikely name of Veronica 'Vonka' Pinke and she possessed all the bells and whistles one would expect of the contemporary heart-throb: hair 'like autumnal chestnuts', eyes that 'sparkled like sapphires', a nose which 'tilted at the tip', a smile – well, you get the pic.

'I suppose there's a snag?' I asked, for there's often a snag with Gussie Fink-Nottle, and always a snag with peacherinos.

'Two, actually: Evadne and Lancelot.'

'Eh?'

'Her Ma and Pa.'

This sounded like one large, amalgamated snag, but Gussie informed me otherwise.

Lancelot Pinke, he said, represented a very conventional type of snag: doggedly protective of his only daughter, with a feline suspicion of any and all suitors. Such sentiments are only to be expected, and usually prove no great hazard to the well-polished Dronesman – not that Gussie is polished *per se*, but he can usually be trusted to use the right fork and not wash his feet in the soup.

Evadne Pinke, however, was an entirely more dubious kettle of fish, for in addition to being kind, doting, and soppily maternal, she was – and I quote – 'fundamentally zig-zag in the steeple'.

Every decision the woman made was guided by a hectic swarm of spiritual piffle, and her checklist of superstitions included black cats, pavement cracks, whistling sailors, red beards, the colour purple, the sound of thunder, twins and triplets, new shoes, loose threads, frosted glass, and chipped buttons. She once refused to leave a restaurant until she had spotted a *second* magpie – a vigil that dragged on for nine expensive days.

'So, to up-sum: Pater is bad and Mater is mad, and you need to snake-charm both?'

'And I need your help.'

'Mine?'

'You're good with parents.'

'*Am* I?'

'You're better than me.'

This was undeniable.

'So, you'll come up to Cambridge to plead my case?'

'Cambridge? Why Cambridge? Who said anything about Cambridge?'

'That's where I met her. That's where she lives. That's where I work.'

'First Monty and now you!' I shook my head. 'When did this mania for honest toil infest the Drones?'

'In my case, ever since my allowance was stopped.'

Gussie explained that his parents had warmly approved of the Emerald alliance (presumably because it meant his imminent departure for the New World), and had taken such a dim view of him calling things off that they had cancelled his quarterly cheques.

'But before I introduce Vonka to my people, I need her people to play ball.'

I was still stuck on him having a job.

'What on earth, Gussie, are you qualified to do?'

'I teach.'

'Ha!'

'At a crammer's called Pinke's Academy.'

'Wait ... *Pinke's* Academy? As in Vonka Pinke, Lancelot Pinke, and the loony Evadne Pinke?'

'That's right,' he beamed. 'I've fallen in love with the boss's daughter.'

'You've fallen into a Victorian melodrama is what you've done.' I buttered myself another roll. 'And anyway, what on earth are you qualified to teach?'

'Almost nothing! But it turns out you only need to be a page ahead of 'em in the textbook. These are hardly ambitious students; if they were, they wouldn't be sweating at Pinke's. In fact, they rather remind me of us, when we were their age.'

'Sounds gruesome.'

'Most of them aren't so bad, though one is a stinker of the first water. More importantly, though: can I count on your help? Term starts on Wednesday, and we should strike while the what-not is hot.'

It occurred to me that a jaunt up to Cambridge would get me out of the house while Dicks & Rudge were wallpapering my bedroom – though I had rather been looking forward to a week of clubbable indolence, and the chance to work on my darts.

'Let me sleep on it, Gussie. But it might, I suppose, be amusing.'

'At-a-boy!'

I swirled the heeltaps of my claret. 'You know, Bingo Little used to tutor.'

'He told me.'

'You should ask him for some tips.'

'I did.'

'What did he say?'

'Don't.'

I arrived home well after midnight to find, propped against my porcelain bust of W. G. Grace, a telegram:

WILL K-C AND A-H MEET 9-D
TOMORROW 10:30 A.M. ALBANY

This was obviously a summons I couldn't refuse, and I rather regretted allowing Gussie to order the second brace of brandies.

2.

TUESDAY

No man can awake to glad confident morning when Reginald Jeeves is upset.

By his coolness of tone as he wished me good morning, and his briskness of manner as he set down my tea, I knew with dark foreboding that a price would be paid for my *Periwinkle* rebellion. Indeed, as I shaded my eyes from the abruptly drawn curtains, I began to wonder if I had seriously goofed. A fleeting victory was all w. and g., but what if this proved the final straw, camel-wise, for a valued retainer who, lest we forget, once threw in the towel when I was briefly bewitched by the twang of the banjolele?

The *entente* was still pretty *uncordiale* as I sat down to breakfast – though, to be fair, Jeeves had not permitted his manifest annoyance to diminish his standards one jot. The eggs were soft, the bacon was crisp, the kedgeree was spiced to perfection, and, as requested, there was a freshly ironed copy of *The Times*, folded open to the crossword, with a pencil honed ready for war.

I attempted to spark a glimmer of warmth.

'I see we've been summoned to a meeting.'

'Yes, sir.'

'With 9-D.'

'Indeed, sir.'

'At his Albany digs.'

'So I gather, sir.'

'Intriguing, eh?'

He evidently considered the question beneath his dignity, so I changed tack.

'Have you done today's puzzle?'

'No, sir.'

'Splendid,' I reached for the paper, 'we can tackle it together.'

'If you insist, sir.'

'Now, let's see. One Across: *Upset ear doctor, one who changes rooms.* Nine letters ... Hmmm ... Any ideas?'

'DECORATOR, sir.'

'Eh?'

'It is an anagram, sir. An *upset* of the words *ear* and *doctor* – which gives DECORATOR – *one who changes rooms.*'

'Well, it fits. And it means Three Down starts with an R. *Nasty vicar's lot drunk with gin.* Nine letters.' I tapped my pencil. 'Thoughts?'

'REVOLTING, sir.'

'Jolly good.' I ignored his tone. 'What about Twenty-four Down: *Fake father, I hear, is tactless in France.* Four, three ... RUDE something, perhaps? ... RUDE MAN?'

'FAUX PAS, sir.'

Staring down at the pencilled-in words – DECORATOR, REVOLTING, FAUX PAS – I couldn't help but notice a theme. Had Jeeves, the thought flashed across my mind, somehow infiltrated the setting of the *Times* crossword to vent his indignation?

The idea was outlandish, to be sure, but the man does move in the most mysterious ways.

After a number of increasingly insulting solutions (REPUG-NANT, FAT-HEADED, REPTILE) the frost began slightly to melt, and so I decided to broach the dilemma that had been nagging me since last night's encounter with Boko.

'Jeeves,' I said, spinning my pencil in a chummy sort of way, 'the Drones Club needs your help.'

'Indeed, sir?'

I set out the posish in as much detail as I could remember, placing appropriate stress on the hundred-grand bill and the timescale of less than a week. Then, having lit the blue touch-paper of the man's pyrotechnic brain, I sat back to *ooh!* and *aah!*

Squibs don't come much damper.

'I am sorry to say, sir, that nothing immediately suggests itself.'

'Nothing?'

'No, sir.'

'Nothing will come of nothing, Jeeves. Speak again!'

'I am sorry, sir.'

Jeeves's mind is so composed that something *always* suggests itself, and it was evident that his pique was not to be easily paci-fied. If I knew my man, and know him I did, he would 'work to rule' like a union foreman until management caved in to his terms.

There was only one way out of this cul-de-sac, so I poured myself a hot spot of tea to wet the old whistle before eating my words.

'Changing the subject entirely, Jeeves.'

'Sir?'

'I've been having second thoughts about the wallpaper.'

He perked up. 'Indeed, sir?'

'*Jorrocks* might be a tad agricultural for the bedroom, and perhaps I do require something more soothingly *Chevron*.'

Jeeves permitted himself a riotous twitch of the eyebrow.

'I am most grateful, sir. I shall telephone Dicks and Rudge directly after breakfast.' There was a diplomatic pause. 'Returning, sir, to the earlier question of the Drones Club finances, one thought does now occur to me.'

Some minutes later I dialled the Fittleworth residence and, after an aeon of rings, the instrument was answered, not by a voice, so much as the echo in a Turkish bath.

'*H-u-l-l-o.*'

'Boko?'

'*Y-e-s,*' continued the echo. '*W-h-o i-s t-h-i-s?*'

'Bertie.'

There was a gasp, a sort of screeching noise, and a splash.

'Are you in the tub, Boko?'

'I was, but am no longer. Hi-ho, Wooster! What prompts you so early in the ungodly?'

'It's about the tax man—'

He emitted a plaintive cry.

'No, it's good news! I've had an idea.'

He emitted an even plaintiver cry, which I felt was a smidgeon unjust.

'I should have said: *Jeeves* has had an idea.'

'That's more like it. What does Jeeves suggest? And please don't say armed robbery – as I *keep* telling Bimbash, it's a complete non-starter.'

'Jeeves suggests an accumulator.'

Boko gasped. 'An *acca* – Jeeves is sensational! Why didn't that occur to us?'

'Well, you were pretty rum-punched. So, is it a goer?'

According to Boko it was.

All we had to do was pick a gang of winning horses running in the next few days. Then we'd sequentially 'reinvest' the profits from each race until they'd accumulated into a sum sufficient to cover our daunting debt. Of course, we'd also need to find a biddable bookie.

'What about that chap Bingo swears by?' I suggested.

'Charles Pikelet? He'll have to swear pretty loudly. "Charlie Always Pays" did a flit to New Zealand with the briefcase from Ascot.'

'Yoicks!'

'I wonder if Leviathan might be a goer?'

'Leviathan is ... a horse?'

'A turf accountant, a.k.a. William Edmund Davies, who seldom turns down an accumulator, and whose stubs are safer than sterling.'

'Sounds ideal. So all we need now is a list of nags at suitable odds?'

'Exactly. I'll zip out and get the papers.'

'You'll put some clothes on first?'

'Oh, yes. Capital idea.'

I was feeling pretty chipper about knocking off the day's Good Deed while still in the silken jim-jams, when it struck me that I too ought to get dressed. And so I padded back to the bedroom where Jeeves had set out the attire he judged appropriate for a meeting between K-C, A-H, and 9-D – viz. the cashmere navy pinstripe and contrasting silver tie.

I was on the verge of presentability when I remembered I'd left my lucky horseshoe cufflinks on the sitting-room mantelpiece – a negligible voyage which nonetheless took me past the green-baize door to Jeeves's lair.

Eavesdropping has never been a Wooster vice, but my steps did slow to a silent halt when I overheard the word 'wallpaper' followed by an insubordinate chuckle. I pressed my ear to the baize, and was distressed to hear Jeeves rescinding my selection of *Jorrocks's Jaunts & Jollities* with a tone that can only be described as triumphant.

Not every phrase was audible, but rather too many were, including 'most unwise' and 'juvenile enthusiasms'. Humility in victory this was not, and the whole bally episode rankled – if rankled is the word I want.

The rankle was still percolating as Jeeves and I quit Berkeley Mansions and ambulated down Piccadilly towards Albany – a

Georgian block of private apartments where the rich and discreet (and my chum Pongo) stomp their *pieds-à-terre*.

Mentioning our host's name at the lodge, we were directed to a set of rooms off the Rope Walk and, arriving at A2, we knocked and waited. Our call was swiftly answered by an explosion of dazzling tartan, indicating to all within a half-mile blast that we'd come to the right address.

'Mr Wooster,' purred Lord MacAuslan in his silken Edinburgh brogue, 'come in, sit down, and make yourself at home.'

This may be an opportune moment to pluck the needle from the record and explain what brings K-C, A-H, and 9-D together.

A month or so back, in the dog days of summer, the rug was unexpectedly snatched from under my slippers when I learned that the Junior Ganymede – Jeeves's club of butlers, valets, and gentlemen's personal gentlemen – was, and had always been, an arm of British Intelligence.

Senior servants make excellent spies (ask any divorcé), and H.M. Government had been eager to tap this inconspicuous infantry of domestic service to winkle out the intrigue on foreign diplomats, industrialists, and society gadflies. Established in 1878 by the then Earl of Winchester, the Junior Ganymede was now overseen by the elegantly urbane Lord MacAuslan – one of those unconventional Establishment pillars that casts a curious shadow across the international stage.

Not every member of the Junior Ganymede is 'in' on the conspiracy – only proven souls are trusted with the club's *true* mission – but over the decades the organisation has established an expansive web of servants at every station who assist, often unwittingly, with access and information.

I don't think I was ever formally 'conscripted' into the Junior Ganymede, if that's the term of art, but I was more than delighted to pitch in, alongside Jeeves, to stymie my old nemesis Roderick Spode, the seventh Earl of Sidcup. Not content to lead a gang of black-shorted goons (preposterously called the Saviours of Britain), Spode had decided to dip his toes into the murky waters of Italian Fascism. It was my pleasure to stamp on these mis-shapen tootsies by helping to intercept the new book code he was to use for clandestine communication.

This caper, which unfolded across London's clubland, intro-duced me to the ways and means of the Junior Ganymede, and gave me a taste for what Jeeves calls 'quiescent espionage', by which I think he means: they also serve who only lounge and drink.

As soon as *l'affaire Spode* had concluded, Lord MacAuslan summoned me to Edinburgh, where Jeeves and I were to 'assist' the Ganymede at a shooting party on the Duke of Lauderdale's estate. Sadly, the Italian bigwig whose footsteps I was set to be dogging never pitched up – and so, in conse-quence, I'd spent several lazy days watching Jeeves haul trout out of Loch Leven.

'Yes, yes,' I hear you object, 'fishing is all very well, but what of those peculiar initials?'

Well, as I discovered almost by accident, senior officers of the Junior Ganymede are allotted code names based on playing cards: Jeeves is the Ace of Hearts, Lord MacAuslan the Nine of Diamonds, and I am the King of Clubs.

Hence K-C and A-H were meeting 9-D.

'Is it too early for a drop of sherry?' asked Lord MacAuslan, heading across to the tray.

It *was* a tad previous, to be perfectly honest, but who was I to come between a Scotsman and his dram?

'I don't see why not, so long as it's pretty dry.'

'Fino is fine-o. Jeeves?'

'That would be most agreeable, my lord.'

Having dispensed with the decanter, Lord MacAuslan adopted his traditional mantlepiece perch and extended his arms like a lazy but limber buzzard.

'I wonder, Mr Wooster, if you have plans for the week ahead? Plans you cannot escape.'

I turned to Jeeves with an enquiring eye.

'Nothing that might not be cut, sir.'

'Well then, MacAuslan, I am yours to command.'

'Excellent. I'd like you to join me in Cambridge tomorrow.'

'Not Scotland?'

Lord MacAuslan's face fell. 'Once again, Mr Wooster, I am most profoundly apologetic—'

'I jest, of course. It's hardly your fault if Peppino What's-his-name stepped on a jellyfish.'

'I'm glad you understand. Espionage is so very often a question of missed connections, crossed wires, and trifling accidents.

Now, returning to Cambridge: we've a small job of work at the University, and consider you the ideal candidate.'

'Really? I'd have thought the Ganymede was burrowed pretty deep into the panelling of Oxbridge.'

'We do have a few contacts among the senior Fellows as well as informal connections with porters, groundsmen, gyps, bedels, and bedmakers. However, we have no one who can pass among, and mix within, the student congregation. For this we need someone who will fit in, but not stand out. Someone who knows the ropes, but is not themselves known. Someone who, perhaps, went to Eton and Oxford.'

'Half a mo! I went to Eton and Oxford.'

Lord MacAuslan blinked a couple of times. 'We know.'

'Oh, yes, you would. But am I not rather ancient to be an undergrad?'

'We were thinking of making you some kind of postgraduate-cum-research-fellow. No need to be too specific, of course. You won't be there for more than a few days.'

'And what am I supposed to be researching?'

'We thought, theology. Clergymen are always popping up in unexpected places, looking ageless, timeless, and oddly anonymous. And you did win that school prize for Scripture Knowledge.'

'How ever d'you know that?'

Lord MacAuslan glanced briefly at Jeeves. 'You may have mentioned it, once or twice. There is also the question of disguise.'

'Let me stop you there: I draw the line at Pierrot costumes.'

'As does His Majesty's Government. However, given your the-
ological studies, you should probably be dressed as a cleric.'

'Won't a Bible-pounder rather sore-thumb it?'

'It's a curious thing: the more conspicuous a person is, the less
one notices him, especially in uniform. And there's the additional
benefit of people's natural hesitation in approaching the clergy,
for fear of becoming *cleeked* in conversation.'

I nodded in heartfelt recollection of the many occasions I'd
suffered 'vestibule paralysis' with a loquacious vicar after Sunday
service.

'Well then, m'lord, what's the mission? Who's the mark?'

'It concerns two undergraduates, one at Trinity, one at Caius.
But I suggest we leave the detailed briefing until tomorrow. I
wanted first to check your availability and willingness, given the
urgency.'

'Urgency?'

'Michaelmas term begins today, and the first week of a new
academic year is always pretty chaotic. Such chaos aids our
purpose admirably: scores of new undergraduates, dozens of
graduates, a handful of junior Fellows. Most of the dons remain
aloof, of course, so the only people who *really* know who's who,
and what's what, are the porters. And this is where we turn to
Jeeves.'

Turn to Jeeves I did. 'Don't tell me you used to be a porter?'

'No, sir. Although my second cousin was once the Fellows'
Butler at Peterhouse.'

'The plot thins. So, MacAuslan, where will we all be staying?'

'I will be at Trinity, my alma mater. You will be at Caius, in the bijou set of a Fellow on sabbatical. And Jeeves will be— Actually, Jeeves, where *will* you be?'

'I have provisionally booked a suite of rooms at the University Arms hotel, sir, which will provide a base of operations that is convenient, commodious, and relatively anonymous.'

It was only a little later, as our meeting drew to a close, that it struck me: *provisionally booked* ... just how long had Jeeves known of this Ganymedean caper in Cambridge?

We stepped out into a Piccadilly bathed in the glow of an Indian summer, and while my man toddled off to acquire dust-sheets for the arrival of Dicks & Rudge, Lord MacAuslan flagged down a taxi. As I followed him into the back of the cab, I heard him request a Covent Garden address that rang a familiar bell.

'I say! You don't also use the Cohens?'

'Naturally, Mr Wooster. They've been with the Ganymede for decades.'

It has been said, by authorities unimpeachable, that the world is a jolly small place and, at that precise moment, I was inclined to agree. The theatrical costumier Cohen Bros. is held in the highest standing by Dronesmen of all sizes, who turn to its services whenever summoned to a fancy-dress shindig. Over the years, Irving, Lou, and Isadore Cohen (the Bros. that comprise Cohen Bros.) have kitted me out as a Roman senator, a Viking warrior, a caveman, a Cavalier, Robin Hood, Friar Tuck, *and* Maid Marion – and this is merely to touch upon the cavalcade of get-ups they stock.

It was a surprise, therefore, but not a shock, to learn that Cohen Bros. were mixed up with the British Secret Service – for what could be handier to a gang like the Ganymede than access to quick-change disguises?

We entered via the tradesmen's door on Rose Street, and came across Irving Cohen tying up parcels with his family's famous blue-and-white twine. He looked up from his labours and clapped his hands in delight.

'Isadore,' he sang out, 'you'll never guess who's here.' He paused. 'Are you two *together*?'

Lord MacAuslan nodded, and Mr Cohen beamed.

'Wonderful, wonderful! Another branch on the tree. First things first, Mr Wooster: how did our postman costume suit your young friend?'

'Almost too well. People insisted on handing him parcels, and he was bitten by more than one dog.'

'Splendid, splendid! Now, my lord, how may we be of service?'

'Mr Wooster is temporarily taking Holy Orders.'

'Interesting, interesting! Follow me.'

For reasons of respect and propriety, Cohen Bros. quarantine their clerical garments in a private, locked room, lending them to non-theatrical clients in only exceptional circs – more often than not, Mr Cohen divulged, when a clergyman has mislaid his luggage.

'Where do they all come from?' I asked, strolling along the rows of ecclesiastical copes and capes.

'Most are from productions, some we have made, and a few are the result of, shall we say, misfortune.'

'Misfortune?'

'With each unfrocking,' Mr Cohen shook his head, 'a redundant frock.'

I ran my finger along the racks, before spying a bright red cassock with a brilliant silver badge.

'What about this sumptuous raiment?'

'You have an excellent eye for cloth, Mr Wooster, but I fear you will stand out, instead of blending in. That piece is traditionally worn by Honorary Chaplains to His Majesty.'

'And this?' I held up a fabulous specimen in white and gold. 'Is this traditionally worn by anyone?'

'Oh, indeed,' Mr Cohen bowed reverently. 'His Holiness the Pope.'

Anticlimactically, the apparel Lord MacAuslan eventually approved was nothing more spiffing than a couple of ill-fitting sack suits, a handful of dog-collars, and a tattered gown of ambiguous academic provenance.

Irving, like me, was clearly disappointed by this selection, but, ever the professional, the customer was never wrong.

'I shall have these sponged and pressed immediately, and sent to ... ?'

'Gonville and Caius College, Cambridge,' said Lord MacAuslan. 'For the attention of Reverend Wooster.'

'Marvellous, marvellous!' He lowered his voice. 'Now, my lord, how did *your* latest costume fare?'

'Rather well. Tsar Boris III was hoodwinked completely.'

I parted company with Lord MacAuslan on the corner of Garrick Street and New Row.

'Until tomorrow, Mr Wooster. Though I believe you're about to meet my niece?'

'We dine at The Savoy at one.'

'Do please send her my love.'

With an hour to kill before this daunting appointment, I decided to quell my butterflies by browsing the flower stalls in Covent Garden market. I was whistling down King Street, wondering whether a dozen roses would be *de trop*, when I paused to admire a colossal pavement chalking of *The Last Supper*. It had all the majesty of Leonardo's original, save for one alarming detail: an unfortunately located iron drain, which gave the Son of God a toothy grin that bordered on the heretical.

Kneeling on the flagstones next to this flawed masterpiece, stippling in the grains of salt spilled by Judas Iscariot, was a scruffy chap in a motley suit. As he turned to cadge a donation, I saw it was an old pal from the Drones.

'Hell's bells! Montague Montgomery, as I live and breathe.'

'Wotcha, Bertie. What d'ya think?'

'It's magnificent, Monty!' And, really, it was – suspiciously so. 'I'd no idea you could draw, or chalk, or whatever this is.'

'I can't,' he grinned, getting to his feet and brushing the dust from his knees. 'I'm just the frontman. I rent this off a screever called Bert.'

Screevers, he explained, are journeyman artists who wake at first light to chalk their repertoire of artistic, religious, and comical scenes on pavements across the West End. Then, each morning, frontmen like Monty purchase these pitches for the day, crouching down to add the 'finishing touches' to works they'd be unable to chalk in a lifetime of trying.

'So, it's a swindle?'

'It's most certainly not! I don't *say* I chalk the pictures. I just sit beside them – covered in chalk, with chalks in my chalky hands – and the public, bless 'em, jump to a useful conclusion.'

Say what you like about Monty, and many people do, but there's an entrepreneurial streak to the chap that sets him apart from the run-of-the-hive Drones. Only a few months back he'd been washing bottles, working in a nightclub, *and* promoting snuff by means of a sandwich-board. More recently, he'd discovered a theatrical bent – in fact, the last time I'd seen him was on-stage, as the Cockney seaman Benskin Muchmore in a dirgeful production called *Flotsam*.

'Whatever happened to your play, Monty?'

'Don't you read *The Stage*?' He was hurt. '*Flotsam* was a smash! A five-week box-office frenzy. But the run just ended, and there wasn't a house free for the transfer.'

'So instead you're chalking pavements?'

'Until I find a role that suits my range.' He stretched his arms and rolled his neck in an ostentatiously thespian manner. 'Look, business is slow, why don't we pop along and rinse the tonsils?'

'*Très bonne idée* – I need some pre-lunch bottle-bravery.'

'A girl?'

'What else?'

Monty picked up his earnings and packed up his chalks.

''Ere, Alfie,' he called over to a chap lounging against some railings. 'Keep ya minces on da Vinci? Won't be more than 'arf.'

'Where to?' I asked.

'The Garrick!' Monty beamed with pride. 'I've just joined.'

'How can you possibly afford the membership of a second club?'

'I can't. But here's the rub: I can't afford *not* to be a member.'

This was the logic of the laughing academy. Only someone as barmy as Monty would pay for one of London's grandest clubs by scrounging for pennies just a chip-shot from its door.

'Look, Bertie, I need theatrical work, and for theatrical work I need theatrical contacts, and where do theatrical contacts congregate?'

'The theatre?'

'The Garrick! *Ipso* – as they say in Paris – *facto*.'

'Aren't you rather unkempt for such an august estab.?'

'It's an actors' club, Bertie. They don't do kempt.'

Even so, he took from his pocket an eye-watering salmon-pink and cucumber-green club tie, which he mangled round his collar in the vague approximation of a half-Windsor.

It had been many moons since I'd swung through the Garrick's portals, and I'd forgotten how dashed congenial the old place was. The head porter Richard greeted Monty like a long-lost friend – as did all of the members we met on the stairs – and Massimo, the maître d', shook up a couple of She Stoops to Conquer snifters without a syllable being spoken.

'This *is* civilised,' I said, relaxing into a low chair overlooking Floral Street.

'Ain't it? And the food is *de*licious.'

'Poverty treats you well, Mr Toad.'

'You've got to speculate to accumulate.'

'Why do people only ever say that before pouncing for my wallet?'

'It's funny you should—'

'Oh no,' I silenced him with a wagging finger. 'No, no, no. Not for all the diamonds in De Beers.'

'I'm not *asking* for money! In fact, I would pay *you*.'

This seemed so outlandishly improbable that I bade him continue merely to see what colour yarn he might spin.

'You're a man about town, Bertie ... '

'One doesn't like to brag.'

'Circulating in society ... '

'The mantelpiece has some stiffies.'

'A playboy of the West End world ... '

'Enough of the apple sauce. What *precisely* are you after?'

'Gossip.'

'Gossip?'

'Gossip.'

It transpired that Monty had, somehow, contrived to be hired as the *Daily Sketch*'s new 'diary columnist', a position that entailed penning eight hundred words of society tittle-tattle each and every day, excluding the Sabbath. The post was apparently perfect for a man with theatrical ambitions (and a slew of the oddest of odd jobs), since most of it could be dictated to the copy-takers down the line of whichever drinking hole he was sunk in.

'I have chosen as my pseudonym, "Iceberg".'

'Because you're incredibly dense?'

'Because I'm *"Exposing Society Below the Waterline"*.'

'Ha! You must be among the least-connected chaps in London.'

'Among the most hard up, though. I've only been doing it a fortnight, and I've managed to pad the column with green-room anecdotes and rewrites from *La Vie Parisienne*.'

'Since when do *you* speak French?'

'I have sisters. But my editor is getting suspicious, and I'm on the verge of desperation.'

'Why don't you just make things up? I bet no one would twig if you invented a dowager duchess or two.'

'That's what the last chap did – and let me tell you, Fenchurch-Smythe came to a pretty sticky end. So now even the smallest detail is checked and double-checked.'

'I'm not sure how I can help. I'm off to Cambridge for a spell and—'

Monty clapped his hands. 'Perfect! They adore Oxbridge antics: cheating students, godless chaplains, Union hecklers, May Balls ... '

'It's October, Monty.'

'Blind me not with details. Get me the juice!'

'I'll do what I can, but I make no promises. By the way, you dangled something about payment?'

'Ah, yes. I've devised a nifty system: every story you give me, assuming it runs, counts as one point – two points if it includes a divorce, three if it includes a royal. When you've earned six points, you get a bottle of club claret.'

'Your generosity overwhelms, Monty.'

'Oh, d'you think it's too much?'

'No.'

*   *   *

I pitched up at The Savoy on the stroke of one and, being the first at our table, annexed the outer chair – giving Iona 'the room', and allowing me discreetly to clock her arrival in the mirror. She appeared a few minutes later, the epitome of gamine charm, followed promptly by the bottle of Krug I'd ordered.

As a rule, Bertram Wooster is not unduly befuddled by the fairer sex. There have been a handful of *affaires de coeur*, and a terrifying number of escaped engagements – twenty-two near-Mrs at the last official count – but while most of my chums can't wait to break into jail and tie the noose, given my choice between 'wedded bliss' or eighteen holes of birdie golf, the jury's never out for long.

The verdict concerning Lord MacAuslan's niece, however, was slower in coming – indeed, in the brief time we'd known each other, Iona had seriously threatened the dissolution of my long-established monastic order.

It's not that she's tall, dark, and lissom – though she's all these things in triplicate. It's that her amused and amusing *sang-froid* strikes that beguiling balance between simpering blancmange

[Exhibit A: Madeline Bassett] and screaming drill-sergeant [Exhibit B: Florence Craye].

Cool, detached, able to pilot planes and impersonate aunts, Iona MacAuslan is the cat that walks by herself. Oh, and you recall the Junior Ganymede's playing-card code names? Well, Iona is Q-C.

The Krug was popped, we toasted her health, and there followed a rather agonising intermission, during which the room's resident elephant could hardly be ignored.

'So, Iona ... Edinburgh.'

'I hear it was a wash-out, Bertie. I'm sorry for that.'

'Work-wise it was; weather-wise it was splendid. And, if you hook as much brown trout as Jeeves, fish-wise it was bliss.'

'Don't you like angling?'

'Within reason. Like house guests, fishing rather stinks after two days.' I steeled myself with another sip. 'The thing is, I had rather hoped to see you in Scotland.'

'And I, you.' She wrinkled her nose in disappointment. 'I was looking forward to it. Maddeningly, something came up in Le Touquet.'

I glanced about and whispered, 'A Junior Ganymede something?'

'Yes,' she whispered back. 'Why are we whispering?'

'Did you have fun?' (I felt the 'without me' was understood.)

'Not especially. I spent five days sipping coffee in the Café de la Poste, waiting to photograph a man who never turned up.'

'Oh! You too?'

'Such is spying: more thirty-nine cups than thirty-nine steps. Still, it gave me a chance to polish off the crossword.'

'The *Times* crossword?'

'Certainly. When I could find a copy.'

'Fiendish, isn't it?'

'Is it?' she smiled.

'Have you done today's?'

'Of course. I hope you got Twenty Down?'

'Remind me.'

'*Some affection admitted for island.* Four letters.'

'I'm, er, still working on that one.'

'Oh!' She dived for her handbag. 'I bought you a gift.'

She handed me a small, heavy, tissue-papered object, in the exact same dimensions as ...

'The Eiffel Tower?'

'You guessed!'

I was confused. 'They have one in Le Touquet?'

'No, Bertie. But they have an absence of anything else worth casting in bronze. Think of it as an apology, and maybe also—'

'Your menus,' interrupted a waiter, somewhat hobnailing the moment.

'So,' I snapped a breadstick, 'what tempts you down to the Smoke? Apart from lunch with me.'

'I'm spending a day with the paper-hangers.'

'I know *just* how you feel! Jeeves was adamant: either that wallpaper went, or he did.'

Iona's grin indicated we were speaking at cross-purposes, and she explained that her 'paper-hangers' referred not to bedroom décor, but to the Junior Ganymede's document department: a flock of boffins in a Fleet Street basement who forge passports, letters, visas, banknotes – pretty much anything involving paper and ink.

'Sounds handy. Any chance of a fistful of fivers?'

'I could probably slip you a few hundred lira. Or a new birth certificate, should you fancy changing your name?'

'I should say not! According to Jeeves, "Bertram" is German for "bright raven" – which I've always thought terribly fitting.'

'That brings me to the other reason I'm here.'

'To visit the Tower of London?'

'To interview the man you and Jeeves suggested.'

A month or so earlier, very shortly after we'd first met, Iona had asked me to suggest a suitable manservant who might serve her as Jeeves serves me. Although I'd warned her that the finest retainers are as tricky to locate as they are actually to retain, the name Crawshaw sprang to mind as one who might be up to snuff. Jeeves gave his nod of approval, and Iona had evidently pursued the recommendation.

'You made contact with Algernon Crawshaw?'

'I did, and I'm meeting him later tonight. In fact, I wanted to ask if you might come along? You know far more than I about butlers and valets.'

'You mean: gentlemen's personal gentlemen.'

'Oh Lord,' she laughed, 'don't start on *that* again!'

'My mission, Iona, is to educate.'

'But if I did hire Crawshaw, I'd hope to set off on the right foot. I don't want to be one of those *spyachles* who's crushed by their staff.'

'What's a *spyachle*?'

She pondered the question. 'Not quite as bad as a *minnie's-man*.'

In time – after cheese, biscuits, coffee, and port – the bill arrived.

Iona reached for the salver. 'Let me.'

'Quite impossible.' I slid the salver away. 'You are my guest.'

A comically polite tussle ensued, before Iona issued an unexpected threat. 'Why don't we play Russian Roulette?'

'Isn't that a tad excessive? I mean to say, it's only lunch.'

'Not with bullets, Bertie! Visiting cards.'

'Eh?'

Iona's version of Russian Roulette was a game of her own invention, devised to add spice to the reckoning when dining with friends. When the bill arrives, every diner places their visiting card face down on the table, and the waiter is instructed to 'pick a card, any card'. Whoever's card is selected then pays for the entire party, which, depending on the number present and the calibre of the wine, can prove almost as fatal as the game's original Moscow rules.

We took out our cards.

'This won't wash,' I said, indicating the disparity in sizes – mine being a Gentleman's Third, hers a Reduced Small. 'No waiter would *knowingly* choose a lady's card.'

'Easily fixed!' Iona tucked the cards under her napkin, so just a corner of each was exposed. 'Now, let's find our assassin.'

The maître d' was far from amused. Russian Roulette was *not* the kind of stunt one pulled at The Savoy, he indicated with nostrils aquiver, indeed he was only prepared to tolerate the outrage on account of the unusually magnetic allure of my companion.

Refusing actually to touch the cards, he pulled the trigger with a tap of his pen and, as Iona slid out his selection, it was immediately clear from its size and shape that she'd lost.

'Cruel bad luck!' I commiserated, thinking what a fabulously bankrupting game this would be at the Drones. 'You can't win 'em all.'

'Really?' she grinned, handing back the bill to the maître d'. 'You can put this on my uncle's ticket.'

Having arranged to meet later at her uncle's Albany set, Iona and I parted ways – she eastwards, back to her forgers; I westwards, towards a forgiving sofa at the Drones. But, as I drifted along the Strand towards Nelson's Column, I couldn't help mull upon Iona's anxiety not to become a *spyachle* or worse, apparently, a *minnie's-man*.

Was I, perhaps, too much at *my* man's beck and call?

Certainly, various aunts have levelled this accusation over the years, not least Aunt Agatha, who, with all the charm of a ransom note, once called me 'the ugly second monkey' to Jeeves's 'autocratic organ grinder' – which, I don't mind admitting, stung.

My pace accelerated as the iron entered my soul (aided and abetted by a glass of the '86 Fonseca) and by the time I'd located a phone box, consulted the directory, and inserted a coin, my dander was at high tide.

A female voice answered. 'Dicks 'n' Rudge, how may I help you?'

'Wooster here, 3A Berkeley Mansions.'

There was a snicker. 'Oh, yeah. I 'eard about you!'

I didn't entirely appreciate her tone, but persisted nonetheless.

'I'd like to change my wallpaper order.'

'Hang on, you'll 'ave to speak to the boss.'

The line went silent before Charlie, or possibly Fred, appeared.

'Afternoon, chief. I hear we've changed our mind – again.'

'Indeed so: back to the hunting scene, please.'

He sighed. 'So, just to be crystal: it was *Jorrocks,* then *Periwinkle,* but now it's back to *Jorrocks*?'

'Exactly.'

'Ain't your butler gonna raise merry hell?'

I assumed a lordly tone: 'No valet should be a hero to his man.'

'Whatever you say, guv,' Charlie yawned. 'All the same to me, 'cept the price.'

On leaving the phone box it struck me that, if I was anyway visiting Cambridge under the Ganymede's cloak, I might also be able to assist the romantic fortunes of one Gussie Fink-Nottle. And so I spun on my heel and inserted a second coin.

A brief while later, I was ambling down Jermyn Street with a satisfied sense of 'mission accomplished', when a woodpeckering *rat-a-tat-tat* caused me to glance up from the pavement and peer through the window of Fortnum & Mason's tea-room.

There I saw, much to my horror, Madeline Bassett flailing her limbs in the manner of an unhinged windmill. Seeing that eye contact had been achieved, she raised her cup, jabbed at it like a deranged baboon, and beckoned me urgently inside.

For those unfamiliar with the lie of the land, the 'Mad Bat' is something of an old flame – i.e. one who very nearly burned down the edifice of my bachelor bliss. Indeed, in the course of our familiarity we've been engaged on at least four occasions (I say 'at least' because maidens like Madeline routinely betroth themselves without troubling to notify the co-respondent party). Recently, however, this specific threat of marital immolation had been doused by Madeline's very public engagement to the pocket-dictator Roderick Spode, and her eagerness to acquire the ludicrous title of Lady Sidcup.

I was, therefore, only moderately on the *qui vive* as I entered the tea-room, slapped on a smile, and pulled up a pew.

Before I'd managed a word of hullo, she pounced.

'You're in love!'

'What? No!'

'Come now, Bertie! You can't pull the lambswool over *my* Bo-Peepers. I spy a glow – the *rubiest* glow – like the blush on a cherub's cheeks when nuzzled by a butterfly's nose.'

(She tends to speak in such stomach-churning tones; try not to let it upset you.)

'First, Madeline, butterflies don't have noses, they have probosces – this much one learns at school. Second, *if* there's a glow, and I'm not conceding the point, it comes from nothing more ruby than port.'

Madeline wasn't listening. 'I wonder who— Wait! Don't tell me it's *Florence*?'

'I've not seen Florence Craye for weeks.'

'So there *is* someone!' She wriggled with glee. 'Oooh! I'll bet it's that Scottish girl I saw you with in Berkeley Square – Fiona? Briona? Something like that.'

'I don't know who, or what, you're talking about.'

Jeeves is fond of quoting a chap called J. Alfred Prufrock who is forever complaining of 'insidious arguments' inside 'tedious tents'. Until now, I'd never really understood what the old boy was on about, but something about Madeline's needling tone rather clicked with the poor chump's predic. I've no idea how J. Alfred P. deals with this dilemma, but my solution was to summon the largest available slice of peach pavlova.

'Peaches!' Madeline squeaked with excitement. 'You *must* be in love! Men only ever dare eat peaches when struck by the arrow of Eros.'

Already exhausted by this mawkish drivel, I deployed the tried and tested strategy of distraction.

'Tell me, Madeline, what's Spode up to these days? Marches and rallies and shouting at tailors?'

'Yes, actually. Work keeps him terribly busy.' There was a catch in her voice. 'At least, that's what he tells me.'

'Trouble in paradise?'

Her eyes began gently to mist. 'Onto each petal some dew must fall.'

'There, there,' I soothed, praying she'd not crank up the tear-pump. 'I'm sure it's nothing.'

'Sometimes, Bertie,' she pulled from her sleeve a hideous mauve handkerchief and began dabbing her eyes, 'sometimes I wonder if Roderick is less interested in the tender shoots of our precious love than he is in fomenting a Fascist dictatorship.'

'I hardly think *that's* likely,' I said, thinking quite the reverse. 'After all, you're getting hitched in, what, just over a month?'

'Are we?' she said, absently.

'Of course you are! The invite has pride of place on my mantle-piece, for which I should say thank you.'

Madeline was in another world. 'He never plays with the kittens I gave him.'

'How very odd.'

'Rachele and Benito.'

'Eh?'

'Like the Mussolinis.'

I spluttered on my oolong.

'But surely, Madeline, if he bought you *that*?' I indicated the monstrous, jewel-encrusted brooch pinned to her jacket that depicted, as far as one could tell, a top-hatted leprechaun perching on a toadstool, fishing for rainbows.

'You spotted it!'

'It's ... impossible to miss.'

'As a matter of fact, I commissioned this myself to make a certain someone jealous. But Roderick's not said a *single* word about it. I don't think he's even noticed.'

'I find that hard to believe.'

'Perhaps,' Madeline mused, suddenly and suspiciously more perky, 'you might have a teeny-weeny word with him?'

'*Me?* Talk to *Spode?* About *you?*' The idea was preposterous: like asking a nail to intercede with a hammer on behalf of a plank.

'Roderick respects you *ever* so much, Bertie.'

'Ha!'

'As do I – *ever* so much.'

As she gazed up at me from under her fringe, klaxons began hooting. As I knew from bitter (and recent) experience, were I not scrupulously vigilant, Madeline's fickle affections would leap from Roderick Spode to yours truly – like fleas escaping fire, and with equally plaguing results.

'I will do what I can,' I solemnly swore. 'You can depend on me.'

And if I had my fingers crossed behind my chair, who but the waitress would see?

It took a second slice of peach pavlova to extricate myself from the undertow of Madeline's romantic riptide, but once finally free I hoofed at a pace up Piccadilly Arcade (stopping only briefly to window-shop the dress shirts in Budd) towards the inviolable sanctuary of the Drones.

I could tell from the war-cries echoing around the lobby that the pre-cocktail hour had already begun in a serious way and so, with a conspiratorial tap of the nose to Bashford, I slipped down to the basement, cut through the luggage room, and clambered up the back-stairs to the solitude of the third floor.

It was a stroke of luck that, just before seven, Bimbash *et al.* burst raucously into the Silence Library, or I'd have dozed straight through my next appointment.

*   *   *

Re-entering Lord MacAuslan's Albany set proved something of a challenge, on account of a landslide of boxes and bags that littered the floor.

'I've been shopping,' Iona gestured, by way of unnecessary explanation.

'Did you leave anything for anyone else?'

'One or two items that weren't to my taste – it seemed kind. Now, may I get you a drink?'

She could, and she did, and we sat – Iona kicking off her shoes and tucking her stockinged feet up under her knees.

'How were the paper-hangers?' I asked.

'Diligent. Extremely diligent. They take their job very seriously, which is only right, but to the exclusion of any levity. I jokingly suggested we misprint a sheet of postage stamps and split the auction profits, only to receive a lengthy sermon on the sanctity of the Royal Mail.'

'Probably a good thing I didn't tag along.'

Iona agreed and glanced up at the clock. 'Look, before Crawshaw arrives, is there anything I should know about him?'

'There's not much to tell. I met him a few years ago and thought he was jolly polished, and Jeeves judges him fit for active service, so ... '

There was a knock at the door, which, as Iona was shoeless, I rose to answer. I guided Crawshaw into the sitting-room, poured him some water, and the interview commenced congenially, if a little haphazardly.

'And where are you from?' asked Iona, by way of breaking the ice.

'Dublin, miss.'

'You don't have an accent.'

'Begorra, miss, I can.'

'And Algernon's not a very Irish name.'

'Ah, well, miss, you see my father was terribly earnest.'

'Are you scared of flying?'

Crawshaw blinked at the *non sequitur*. 'I ... well ... I really couldn't say, miss, having never flown. But from down here, it looks more thrilling than frightening.'

'Do you have any pastimes?'

'The wireless, miss. And, when I can, the theatre. That's my true passion.'

'Do you drink?'

He looked a tad abashed. 'Yes, miss.'

'Excellent! I do so hate being judged. Smoke?'

'The occasional cigar, miss. Strictly out of doors, of course.'

'Not on my account; it always reminds me of my Uncle Abernathy.'

'Wait,' I interjected, 'you have an Uncle Abernathy?'

'Abernathy Brocagni Dunwoodie MacAuslan.'

'And he's a warrior chief?'

'Scotland's Lord Advocate – so, close. Now, let me think, what else?'

I raised my hand. 'What would you do, Crawshaw, if your master – *mistress*, I should say – purchased a garment of which you disapproved?'

'What type of garment, sir?'

'Oh, I don't know – say, a hat.'

'And what type of hat, sir?'

I turned to Iona with a grimace.

'A soft cloche,' she improvised, 'in tan velour.'

Crawshaw nodded. 'Along the lines, miss, of the slouch cap worn by Miss Greta Garbo in *A Woman of Affairs*?'

'Exactly!' Iona was as impressed as I was nonplussed.

'Well, miss, I would not seek to *dissuade* you from such a hat – even if it is a season or two past its prime – but I might propose a more suitable style.'

'Such as?'

Crawshaw studied Iona's features with a discerning eye. 'Some might say an Empress Eugénie, miss, but they have become very commonplace. No, I would suggest a peaked Tyrolean, in blue felt or emerald suede.'

Iona scampered over to where her purchases lay strewn and rummaged around for a while before locating an Aage Thaarup hatbox. From this she unwrapped a navy felt Tyrolean peak, gilded with a yellow feather, which she set on her head at a jaunty four o'clock.

'Like so?' she curtsied.

'*Very* much like so, miss.'

After this bravura display of millinery tactics, the rest of the interview sailed by. Crawshaw seemed sound on the things that mattered, and eager to divide his duties between Edinburgh, London, and Continental locations unknown.

'One last thing,' I said, as we stood to say our goodbyes. 'You're a member of the Junior Ganymede, yes?'

'I'm what they call a "noviciate", sir. Not yet experienced enough to be fully fledged, but one or two senior members have taken me under their wing.'

'Including Jeeves?'

'Mr Jeeves is a little *too* senior, sir – I can but hope.'

'Well,' asked Iona, once we'd seen him out, 'what's the verdict?'

'Sound chap, I'd say. Very polished.'

She hesitated. 'A little *too* polished, perhaps?'

'Trust me, Iona, when it comes to gentlemen's personal gentlemen there's no such thing as *too polished*. You might as well say Anatole's cooking is *too good*.'

Iona laughed. 'I defer to your expertise, and will engage him tomorrow. He can start on the first.'

'Excellent. Say, I'm biffing off to the Quarrelsome Crab for a spot of late supper. Can you be tempted?'

'Two meals in one day?' She shook her head. 'Tongues will *claik*! I'd better stay and alphabetise my acquisitions.'

*   *   *

The Quarrelsome Crab is a curious club, which, over the years, has niftily perfected the art of reincarnation. Its origins are lost in the pea-soupers of time, but I first joined the place when it sailed under the flag of The Bitter Pill. Almost immediately it mutated into The Feverish Cheese, before becoming The Frozen Limit, The Startled Shrimp, The Mottled Oyster, and then, very briefly, The Last Gasp.

This 'schizophrenic metamorphosis' (Jeeves, of course) is usually blamed on the boys in blue, who pile into a van and bust the joint whenever life down at C Division gets dull. But darker forces may also be at work, for each new neon name prompts the design of a corresponding ashtray, which the management flog for exorbitant sums. (The Drones has an impressive collection of these ashtrays – some purchased, many purloined – displayed under glass next to our cache of 'liberated' opera specs.)

There was a brief attempt to revive The Frozen Limit when The Last Gasp was raided, but the name had been nabbed by one of Soho's more unyielding criminal gangs. And so the Quarrelsome Crab was born – for how long, though, was anyone's guess.

I blew in just before nine, and bellied up to the bar.

Although the place was pretty tranquil for a Tuesday, the band was still giving it the big trombone, and the table-telephones were flashing as flirtatiously as ever.

I dialled a chum drinking alone at Table Thirty-six, only to be told (in the saltiest of terms) to vacate the line, as he was hoping for a call from Table Eight. I craned my neck to get a glimpse of the party in question, before concluding she fully justified his Anglo-Saxon invective.

A short while later I was Tabascoing an ice-shelf of oysters when a cloud of chalk burst onto the scene, closely followed by Monty Montgomery.

'Have you heard?' he gasped, managing to haul a barstool, signal the barman, light a cigarette, and unfold the *Evening News* in one elaborate flourish.

'It's hard to say, old fruit. Can you be a dash more specific?'

'About the robbery!'

'Eh?'

He directed my attention to the red ink of the stop-press column:

MAYFAIR HOTEL DIAMOND HEIST

Four young men lured a Mayfair jeweller to the Mount Street Hotel this afternoon, before robbing him of diamond rings valued at £16,000. The dinner-jacketed assailants, described by hotel staff as 'well spoken' and 'public school', wore distinctive red-and-white polka-dotted cummerbunds. Police have appealed for witnesses.

'I'm sure it's just coincidence.'

'Coincidence my foot!' Monty scoffed. 'Remember all that trouble?'

I did.

Some years back, the Drones had been shaken to its pips by a bitter dispute concerning the colour of the club's tie. Many of the younger members contended that the long-established plum-purple was 'ditchwater dreary' and demanded we adopt a replacement of crimson with white dots. So acrimonious was the debate (Lord Mueffling challenged the entire library committee to a duel) that a referendum was called to settle the q. for a generation. Unsurprisingly, the status quo was upheld but, as a gesture of goodwill to the juvenile contingent, an optional red-and-white spotted cummerbund was approved for formal events, and very soon the 'Crimson Polka' became as synonymous with the Drones as the Jolly Roger is with pirates.

I sluiced a thoughtful oyster. 'You can't seriously believe anyone from the club is involved in the robbery?'

'It's unlikely, even with the oiks the membership committee keeps admitting.'

'Very droll, Monty. Anyway, who in the Drones would be dim-witted enough to wear a club cummerbund to a diamond heist?'

Even as these words were passing my lips, more than a dozen dim-witted names leapt to mind.

The telephone flashed, and I plucked the receiver.

'Barstool Six. How may I direct your call?'

'Boko, here. Table Fifty.'

'Hullo, Boko. Have you heard?'

'About what?'

'The diamond heist.'

'Of course I've heard! Everyone's heard. I *knew* those cummerbunds were an incident waiting to happen. But I'm calling about the accumulator. We've finalised a list of nags, if you wanted to come and glimpse?'

'I'm oystering with Monty at the mo, but why not pop round for matins tomorrow, and we can rope in Jeeves?'

'Excellent idea. Look, I'm here with the committee and we wondered if you'd like to chip in for a congratulatory bottle of—'

I replaced the receiver.

'What was all *that* about?' asked Monty, helping himself to a bivalve.

I was on the verge of spilling the beans on our last-ditch tax-bill wager, when I remembered Boko's plea for discretion.

'Nothing spesh. Just a man about a horse.'

A gentle but insistent mist of precipitation prompted me to taxi back to G.H.Q., where I discovered Jeeves hiding *objets d'art* from Dicks & Rudge.

'All quiet on the Western Front?'

'Remarkably – if sir will pardon the pun.'

(Often with Jeeves it's best just to nod wisely; I nodded wisely.)

'Except to say, sir, Miss Bassett telephoned.'

'With threats of *something, something* – remind me, it's late.'

'With threats of pain and ruin to despise? No, sir. She was, however, eager that you not forget your promise.'

'Ugh!' I collapsed onto the sofa. 'What's wrong with people?'

'A question, sir, which philosophy—'

'That was rhetorical, Jeeves.'

'Very good, sir.'

'I mean, having made the blunder of getting spliced, why can't people stick to their guns and quit the race? Why do they keep popping back up like poisonous mushrooms?'

Jeeves paused briefly to check if this too was rhetorical. 'May I take it, sir, that Miss Bassett and the seventh Earl are disengaged?'

'Not quite. But they're sailing perilously close to the rocks. Doubtless I will be imploring you to unsoup me in the foreseeable – but not tonight. Tonight that brace of beetle-brains can go hang.'

'Very good, sir. Shall I fetch you a night-cap?'

'You shall! What does one drink after Guinness and oysters?'

'More Guinness, sir. Or champagne.'

'Anything but absinthe.'

He was gone and back in a twinkling.

'Turning to happier matters, Jeeves, Iona has this very evening hired Crawshaw.'

'I'm gratified to hear so, sir. I hope they will prove compatible.'

'Like us, you mean?'

He popped the split of Bolly. 'Precisely, sir.'

'How well do you know the man?'

'Not very well, sir. But by all accounts Mr Crawshaw is a most enterprising and imaginative individual – characteristics that seem likely to suit Miss MacAuslan.'

'Very true. By the way, Crawshaw says he's some kind of pro-bationary member of the Junior Ganymede?'

'A noviciate, sir.'

'But just the Curzon Street club, right? Not *our* gang – not the MacAuslan gang?'

Jeeves looked aghast. 'Oh no, sir. I'd say Mr Crawshaw needs many more years of proven service even to be considered for such a sensitive position.'

'Oh, one thing more: in addition to extra copies of *The Times*, we need to start taking the *Daily Sketch*.'

'Very good, sir.'

'Monty's just become its latest gossip columnist.'

Jeeves's left nostril twitched in amusement. 'I was not aware, sir, that Mr Montgomery was especially well connected in society?'

'Well, exactly.'

Insomnia is not an affliction that traditionally burdens the Wooster line: as soon as the hayloft touches the feathers, darkness descends on the land. Others, of course, are not so fortunate. Freddie Widgeon, I happen to know, is up and down like a lift attendant – not surprising, given the hellish state of his backhand. And Ginger Winship is frequently obliged to swipe his uncle's sleeping draughts, which knock him out for days at a stretch.

That night, however, I was unable to find the cool side of the pillow.

It didn't help that my bedroom had been stripped of all but the barest essentials, nor that I knew a wallpaper bust-up with Jeeves was looming over the dado. And so, after an hour of diligently herding sheep, I admitted defeat, turned on the lamp, and reached for my now dog-eared *Times*.

What had she said? Twenty Down.

Some affection admitted for island.

Four letters.

Hmm.

REEF fitted, but was it an *island*?

And why *affection*?

Or *admitted*?

And why just *some* affection?

I stared at the grid until my eyes grew heavy, the letters began to swim, and (as I discovered the next morning) the nib of my pen pooled navy-blue ink across the pillow.

3.

WEDNESDAY

There's something about a morning cigar that sets a chap up for the day.

Puffing away in the wee small hours, surrounded by dead soldiers and walnut shells, has its charms, undeniably – but, more often than not, one awakes the next morn with a mouthful of ashen regret. A cheroot for elevenses, however, accompanied by a pot of hot java, stiffens the sinews and jangles the nerves in a delightfully up-bucking way.

(I was bequeathed this tradition by my eccentric Uncle Henry, who, forbidden by Aunt Emily from smoking in the house, hailed each morning a taxi to cab him round St James's Park while he kippered himself with a Perfecto Sublime.)

Jeeves had just cut and lit my a.m. Havana when the doorbell made itself known.

'Is anyone expected?'

'No, sir.'

'We are At Home to all but aunts.'

'Very good, sir.'

He trickled out, there was a click and a clunk, and Boko popped his phiz round the door.

'Bad time?'

'Not at all! I forgot you were biffing by. Care for a stogie?'

'Rather.'

I agitated the communicator.

'You have the runners and riders?'

'Yup, at just the right odds – but also a niggling hitch.'

Jeeves materialised. 'You rang, sir?'

'A big 'un from the humidor for Boko, please, some fresh coffee, and then we'd like to ransack your noggin.'

'Very good, sir.' He dematerialised.

'We should wait for Jeeves before we tackle bloodstock.'

'Eh?' said Boko, who was furtively browsing my mantlepiece.

'Wait for Jeeves: we should.'

'Fairy-snuff— I say!' He plucked an invite and waved it aloft. 'Madeline and Sidcup *finally* getting spliced? Mayfair can sleep easy.'

'We'll see. I'm not counting my chickens until that foul duo is matched.'

'Very wise.' He turned and spied my copy of *The Times*. 'I didn't know you did the crossword.'

'I dabble. D'you?'

'No fear. Too reminding of Latin tests and Greek unseens. But sometimes I like to fill in the little squares with words of my own invention.'

Marvelling afresh at how the Drones Club finances became entrusted to such a thundering dolt, I returned to the matter in hand.

'You mentioned a hitch, Boko?'

'It's moolah, of course.' He sat down with a groan. 'According to the odds I've haggled with Leviathan, to win the hundred thou required, we need to stake five hundred.'

'That's hardly niggling,' I protested, 'since we're effectively bonfiring banknotes in the street.'

'The committee's been hunting behind the cushions for a hundred apiece – but that leaves us a hundred short.'

He gave me a look.

I gave *him* a look.

'Why me? Why not Oofy Prosser, or one of the club's other jingle-boys?'

'We thought you'd be pleased! It was your idea after all.'

'It was *Jeeves's* idea,' I credited-where-credit-was-due. 'But can't we just borrow the stake from petty cash?'

'I did enquire, but apparently it's considered *fraudulent conveyance*. And anyway,' he lowered his voice, 'I'm keen to keep things on the q.t. We don't want the investment committee falling into disrepute.'

'Disrepute? Ha! Listen, Boko—'

I was saved from uttering curses I'd live to regret by the arrival of tobacco and coffee.

'Jeeves,' I said, tapping the ash from my cigar, 'we have the horses for your accumulator, and rather hoped you'd give them a dekko.'

'I'd be happy to help, sir.'

Boko presented his list like a schoolboy handing in prep, and Jeeves perused it with a headmasterly eye.

The accumulator Boko had scenarioed comprised five races run over four days, all of which needed to be won outright, at aggregate odds of 200/1. (By a sinister coincidence, these were the exact same odds I'd been given at the last Drones Club cat-herding derby, where I'd lost both the race and, for several nerve-racking days, my elderly neighbour's cat.)

Although I was insufficiently immersed in the form book to make head or hoof of Boko's bets, Jeeves was uncommonly impressed.

'This seems a most judicious selection, sir, given the odds required. Though I do have some qualms about the 4:45 at Newmarket.'

'Gawking Girl – why, what's wrong with her?'

'I happened to observe Gawking Girl in the ring at Plumpton, sir, and even to a non-veterinary eye she appeared bone-spavined, elbow-capped, knee-sprung, moon-blind, splay-footed, and quite hideously parrot-mouthed.'

Boko laughed. 'Is that all?'

'No, sir. There was also a florid presentation of fistulous withers.'

'Ugh!'

'If you will forgive the liberty, sir, I do have an alternative suggestion.'

'I'm all ears.'

'No, sir. I'm All Ears runs in the 2:20, and does not favour a right-handed course. For the 4:45, I would recommend Inch Arran.'

'Really?' Boko scoffed. 'He's sat on the carpet for the last five races.'

'Precisely, sir.'

'Oh-*ho*! Is this the feedbox noise?'

Jeeves adopted his Mona Lisa smile. 'I really could not say, sir.'

'Well, they've the same odds, so Leviathan shouldn't quibble.' He made the necessary adjustments and handed back the card. 'So, we're good as gold with this?'

Wed.	Fontwell	2:30	Monaveen	8/5
Thurs.	Sandown	1:30	Double Star	6/4
Fri.	Kempton	2:00	Manicou	5/2
	Aintree	3:20	The Rip	6/5
Sat.	Newmarket	4:45	Inch Arran	3/1

'Gold may be optimistic, sir. But I am relatively sanguine.'

'Well, let's hope your intel is sound.'

Jeeves nodded sagaciously and melted away to finish the packing.

Boko, meanwhile, had sprung to his feet and was bouncing round the room like a jam-jarred wasp.

'Well, Bertie, that's the quadrupeds settled.'

'Touch wood.'

'But the question remains: are you good for your slice of the boodle?'

I hemmed and hawed, and blew an equivocal smoke ring. A hundred quid was a sizeable sum to stake on a bet that (Jeeves's guarded optimism notwithstanding) would probably boil down to glue. But then again, a life devoid of the Drones Club buzz would be unbearably humdrum and flat – I mean to say, one might as well move south of the Thames.

Sensing my doubt, Boko upped the ante. 'Furthermore, Bertie, as a token of our appreciation, we'd be delighted to co-opt you onto the investment committee.'

This was the clincher.

'I'll put up a hundred on the strict understanding *that* never happens.'

'You're a prince among men! Now, let us sally forth.'

'Sally forth? Sally forth where?'

'To place our bets. The first race is in a few hours, so we need to get our ducats down before Leviathan snips his odds.'

The plan had been to zip off to Cambridge *toot sweet* and pause for refreshment at some picturesque wayside inn – but there was no reason, I supposed, why Jeeves couldn't motor down with the impedimenta, allowing me to follow on by train, in time for our meet with MacAuslan.

'Very well, Boko. So long as our errand is over by lunch.'

'We might even lunch there,' he said, cryptically. 'Don't forget your chequebook!'

*　　*　　*

After a rattling journey east – down Fleet Street, past St Paul's, and along Cheapside – our taxi squealed to a halt outside a distinctly grubby purveyor of fish and chips. We made our way in and stepped up to the counter, where a white-jacketed fryer stood elbow-deep in battered haddock.

'Chips to four plaice,' murmured Boko in a confiding tone, at which our fishy friend jerked his head towards a door marked KEEP LOCKED.

Passing through this (unlocked) portal, we climbed a set of rickety stairs, at the top of which stood a second door, significantly more sturdy, decorated with a skull and crossbones and the cheerful greeting: INDUSTRIAL POISON.

Boko gave a Masonic knock, opened his cigarette case, and pushed a Balkan Sobranie through a narrow hole drilled in the woodwork. After an intricate sequence of unlockings and unlatchings, the door inched open and we were ushered into a chaotic office populated by an army of touts, runners, look-outs, and, judging by their stature, jockeys.

The room's dominant feature was Leviathan himself, who basked like a lustrous shark behind a desk littered with betting slips, ledgers, and bundles of cash. In contrast to the riot of sartorial excess around him, Leviathan wore a funereal double-breaster, offset by a buttonhole gardenia the size of a melon.

'In the nick of time, Mr Fittleworth,' said this gargantuan, demonstrating the tricky art of speaking while inhaling a cigarette. 'I assume you have the readies?'

'I have cheques,' said Boko. 'Will they do?'

'Kites, eh?' Leviathan tutted like an indulgent uncle. 'If you must. It keeps the tax man happy to see *something* kosher on the books – but we don't want him *too* happy, now do we?'

'Also, I'd like to make a change to the last race.' Boko unfolded his list, and handed it over.

'Inch Arran?' Clearly, Leviathan hadn't heard whatever Jeeves had heard or, if he had, didn't credit it. 'You sure?'

'Never *sure*,' admitted Boko, handing over five cheques for a hundred a piece, including the one I'd scrawled in the back of the cab. 'Always hopeful.'

Leviathan passed the cheques to one of his associates, and leaned back luxuriantly.

'You interested in birds, Mr Fittleworth?'

'Well ... ' said Boko, unsure of the conversation's trajectory.

'*Prints* of birds, to be precise.'

'Prints?'

'Oversized, hand-coloured, very rare.'

'And these birds are ... ?'

'American.'

'Right.'

'Nineteenth century.'

'What?'

Deciding it was quicker just to show us what he meant, Leviathan heaved himself to his pins and manhandled onto the desk a vast morocco-leather portfolio.

'It's a new side-line I'm exploring – antique prints and engravings. Very rare. Very select. Very *hush-hush*, if you catch my drift.'

'I say!' gasped Boko. 'These are breathtaking.'

And they were.

Although Jeeves has a well-developed ornithological bent, and is seldom happier than when creeping through the rushes in search of a crested grebe, to my untutored eye one fine-feathered friend looks much like the next. But even I could discern that *these* birds were something quite out of the ordinary – the pains-taking detail and dazzling colours were one thing, the sheer scale of them quite another.

'Hefty, ain't they?' nodded Leviathan. 'The trade calls it "double elephant" – the paper, that is, not the birds. Don't think this geezer ever painted elephants, but imagine the *size* if he did!'

Boko was smitten and, as Leviathan turned the pages, he incanted the inscriptions with awe.

'The Worm-eating Warbler . . . the Long-legged Avocet . . . the Esquimaux Curlew . . . the Red-breasted Merganser . . . '

He was particularly enamoured of a beaky cove known as the 'Ferruginous Thrush' (which sounded to me exactly like one of Jeeves's dismal wallpaper patterns).

'What d'you say, Bertie? Shall we go halves and buy it for the Drones snooker-room?'

'I suppose it depends on how much he's asking.'

Leviathan slammed shut the portfolio and stared at me.

'Say that again!'

'Say what again?'

'What you just said!'

'*I suppose it depends on how much he's asking?*'

'It's bloomin' uncanny. Say "I fancy Apple Scrumping in the 5:15 at Brighton".'

'No!'

'Say it!' hissed Boko, eager to keep Leviathan on-side.

'*I fancy Apple Scrumping in the 5:15 at Brighton,*' I parroted, with a sliver of sarcasm to protest at this ventriloquistic abuse.

'Coo!' said one of the jockeys. 'It's like 'e's in the room.'

'Who?' I asked, irked to be the butt of such cryptic flannel.

Leviathan didn't answer. He leaned over the desk, and fixed me with a beady eye.

'I wonder if you might do me a little tickle?'

'Now look here—'

'He'd be delighted!' cried Boko. 'Anything!'

This 'little tickle', it transpired, involved impersonating a disbarred solicitor called Arbuthnot Scratch, whom Leviathan dispatched to negotiate terms with his 'well-to-do' clientele: the businessmen, clergymen, politicians, and judges who preferred a bookie who'd gone to the same school as them, or at least sounded like he had.

'A few of 'em like slumming it with a *bona fide* scoundrel,' Leviathan grinned. 'They think I'm pukka, see. But Scratchy holds their hands when I'm a little *too* pukka.'

'If this Mr Scratch is so adept,' I sniffed, 'why do you need me?'

Leviathan unfolded a copy of the *Daily Sketch*, and pointed to a headline:

BETTING KINGPIN NABBED IN NIGHTCLUB RAID

'He's not really a kingpin, Scratchy. More of a king prawn. But he is handy. Just like you could be. Man of your talents. Man with your posh tones.'

The more Leviathan smiled and cajoled, the more I sensed myself lured out onto thin ice. Bunging a hundred to save the Drones was one thing; impersonating a freshly collared con man was quite another. How the former had tripped so abruptly into the latter was a question I'd be asking the instant I was free from this den of insanity.

Boko, as is so often the case, was no damn use whatsoever. 'Of course he'll help! What d'you need him to do?'

'Just repeat whatever I say.'

Before I'd time to prepare a defence, Leviathan had seized one of his six telephones, put through a call, and handed me the receiver.

After a couple of rings the line was answered by a deep, domestic voice.

'It's a footman,' I whispered.

'Ask if the lady of the house is in.'

I did. She wasn't.

'Tell him you'd like to leave a message.'

'Which is?'

Leviathan consulted his ledger: 'Eau de Cologning at 6/1, if it's less than two hundred quid.'

I repeated this down the line, and the flunky repeated it back with a weary tone that suggested he'd had more than enough of his employer's 'endearing little ways'.

'See, Mr Wooster?' Leviathan replaced the receiver. 'That wasn't *too* naughty a tickle, now was it?'

'I suppose not.'

'In fact, I'd say you were a natural.'

I blushed.

'I don't know how you're fixed for graft, but if you fancied more in this line, I could put you on a tasty commish. Say three percent? Cash on the nail, of course. None of your flying kites.'

He gave Boko a look, and pointed to a piece of needlepoint framed on the wall:

Punctual payment with a pleasant courtesy of words.

'That's awfully generous, Mr Leviathan, but I'm simply rushed off my feet at the moment. Might I enquire, though, in this spirit of cooperation, which unfortunate fish I've just hooked on your behalf?'

Leviathan shrugged; it was no skin off his cauliflowered conk.

'One of our regulars, actually. A party called ... ' And then he paused, thinking better of simply giving away a tradeable commodity. 'Tell you what, my old son, you do me a few more tickles, and I'll give you all the names you want.'

*　　*　　*

Declining Boko's untempting offer of the 'cod and saveloy special', I hailed a taxi to King's Cross Station, where I purchased a Chelsea bun and a single to Cambridge. After a morning's turf-roguery, it was a blessed relief to bag a window seat in an empty compartment and unfold *The Times* – whereupon my eye was caught by the headline:

MAYFAIR GRIPPED BY DIAMOND THEFT

Despite having considerably more juice than the *Sketch*'s stop press, I was relieved to see that The Thunderer didn't judge our

Crimson Polka to be worth more than a passing remark. Perhaps, I mused, turning to the crossword, the Drones would dodge this cummerbunded bullet after all.

I was getting to grips with Thirty-two Across when, with seconds to spare, the compartment was rushed by a stampede of passengers: a stern gent in heavy tweeds, a harried mother with her sticky child, an elderly matron in fur and pearls, and (somewhat incongruously for first class) a nun in a wimple.

As the last to board, this Wimpled Nun was obliged to cram herself into the narrow, rear-facing seat next to the corridor. Ever Sir Galahad, I silently gesticulated we might swap places – an offer she accepted with belligerent push and an unchristian absence of thanks. (Mr Tweed, however, gave me an approving nod, as if to say the younger generation was not *completely* hand-carted hellwards.)

We pulled out of the station with a long, low whistle, and I set about decoding: *A pro putt almost acceptable* (2,2,3).

Soon, though, my train of thought was derailed by the Sticky Child opposite, who, having been scolded for tapping, whistling, and jiggling his feet, began aggressively rustling a bag of boiled sweets. I glanced up from my doodles to give him a Forbidding Stare, which, far from quelling the beast, merely inspired him to ferret out a peppermint bull's-eye and fling it at my face. Despite having short, pudgy arms, the little chap's line and length couldn't be faulted, and his missile made its mark on the bridge of my nose.

Mortified by her son's incivility, the Harried Mother snatched the bag from his hands and, by way of apology and punishment, passed the sweets around the compartment. (Mrs Fur-and-Pearls politely demurred; the Wimpled Nun took twelve.) The Sticky Child, outraged at this plundering of his treasure, spent the rest of the journey catching my eye and poking out his tongue.

Returning to my paper, I couldn't help but notice that Mr Tweed had just solved Thirty-two Across. Reasoning it was only a matter of time before I too cracked this nut, and since our proximity effectively made us team-mates, I pencilled in UP TO PAR with a gratifying sense of achievement.

At Royston, the Harried Mother and her Sticky Child departed, and we were joined by a boorish, red-headed thug who threw into the compartment an almost endless inventory of suitcases, sporting paraphernalia, trunks, and musical instruments.

'D'you mind?' protested Mrs Fur-and-Pearls, breaking the silence that had lasted since London.

'Not really,' said the Thug, hurling through the door a second set of golf clubs, an oyster rake, and an accordion.

Having made himself expansively comfortable across both empty seats, the Thug took out a meerschaum pipe and, as the train picked up speed, began filling it with a dark and pungent shag. Every so often he'd tamp down the tobacco and test the draw through his fat, moist lips – a performance that was as mesmeric as it was vile. Once the bowl was packed to his satisfaction, he clamped the stem between his teeth and began sucking on it noisily, daring his fellow travellers to object.

Irritating though this all was, the Thug wasn't *technically*— and then he took out a box of Swan Vestas.

For a while he simply maraca'd his matches to the track's *click-ety-clack*, but soon he tired of taunting us and struck a flame.

'Now look here,' said Mr Tweed, 'this is a no-smoker.'

'Is it?' said the Thug.

The compartment erupted into a windmill of arms, jabbing in every direction at the multitude of signs.

'It's only one stop,' grinned the Thug, lighting his pipe with exaggerated pleasure. 'Hardly worth *whining* about.'

'I shall call the guard,' said Mr Tweed.

The Thug extended his foot across the door and let the train's *clickety-clack* speak for itself.

This hostile stalemate became staler still as the meerschaum's fug grew increasingly dank. Don't get me wrong, I like a pipe as much as the next man, so long as the next man isn't Gussie Fink-Nottle, who insists the fumes unsettle his newts, but within minutes our compartment resembled the interior of a Hebridean smokehouse.

'Shall I maybe open the window?' asked the Wimpled Nun.

'No,' shouted the Thug, as the rest of the compartment urgently nodded 'Yes'.

Calculating that people seldom strike vestals in full fig, the Wimpled Nun slid down the glass and a welcome tornado blew in.

In time, regulars for Cambridge began to recognise the landscape and ready their belongings – the Thug included, who stood to rebuckle the straps of what looked like a collapsible canoe. As he did so, he placed his meerschaum on an armrest and – quick as a flash – I stretched across the narrow aisle and snatched it. Leaning back in my seat, I passed the pipe to Mr Tweed, who smuggled it under his *Times* to Mrs Fur-and-Pearls, who conveyed it back across the aisle to the Wimpled Nun, who flung it out of the window.

The Thug resumed his seat.

'Where's my pipe?'

Clickety-clack ... Clickety-clack ...

'Who took my pipe?'

'Almost one o'clock,' said Mrs Fur-and-Pearls, either by way of cunning distraction or through stone-deaf confusion.

'WHAT?'

Clickety-clack ... Clickety-clack ...

And then, with a long, low whistle, the train drew into Cambridge.

Deciding it would be gallant-spirited if I were the player to exit pursued by a bear, I dodged past Mr Tweed, clambered over the Thug's belongings, unlatched the door, and jumped down to the platform.

'Hey, you!' shouted the Thug over the heads and hats of the surging crowd. 'Wait!'

Wait, dear reader, I didn't.

I weaved a path through the throng of bodies, until I reached—

'Tickets, please,' said the inspector, blocking my path.

I patted all the obvious pockets, including the ticket pocket, which, to my certain knowledge, has never been used for anything even vaguely ticket-related, but to no avail.

'Hey, you!' The Thug was closing in. 'Wait!'

Caught between the immovable objections of a uniformed inspector and the unstoppable force of my brutish pursuer, I froze.

And then Mr Tweed appeared.

'D'you see that chap behind us?' he said to the inspector. 'The one waving?'

'Friend of yours, is he?'

'My son, actually, and he's got our tickets, which explains his excitement. We *could* stand here until he gets through the crowd, but ... '

'That's all right, sir.' The inspector waved us through. 'I'll collect them when he comes.'

'I don't know how to thank you,' I gasped, as we sped to the cabs.

'Don't mention it,' said Mr Tweed. 'One of the perks of being a judge is learning the tricks of the trade.'

*   *   *

Having taken an expensively scenic tour of Cambridge landmarks, my taxi juddered down Trinity Street and deposited me outside Gonville & Caius. I entered the lodge to find a black-suited porter, with his back towards me, methodically filing correspondence into a warren of pigeonholes.

After a lengthy interval of ignoration, I jangled my pocket change.

'*One* minute, sir,' said the porter severely, before condescending, quite a few minutes later, to turn round.

'My word!' I exclaimed. 'Jeeves!'

I was about to enquire what, on God's green earth, gave – when two undergraduates strode laughing into the lodge.

Jeeves gave me a meaningful look. 'How may I help you, sir?'

'I'm Reverend Wooster,' I said, unleashing the ecclesiastical manner I'd been rehearsing *en route*. 'Here to pick up my key.'

'Certainly, Reverend. I will just attend to these two gentlemen, and then show you to your rooms.'

We climbed to the very top of N Staircase, where Jeeves unlocked the outer oak of my set. Stepping inside, it was clear that Lord MacAuslan hadn't been exaggerating – the rooms were indeed bijou, but they were also crammed to bursting with resplendent African art.

'Holy smoke! It's like a tiny museum.'

Jeeves nodded. 'The set is usually occupied by the anthropologist Professor Evelyn Evan-Evans, sir. I gather he is presently beleaguering the Nuer people of the Nile Valley.'

'Let's hope they count the spoons before he leaves. The Prof looks to have extremely sticky fingers.'

I wandered into the bedroom and up to an alcove of sash windows that afforded a stunning, if vertiginous, rooftop panorama of the Senate House, the University Library, and the spires of King's College Chapel.

The bedroom's *other* panorama, equally stunning and vertiginous, was afforded by its wallpaper – which bore a striking similarity to the wallpaper I'd secretly reordered the day before. Its hunting design was a tad more 'safari' than my *Jorrocks's Jaunts & Jollities* (there were, for example, significantly more zebras than you'd see at the Quorn or Pytchley), but the overall effect was depressingly similar – and I immediately saw the world of difference between a sample sheet of foolscap and an entire, enveloped room.

I was startled by Jeeves's cough.

'It is somewhat reminiscent, sir, of an exotic Hieronymus Bosch.'

I'd no inkling who, or what, the man was on about, but seeing how terribly smug he looked, I thought it prudent to lay the groundwork for my *Periwinkle* betrayal.

'What piffle! It is spirited and joyous. Full of life. I couldn't be happier.'

'Very good, sir.' He placed a blue-and-white-stringed Cohen Bros. parcel on the bed. 'If you will change into your clerical attire, sir, we should be leaving very shortly.'

*　　*　　*

Jeeves unlocked the gate to Trinity's Fellows' Garden with a key from an unfamiliar bunch, and steered me across the lawn to what is known by us ink-slingers as a 'leafy bower'.

Beneath said bower sat Lord MacAuslan, elongated along a bench like an Anglepoise lamp, perusing a volume of Walter Scott and sporting his trademark tartan buffet. Next to him, equally elegant, though reading *The Times* and dressed for riding, sat his niece.

'What-ho, MacAuslans! And a particular *what-ho!* to you, Iona, since I'd no idea you'd be joining us.'

'Not a disappointment, I hope?'

'Quite the other thing. But you didn't mention it at lunch.'

'It's called the Secret Service for a reason, Bertie.'

Lord MacAuslan saved my blushes by bidding us to sit.

'Mr Wooster – *Reverend* Wooster, I should say – welcome to Cambridge, and thank you once again for assisting us.'

'Happy to oblige.'

'As I said yesterday, we have in our sights two undergraduates, both now in their final year. The first is a *sneekit* rascal called Adrian Whipplesnaith. He's reading modern languages at Trinity and is desperate to be "recruited" by someone – anyone, really. He keeps popping up at odd societies, making cryptic interventions, and attempting meaningful handshakes.'

'And here he is,' said Iona, handing me a glossy photo.

Even in black and white, Whipplesnaith's red-headed bulk and thuggish demeanour were instantly familiar.

'I've just met this chap!'

'Really?' Iona looked concerned.

I described my eventful train excursion.

'Would he recognise you?'

'Possibly – though it was all pretty haywire, and I wasn't yet Rev'd up.'

Lord MacAuslan turned to Jeeves. 'Should we maybe call it off?'

'I think not, my lord. The risk would be that Mr Whipplesnaith had deduced he was of interest to the Ganymede – and I venture to suggest the defenestration of a meerschaum pipe is unlikely to inspire such a conclusion, even in the most paranoic.'

'Well, let's hope so. Anyway, our immediate concern is not with Mr Whipplesnaith, who is as disposable as he is deplorable, but with the threat he poses to Mr Orsini, for whom we have greater expectations.'

Iona handed me a photo of a nondescript chap in cricketing whites.

'Fabrizio Orsini,' Lord MacAuslan continued, 'is at Gonville and Caius, also studying modern languages, and he dreams of joining the Foreign Office. Despite his academic mediocrity, this is a dream we are eager to make come true.'

'I assume there's a Ganymedean motive for such largesse?'

'There is. Although Fabrizio is himself English, his father, Tonello, is a senior figure in the Italian finance ministry, and we have reason to believe he is not enamoured of his country's current political direction.'

'So we're coddling the son to nobble the father?'

'Precisely. However, Mr Orsini is being blackmailed by Mr Whipplesnaith.'

'Incriminating photos? It usually is in the Rex West novels.'

'Actually, yes,' said Iona. 'But not what you might expect. Have you ever heard of night climbing?'

'It rings a bell,' I said vaguely – though, in truth, it clanged Big Ben.

82

Night climbing, as the name suggests, involves climbing by night – not the fruit trees or garden walls of one's youth, but the ivy-clad brickwork and crenellated spires of ancient monuments. Modern architecture is all well and good, I suppose, but give me the leaded dome of the Radcliffe Camera, or the Bod's Tower of the Five Orders, and I'm up and across 'em like a spring-heeled gazelle. Well, I used to be in my Oxford days, when I was an eager, if discreet, night-climbing buff.

'Sometime last term,' Lord MacAuslan continued, 'Mr Whipplesnaith took a photograph of Mr Orsini night-climbing on the roof of Pembroke Chapel. In the normal course of events, the disclosure of such a document might have resulted in Mr Orsini being gated for a period, or perhaps fined. However, the University authorities have recently decreed night climbing a sending-down offence – and it is this which prompted Mr Whipplesnaith to launch his campaign of intimidation and extortion.'

'What does he want?' I asked. 'Cash?'

'So it seems, which is curious since Mr Whipplesnaith is already the wealthy heir to his family's powdered-soup fortune. We suspect, however, his real aspiration is to join Mr Orsini's club.'

'Don't tell me, the Pitt?'

Lord MacAuslan nodded. 'Mr Whipplesnaith has tried to join the Pitt on several occasions, presumably to further his murky political ambitions. But the membership committee, on which Mr Orsini sits, considers him utterly beyond the pale.'

I nodded: membership committeeing is far more taxing than anyone imagines.

'We can engineer Mr Orsini into the Foreign Office no matter how disappointing his degree. But were he to be expelled, the ensuing publicity would make his employment impossible. So we need to obtain Mr Whipplesnaith's blackmailing negative, and for that we need you.'

'Right. Well. Gosh. Sounds like fun. So, what now?'

Lord MacAuslan turned to Jeeves.

'We wait, sir. Mr Whipplesnaith is, as we speak, moving his myriad belongings into his rooms in New Court, and the conditions for a burglarious intervention are not yet propitious.'

Lord MacAuslan put his hand on my shoulder. 'But don't drop your guard, Reverend Wooster. I expect to fire the starting gun on Friday night.'

Leaving the MacAuslans to their leafy bower, Jeeves and I strolled back across the lawn, where we were accosted by a wild-eyed chap in a mismatched suit, holding an enormous bobbin of twine.

'Might I intrude, gentlemen?' He had the well-clipped English of a native German. 'What do you say, please, about this path?'

'Path?'

'Yes. This path in the grass. On which we stand.'

'Er ... '

'I could not agree with you more.' He shook his fist furiously. 'The path is terrible. *Every* path here is terrible. The garden looks like ... *a birthday cake!*'

'I see,' I said, though I decidedly didn't.

'Will you assist, please, for just one moment?' He took from an inside pocket a worn blue notebook, and located a stump of pencil from behind his ear. 'I am planning a new design for these paths and must urgently take some measurements.'

Before I might conjure any reasonable objection, our new friend had guided Jeeves to a spot in the centre of the lawn and handed him the twine's loose end.

'Stand here, please, and hold this.'

Me, he beckoned to follow him as he played out his spool in an easterly direction, counting off a hundred paces, before tapping a spot on the grass with his foot.

'Stand here, please, and hold this.'

He wrapped a loop of twine around my thumb and then marched off to the north, loudly enumerating his steps as he unspooled his bobbin, twice round an ancient oak and off out of sight.

I stood staring at his departure, expecting, at the very least, some sort of encouraging cry. But silence reigned and nothing happened. Silence reigned for a further five minutes, and eventually I called across the lawn to Jeeves.

'Do you think he's coming back?'

'I am not overly optimistic, sir.'

'Hmm.'

In time, two elderly, black-gowned Fellows entered the garden; one was inordinately fat, the other cadaverously thin.

'Excuse me, gentlemen,' Jeeves called across the lawn, 'might you be able to assist us?'

The men diverted their trajectory and stalked towards me with a distinctly hostile step.

'Yes?' the fatter Fellow demanded. 'What do you want?'

'Well ... ' I faltered, having no inkling of Jeeves's plan.

'Is this a rag, young man? I have the lowest possible regard for student antics, and refuse absolutely to be ragged.'

His colleague was of the same angry mind. 'The Dean is quite right. Furthermore, this garden is out of bounds to all but Fellows.'

I'm afraid to say my mouth rather flapped open ('like a rain-drenched wind-sock' an aunt once said) before Jeeves intervened.

'We are from the Ordnance Survey,' he shouted, 'and have permission to gather preliminary mapping coordinates for a proposed retriangulation.'

'Retriangulation, eh?' the thin man mused, before shouting, 'Where's your theodolite?'

'In the automobile,' Jeeves shouted back. 'In fact, sir, this explains our request for assistance. If you might momentarily hold our positions on this line, we will return with our equipment and complete our calculations.'

The Fellows exchanged a doubtful glance, before finally relenting.

'I suppose it's all right – if it's for the Ordnance Survey.'

'Thank you, sir. Now if one of you might take my place over here, and the other where my colleague is standing, we will be just a few minutes.'

Jeeves made an elaborate show of correctly positioning the Fellows, adjusting the twine an inch or so back and forth, before bowing in thanks and whisking me off towards freedom.

We were almost at the garden's gate when one of the Fellows cried, 'STOP!'

We turned round.

'Why is a clergyman working for the Ordnance Survey?'

Jeeves's reply was instantaneous.

'Spiritual outreach, sir.'

'That was quick thinking,' I said, as we ankled back to town through the gardens of Clare.

'Thank you, sir.'

'I wonder how long they'll wait. But, tell me, who was that queer cove with the spool of twine and the German accent?'

'The *Austrian* accent?' Jeeves gently corrected. 'I may be mistaken, sir, but I think that was the philosopher Ludwig Wittgenstein.'

'So, not an unhinged gardener?'

'Dr Wittgenstein is the author of the *Tractatus*.'

'A short history of farm machinery in the Ukraine?'

'The *Tractatus Logico-Philosophicus*, sir, concerns itself with a picture theory of language. The title, as you may recall, is a reference to an earlier work by Baruch Spinoza.'

'Ah, yes, your chum Spinny. But why is Earwig Whatsisname so h. under the c. about garden paths? Seems a little *ultra vires* for a philosopher, or do I mean *infra dig*?'

'I could not say, sir. And whereof one cannot speak, thereof one must be silent.'

By this time we'd reached Clare Bridge, and I stooped beneath a yew tree to collect two sturdy twigs.

'What d'you say, Jeeves: fancy a game of Poohsticks?'

It's seldom that I or, indeed, anyone steals a march on Jeeves, but the look on his face as I held up the sticks was one for the family album.

'I beg your pardon, sir?'

'Poohsticks? Winnie-the-Pooh? A. A. Milne? Don't tell me you've never come across *Winnie-the-Pooh*? Or *The House at Pooh Corner*?'

I didn't think there was a book in existence that Jeeves had not read, digested, and in great part memorised, yet it was clear from his incredulity that I was speaking the richest banana oil. And so I briefly sketched out the Hundred Acre Wood hypothesis, from Pooh and Piglet to Owl and Eeyore – not neglecting, of course, Christopher Robin or Rabbit's Friends and Relations.

Jeeves tilted his head like a confused whippet.

'Winne-the-Pooh is a bear, sir?'

'He is.'

'And Piglet is a piglet, sir?'

'Indeed.'

'And there are two kangaroos, sir?'

'That's right.'

'In East Sussex, sir?'

'Yup.'

'I hope you'll forgive the observation, sir, but this all seems highly improbable, ethno-zoologically speaking. Moreover, to approach the matter from a Darwinian perspective, why would the stronger animals not simply eat the weaker ones?'

'They're children's books!' I cried, thankful I hadn't broached the subject of heffalumps. 'Were you never a child?'

'Briefly, sir. The predicament proved unavoidable.'

'And were there no such books in the Jeevesian household?'

'I recall *Der Struwwelpeter*, sir – a German cautionary tale in which various children are punished for their moral failings.'

You could see where the man had amassed his brains, but you had to wonder if the knowledge was worth the recurrent nightmares.

I pressed on.

'So, Poohsticks – fancy a game?'

'Possibly, sir. How does one play?'

Briefly, I set out the rules and regs, giving him his choice of twig, and we took up positions on the upstream side of Clare Bridge.

'On three, Jeeves. One ... two ... *chuck*!'

It was, I suppose, inevitable that Jeeves had a natural flair for Poohsticks, and I wondered if there was a German word for one who, in an instant, transforms beginner's luck into professional expertise.

Time and again his twigs caught hidden eddies and sped ahead of my sluggish logs, which, inevitably, became tangled in bindweed or, inexplicably, sank without trace. Best of three turned into best of five, and then best of seven, and by the time Jeeves had scored nine straight victories I had run out of patience – and twigage.

'What a remarkable game, sir,' Jeeves declared as we trooped back to Caius. 'I shall seek out the works of Mr Milne without delay.'

*　　*　　*

I met Gussie, as planned, outside his rooms in Rose Crescent, before heading off to The Eagle to meet his peacherino. We were ambling past Great St Mary's, confidentially discussing Boko's accumulator, when I spotted, stepping out of Ryder & Amies, my young and ne'er-do-well Cousin Thos.

'Oh, God!' I cried, seeking to hide myself behind Gussie, at the exact same moment Gussie also cried, 'Oh, God!' and sought to hide himself behind me.

'What d'you mean?' I gasped, as we spun round each other. 'He's *my* cousin!'

'Quite possibly,' said Gussie, ducking down behind me. 'But he's *my* pupil.'

We were still embroiled in this tangle-footed fox-trot when the cuz. in question stepped up.

'Hullo, Cousin Bertie. Hullo, Mr Fink-Nottle. What are you doing here?'

'Well—'

'And why are you dressed as a priest?'

This was an excellent question, and I was pondering why Gussie had failed to ask it earlier, when the air was rent asunder by a goose-pimpling shriek.

'BERTRAM!'

It would have been superfluous to revolve the lemon, for I knew in a flash that the voice behind this verbal assault belonged to my aunt (and Thomas's mother) Mrs Agatha Gregson – five feet nine of barbed-wire entanglements, the Beast of Belgravia Square.

People talk of giddy aunts, holy aunts, and even sainted aunts, but, if you ask me, aunts is aunts – and aunts is trouble. I seem to have scores of the blighters, dozens for each deadly sin, and the overwhelming majority are as welcome as Pharaoh's plagues. If they're not correcting your grammar or complaining about your clothing, they're criticising your pals or calling you feckless. Frankly, it's exhausting, and something should be done.

This isn't to say there aren't occasional sunbeams of warmth. Aunt Dahlia, for example, is generally good and deserving, and when she's bad and ill-deserving there's always her chef, Anatole, to oil troubled waters with foodstuffs fit for the gods. Of course, the only things Aunt Agatha eats are rusty nails and shards of glass, washed down with the tears of her foe.

'Pippety-pip, aunt o' mine. What a topping surprise!'

'Do *shut up*, Bertram.'

'Right-ho.'

She swivelled to Gussie. '*Who* are *you*?'

'Mama,' interceded Thomas, with suspicious civility, 'this is Mr Fink-Nottle. He's my tutor.'

Aunt Agatha gave Gussie the once-over, and was clearly unimpressed.

'A tutor called Ink-Bottle? Is that supposed to be clever?'

'Well ... *ahhh* ... '

'In what do you tutor my son?'

'Well ... *ahhh* ... you know ... *ahhh* ... this and ... *ahhh* ... that.'

Although Gussie tends to vagueness at the best of times, the particular inanity of his responses owed much to the savage assault that had been launched on his ankles by McIntosh – Aunt Agatha's increasingly malicious Aberdeen terrier.

'*This and that?*' Aunt Agatha spat. 'For the exorbitant fees I pay Lancelot Pinke I expect a little more—'

She stopped and went puce with rage.

'DID YOU KICK MY DOG?'

There is, of course, only one possible answer to this question.

Naturally, Gussie failed to supply it.

'I merely nudged him with my foot,' he explained, foolishly assuming that truth and reason cut any sort of auntly mustard.

'YOU KICKED McINTOSH!'

'I *guided* McIntosh. Very gently.'

Aunt Agatha turned to her son. 'KICK HIM, THOMAS!'

Now, this was a tester. Not in his wildest dreams could Cousin Thos. have imagined being given permission, let alone a direct order, to physically assault one of his teachers. Yet, at the same time, he had the feral sense to know that, despite any number of witnesses, he'd inevitably be punished for the crime.

'I'm not sure that's a good idea, Mama,' he said, quite possibly for the first time in his life.

Aunt Agatha sighed, and handed him the lead. 'Do I have to do *everything* myself?'

Gussie, now unsnarled from the fangs of McIntosh, decided that loitering *in situ* to be kicked by a pupil's mother corresponded neither with the letter nor the spirit of his employment.

'Heavens!' he said, retreating diagonally like a dressage pony. 'Is that the time? Well, I shan't detain you any longer, Mrs Gregson. It was a pleasure. I can see where Thomas gets his pluck!'

And with that, he stood not upon the order of his going but legged it towards The Eagle at something approaching a sprint.

I watched him depart with envious eyes, before Aunt Agatha hinted she desired my attention by stabbing me in the thigh with her brolly.

'Why are you dressed as a clergyman?'

'Am I?'

'*Aren't* you?'

I reflected on my options. 'I suppose I am.'

'Well, that's both of us a minute closer to the grave with nothing to show for it. I do wish you'd be a little less vapid.'

One of these days I'd like to meet the chump who said 'people mellow with age like fine wine' and shake him warmly by the throat. For while Aunt Agatha had unquestionably aged, she had not done so in the manner of good burgundy, so much as bad hock turning into worse vinegar.

'I expect it's one of your idiot fancy-dress affairs?'

'It is,' I lied, grateful for the alibi. 'But what brings you to Cambridge?'

'I'm visiting ugly-mug here, who is cramming at Pinke's Academy and being tutored by your dog-kicking friend.'

'Weren't you at Pevenhurst?' I asked Thomas, who merely shrugged in sullen reply.

'He was, until that damfool headmaster "suggested" he leave. Stuff and nonsense, if you ask me. All boys are interested in fire. Only natural at his age.'

Thomas had the good grace to look a little sheepish at this, and I could only imagine which glorious timber-framed antiquity had been razed to its stumps by his furtively concealed matchbox fixation.

'Nonetheless,' Aunt Agatha conceded, 'I'm not *entirely* displeased to see you, Bertram, for you have recently been much on my mind.' This boded ill. 'What are your plans for luncheon tomorrow?'

I opened my mouth to conjure a prior engagement, but she was too quick.

'Nothing? Very good. You shall lunch with me.' She gave my dog-collar a final, distasteful glower. 'And I expect you to be properly dressed.'

'But—'

'Take it off,' she ordered, 'or I shall make myself *most* disagreeable.'

Wondering what such a threat could possibly involve, I slipped a finger under my collar, and slid out the band.

'You may find it amusing to ridicule the Church, Bertram, but I do not.'

Thus dismissed from my papal audience, I reeled along to The Eagle, where, in a dark and intimate alcove, I spotted Gussie in animated conversation with a striking brunette. Well, she was animated – he was silent as a man being shaved.

'Bertie!' he beckoned, delighted by the arrival of reinforcements, 'Come and say hullo to Vonka.'

So this was Emerald's replacement.

'What-ho, Vonka. It's a pleasure to meet you.'

'Likewise, I'm sure. I've heard an awful lot about you.'

'All good, I trust?'

'Well,' she paused, 'I did think you'd be wearing a monocle.'

'Why does everyone say that? I've never worn a monocle in my life!'

Looks-wise, Vonka resembled the kind of dame forever being tied to railway tracks, though in her case the cinema-going masses would doubtless cheer for the wax-moustached villain if it meant a moment's peace from her war of words.

If beauty is in the eye of the beholder, and that ship has pretty much sailed, I'd like to put in a word for the beholder's ears. Some girls are tranquil, you see, and some girls are chatty, but

Vonka Pinke never, ever stopped talking. Nineteen to the dozen fails to do justice to the speed and flow of her incessant chatteration, and attempting to edgeways into her onslaught of words was a little like playing ping-pong against a hail-storm.

On the rare occasions I did manage to chip in, she anticipated every turn of my phrase, and sprinted off with the conversational ball.

Gussie gazed at his girlfriend in lovestruck silence (not that he had much choice), presumably entranced by her ability to speak without breathing, like one of his 'lungless salamanders'.

Every now and then he shot me a glance that said: *Isn't she marvellous?*

She's certainly something, my glances replied.

Mindful of the cost of paper and ink, I'll spare you the complete transcript of Vonka's monologue, but the headlines were these: an only child; keen on riding, with a love of dogs and a loathing of cats; agnostic about newts, but keen to be convinced (here Gussie blushed like a grape); gainfully employed at the University Library, where she wielded an inky date-stamp; and a reluctant Gemini – which was as far as she went in sharing her mother's many and various superstitions.

The mention of Mrs Pinke allowed me to jam a foot in the conversational door.

'I gather your mother has—'

'Objections to our engagement? Yes, she has two. The first is that Gussie drinks, which is easy enough to conceal. I've been concealing it for years. The second is more squirrelly: she doesn't approve of his birthday.'

'What's wrong with—'

'His birthday? It's not *preordained* with mine.' Vonka unfolded a slip of paper. 'You see Gussie is a *Potamogeton perfoliatus* whereas I am a *Dionaea muscipula*.'

My heart sank. 'Don't tell me she's reading—'

'*Fortune-Telling with Flowers*? Oh yes. It's by her bed. She takes notes. She's crazy about it.'

This appalling book had spread like tangled knotweed through fashionable (i.e. gullible) society since its publication – and in a few short months it had done more to uproot the romantic order than any number of private eyes or lipsticked collars. I knew of several engagements broken off, or forced into being, on account of 'flower-bed compatibility' – the preposterous idea that 'birth flowers' govern one's destiny. Indeed, I, an *Aster amellus*, had only escaped the poisonous tendrils of a *Convallaria majalis* because *Fortune-Telling with Flowers* called us an 'imaginable' but not an 'envisaged' match. Whatever that compost meant.

I was thinking how tricky it would be to disabuse Mrs Pinke of her botanic inanities, when I remembered Iona's Junior Ganymede 'paper-hangers'.

I raised my hand for permission to speak, which, in time, was grudgingly granted.

'Don't ask me how, Vonka, because I am sworn to secrecy, but ... ' I risked a pause for dramatic effect ' ... I can probably forge Gussie a new birth certificate!'

The effect was undramatic.

'To give him a different birthday,' I clarified.

Vonka shook her head. 'That cat won't jump. Mama checks every candidate's birth certificate before Papa offers them a job.'

'What about—'

'Pretending he has an identical twin?' She rolled her eyes. 'Why are men so obsessed with that idea?'

'All right then, I give up. Time to consult the oracle.'

'Who?' asked Vonka.

'Jeeves,' said Gussie, speaking for the first time in weeks.

Unfortunately (or otherwise, depending on your affection for tinnitus), Vonka was obliged to return to her dusty stacks, and so Gussie and I headed off *à deux* to the University Arms hotel.

'Well?' he asked, his eyes aflame. 'What d'you think?'

'Of Vonka?'

'Of course!'

'I'm a little surprised she works in a library.'

'Eh?'

Although I was baffled why Gussie aspired to marry a girl as strident as a cattle auctioneer and as tedious as a twice-told tale, only a fool attempts honesty with a man in love. In my experience, the blunter one is in enumerating the deficiencies of an affianced, the more likely that marriage becomes – placing you on the wrong side of a wronged wife until divorce do them part. 'Give it to me straight' is a trap, you see – so no matter how plangent the tone, or doleful the gaze, at all costs lie.

'I'm serious,' said Boko. 'Give it to me straight.'

'I think Vonka will make you very happy.'

'Thank you, Bertie, that means a great deal. I've already started saving for the ring. She says she likes red, so a ruby, perhaps? Or a garnet? But surely diamonds are the safest bet?'

'There's always the Blarney Stone.'

'Oh! Would that suit her?'

'More than you can imagine. Listen, tell me about tutoring Cousin Thomas. Just how bad is he?'

'Hellish. I don't care that he smokes – they all do that – but I strongly suspect him of setting fires. His last piece of prep simply reeked of paraffin, and I swear several of the pages were charred round the edges.'

'Even in the cradle there was a whiff of brimstone.'

'And he wrote a *terribly* insulting essay about newts. I had to look up many of the words and, really, I was shocked. Can you have a chat with him? He's your flesh and blood, after all.'

'I hardly think my counsel will prevail – it's never done so in the past.'

As we approached the University Arms, Gussie pointed to a crab-like figure beetling out of a chauffeur-driven Rolls.

'Ain't that your aunt?' He shrank back at the memory of their recent skirmish.

It was. And there was McIntosh drawing blood from a doorman's ankles to banish any doubt.

'I should've guessed she'd be staying here,' I lamented. 'We'll have to come back later in case she loiters in the lobby.'

'Why don't we use the staff entrance?'

'I doubt they'd let us in.'

'They'll let me in,' he grinned. 'I work here.'

'No, Gussie, you work at Pinke's Academy for juvenile arsonists. This much we've established.'

'But I *also* serve room service here. I can't possibly crack a crust on what old man Pinke calls a wage.'

'You, Gussie, serve room service?'

'Only breakfasts, and only at the weekends.'

'This is too deliciously *too* for words!'

'Nothing wrong with serving room-service breakfasts, Bertie. You meet some very nice people serving room-service breakfasts.'

Having navigated the hotel's labyrinthine staff quarters and back-stairs, we arrived at the Perseus Suite – a sprawling set of floral rooms that was serving as Jeeves's bedroom, my backup emergency bedroom, and the Ganymede's base of ops.

I opened the door to discover Jeeves, shirt-sleeved, with his feet up, deep in a copy of *The House at Pooh Corner*.

'I am most terribly sorry, sir.' He sprang to attention and flowed back into his coat. 'I had not anticipated you would require me.'

'It is I who should apologise, Jeeves, for disturbing your afternoon off. Enjoying A. A. Milne?'

'He is most diverting, sir. I am learning that Tiggers don't climb trees.'

'Splendid! Look, I hope you don't mind, but Gussie here is up to his stud in the soup *du jour*.'

'I would be happy to assist, sir.'

'It's a long shot, I know,' Gussie grimaced, 'and I feel a fool for asking ... *but* ... can you change the date of my birth?'

Jeeves emitted not a flicker of surprise. 'I fear, sir, you flatter my abilities. Perhaps, though, an alternative solution might present itself were I to know the broader circumstances of your dilemma.'

And so, perching on the edge of a chair, Gussie set out the scope of his plight – from the crackpot advice of *Fortune-Telling with Flowers* to the unhinged mind of Evadne Pinke.

Jeeves listened with Solomonic attention before handing down his judgement.

'In my experience, sir, it is bootless to reason with the superstitious. Those who are convinced that the fault is in our stars seldom take kindly to more terrestrial explanations.'

'So, I'm doomed?'

'Not necessarily, sir. My suggestion is that you appeal to a higher power.'

Gussie was alarmed. 'You mean ... *God*?'

'No, sir. Another fortune-teller – one who might convince Mrs Pinke that floral birthdays should admit no impediment to the marriage of true minds.'

A smile inched across Gussie's face, transforming it from lugubrious haddock to exuberant flat-fish.

'Clever, Jeeves. Very clever. I happen to know she consults a clairvoyante called Madame Paladino every Thursday morning. I see it all unfold from my bedroom window on Rose Crescent.'

'That is most providential, sir. Perhaps this clairvoyante can be persuaded to advocate your cause in return for a nugatory *unguentum aurem*.'

Gussie turned to me. 'Whashesay?'

'He says: We can probably bribe 'em. But, really, Jeeves, this all sounds hopelessly far-fetched. Don't these spiritual johnnies swear some kind of hypocritic oath?'

'Hippo*cratic* oath, sir? Though in some respects your neologism is apt: persons who claim mystical powers often enjoy remarkably ambidextrous moralities when presented with opportunities for enrichment.'

Gussie turned to me again. 'Whashesay?'

'He says: We can probably bribe 'em.'

'But how? I've never bribed anyone in my life, let alone a clairvoyante. Presumably they'd see me coming?'

'Perhaps it would be best, sir, if I broached the matter with Mrs Pinke's clairvoyante on your behalf?'

'You'd do that?'

'Of course, sir.'

'I say!' Gussie beamed. 'How terribly A.B.C.D.!'

It was Jeeves's turn to look confused.

'Above and Beyond the Call of Duty,' I translated.

Gussie departed soon after, to do whatever it is Fink-Nottles do on Wednesday afternoons, and I kicked off my shoes to spend a little time with the crossword. I rejected Twelve Across and Sixteen Down as monstrously polysyllabic, and was pondering a five-letter word for *Medic with singular low hum*, when I remembered my news.

'I say, Jeeves, you'll never guess who I bumped into on King's Parade.'

'Given the multiplicity of alternatives, sir, I fear you have the upper hand.'

'Aunt Agatha! Here in Cambridge!'

'How very distressing, sir.'

'I mean to say, if familiarity breeds contempt, then family breeds ... '

'Contumely, perhaps, sir?'

'If you say so. Sounds made up to me. Anyway, Cousin Thomas is now studying at Pinke's Academy.'

'Ah, yes, sir,' Jeeves nodded. 'I recall reading about the Pevenhurst arson.'

'And get this: he's being tutored by Gussie Fink-Nottle.'

'Quite the meeting of minds, sir.'

'You said it.' I tossed the paper aside with a yawn. 'Rouse me in time to shave before supper.'

I awoke with a start, to find Jeeves at my side.

'Is it today?'

He frowned. 'In a sense, sir, it is always "today".'

'I mean, is it the same day as it was a little earlier?'

'Yes, sir.'

'I've just had the most remarkable dream.' There was an awkward silence. 'Do I detect a lack of vim for the young master's reverie?'

'Perish the thought, sir. I await the substance of your crepuscular fugue with the keenest of interest.'

And so I let him have it, with both crepuscular barrels.

'I was at a dinner, possibly in Oxford, with MacAuslan and a gang of the Ganymede chaps. They were discussing some kind of "secret signal" that would be communicated by wearing red socks. Anyway, the dinner was being cooked—'

'Excuse me, sir.' Jeeves rarely interrupts, so I knew this would be vital. 'Did I hear you say "socks"?'

'Red, for the wearing of.'

He looked askance. 'I could not recommend red as an acceptable hue for hosiery, sir.'

'It was a dream, Jeeves! I was asleep!'

'Even so, sir, red is *not* worn. Black, navy, or charcoal grey are all suitable – depending on the day's attire – and white, of course, for tennis and similarly athletic pursuits.'

'Right, well, thanks for that. Now, returning to my dream. We were at dinner, Anatole was cooking, and the menu was remarkable: *Caviar Frais, Hareng fumé, Rôti de boeuf avec pointes d'asperges à la Mistinguette, Timbale de ris de veau Toulousaine,* and *Toast au fromage fondu avec marmalade.*'

There was another awkward silence.

'Well, Jeeves?'

'Sir?'

'What do you think it *means*? What does it *suggest*?'

'I hesitate to draw too definitive a conclusion, sir, but it might suggest you were hungry.'

'Interesting. Now I come to think of it, I haven't yet had lunch. Perhaps there's something to this dream-interpretation malarkey.'

'I am sure Professor Freud will be cheered by your approbation, sir.'

'The blighter who wrote *The Monster from Within*?'

'In a sense, sir. On an unrelated matter, you may be interested to know that Monaveen won.'

'Is that a crossword clue?'

'No, sir – the first horse in Mr Fittleworth's accumulator. He, by which I mean Monaveen, not Mr Fittleworth, romped home, as they say, in the 2:30 at Fontwell.'

Frankly, I wasn't sure if this was news to cheer at all. One down, four to go, and all that – but it did rather prolong the agony of inevitable defeat. Like ripping off a plaster, or jumping into the Cornish waves, equine disappointments are best confronted with quick resolve and a stiff drink, not dragged round the houses like one of Barmy's jokes.

'When's the next race?'

'Tomorrow, sir. The 1:30 at Sandown. The word along the rail is that the hard going will suit Double Star, and the jockey has—'

'*This* jockey,' I rose from my chair with a yawn, 'must dress for dinner.'

*   *   *

I rendezvoused with Lord MacAuslan outside Trinity porter's lodge – whereupon he promptly read my mind.

'The kilt is in London, Mr Wooster, but I trust these *trews* will suffice?'

'At least we know I'm not colour-blind.'

'And I see you've stuck with the clerical collar.'

'Jeeves was adamant: no priest worth his psalter wears a dicky-bow to High Table.'

We made our way across Great Court to pre-prandial drinks in the Fellows' Parlour, which was so crammed with gowns of every hue that I was momentarily transported to the academical racks of Cohen Bros.

Lord MacAuslan found two schooners of unspeakable sherry, and had just guided me to an inconspicuous corner when the room was silenced by a tapped glass.

'Has anyone seen the Dean?' a voice called out.

'I saw him this afternoon, Master,' said a chap nearby, 'walking with the Senior Tutor towards the Fellows' Gardens.'

'Well, neither has made it back.'

'Come along,' said Lord MacAuslan, abandoning his sherry, 'I'd better introduce you.'

The Master was a tall, languid, self-satisfied sort of chap, with an impatient air and a black patch across his right eye. (The *diablerie* of this adornment rather evaporated when Lord MacAuslan informed me that the oyster had been sacrificed settling a bet that champagne could safely be sabred *towards* one.) He greeted Lord MacAuslan as an old friend.

'Torquil, my dear chap. I saw your name on the list. To what do we owe this honour?'

'I've to consult some volumes in the University Library, Master, and thought I'd exercise my dining rights.'

'Splendid! Too few do, which means we're stuck night after night with dullards like the Bursar. And who is your colleague?'

'May I introduce Reverend Wooster.'

'How d'you do, Master.'

He regarded my collar with disdain. 'Why are you gospel-grinders so damn timid about dressing for dinner?'

This was one of those times I wished Jeeves might emerge from the crowd to win the argument for me, but further hostilities were avoided by the banging of a gavel and the announcement that dinner was served.

High Table seating is a tricky affair, Lord MacAuslan explained, the art being to ensure one isn't trapped by any of the 'Bore Quartet' – Drunks, Lawyers, Limpets, and Mutes. With the exception of stumbling Drunks, members of the B.Q. are notoriously tricky to spot from a distance, and the danger is multiplied when the species interbreed. (It's theoretically possible to meet a Drunk Mute Limpet Lawyer, and statistically probable at the Athenaeum.) The only *formal* formality is that the Master selects his neighbours before heading into Hall – after which, it's every man jack for himself, and one needs quick feet and sharp elbows to swerve into a bearable seat.

Lord MacAuslan, an old hand at the game, deployed the ingenious technique of introducing bores to each other as the procession crocodiled up the stairs, causing snarls of traffic that he ruthlessly exploited. Sadly, we were heavily outgunned by the B.Q. that night, and had to take what tedium we were given.

I ended up several places along from my host, and diagonally opposite the Master, who glared at me with his one operative eye, and made an odd sort of gesture. Not really knowing the High

Table form, I replied with a nod, and he gave me a grim smile of thanks before announcing to the table:

'In the Dean's unscheduled absence, Reverend Wooster has kindly agreed to say grace.'

As I opened my mouth to protest, the gong was struck and two hundred students fell silent. Realising the honour was now inescapable, I steepled my hands in a vicarly fashion, and launched in.

'Our Father—'

The Bursar snapped his fingers furiously. 'In *Latin*, dammit!'

I don't know about you, but Latin has always been a hate-love sort of affair for B. W. Wooster. Like any schoolboy worth his tuck, I relished nothing more than parading around an ice-cold dorm bellowing at full lung: *Bellum-bellum-bellum-belli-bello-bello-bella-bella-bella-bellorum-bellis-bellis*. But with such declensions firmly roted in the hatbox, the study of Latin became increasingly detached from the life of a conker-pocketing shirker with little on his mind but the cricket:

Iulia aquam ad nautam portat.
Julia does indeed carry water to the sailor. Too often for my liking.

Apollone tu Delius spolio audeo?
You bet I dare plunder Apollo of Delos!

Hic ego aut omnino falsus, aut certe parvus opinio sum confido.
Nope – not a clue.

Faced now with a Hall of hungry eyes upon me, I stared up at the ceiling and strove to recall the words I'd heard many scores of times at Oxford.

'*Te Deum Patrem colimum*—'

'*COLIMUS!*' corrected an angry voice from behind me.

I started again.

'*Te Deum Patrem colimus …*'

And then, like an actor drying on stage, my mind went completely blank. Not only did all the Latin I'd ever acquired vanish from the grey cells, so did most of my English, and my face began to tingle with vermillion pins and needles.

Sensing that something was gravely amiss, one of my neighbours leaned across the table and whispered, '*Te Laudibus prosequimus*,' which I echoed with solemn reverence, but even this failed to ignite the engine's auto-starter.

And then a helpful undergraduate nearby supplied the next cue – '*Ave atque vale*' – which I gratefully repeated, and the next – '*Timeo Danaos et dona ferentes*'.

Soon the Hall became one giant prompt box, feeding me with lines to repeat.

'*De gustibus non est disputandum.*'

'*Ignorantia juris non excusat.*'

'*Post hoc, ergo propter hoc.*'

'*Mens sana in corpore sano.*'

Admittedly, some of these lines sounded oddly familiar (and, indeed, familiarly odd), but having embarked on this panto of audience participation, there was no retreating from the stage.

And so I parroted all that was shouted, in as reverent a manner as I could muster.

'*Cum grano salis.*'

'*Panem et circenses.*'

'*Vox populi, vox Dei.*'

'*Habemus papam.*'

Finally, a voice at the very back of Hall bellowed, '*Apologia pro vita sua.*'

Thinking this sounded like a suitably devotional full stop, I repeated the line with emphatic force, and concluded my grace with a godly and sober 'Amen'.

'AMEN!' roared two hundred souls, before bursting into wild and uproarious applause.

I'd like to report that the rest of the meal was any less agonising than its liturgical preamble, however the chap on my left very pointedly 'turned', and I was limpeted by a professor of English whose formidable lisp was matched only by the feebleness of his R's.

'Do you appwethiate werth, Wevwand Woothter?'

'Werth?'

'Yeth, werth! Poemth. Thoneth, villanelleth, hewowic poemth, poemth of womanth!'

'I know "A Charming Young Dancer from Delhi" if that butters the cabbage?'

'Doggewel ith not werth, Wevwand Woothter. Doggewel ith damnable!'

'Right-ho.'

He went on to dispense an earful of assertions (and an eyeful of saliva) on the function, form, and historical significance of poetry, which dragged on through the tepid soup, the oily fish, the gristly chops, and the woody rhubarb crumble. Indeed, I only managed to silence this unconscionable stream by swearing up and down that I would purchase, without delay, at least one copy of his self-published anthology, *Weasel Words*.

As the servants cleared the final plates, three loud blows were struck against the panelling, and the Hall fell silent.

'Gentlemen,' said the Master, rising to his feet and hitching a thumb into his waistcoat, 'it is customary, at the start of a new academic year, for the Master to say a few words.'

A low groan was emitted from those who had endured these 'few words' before, but the Master was deaf to reproach. After a soul-crushing diatribe on the fragility of college plumbing, the sanctity of library tickets, and the best way to mothproof one's gown, he sat down to barely polite applause. But then, as if remembering he'd left the bath running, he jumped back up.

'There is one more thing, gentlemen, and I address this especially to those who have just joined our little community: *night climbing*.' (A few brave souls cheered.) 'In the past, certain individuals have made a sport of scaling by night the roofs of this college and other buildings. This is dangerous, disrespectful, and not to be tolerated. At the last meeting of the Regent House, it was unanimously agreed that *any* member of the University discovered night-climbing will be sent down. No gating. No fines. No rustication. No excuses. Gentlemen, you have been warned: *expulsion*.'

This time the Master sat to a sand-dance of shuffling feet, before one piercing whistled echoed round the room.

'Who whistled?' shouted the Bursar. 'Licence is given to many things, but never whistling.' He summoned a steward. 'Find that man ... and fine that man.'

The gong was struck, the congregation rose, and the Master gave me a filthy, monocular stare before snarling '*Benedicto benedicatur*' and sweeping out of Hall.

We recombined for dessert in an ancient panelled room, heady with the scent of port, Stilton, and beeswaxed oak. For obvious reasons of self-preservation, I engineered a seat as distant from the Master and Bursar as geographically possible; indeed, I was so far below the salt that Lord MacAuslan was lost in the shadows.

I was in the midst of an intriguing conversation with a chap called Charlie on the best way to extinguish candles (place your thumb in front of the flame before blowing, was his ingenious advice) when my elbow was tapped by a neighbour.

'Excuse me,' he said, in a nasal sort of voice, 'but do you know the Bishop of Norwich?'

'Don't think so – though I did once meet the Vicar Apostolic of Brazzaville.'

'What I mean is, why don't you stab yourself and pass the dagger?'

'I don't follow you.'

'No, *I* follow *you* – that's my point.'

'Eh?'

'Pass. The. Damn. Port.'

I reached for the decanter with an alphabet of apology, and was about to slide it to the left when my arm was stayed by the chap on my right.

'I say, any chance of a back-hander?'

'Does everyone here speak in riddles?'

'A back-hander: you can pour me a glass out of turn, but I can't pour one myself. And if I wait for the damn thing to circulate, I'll be sober.'

Touched by this heartfelt plea, I dispensed the requested refill – but clearly with insufficient generosity.

'Play fair, Reverend, that's only a buzz – make it a brimmer!'

And so I topped *both* of our glasses up to the meniscus, which proved provident, for the chap on my left snatched the decanter and we never saw it again.

As this storm with the port was blowing over, I became aware that an argument had silenced the table.

Inevitably, the Master was holding forth.

'Nonsense!' he declared. 'When it comes to athletic pursuits, women are the inferior sex, plain and simple. Indeed, I'll wager a case of college claret – the *good* college claret – that no sport exists where men and women can compete on equal terms.'

After my graceless performance earlier, I'd vowed to keep well away from the enemy lines, but something in the Master's tone, combined with memories of Aunt Agatha thwacking me into the rhodos, caused me to blurt out the word 'Croquet!'

'Who said that?' the Master barked.

'I did.'

He peered down the table. 'Oh! Still here, Reverend Wooster? How *very* brave.'

'Reverend Wooster is my guest,' said Lord MacAuslan, riding to my rescue.

'And is your guest a betting man, Torquil?'

'He's a man of the cloth, Master, though I stand ready as proxy for any wager he might be called to answer.'

'Croquet is a question of physics and mathematics – two subjects women are incapable of grasping.'

'And yet,' smiled Lord MacAuslan, 'and yet.'

'I assume your guest is willing to test his ridiculous assertion in a doubles match?'

'Certainly.'

'Well then,' said the Master, 'let's hope the Reverend's croquet is less humiliating than his classics.' And he summoned the Fellows' Betting Book to formalise our wager in ink.

'Was that entirely wise?' I asked Lord MacAuslan as the evening broke up. 'I can't imagine for a moment that Aunt Agatha will be persuadable, and I don't know any other female croqueteers in Cambridge.'

'Why would we stoop to aunts, Mr Wooster, when we're so handsomely *plenished* with nieces?'

I was wending my way back to the porter's lodge when a crooked figure stepped out of the shadows and aggressively blocked my path. Unable to make out his features, and fearing it might be Adrian Whipplesnaith seeking revenge for his meerschaum pipe, I raised my fists in the approved Queensberry manner and braced myself for a blow.

'Wevwand Woothter!'

I dropped my dukes.

'I have that wolume of *Weathel Wordth* you were tho werry enthuthiathtic to pwocure! I pwethume you can wecompenthe me with weady money?'

With an hour in hand before Caius bolted its doors – and in no hurry to return to my minuscule mausoleum of stolen tribal art – I drifted across to 7A Jesus Lane for a finisher at the Pitt.

The University Pitt Club (as you might guess) was established in honour of William Pitt the Younger, and (as you might not) occupies the neoclassical premises of an insolvent Turkish baths. It's not quite as boisterous as some of the Oxford establishments – certainly not the glass-half-broken Bullingdon Club – but its members are occasionally roused to rannygazoo, most often during May Week, when balls are crashed, picnics raided, and Bumps races bombarded with prawns.

I slipped off my collar as I entered the bar, and introduced myself as a reciprocal from the Drones – whereupon I was invited to join an ebullient table of chaps, all of whom were shod in fluffy bedroom-slippers.

'The last gang I saw in footwear like that,' I said, 'was the Hysteron Proteron.'

'We *are* the Hysteron Proteron!' sang a chorus of voices.

'I thought it was an Oxford club?'

'It is,' said the president, who introduced himself as Lord Pallot. 'I brought it across after getting sacked from Balliol.'

The thesis of the Hysteron Proteron is deceptively simple: once a term, its members live a day backwards. They rise at six, slip into black tie, and take brandy and cigars while playing bridge. Then they 'breakfast' on a five-course supper, with matching wines, before a lazy morning of snooker, darts, tennis, or golf. Lunch is an oasis of stability, but supper (eaten in jim-jams and accompanied by teddy bears) is a full-board breakfast from devilled kidneys to porridge oats.

Trust me: the whole charade is as stomach-turning as it sounds, and on the few occasions I partook at Oxford, it took me a fortnight to rediscover my sea legs.

'If today is Hysteron Proteron Day,' I queried, 'shouldn't you all be in pyjamas?'

'Friday's the actual day,' said the club's secretary, a chap called Baxley 'The Baron' Salmon. 'Tonight we plan and plot – and climb.'

'Climb?'

Lord Pallot pulled out of his satchel a pair of ink-black, rubber-soled shoes.

'What a coincidence,' I exclaimed. 'Only this afternoon I was discussing night climbing with ... some chums.'

'Care to join us?' He glanced down at my patent-leathers. 'I'm sure we could find you something with a little more grip.'

I explained that my night-climbing days were long gone, and the conversation turned to other matters – notably, how they might join the Drones after graduation, or on being sent down – until the time came for them to lace up, and for me to head back to Caius.

As I rose from the table, I spotted a familiar face sitting alone in the far corner, reading the paper.

'Who's that chap over there?'

Lord Pallot glanced over his shoulder. 'Orsini. Third-year linguist at Caius. Chairman of the membership committee. Sound chap and a first-rate night climber. Shall I introduce you?'

'Oh, no, thank you. He just looks like a friend of a friend.'

4.

THURSDAY

I was woken from a deep, dreamless slumber by the sound of my outer oak being banged upon and then unlocked.

'Cock-a-doodle,' a throaty female voice sang out. 'Rise 'n' shine!'

If this was a burglar, I thought, she had an unusually chipper *modus operandi*.

'We've left you till last 'cos you're new. But the room's gotta be done. Ain't that right, Diane?'

'That's right, ma'am!' a second voice sang out. 'Gotta be done.'

'Don't want you wastin' the morning. Ain't that right, Diane?'

'That's right, ma'am. Wastin' the morning.'

'The rain's gone, and it's gonna be a bright sunshiny day. Ain't that right, Diane?'

'That's right, ma'am. Lovely day.'

This raucous dialogue became louder and shriller as it approached my bedroom door, which, without warning, swung open.

'Hope you're decent!'

In burst an enormous woman of mature years who, even to my sleep-drenched senses, was the spitting image of the all-in wrestler who used to deliver my coal.

I bolted upright, clutching the bedsheets to my neck.

'Hullo, dearie! I'm Christine, your bedmaker. This is my help, Diane.'

A slim young girl circumnavigated her boss's formidable girth and stepped into the room, whereupon my eyes nearly sprang from their sockets – for, standing before me, dressed like a maid with her hair in a net, was Iona MacAuslan.

Christine nudged her with a fleshy elbow. 'Say hullo to the nice man, Diane.'

'Hullo, nice man,' Iona twinkled. 'Smashing pyjamas.'

'Er, thank you.'

'Don't mind her, ducks, she's new.'

'I see. Well, best of luck.'

Christine leaned on her mop. 'I hear you're a priest?'

'Something like that,' I said, slowly sinking down under the covers.

'Do you hear confessions?'

'Not right now.'

''Cos there's a few things I want to get off my chest.'

I glanced at Iona, who did little to help my composure by goggling her eyes like Buster Keaton.

'I've seen a lotta things,' Christine continued.

'Well—'

'I've *done* a lotta things.'

'Right—'

'Things you would *not* believe.'

'Perhaps,' I said, pinching myself under the bedclothes, 'we might arrange a time to talk?'

'Reckon I'm going straight downstairs,' she pointed to the floor.

'The basement?'

'HELL!'

Then, suddenly, as if a switch had been flicked, Christine was back to her warm and sunny self.

'Righty-ho, we'll do the study first. Let you get respectable. But don't be all day.'

'Actually, what time is it?'

'Time you was up, priest or no priest! Ain't that right, Diane?'

'That's right, ma'am. Priest or no priest.'

I dressed at speed, and was almost out of the door when I remembered my luncheon subpoena from Aunt Agatha. And so I ditched the dog-collar for a tie of knitted silk before hoofing it across to my other set of rooms at the University Arms hotel.

Here I was delighted to discover that Jeeves – ever indulgent of his master's vice – had ordered an unstinting breakfast of eggs, bacon, sausage, and kippers. Sadly, the lion's share of this feast was in the process of being polished off by Gussie Fink-Nottle, who, arriving promptly for the first time in his puff, had appointed himself Early Bird and commandeered my worms.

'Hungry, Gussie?'

'As the proverbial. Try the scrambled eggs.' He pushed an empty dish in my direction. 'They're fluffier than you can imagine.'

I salvaged a crust of toast and a sliver of bacon from the crumbs he'd let fall, and fashioned myself a far from agreeable sandwich.

'Did you leave any coffee?'

He weighed the pot. 'Half a cup? Probably cold.'

I was on the verge of dispensing a few cold words on the subject of bedbugs, leeches, and other bloodsucking parasites when I spotted at Gussie's elbow my copy of *The Times*.

'You've finished the crossword!'

'Yup.'

'How?'

He looked surprised. 'It's not *that* hard!'

Shock competed with envy, and a dash of indignation.

'Give it here.'

He handed me the paper like a man tipping his barber, munching on a sausage all the while.

Even after I'd scraped away the smears of butter and gobbets of jam, it took me some time to figure out what Gussie had done. Every square of the crossword was indeed filled in, but with seemingly random letters forming words of utter gibberish. Only when you read the grid like a book – from left to right, top to bottom – did it become clear that he'd simply repeated the phrase: ALL WORK AND NO PLAY MAKES JACK A DULL BOY.

I tossed the paper back across the table.

'Congratulations, Gussie. You outshine yourself.'

'Thanks, old man. Shall we get another round of snorkers?'

Declining to entertain Gussie's sausage compulsion any further, I summoned a flagon of fresh coffee, and set about the agenda's solo item.

'So, Jeeves, is the fix in? Will Mrs Pinke's fortune-teller be puffing Gussie to the stars?'

'Up to a point, sir. As I predicted, Madame Paladino was eager to participate in the deception, in return for a surprisingly meagre financial inducement. She did, however, express unusually professional qualms about dissembling to a client of long standing.'

'In words of one syllable, Jeeves?'

'She will not lie to Mrs Pinke,' he staccatoed at dictation speed, 'but has gone out for the day and lent me a key to her shop.'

'A *key*? What good is a key? Someone needs to be there *in person* to give her the old razzmatazz-ical – Barnum and Bailey her.'

'That thought did occur to me, sir, which is why . . . '

His gaze drifted across the room towards a brown-paper package tied up with string – blue-and-white string.

'Oh, no,' I groaned. 'Not again!'

'Not again, what?' asked Gussie.

'Jeeves wants one of us to assume the role of fortune-teller.'

Gussie clapped his hands like the seal he so often resembles. 'That is splendacious! I mean, *obviously* it can't be me, because she's met me hundreds of times, but *you* would be perfect.'

'First, splendacious is *not* a word. It's *never* been a word, and I wish you'd stop pretending it *is* a word. And second, the entire fandangle is far, far too risky. Don't forget I'm joining you at the

Pinkes' for supper tonight. What if Mrs Pinke recognises me over
the *hors d'oeuvres*? What then for your engagement to Vonka?'

Gussie put his hand on my shoulder. 'The Bertie I've known
from our days in short trousers – Daredevil Bertie – would do
anything for a chum in a spot.'

'It's no use buttering me up,' I complained. 'Not after you've
snaffled my toast.'

The problem was: Gussie wasn't wrong.

(Not a sentence I take pleasure in writing, nor ever expected
to write. But there it is: even a stopped Fink-Nottle can be trusted
twice a day.)

We Woosters have a Code, you see – Never Let a Pal Down
– and that Code runs through us like veins in a Gorgonzola.
Generations of my forebears have forborne any number of indig-
nities in the name of camaraderie, even if – or especially when –
the comrade in question is a love-struck Romeo.

'Very well,' I groaned, 'I'll don the disguise. But one day the
boot will be on the other foot, and I shall ask of *you* a favour –
what it is yet I know not: but it shall be the terror of the Drones.'

'What was that?' said Gussie, chomping on a morsel he'd
exhumed from under a cloche. 'Something about feet?'

My riposte was forestalled by a knock at the door, which,
when answered by Jeeves, presaged the entrance of a shy young
waitress bearing my coffee.

'Perhaps, miss,' I gestured to the detritus before us, 'you'd be
kind enough to clear some of this?'

'Very good, sir.'

As she set about Gussie's destruction, it was impossible not to notice the poor girl was racked with nerves – a trembling state that caused her to drop, spill, or clatter almost everything she touched. Plates clanged into platters, spoons fell to the floor, and the milk jug was knocked across *The Times*, causing Gussie's WORK and PLAY to interbleed like Monty's rainswept chalks.

She giggled awkwardly at every mishap, glancing up at Gussie and Jeeves, before abandoning the task, grabbing her tray, and fleeing the room in a cloud of apology.

'What a remarkable girl.'

'She's called Mabel,' said Gussie. 'Mabel Chitt.'

'You *know* her?'

'Of course! We work together at the weekends. She was evidently rather surprised to see me as a guest.'

'Evidently.' I turned to Jeeves. 'Shall we take a gander at this costume?'

He was gazing into the middle distance with a look of ... well, I'm not quite sure.

'Jeeves?' I said, after a beat or two. 'The costume?'

'Yes, sir, of course. Forgive me.'

It's hard to express the shock and chagrin I felt on unwrapping the Cohen Bros. parcel to discover, not the heavy velvet robes of a noble wizard, but the diaphanous wisps of a dainty clairvoyante.

'I'm to play a *woman*, Jeeves?'

'I judged it prudent, sir, not to disconcert Mrs Pinke by introducing an excess of innovation into the *mise en scene*.'

'Did you now?' I scoffed, for scoffing was what the *mise en gubbins* demanded. 'Won't Mrs Pinke be a teeny-tiny bit disconcerted by — oh, I don't know — my unshaven face?'

'No, sir.' He handed me a heavy gauze veil. 'Not if you wear this.'

'And my voice?'

'I suggest you adopt a falsetto register, sir.'

I gave a hollow, mirthless laugh. 'Brilliant, Jeeves. Just brilliant.'

Gussie, proving himself the foulest of fair-weather friends, ganged up against me. 'Buck along, Bertie! Remember at school, when I was Goneril to your Regan? You were pitch perfect then.'

'You mean, before our voices had broken?'

'Oh, yes. There is that.'

I reflected upon my options. True, this hideous costume was hardly 'What the Well-Dressed Man is Wearing', but then again, it would afford me considerable protection against identification at supper, or should the balloon go up. Also, time ticked by, and it seemed unlikely we could locate a more dignified replacement before the evil hour.

'Very well. But I'm not prepared to pass through Cambridge dragged up like Widow Twanky. I shall change in the shop.'

Jeeves handed me the key.

'You're not coming to spectate?'

'No, sir. I shall stay and conclude matters here.'

'Jolly good— Wait a sec! What's my name?'

'Your name, sir?'

'My clairvoyante name. Don't I have to call myself something appropriately mysterious, like they do in the films?'

Jeeves pursed his lips. 'Perhaps, sir, you might adopt the persona of Madame Sosostris.'

'*Sosostris.*' I rolled the word around my tongue. '*Madame Sosostris.* Is that a suitably psychic sort of name?'

'I would say so, sir. It enjoys the imprimatur of Messrs Huxley and Eliot.'

'Are they also clairvoyants?'

'In a manner of speaking, sir, yes.'

*   *   *

The door jangled open, and Mrs Pinke stepped into the shimmering half-light.

'Madame Paladino?' Her voice was quavering and shy.

I waited a beat for dramatic effect, before emerging from the shadows (like Bela Lugosi in *Chandu the Magician*).

'I am Madame Sosostris,' I intoned theatrically. 'Clairvoyante, occultist, sayer of sooths.' I clocked her look of disappointment. 'Madame Paladino is at home with a bad cold.'

'Your voice is awfully deep, Madame Sosostris.'

'I too have a bad cold.'

'Must be something going around.'

I guided her to the seance table, which Gussie had thought-fully decked out with a flickering candelabra, and we sat.

'Tell me, oh seeker of truth, how may the Spirits guide you this morning?'

'Shouldn't I cross your palm?'

'Eh?'

'Madame Paladino always says silver guides the Spirits to their voice.'

'And who I am to argue?'

'You have to say it, or it doesn't work.'

'Cross my palm.'

'You have to say it *properly*!'

'Cross my palm with silver,' I warbled, struggling rather to get my voice at an appropriate pitch.

Mrs Pinke unearthed a coin from the depths of her handbag and pressed it into my hand.

'Thank you. Now, how may the Spirits guide you this morning?'

'It's my daughter, Veronica. I'm anxious—'

'Speak not! We shall see what the Spirits know.'

I took her hand in mine (as Mischa Auer took Phyllis Barrington's in *Sinister Hands*) and closed my eyes.

'Is there anybody there?' I warbled. 'Be not afraid, ye Spirits of the Spirit realm. Knock to indicate your presence.'

Silence rang out. What the hell was Gussie playing at?

'*Knock*,' I repeated a little louder, opening one eye and giving Evadne a reassuring nod, 'to indicate your presence.'

Finally, Gussie knocked.

'We have a connection! Thank you, operator. Will you knock once for "Yes", and twice for "No"?'

Knock.

'May we seek your wisdom?'

Knock.

'Do you know this lady?'

Knock-Knock.

'But you sense her predicament?'

Knock.

And then a blood-icing yowl emanated from behind the beaded curtain which, to an ear as trained as mine, sounded exactly like a newt-fancying Dronesman catching his finger in a hinge.

Mrs Pinke gasped. 'What does *that* foretell?'

Sheer damned inanity was what I wanted to say, but the only word that sprang to mind was, 'Maybe ... '

'*Maybe* the spirits sense my predicament?'

She had a point.

'Maybe it's the plumbing. Let us seek another path.' I glanced at the shelves for inspiration. 'Shall we consult the Tarot? Or the dice?'

Mrs Pinke's eyes shone with excitement. 'Might we try ... ' she hesitated, plucking up her courage, ' ... the *orbuculum*?'

I very much hoped that the ensuing silence indicated awe on my part, rather than total ignorance, and then my eye fell on a faded poster for 'Alexander the Orbuculum Seer', which depicted a turbaned man looming menacingly over a crystal ball.

'Of course!'

Madame Paladino's orbuculum was both heavier than it looked and – as I discovered when it thudded to the carpet – sturdier. Once it was safely in the centre of the table I waved my hands over its contours with a flutter, and shrouded it with my voluminous veil. (To be honest, I was rather pleased with my performance, which owed much to Nellie Savage's 'Madame Mystera' in *The Hole in the Wall*.)

I took a deep, mystical breath before ducking under the covers and launching in.

'What do you see?' asked Mrs Pinke, eagerly.

'I see clouds ... '

'Oh.'

'But they are parting ... '

'Ah!'

'I see a girl ... '

'Vonka!'

'She's very talkative ... '

'*Lively*, you mean?'

'No. Talkative. Very, *very* talkative ... but now I see a man!'

'Ooh!'

'Dark ... spectacled ... and, between you and me, a little fish-faced ... '

'Augustus!'

'They are in love ... '

'They *are*!'

'But, I see an impediment ... '

'Oh, no!'

'Can it be ... '

'*What?*'

'A flower bed?'

'It can!'

'Does a flower bed divide their love ... ?'

'It does!'

'A flower bed of ... *affinity*?'

'Yes!'

'Wait!'

'What?'

'I see movement ... '

'Oh!'

'The clouds are shifting ... '

'Hooray!'

'The girl is crossing the flower bed ... somehow floating ... '

'*Floating?*'

' ... over the flowers that divide them ... '

'Oh!'

'Into the arms ... of her love.'

'The impediment is gone?'

'Yes.'

'They are preordained?'

'Yes.'

'An engagement?'

'Yes.'

'A *love* engagement?'

'Yes.'

'Can it be true?'

'Yes.'

'You *know* it to be true?'

'Yes.'

This went on for quite a while – 'Are you sure?' *Yes.* 'Quite sure?' *Yes.* 'Certain?' *Yes.* 'Certain-certain?' – *ad nauseam* and very nearly *infinitum*.

Eventually, Mrs Pinke was persuaded that mere flower beds should prove no obstacle to the blooming of true love, and she burst into tears of joy.

'I'm so pleased. He's such a very nice boy, Augustus.'

'Is he?' I murmured, a little too loudly as it turned out.

'*Isn't he?*' she gasped. '*Why? What do you see?*'

'Nothing, nothing. I meant to say: He is.'

She exhaled in relief, and took from her purse another coin.

'Now, Madame Sosostris, let me cross you in farewell.'

'Eh?'

Mrs Pinke explained that for a reading to 'fix', silver must cross at the conclusion as well as the commencement of each consultation. This sounded suspiciously like a Supertax of Madame Paladino's special invention, but who was I to throw stones in the glasshouse of fraud?

As I extended my arm across the table, my hand was briefly illuminated by a rainbow of light bouncing off the crystal ball.

Mrs Pinke squealed in delight and lunged at me. 'Your *palm*!'

'What about it?'

'Such beauty! Such proportion!' She pulled my hand closer. 'I've never *seen* such a Mount of Venus.'

'Which means?' I asked, curiosity causing me to slip out of character.

'Surely you know?'

'Yes, of course! But what do *you* see?'

'Yours, Madame Sosostris, is a Solar Hand – indicating grace of body and mind, and a love of riches and honour.'

'Jolly good.'

'The Line of Saturn is pure through the Plain of Mars – indicating uninterrupted success, notwithstanding any amount of imprudence.'

'No argument there.'

'And the Life Line begins shallow, but becomes deeper with age – indicating a childhood of adversity, but an adulthood of tranquillity.'

This was all ringing strangely true, and I began to wonder if there might be something to the whole flapdoodle when I remembered that, for all her faith in the Spirit Realm, Mrs Pinke had failed to tumble that the hand she was holding belonged to a man, dressed as a woman, masquerading as a clairvoyante.

'The Heart Line is long and strong,' she continued, 'but often crossed – indicating many dalliances, but no fixed alliances.'

'Too true.'

'But see here!' She twisted my palm painfully into the light. 'An unmistakable cross on the Mount of Jupiter!'

'The Mount of Jupiter?'

'The Mount of Jupiter!'

'Remind me ... '

'True love, Madame Sosostris! Finally, after years of questing, you have found true love!'

I guided Mrs Pinke from the half-light of our seance into the sunshine of Rose Crescent, flipped the sign from THE EYE IS OPEN to SEER TOMORROW, and headed back through the beaded curtain to give my so-called partner a piece of my mind.

He was sitting by the sink with his hand in a bowl of ice.

'And where were you, Gussie? I got six measly knocks and then you vamoosed.'

'Sorry, old man. I trapped my finger in the hinge.'

'Leaving me alone with the batty Mrs Pinke? Thanks awfully.'

'But did it work? Are Vonka and I engaged?'

'Naturally,' I bowed. 'I played my part to perfection.'

'And Evadne won't recognise you at supper tonight?'

'Not a chance.'

Gussie beamed. 'Jeeves is a marvel. I must remember to slip him something.'

'*Jeeves?* It was your pal Bertram Wooster who put in the hard yards. Just look at me.'

Gussie eyed my outfit with distaste. 'The less said about that the better.'

I was musing on the winter wind of man's ingratitude – serpents' teeth, and all that – when I noticed the time.

'Oh, Lord, lunch! I must change into civvies.'

'Isn't eleven fifteen a shade early for lunch?'

'Not for lunch with an aunt.'

*   *   *

Knowing Aunt Agatha's tyrannical approach to punctuality, I arrived at the chop-shop a good five minutes early, only to spot the old raptor in a far distant corner, glaring at the clock.

'Nice of you to join me,' she scowled as I took my seat and unflapped a napkin. 'It's a shame you couldn't find time to shave.'

Aware that any attempt at mitigation would merely infuriate the court, I apologised for my tardiness, and hid my hirsuteness behind the extensive *à la carte*.

Aunt Agatha snapped her fingers across the empty restaurant and, in time, a waiter appeared.

He glanced at his watch. 'Good *morning*, madam. To start?'

I was about to enquire which kind of Madeira would best complement the *Pâté de lièvre à la sauce Jaoudi*, when Aunt Agatha snatched the menu from my hands.

'Nothing! We will both have the Dover sole. No butter, no oil, no salt, no lemon, and no potatoes.'

The waiter took this all in his stride and then, with an irony that, had he but known, bordered on the suicidal, enquired, 'Parsley?'

'Don't be absurd!'

'And to drink, madam?'

'Water. No ice. No fruit.'

'Very good, madam.'

'Oh, and a single sausage for McIntosh.'

'McIntosh, madam?'

'McIntosh!'

The waiter followed Aunt Agatha's gaze under the table, where McIntosh sat conscientiously shredding my laces.

'No dogs allowed in here, madam.'

'Poppycock! McIntosh isn't a *dog* – he's McIntosh!'

The waiter shared with me a pitying look as he collected our menus and set off to alert the chef of the Herculean labour he'd been set.

'Now, Bertram,' Aunt Agatha straightened her knife with surgical precision, 'which would you prefer first: the good news or the bad news?'

With a sinking certainty that the difference would be invisible to the naked eye, I opted for the former and steeled myself for the inevitable blow.

A milk-curdling smile cracked her lips.

'Congratulations. You're to be married.'

I don't know if you've ever found yourself in a dentist's chair, blinded by lights, mouth clamped agape, with a screaming drill descending towards a tender flap of gum, but if you have, you'll know the brand of icy terror that drenched me like a bucket of sleet.

I mean to say, it's bad enough being match-made by a romantically inclined chum who has only your happiness at heart, but the skies take on an apocalyptic hue when Cupid comes bearing a scythe.

I scanned the room for any kind of analgesic, and would gladly have stolen wine from a neighbouring table, had any been available. But one of the drawbacks of lunching when sensible folk are still dunking their soldiers is that you're usually dining alone.

'Well?' Aunt Agatha secured my attention with the tines of her fork. 'Aren't you going to thank me?'

'Of course! Absolutely. Goes without saying,' I filibustered. 'Might I know something of my bride-to-be?'

'Her name is Lottie. Or Dottie. I have it written down somewhere.'

'You don't know her *name?*'

'Don't be impertinent. We only met on Monday.'

'And from this Monday meeting, you're somehow certain she's my soulmate?'

'I don't believe in soulmates, Bertram, and neither should you. I believe in practicalities. You are much too old – and far too wayward – to remain unwed.'

'Is there any trivial detail you might vouchsafe about the future Mrs Wooster?'

Aunt Agatha sighed, as if asked to recite the Old Testament. 'She is several years younger than you, which is ideal. Educated, which is tolerable. And employed, which is unfortunate. But she comes from a very respectable pedagogical family.'

'Ped-a-*what*-icle?'

'Exactly. Time there was something other than music-hall songs between your ears.'

Our lunch, such as it was, arrived.

'Is she pretty?' I enquired, making quick work of the tasteless fish. 'My new wife?'

'I really couldn't say.'

'Well, who would play her in the movies?'

'What a ridiculous question. One day, Bertram, the wind will change and you will stay flippant for ever.'

'And am I to meet this mystery woman before the ceremony? Or is she to be unveiled at the altar like a municipal statue?'

'I did invite her for lunch today,' Aunt Agatha sniffed, 'but she seemingly has to work. So instead she will be joining us for breakfast at my hotel this Saturday.'

'That sounds a little early. Love seldom clicks over kippers.'

'What nonsense. Have you never heard of the wedding break-fast? And if you behave like a gentleman, which I *insist* that you do, there will be an engagement by luncheon.'

Not without a ring, I silently schemed.

'I even have a ring for the occasion.'

'Dear Aunt, you think of everything.'

'And now,' she smiled acidly, 'for the bad news.'

I racked the attic for what could possibly be worse than this deranged and indecent proposal, but came up with zip.

'You are to dismiss Jeeves.'

I wonder if you recall what I said a page or so above about teeth? Well, take that as gospel, but for 'dentist' substitute 'grave-digger'.

Aunt Agatha has never seen eye to eye with Jeeves, and not just because he looms over her by more than a gimme. As a species, aunts are unprepared for anyone who declines to shrivel before them like ants under a schoolboy's magnified sunbeam. And Jeeves, to the best of my k., has never shrivelled before anyone.

The situation is not helped by Aunt Agatha insisting that Jeeves is a valet – a position he admires, but does not hold. As I've often had cause to explain, Jeeves is neither a valet nor a butler, but a Gentleman's Personal Gentleman – a breed apart in the hierarchy of the servants' hall. Assuredly, G.P.G.s can valet up a storm should the need arise, and will turn their hand to any respectable request – from buffing up shoes to flushing out snipe. But they do so on their own terms, and with a healthy glug of *amour propre*. It's not for nothing that 'gentleman' appears at either end of the G.P.G. equation, as the savvy employer does well to remember.

Naturally, Aunt Agatha tolerates none of this. To her, servants should simply serve – ideally in a servile sort of way – and, unlike children, of whom she is also not fond, they should neither be seen nor heard.

The idea of seeking *advice* from a servant (as I have been known to consult Jeeves *de temps en temps*) would be as unthinkable to Aunt Agatha as tipping them on Boxing Day. This explains why she sees off domestic staff with the ruthless efficiency of the Grim Reaper, and why those that remain under her roof only do so when slipped the occasional coin by her better half.

'I can't dismiss Jeeves!' I protested. 'I spend most of my waking hours ensuring he doesn't dismiss me.'

'You can – and you will. You have until Monday.'

'Or?'

'*Or?*' Aunt Agatha drew slowly from her chair like a hypodermic syringe, before plunging in the poison. 'Or I shall dismiss him myself.'

I watched her drag McIntosh out of the restaurant, feeling like a cat rapidly burning through life-insurance policies.

The unpalatable truth was that Aunt Agatha had a point: one day the wind might change, and if I didn't keep my wits about me I'd be married *and* manservant-less in a single stroke. (So common is this one-two assault on the bachelor life that when some newly wedded Dronesman penknifed into the bar '*Not so much gaining a wife as losing a valet*', the general committee voted to varnish the carving as a cautionary tale to others.)

Of course, the fact that Aunt Agatha's double-bladed threat was just the kind of three-pipe problem only Jeeves could unravel, proved just how much I relied on the man to cluster round and unpickle me.

I was snapped out of my melancholy by the unexpected appearance of a ham-and-cheese sandwich and a glass of beer.

'Something from the kitchen,' said the waiter, gently. 'On the house.'

*   *   *

I returned to the Perseus Suite to find the target of Aunt Agatha's wrath needle-and-threading a waistcoat button. Glancing up at my arrival, he laid down his endeavours and buttled over to attend to my hat.

'Good afternoon, sir.'

'Bad afternoon, Jeeves. Calamitous afternoon.' I sank into a sofa. 'Would you prefer Aunt Agatha's ghastly news, or her appalling news?'

'Whichever you consider most exigent, sir.'

'I am to be married.'

'Congratulations, sir.'

'And you are to be sacked.'

'I shall be sorry to leave your service, sir.'

'That's it?'

'Sir?'

'You're not aghast?'

'No, sir.'

'But these are calamities!'

'I think not, sir. Assuming, that is, you do not wish to dismiss me from your service, nor marry your aunt's postulant?'

'If postulant is anything like pestilent, I plead Not Guilty.'

'Very good, sir. I shall order tea.'

I'm well accustomed to Jeeves being as placid as a millpond, or whatever placid thing poets are keen on nowadays, but it's always rather a poke in the eye to see the man so damnably calm when I am a thing of sound and fury.

'Tea! That's it? No grand plans, just warm words and hot water?'

'With aunts, sir, as in chess, it is an error to anticipate an endgame before the queen has moved.'

'You mean: cross bridges on arrival?'

'Yes, sir. And, if you will forgive the observation, this is well-surveyed terrain.'

'You mean: we've been here before?'

'Precisely, sir.'

To those who say 'A problem shared is a problem halved', I say, 'Meet Jeeves' – for the man doesn't halve problems, so much as coax them out for a Sunday stroll, cosh them across the nape of the neck with a brick in a sock, and bury them by moonlight in a shallow grave.

(I'll admit to feeling the slightest twinges of guilt about betraying such a staunch ally in the matter of his *Periwinkle Chevron*, but the deed was done and the die was cast, and I'd have to double-cross *that* bridge on arrival as well.)

'On an unrelated matter, sir, I wonder if you have had time to peruse the newspapers.'

'Not since Gussie defaced my crossword – why?'

'This story was not reported in *The Times*, sir.'

He handed me a copy of the *Daily Sketch*, ironed open at page three.

MAYFAIR DIAMOND HEIST:
DRONES CLUB IMPLICATED

Speculation is mounting that the Drones – a private gentlemen's club in Mayfair – may be implicated in Tuesday's diamond robbery at the Mount Street Hotel. According to Scotland Yard, the distinctive polka-dotted cummerbunds worn by the four assailants form part of the

Drones Club's official regalia, and are available only from the London tailors Hubbard & Legg.

'Oh well. 'Twas only a matter of time.'

'Indeed, sir. But you may also wish to glance at the final paragraph.'

I ran my eye down to the coda.

Lloyds of London have offered a £1,500 reward for information leading to the recovery of the diamond rings, or the arrest of those responsible for the attack on the jeweller, who has been identified as Mr Lambert Lyall.

'Good Lord! I must call him. Is there a book to hand?'

'In anticipation of your concern, sir, I made enquiries at the front desk.'

He handed me a number, and I strode to the telephone and dialled.

'Lambert Lyall,' a known voice answered. 'How may we serve?'

'Ahoy there, Lambert, it's Bertie.'

'Mr Wooster! What a gladness.'

'I'm shocked to find you at work after your recent distress.'

'Just a few bumps and bruises, sir. All in a day's work.'

'I'd no idea bejewelling was so fraught. Look, I've just read in the *Sketch* that the police suspect the Drones—'

'Let me stop you there, Mr Wooster. I don't for a second credit any of that cummerbund nonsense. In fact, I assured the police my assailants weren't *real* gentlemen.'

'You seem jolly sure.'

'When I knocked at Room 305 of the Mount Street Hotel, the door was opened by a young man smoking a Havana cigar.'

'So?'

'The cigar's paper band was still attached.'

'How perfectly atrocious!'

'Quite. The police, however, dismissed this detail as irrelevant.'

'Poirot would have seen the clue's value,' I said. 'Also, Father Brown.'

'Sadly, today's policeman is not as well read as he once was. Actually, Mr Wooster, it's funny you should telephone, as I'd planned to be in touch.'

'Really?'

Although my tone was casual, I suddenly feared there might be an unpaid invoice lurking in the shrubbery. As you'd imagine, Jeeves is pretty slick when it comes to life's bureaucracy – but, as he often reminds me, he can only work with what he's given, and so when vital correspondence is crumpled up and lofted skilfully into the old wagger-pagger-bagger, his well-tempered system rather grinds to a halt.

'You know I hate to gossip,' Lambert Lyall continued confidentially.

'Absolutely.'

'And would *never* reveal the particulars of a commission in the normal course of events.'

'Heaven forfend!'

'But a few weeks ago, your acquaintance Miss Bassett bespoke from us a rather unusual brooch—'

'Leprechauns, toadstools, rainbows?'

'You've *seen* it?' He sounded dismayed.

'It can't be unseen! But I'd no idea it was by the hand of Lambert Lyall.'

'I *very* much hope we might keep that between ourselves.'

I explained that Madeline Bassett was attempting to catch the eye (also: steady the nerves, jog the memory, tweak the nose, force the hand, and tug the heartstrings) of her fiancé Roderick Spode, with whom relations had recently cooled – but Lyall was not so sure.

'Much as it pains me to contradict you, Mr Wooster, Miss Bassett never once mentioned Lord Sidcup when bespeaking that brooch.'

'How odd.'

'Indeed, sir. The name she mentioned was yours.'

I replaced the receiver in something of a daze, my ears still ringing in shock.

'Did you get all that, Jeeves?'

'The salient points, sir. Mr Lyall has a penetrating vocal style.'

'Well, let's not panic. I simply need to steer well clear of Madeline and Spode for a decade or so. That should be simple here in Cambridge, and then, when this Ganymede hoo-ha is over, we can sail to Argentina and disguise ourselves as grouchos.'

'*Gauchos*, sir?'

'Either, I assume, would work.' And then my memory was jogged. 'On the topic of disguises, Jeeves, I've a crow to pluck with you.'

'Sir?'

'About that clairvoyante's costume, which was delivered by the Brothers Cohen – early this morning?'

'Late last night, sir.'

'So you ordered it yesterday?'

'Yes, sir.'

'But you didn't tell me about the impersonation yesterday.'

'No, sir.'

'You sprang it on me over breakfast, as a *fait à prix fix.*'

'*Accompli*, sir? Yes, sir.'

'And may I ask why?'

'I estimated it kinder not to burden you, sir, in case the prospect of the deception marred your evening.'

Such consideration rather spiked my guns.

'Oh. Well, that's thoughtful, I suppose. But next time – *if* there's a next time, and I trust there's *never* a next time – I expect to be consulted. Especially if it means I get to go as a wizard.'

'Of course, sir. Might I enquire if the deception proved successful?'

'It was an immaculate deception – no thanks to Gussie – and my impersonation of Bela Lugosi was a sight to behold. All that matinée-idling at the flicks did not, *contra* Aunt Agatha, go to waste.'

There was a knock at the door, which Jeeves floated across to answer. He returned with a telegram:

DOUBLE STAR WON.
X FINGERS FOR MANICOU. BOKO.

'We live to fight another race— Hang on! How does Boko know I'm in Cambridge, let alone at this hotel?'

'I could not say, sir.'

'Apart from you and the MacAuslans, no one else knows I'm here ... *Of course* – Gussie.'

'With reference to Mr Fink-Nottle, sir, I was interested to learn that he is now employed at this hotel.'

Jeeves is 'interested to learn' the way others are 'excited to lose a limb', and it was obvious he was irked by Gussie merely playing at his vocation.

'Only at the weekends,' I reassured, 'and only serving breakfasts. Mind you, I can't imagine it'll last. He's not exactly the Admirable Crichton, what?'

'No, sir. Not exactly.'

'Right, time to put in some hard graft on the crossword.'

An hour or so later I was woken by Jeeves, who informed me Iona MacAuslan was on the line.

*   *   *

We met at The Eagle, in the same quiet alcove where I'd first endured Vonka.

'Ahoy there, Iona – or should I say *Diane?*'

'Sorry about that,' she grinned. 'One of my Cambridge covers.'

'*One* of?'

'In the mornings I'm Diane the Bedder, keeping an eye on Orsini. And for the rest of the day I'm Helen Marion of Girton, keeping an eye on Whipplesnaith.'

'Sounds confusing.'

'Not if you can count to two, Bertie.'

'It's touch and go at that hour. And I think you might have warned me you'd be breaking down my door.'

'And miss your pyjamas? Not a chance! What colour do you call that, anyway?'

'Heliotrope.'

'My only regret is not having a camera.' She took a sip of her Gin and It. 'So, busy morning?'

I outlined the improbable sequence of events that had tran-spired since we'd met.

'But you should have asked me!' she cried. 'I could have impersonated a clairvoyante in my sleep. Or, indeed, while you slept.' She adopted an air of spiritual stupor and spoke in a tremu-lous voice: '*I do not tell fortunes . . . I convey messages from those who have passed beyond.*'

'I say, Iona, that's absolutely ripping!'

'It's Nellie Savage in *The Hole in the Wall.*'

'I know! Madame Mystera was my model for Madame Sosostris.'

'Great minds. Perhaps you didn't need me after all.'

'Ask around, Iona – I need all the help I can get.'

She laughed. 'By the way, Madame Sosostris was an awfully brave name to choose. Witty, of course, and clever. But brave.'

'Eh?'

'Let's hope Mrs Pinke never reads *The Waste Land*.'

'*The What Now?*'

'T. S. Eliot.'

I'd not an inkling what she was on about (*Brave? Clever? Witty?*), but Jeeves had some explaining to do.

'So, Iona, is this a social call, or do you have news?'

'Always social, but the news is: no news yet. Friday night still seems likely, but Whipplesnaith is acting even more erratically than usual, and we need to be sure of his allegiances before the trap is sprung. Our friend Adrian seems to be involved with the Saviours of Britain.'

'Spode's Black Shorts have infiltrated Cambridge?'

'With a vengeance. It's a little unclear who is organising and funding them, but they're going round the colleges to sign up impressionable freshers – and immature finalists.'

'So what do you need me to do?'

'For now, absolutely nothing.'

'I think I can manage that. For centuries we Woosters have done absolutely nothing under much more trying conditions.'

'I knew we'd picked the right man.'

Just then I happened to spot a chap I recognised. He was carrying from the bar three pints of bitter in the approved triangle grip, and he held between his teeth a pickled egg.

'See that cove yonder?'

Iona followed my gaze. 'Egg man?'

'He's a famous Austrian philosopher. Hedwig Lichtenstein. Wrote a book about a tortoise, and gets enraged by garden paths.'

Iona laughed. 'Do you perhaps mean Ludwig Wittgenstein, who wrote a book called the *Tractatus*?'

'Some of the details are hazy, I'll admit, but not the garden paths – about those I am certain. I've not seen anyone so vexed about a lawn since Sutcliffe and Hobbs made a hundred and seventy-two at the Oval in '26.'

There was a pause.

Cricket takes girls in different ways, you see: some do; some don't.

Iona didn't.

'Well,' she said, scooping up her belongings. 'Things to do, people to spy on.'

'But we're meeting tomorrow? Half past three?'

'I'll be there: the woman in whites.'

* * *

'This will be gruesome, sober,' Gussie grumbled as we marched across Midsummer Common to supper with the Pinkes. 'Parents are the worst, and Vonka's parents are truly the worsted.'

'Fear not, old soak!' I extracted the hip-flask Uncle Tom had slipped me on the occasion of my twelfth. 'The pocket-pistol is always loaded.'

'Bertie, you're a lifesaver.'

As he pelicanned my brandy in a series of gulps, I marvelled afresh at how this once abstemious innocent had taken to the grape like a duck to *l'orange*. Indeed, by the time we'd reached the Pinkes' front door, he was already a couple of sheets to the wind.

My knock was answered by an elaborate Italian butler who escorted us to the drawing-room and announced our arrival in an accent so impossibly folderolled it took him a full breath to get through: 'Signo*rrrr*e Be*rrrrtrrrrr*am Wooster*rrr*.'

The Pinkes rose reluctantly to greet us.

Having shaken my hand with dismissive inattention, Lancelot Pinke seized Gussie's elbow and pulled him uncomfortably close to his frog-like face.

'I never knew you were T.T.,' he growled.

Gussie blushed. 'C. of E.'

'*What?*'

'What?'

'I asked if you were a pussy-foot?'

'Eh?'

'A water-wagoner? A pledge-man? A bone-dry? A Good Templar? A tack-wallah? A sky-juice quaffer? A badge-wearing member of the Blue Ribbon Gospel Army?'

Gussie turned to Vonka with panic in his eyes.

'Teetotal,' she decoded.

'*Oh*, yes. That's right.' He was back on script. 'Never touch the stuff. Won't have it in the house.'

'You didn't mention this on the application form,' Mr Pinke snarled.

'Was it *on* the application form?'

'Well ... no. Not in so many words. But there is a section for hobbies. Anyway, teetotal: good for you. Can't say abstention's ever been my cup of Darjeeling, but each to his own, eh? The wee wife here is a fan, of course, and it's still a free country, *or so they say*!' And then Mr Pinke's face darkened, and his tone sharpened.

'Dashed inconvenient having to ban the booze *completely* simply to remove any temptation from lily-livered milksops. Rather fouls up supper for the rest of us, and it's *terribly* disrespectful to Chef. So *don't* make a habit of it. Hear me?'

Gussie didn't know where to look after this bizarrely threatening *volte-face*, but luckily for him (if not for me) Mrs Pinke seized the conversational rudder.

'Have we met before, Mr Wooster?'

'I don't think so,' I *profundo*'d as *basso* as my lungs would stretch.

'How curious.' Her eyes narrowed. 'I could have sworn ... Are you on the stage?'

'Stage *door*, more like!' Mr Pinke guffawed, slapping me on the back with teeth-rattling force. 'Stage-door Johnny, I'll be bound, eh?'

'Well,' I obliged, reluctantly, 'you know how it is.'

'Do I ever!'

'It will come to me,' Mrs Pinke wheedled. 'I *never* forget an aura.'

We were introduced to the dinner's other guests – a mournful gang of halitotic dullards, one of whom admitted to being Evadne Pinke's chiropodist, which rather tested my powers of small talk. After half an hour of conversational agony, alleviated by nothing stronger than weak lemon squash, the door swung open and the butler appeared.

He took a deep breath.

'The Earrrrrrrrrrrrrrrrrrrl of Sidcuuuuuuuup.'

I froze in horror before retreating into the curtains.

What in blazes, I silently screamed, was Roderick Spode – *of all people* – doing – *of all places* – here?

In he swaggered like a side of ham: day by day, in every way, he was getting fatter and fatter.

'My lord!' Mr Pinke jumped up from his seat and greased over to welcome his guest. 'We are delighted – nay, *honoured* – you could join us. You know Evadne, of course, and Veronica ... '

'Charming as ever, Miss Pinke.'

' ... and her chap, Augustus Fink-Nottle.'

'We've met,' Spode spat.

'Splendid,' beamed Mr Pinke. 'Old friends!'

'Let's not get carried away,' said Gussie, extending a tepid flipper.

Gussie and Spode had indeed met, and not under the most conviv. of conditions. To take one example, there was the time Gussie had instructed Spode to 'boil his head'; to take another, there was the time Gussie had assaulted the boiled head in question with an oil painting; to take a third, there was the time Gussie had become engaged to Spode's fiancée – but here the calculus gets a little confusing, for Gussie and Madeline had been betrothed on approximately five occasions, none of them ending very happily ever after.

'Of course,' said Spode, his florid nose snuffling round the room like a pig in search of scraps, 'whenever you spot a Fink-Nottle, you can be pretty sure there's a Wooster close by – lurking in the shadows like a thief.'

The jig was up, and so I emerged from the curtains with a carefree wave. 'What-ho! Anyone for tennis?'

'There you are,' Spode glowered. 'I want a word with you later.'

Since the sole purpose of my presence at supper was to chorus Gussie's praises, Vonka had sat me to the left of her mother, whose place setting at the end of the table was encircled by a daisy-chain of salt cellars, arranged like the infield for a leg-theory bowler.

Gussie sat opposite me, to the right of Mrs Pinke and to the left of Vonka – but almost immediately, his brandy-addled gaze was drawn not to his peacherino, but to a shy young maid flitting in and out of the room.

Concentrate, Fink-Nottle! I telepathised as loudly as I dared. *This is hardly the time to philander.*

Mr Pinke kicked off proceedings with a long and fawning speech about how fortunate we all were to be in the exalted presence of Lord Sidcup, before turning to the guest of dishonour and proposing a toast to 'the Saviours of Britain'.

Ordinarily, I'd have refused point-blank to raise a glass to any such treason, but given my delicate romantic mission, and since the only liquid on offer was weak lemon squash, I made an empty gesture over the water, and mumbled something about Britain's 'Saboteurs'.

Lord Sidcup was halfway to his feet to reply to his host's unctuous flattery when a chef crashed in through the door to ladle out the first course – *Consommé royale à la Bowes-Lyon* – and so Spode sat back down, feebly pretending that he always stretched his legs before the soup.

Once all had been served, the maid placed before each guest a half-bottle of Dubonnet. Unsure of the protocol relating to this eccentric condiment, I peered down the woodwork to see Lancelot Pinke upending his bottle into his bowl.

'Régis does his best with the consommé,' he confided, 'but it tends to need a little *encouragement*.'

'Absolutely,' said Mrs Pinke, encouraging her serving with gusto. 'No need to stint.'

I gingerly sampled my soup unencouraged, to find it tasted like headaches feel. The very last thing it needed was further fortification, indeed I wondered if dilution with lemon squash was a discreet possibility.

This intoxicating *bemuse-bouche* set the tone for the rest of the 'teetotal' menu, which read like a water-wagoner's cry for help:

Artichauts au Advocaat
Campari tête de veau
Poulet sauvage Fernet-Branca
Champignons à la Cinzano
Compôte de prunes limoncello

As each new dish was unleashed, I glanced about to share the joke with my fellow guests, but seemed to be alone in my surprise. True, Vonka hardly ate a morsel, but this was because her jaw was otherwise engaged. Ditto Spode, for whom the sound of his own voice was nourishment enough. By contrast, Gussie was sloshing down whatever he could grab – more in thirst than hunger – and soon his frenzied gourmandising caught the eye of our host.

'Got a cobweb in your throat?' Mr Pinke quipped, as Gussie poured yet another dose of Campari sauce. 'More like Sink-Bottle if you ask me!'

Evadne Pinke was less entertained. No son-in-law of hers, she remarked on several occasions, would share her husband's weakness for the grape and grain. That said, it was impossible not be startled by the heavy shovel she herself took to every dish. At one point she caught me staring quizzically at the flood of Fernet-Branca drowning her *poulet sauvage*.

'Alcohol in food,' she declared loftily, 'is merely a garnish.'

Unsurprisingly, given his unquenchable hunger, Gussie's ebullience slid quickly into drunken fatigue, and his conversation became slower and quieter until it petered out altogether. I don't think he was ever actually asleep – sleeping men seldom eat so much – but his eyes were often closed for extended periods, during which his horn-rimmed specs slid down his nose, and his limbs twitched like a dreaming beagle.

Vonka, evidently, found this behaviour utterly endearing, but her mother was clearly alarmed. 'How long have you known Augustus?', 'Have you met his parents?' and 'Is he always like this?' were just some of the maternal googlies I attempted to sweep past square-leg.

Having failed to placate Evadne with the weather, the rugby, and the state of the railways, I finally resorted to family.

'Did you know, Mrs Pinke, that my cousin is one of your husband's pupils?'

'And who is that?'

'Thomas Gregson.'

'Well then, Mr Wooster, that makes you Agatha Gregson's nephew.'

'As night follows day.'

'How lovely for you. Agatha and I have only recently met, but already we're fast friends. Isn't she a scream?'

I was about to agree that 'scream' was the word many associated with my aunt, when disaster almost struck.

As the maid leaned over the table to deliver a third bottle of limoncello, the sleeve of her blouse snagged one of the salt cellars (a tall, pewter medieval knight), toppling it to the table.

Before Mrs Pinke could emit the shriek her mouth had formed, I shot out an arm and caught the tumbling grains in the palm of my hand.

'Does this count?' I asked, carefully upending the knight so not a granule fell to the cloth.

'It does, Mr Wooster! Aren't you *brisk*?'

'All those afternoons at silly mid-off,' I explained, making to brush the salt onto a plate.

'Stop!' Mrs Pinke lunged at my wrist. 'Throw it over your shoulder— *No!* Your *left* shoulder ... excellent ... and now we are safe.'

Mrs Pinke turned to the maid, who was glued to the spot like Lot's wife.

'Really, Mabel, you *must* be more careful! Forgive her, Mr Wooster, she's new, you see, and we've yet to iron out the slovenly habits she picks up at that hotel.'

And then it clicked: Mabel was Gussie's room-service colleague from the University Arms, with whom, his tipsy glances suggested, he was hankering to become ever more collegiate.

I'm not often grateful for Spode's presence, but his cry of 'Disgraceful!' ended this awkward interaction, and provided Mabel with cover to flee.

'What was that, my lord?' Mrs Pinke called across the candelabra, fearful that a black cat or red-bearded sailor had entered the room.

'We're discussing the Mount Street diamond heist, Evadne.'

'How deliciously wicked,' she grinned like a vulture. 'Those Mayfair playboys have it coming, if you ask me.'

'Flogging's too good for them,' said Mr Pinke. 'In my day, they'd be off to Australia.'

'Really, Papa?' Vonka laughed. 'You're fifty-three, and penal transportation ended in 1868.'

'That's the problem with educating girls,' said Spode, bitterly, 'they *never* stop resorting to fact.'

'Actually,' I raised my head above the parapet, 'the rumour is they're not playboys at all, but gangsters playing the part.'

'Need we concern ourselves with Drones Club gossip?' said Spode, dismissively. 'Especially as you seem to be *involved* in the crime.'

At this point, Gussie awoke from his sozzled coma and, for no apparent reason, shouted: 'Bertie's been arrested!'

There was a tense silence, during which I sought to introduce the toe of my shoe to a Fink-Nottle shin.

'Good for you!' cried Mr Pinke, unexpectedly. 'I was in Brixton for a spell – not for long, of course, but time enough to polish the King's iron with the eyebrows. What was your offence? Violent affray? Going equipped? Sedition?'

'Stealing a policeman's helmet!' beamed Gussie with pride. 'On Boat Race night!'

A frostiness swept over Mr Pinke's features.

'I'm not sure I hold with that, Wooster. I mean, crime is crime, but we do need to respect the police. Tricky enough job as it is, without juvenile squits purloining their kit.'

'What utter rot!' jeered Gussie. 'What unmitigated drivel! Coppers adore a cat-and-mouse helmet chase – don't they, Bertie?'

Deciding this was hardly the moment to take sides, I attempted to nod and shake my head simultaneously.

To be fair to old man Pinke, he did well to rise above the insults of a man who was not only a dinner guest and an employee, but his daughter's fiancé.

'I'm sorry, Augustus, I really can't agree. We must respect the British bobby, and give no quarter to immature hooligans.'

And then Spode intervened.

'I once stole a policeman's helmet,' he said, almost philosophically.

'See!' crowed Gussie. 'Even Spudcup here has nicked a helmet! *Spudcup!*'

You could almost hear Mr Pinke double-declutching as he attempted to find reverse. 'Well ... of course, my lord ... when I said *hooligans*—'

'NO!' Spode slapped his palm on the table, causing Evadne to cower over her salt. 'I was wrong, and I *should* have been punished. Helmet theft is the thin end of a slippery wedge. Mark my words: when the Saviours of Britain sweep to power, we will channel such youthful excesses into an efficient and dynamic fighting force. Starting with the layabout playboys of Mayfair.'

The applause that greeted this vile little spasm had a remarkable effect on Gussie, whose intoxication found, if not eloquence, then startlingly fluent insolence.

'SHUT UP!' he cried. 'Shut up clapping! You shouldn't clap the Black Shorts – *blackguards*, I should say. If there's one thing I can't stand – simply *cannot* stand – it's ugly great fools prancing about in footer-bags. You, Spode, should be ashamed of yourself. Big, fat, pink-faced fool waving nasty flags with lightning bolts! Shocking! An absolute disgrace! Did I say shocking? Well, I say it again. Shocking-shocking-shocking. Funny word, shocking, when you say it often enough. Shocking. Shocking!'

As Gussie paused for breath, Mrs Pinke's chiropodist attempted to intercede. 'Now, listen here—'

He got no further.

'Oooooh! The foot quack speaks! Well, Dr Bunion, I hope you washed your hands before sitting down to supper. Touching people's feet all day – it's disgusting! And abnormal. What prompts a man to handle feet for a living? Something dark in the old think-box, if you ask me. Something very dark indeed. You're all the same – corn-cutters and Black Shorts – cads and bounders to a man. Just like Spode here. A bounder's bounder. You should see the way he treats Madeline. Ah! Dear, sweet Madeline Bassett – like the hound – the Bassett hound! Woof-woof! You know who's *really* in love with Madeline?' (I covered my eyes, sensing what was next.) 'Bertie! Bertie Wooster. My pal here. Always has been, always will be. Madeline should marry Bertie – and then he could be Bertie Bassett. He *looks* like a Bertie Bassett, now I think of it. Odd-shaped body. Odd-shaped head. Madeline and Bertie Bassett. What a couple they'd make. But Spode nabbed her first, and Madeline will become Lady Sidcup! Ugh! *Sidcup* – I ask you! Who's ever been to Sidcup? Does Sidcup even exist? I wouldn't put it past Spode to have invented Sidcup. Just the sort of low trick he'd pull. Well, I say it's a shame. A shocking shame. You, Spudcup, are a shocking shame. And a shower. A shocking, fat, pink-faced shower.'

After what felt like a decade, the echoing tick of the grand-father clock was interrupted by Mrs Pinke.

'Shall we leave the gentlemen to their cigars,' she said, 'and maybe Mr Fink-Nottle would like some fresh air?'

I feared that Gussie might stand his ground and fight his corner, but to my immense relief he permitted himself to be lifted from his seat and guided out of the room.

'What an extraordinary performance,' said Mrs Pinke's chiropodist as the men reassembled at the head of the table. 'I can see why he's teetotal – can you imagine him after a drink?'

'I hope you weren't too offended, my lord?' Mr Pinke asked, passing round the humidor.

'Offended? By Fink-Nottle?' Spode grunted. 'The idea's absurd. I strongly suspect he's insane.'

'I can't imagine what my daughter sees in him. But once Veronica has set her mind on something – well, there it is. What d'you say, Wooster, is he off his chump?'

'Gussie? Oh, no. Definitely not. Chump-wise, he's always been one of the soundest. It must have been something he ate.'

The conversation soon shifted from the mental deficiencies of my close friends to the politics of Roderick Spode.

'Are you prepared for tomorrow, my lord?'

'A Black Short is always prepared.'

'Prepared for what?' I queried.

'Lord Sidcup is debating at the Cambridge Union,' said Mr Pinke. 'On the motion "This House prefers Fascism to Socialism".'

So *that's* why Spode was in town.

'And which side are you for?' I quipped.

'Enjoy your tomfoolery while you can, Wooster. You'll be smirking on the other side of your face when the Black Shorts sweep to power and shake things up.'

Fearing he was almost certainly correct, I sank back into my chair and bided my time for a suitable moment to slip out of the room – but not before I'd spotted that the Saviour of Britain was smoking his cigar with the band still attached.

I was padding down the corridor towards the relative sanity of the sitting-room when a hand emerged from the panelling, seized my elbow, dragged me into an ink-black cupboard, and thrust me up against a row of coats.

'My husband doesn't understand me,' Mrs Pinke slurred into my ear.

I silently wondered if anyone could.

'Not like *you* understand me.'

'*Me?*'

'I know who you are.'

'Eh?'

'You are *her.*'

'Who?'

'Madame Sosostris!'

I began to protest that I was no such thing, when Mrs Pinke placed a finger over my lips.

'Hush now, sweet prince. It's no use pretending. I'd recognise that palm anywhere. Such a *dramatic* Mount of Venus!'

Ah. The salt. No good deed goes unpunished.

'But I won't tell,' she giggled.

'Jolly good.'

'It'll be our little secret.'

'Excellent idea.'

'Just you and me.'

'Very wise.'

And then her giggles melted into granite. 'For now!'

She propelled me out of the cupboard with the same finesse with which she'd ensnared me, and I took a moment in front of the hall mirror to straighten my dishevelled bow-tie.

I entered the sitting-room with every intention of grabbing Gussie and vamoosing at speed – but Spode had other ideas.

'Wooster,' he grinned with unnerving bonhomie, patting the cushions as if I were a favoured spaniel. 'Join me.'

'Quite a supper,' I said as I sat, hoping banalities might see me home unscathed.

'Ghastly. Lancelot's a dipsomaniac. But a useful maniac – politically and financially – for the cause.'

I murmured evasively, sensing something nasty in the woodshed.

I wasn't wrong.

'Tell me, Wooster, have you seen Madeline recently?'

'NO!' I cried, far too stridently for *politesse*, but I was eager to place my defence on the record. 'Why?'

'Funny thing is, I've not seen Madeline myself for a while.'

'But you're tying the knot this Christmas! The invite has pride of place on my mantelpiece.' (I thought it best not to mention its previous pride of place on the Drones Club dartboard.)

'Things,' he said pensively, 'are up in the air. Madeline, I fear, is not the woman for a man of my calibre: a man of the people, a man of destiny.'

This was an ill wind, for Spode's engagement to Madeline Bassett was one of those diplomatic triumphs that pacifies two belligerent nations, saving the bacon of plucky neutrals, like me.

'You see, Wooster, the founder of the Black Shorts needs a mate of common stock. A mate the poor, dumb proletariat mass can relate to. A mate who is not, for example, obsessed with leprechauns. A mate like this *very* pretty creature here.'

I looked up to see Mabel approaching with the *crème de menthe* coffees.

'And what is *your* name?' Spode leered.

'Mabel, sir. Mabel Chitt.'

'My lord.'

'It's not *that* strange a name, is it?'

'No, my dear, you address me as "my lord". For I am the seventh Earl of Sidcup.'

'Beg pardon, m'lord,' Mabel blushed, attempting a curtsey. 'Actually, *I* was born in Sidcup – so does that make you *my* lord, m'lord?'

Spode preened the ends of his revolting moustache. 'I think it rather does.'

'Fancy!'

'Perhaps one day soon I might show you the House of Lords – guide you round the red benches?'

'Ooh, m'lord,' she giggled. 'Aren't you a one!'

'You see?' said Spode, as Mabel departed. '*That's* the kind of girl the plebs will flock to. Not some blithering wet blanket who insists that "every time a baby yawns, a kitten gains a whisker".'

I said nothing, praying silence might render me invisible. No such luck.

'The thing is, Wooster, you were spotted at Fortnum's on Tuesday, sharing cake with Madeline.'

'Not *sharing*—'

He raised a sweaty hand. 'I don't mind. In fact, I'm delighted.'

'You are?'

I felt the guillotine's blade just inches from my neck.

'It merely confirms what I have long suspected.'

'It does?'

'You are clearly the best man.'

Relief sprang from every pore.

'Well, Spode, this *is* an unexpected honour. I was best man to old Pendlebury-Davenport when he took on Valerie Twistleton, and my speech was an absolute corker—'

Spode shook his head. 'No, Wooster, you are the best man *for Madeline*.'

'Eh?'

'I want you to marry her.'

Two threats of marriage in under twelve hours is by no means a record – Bingo Little once found himself contracted to five different girls during a single performance of *As You Like It* – but there's only so much comfort to be drawn from statistics.

For obvious reasons, Aunt Agatha's dangling sword was by far the more perilous, but Spode's intervention – ham-fisted as it was – could not simply be shrugged off, for Madeline had always vowed that, somehow, she and I would square off at the altar.

'Now look here, Spode—'

'I'm not *threatening* you, Wooster,' he said, threateningly. 'I'm simply saying this: I know you've been engaged to Madeline an indecent number of times, and I'd hate to see your name dragged through the gutter press.'

'What?'

'If you don't marry Madeline, I shall ruin you.'

Having dispensed this choking oyster, he patted my knee, groaned to his feet, and waddled off to truffle out Mabel.

The evening broke up soon after – not soon enough for my taste, but Gussie proved hard to pry away from a cache of brandy snaps. Since Mrs Pinke had vanished upstairs with 'one of her heads', and Vonka was ear-bending the chiropodist and his wife, we were seen off the premises by Lancelot himself.

'It's a shame you're such a namby-pamby,' he said, punching Gussie's forearm with force to fell a tree. 'We were denied a rather rare Muscadet, and a truly historic Pomerol.'

Gussie was outraged. 'I didn't insist on Prohibition!'

'You didn't?'

'Why would I? Not my problem.'

'Then why didn't we serve any wine?'

'I suggest you ask your wife.'

Mr Pinke went pale with shock, and slammed the door in our face.

'Isn't she marvellous?' Gussie cried, as he stumbled back to town.

'She was marginally less hectoring, I suppose.'

'Not Vonka!' He stopped and glared at me. '*Never* Vonka! Why would it be Vonka? That atrocious harpy has tongue enough for two sets of teeth!'

'You're kidding!'

'It's Mabel! Mabel the *peacherino*!'

'After all I've done to smooth the path – not least today's clairvoyance – tell me you're kidding.'

He spread his arms in exaltation and began to sing, 'I'm in love with the lovely Mabel!' to the tune of 'What Shall We Do with the Drunken Sailor?'

'The only thing you're *in*,' I observed when he'd paused to take a breath, 'is -ebriation.'

'I think not! Apart from your hip-flask, not a drop has passed my lips.'

'And what about that intoxicating meal?'

'Alcohol in food, Bertie, is merely a garnish.'

'Oh, and thanks awfully for dragging me into your Spode tirade.'

He gave me a puzzled look, so I reminded him of his slanderous allusions to 'Bertie Bassett'.

'That's odd,' he said, lighting a colossal cigar, 'I've no memory of saying *anything* during supper.'

Tobacco has an uncertain effect on the very drunk. Some, it sobers up as briskly as an icy plunge; others, it sinks deeper into their slough of debauch. I doubt you'll be surprised to learn that Gussie was one of the others.

It started with a deathly silence, punctuated by dia-phragm-heaving hiccups. Very soon, though, he was as green and clammy as his beloved newts, and the remainder of our journey back to town was interspersed by a series of unfortunate events that no true friend would relate.

Having, somehow, lumbered the drink-stained wretch back to his Rose Crescent rooms, I zipped round the corner to find the gates of Caius unambiguously closed for business.

As a senior (if vaguely defined) 'postgraduate-cum-research-fellow', I would have been well within my rights to lean on the Night Bell and rouse a bleary porter. But I feared such swagger might have stretched the credulity of my clerical cover – especially as I was not untipsy myself.

So, I struck north and prowled the perimeter walls until I found an easy way up.

Breaking into college after curfew is how most of us get bitten by the night-climbing bug. If one can nail such agility after a snootful of port, the thinking goes, how much more nimble might one be sober?

Naturally, one's first few attempts are timid affairs – low roofs in dark alleys proving ideal nursery slopes for the tenderfoot. But soon the dreaming spires beckon and one sees the skyline with fresh, scheming eyes. Instead of staring down at the cobbles, one scans the stonework for routes of ascent (and options for escape) and, over time, one becomes aware of fellow aficionados stealth-ily doing the same.

I should state for the record that I'm hardly a night-climbing ace, indeed I could name many Oxford chums (and one college Chaplain) who are infinitely more dexterous in 'chimneys', 'drainpipes', 'handgrips', 'knee-grips', 'chockstones', 'flanges', and 'overhangs'. That said, I'm not a complete duffer, and can 'under-grip' a 'mantlepiece' with reasonable aplomb, should the need arise.

Fortunately, that night the need had not arisen ... until, that is, I was a few feet from the zenith of my ascent, when a short length of overflow pipe snapped off in my hand. I glanced around the brickwork for an alternative hold, but nothing of use was in reach. And so, with a sigh of fatigue, I began my descent to search for another route up.

No sooner had my toes touched the pavement than my collar was seized by the unmistakable arm of the law.

'Good evening, sir,' a sly voice murmured. 'Are you a member of the University?'

This seemingly simple question, I knew from Oxford, was actually rather a tripper. If my captor was a 'bulldog', I ought to answer 'No' – since the University constabulary has no real power over townsfolk, and little incentive to hand them over to the police. If he was a city copper, however, I ought answer 'Yes' – for a genuine bobby can rarely be bothered with undergraduate antics, unless they stray into newsworthy crimes, like the stealing or eating of swans.

The safest course of action would have been to turn my head and catch a glimpse of my captor's uniform, but, wise to this ancient dodge, the iron grip of authority was firm.

And so I tossed the mental shilling, came up with tails, and replied with bravado: 'Member of the University, Officer? I should say not.'

'I see, sir. In which case, you're under arrest.'

5.

FRIDAY

I won't tire you with the *De Profundis* of my night in St Andrew's Street nick. Suffice it to say, I was shaken awake at a deep-blue hour and handed a mug of hot tea.

'I don't suppose there's a copy of *The Times*?'

'You what?' said my jailor, incredulous.

'*The Times*. I've grown rather fond of the crossword.'

'You ain't got time for crosswords, chum. You're up in a sec.'

I consulted my watch. 'Isn't half past six a tad early for the majesty of the law?'

'It's pheasant season.'

'Forgive me – I don't see the connection.'

'His nibs is shooting this weekend, and you're the last on the list.'

'The last? You mean, he's *already* heard cases this morning?'

'Just the one. Little old lady was up for failing to abate a smoky chimney.'

'I trust justice was tempered by mercy?'

'Not really. She got fourteen days without the option.'

After the traditional courtroom formalities – where I gave my customary pseudonym (Alfred Duff Cooper) and fictitious address (23 Leinster Gardens) – the presiding beak, a dusty bird named Sir Godfrey Winthrop-Young, glanced up from his notes and gave me The Stare they practise each morning while shaving.

Although he clearly intended this glower to intimidate, there was something oddly avuncular in his eyes— and then it clicked: Mr Tweed from the London train!

Thanking my lucky stars, I socked him my warmest hail-fellow-well-met smile of camaraderie ... which did not go down well. And so I mimed smoking and chucking an imaginary meer-schaum out of a window ... which went down even worse. Evidently, he hadn't a clue who I was.

'Prisoner at the bar will confine his hands to his pockets,' he snarled, before calling to the stand my arresting officer and asking him to describe his version of last night's 'incidents'.

Constable Dockery flipped open his notebook and read ploddingly.

'I was proceeding down Trinity Lane, Your Honour, in a westerly direction, h'ascertaining the lock'dness of windows and doors, when I saw, in sil'houette, as you might say, movement on the walls of Gonville 'n' Caius.'

Sir Godfrey peered over his half-moon specs. 'Carry on, Constable.'

'I approached the suspect – sneaky like – to h'ascertain whether 'e was going up or coming down, and when he was in reach, I nabbed him. Then, Your Honour, having h'ascertained he was not a member of the University, I placed him under h'arrest.'

'I see. Is there anything else?'

'Yes, Your Honour. He was carrying a length of lead piping.'

'Lead piping, you say?' The judge made a careful note, and turned to me with a scowl. 'Burglary, young man, is a very *grievous* offence—'

'It wasn't burglary!' I protested.

'You were caught *in flagrante delicto*, with a length of lead piping, and dressed, I see, in a dinner jacket.'

'Dinner jacket?'

'Like the Mayfair diamond thieves – with whom, I note, you share a suspiciously public-school accent.'

This was rich, considering *his* accent was fruity enough to garnish Pimm's.

'Actually, Your Honour, I was merely engaged in a spot of night climbing when the pipe came off in my hand.'

'*Aha!* So you plead guilty to night climbing – a *very* grievous offence.'

I was about to object when the clerk of the court intervened.

'Excuse me, Your Honour, but *is* night climbing an actual offence?'

'Don't be obtuse, man. The offence is aggravated trespass, or something similar.' He swung back to me. 'Now, Mr Duff Cooper, we come to your sentence.'

'But I plead not guilty!'

'Too late! You just admitted the crime from the dock.'

'Hang on—'

Sir Godfrey was furious. 'Do you presume to lecture me on judicial procedure?'

'No, Your Honour, except to say—'

'Guilty!' he shouted, slamming his fist on the bench.

'But—'

'Unless you say Constable Dockery is a liar?'

'Well—'

'Perhaps you *are* admitting to burglary?'

'No!'

'I should hope not. Night climbing is crime enough. Scaling historic buildings does untold damage to fragile structures, not to mention the hazard it poses to members of the public.'

In the face of such judicial derangement, what could one do but appease the bench and pray for mercy?

'Yes, Your Honour.'

'This epidemic of night climbing – of so-called Alpine Fever – is to be deprecated *and punished* in the strongest possible terms.'

'Of course, Your Honour.'

'No matter the challenge of ascending the highest peaks without rope or harness.'

'Absolutely, Your Honour.'

'No matter how thrilling the adventure.'

'Er ... '

'The sensation of solitude, up among the gods. The exhilaration of pitting your strength against the cold, unrelenting brick: every muscle taut, every sinew strained, your senses alive to sound and smell. The touch of the stone echoing memories that cascade down the centuries.'

Like me, Constable Dockery was staring up at the bench in wide-eyed dismay; but the bench was just warming up.

'The sensation of divine redemption up there – *there* – among the gargoyles and spires. The freedom to roam the roofs, to traverse the slates where none but angels tread. Your heart pounding – *pounding* – fit to burst with passion ... possibility ... deliverance ... *destiny*!'

Sir Godfrey Winthrop-Young leapt to his feet, causing everyone in the court to scramble to attention. He silently surveyed the cold, bare room with damp, faraway eyes before gazing up to the skylight where a weak yellow sun broke through the dawn's grey cloud.

'CASE DISMISSED!' he boomed.

I was met on the steps of the court by the Hysteron Proteron – many of whom looked like they'd also spent a night in the cells.

'Hi-ho, chaps! What brings you here?'

'We watched you getting collared last night,' said Lord Pallot, 'from the tiles of Trinity. Sadly, sixty feet above the fray, there was little we could do.'

'When we saw he was a copper,' added Baron Salmon, 'we decided to come and bail you out, but I see we're too late. Was it a particularly salty fine?'

I explained the oddly poetic hairpin of events.

'How dashed uncommon. Who was the judge?'

'Some cove named Winthrop-Young.'

'Well, I'll be!' Lord Pallot laughed. 'That was a fluke.'

Sir Godfrey Winthrop-Young, they explained, was *the* pioneering night climber of his day, and the first man to ascend the

Great Gate of Trinity, alone and without ropes. Notwithstanding his elevated judicial position, old Thropper clearly hadn't shaken his affection for the sport – nor, it seemed, his sympathy for its youthful practitioners.

'Any other beak,' said Lord Pallot, 'and you'd be clinked for a couple of days at the bare min. But seeing as you're now a free man, why not join us for brekker?'

As we set off to the Pitt, I spotted Constable Dockery sloping disconsolately out of the court's side door – his shoulders hunched, his eyes downcast – living proof, if proof were needed, that a policeman's lot is not a happy one.

*   *   *

Breakfast for the Hysteron Proteron means supper, and supper means supper reversed. The meal kicked off with coffee, cigars, and *petits fours*, before proceeding to Welsh rarebit, apple crumble, roast beef, poached salmon, and watercress soup. Each course was introduced with an appropriate toast – from 'Auld Lang Syne' to 'Old Father Time' – and the meal commenced with a vigorous chant of 'Shoes and Socks'.

'What's so special about shoes and socks?' I asided to Baron Salmon.

'It's a classic.'

'A classic what?'

'Hysteron Proteron.'

'Eh?'

'Hysteron Proteron is a rhetorical device meaning "the last put first" or "the cart before the horse" – hence the inverted day.'

'But how is that relevant to footwear?'

'It's the most famous example. "I've put on my shoes and socks" you might say, but actually you put on your *socks and shoes* – in that order – unless you've extremely odd feet.'

Adding further topsy to this profoundly turvy meal, Lord Pallot insisted on a range of 'drinking rules' more often associated with the rowdier elements of college rugger: pointing was prohibited, as were coughing, sneezing, and even the mildest of oaths; 'drinking' was outlawed in favour of 'quaffing', which was itself allowed with one hand only (the permitted hand alternated every half-hour); nothing could be passed without permission from the Chair, which was also required before standing, sitting, or leaving the room; and glasses (which had to be held with one's little finger aloft) might only be filled by the chap sitting opposite.

All of these rules (and many more I've forgotten) were adjudicated by 'Mr Chairman' (Lord Pallot) and enforced by 'Mr Chief Sneak' (Baron Salmon) – and contraventions were penalised by quarter-pint fines of lukewarm bitter, dispensed by 'Mr Weights & Measures' (a cheerful medic called K.J.).

It was over the roast beef that the meal took a curious turn.

'These sprouts are uneatable,' complained Lord Pallot. 'Why are sprouts *always* uneatable? Why do they plant them, pick them, cook them, and serve them if they are going to be uneatable? What, in other words, is the point of Brussels sprouts?'

There was a general harrumphing that sprouts were a pretty shabby trick.

'We should use them as ammunition,' I suggested, 'for Lord Sidcup's debate at the Union.'

Lord Pallot was shocked. 'Sidcup is speaking at the Union?'

'Tonight,' said Baron Salmon. 'On the motion "This House prefers Fascism to Socialism".'

'I don't know about Socialism,' Lord Pallot declared, 'but we do *not* tolerate Fascism. It's bad enough that his Saviours of Britain are going from college to college to sign up gullible freshers, without that fat, ugly brute strutting about in his tasteless shorts. We should attend tonight's debate and heckle.'

Since applause was another fineable crime, this impassioned outburst was saluted with a banging of spoons.

'We should do more than heckle,' said one of the chaps, 'we should stop him debating entirely.'

'Would that be cricket?' another chap objected. 'Freedom of speech, and all that.'

'Why should Fascists enjoy the freedoms they deny others?'

'Who then decides what can and cannot be said?'

'Can *anything* be said then, regardless of decency or truth?'

'So you'd just replace Lord Sidcup with an empty chair?'

'Empty sofa, more like!'

This thorny ethical debate raged on, even unto the soup, and it was quite something to watch the Hysteron Proteron explore the meaning of *veritas* having consumed so early in the day such an impressive quantity of *vino*.

'If a line is to be drawn,' said Lord Pallot, eventually, 'I vote we draw it at Sidcup.'

'But how do we stop him debating? If we simply heckle, won't *we* be the ones who look like cads?'

'What about a mock funeral? Like when someone's sent down.'

'Pass the cream of *ennui*,' said Baron Salmon. 'We get two of those a term.'

'Stink bombs?'

The table was united in apathy.

'Did anyone seen that Laurel and Hardy flick *Two Tars?*'

'When all the cars get jammed and dismantled?'

'That's the one. Well, what if we create a traffic snarl – no, better still, some sort of traffic *diversion* – which takes Sidcup's car on an endless journey round town?'

'We could direct him to Grantchester!'

'Or Newmarket?'

'Or Shingay-cum-Wendy! I've always wondered what happens there.'

'Where's he staying?'

'The Bull Hotel.'

'That's perfect. We can drive him to Wimpole Hall.'

'This is hardly in the spirit of the Hysteron Proteron,' one of the chaps complained, 'unless we drive him backwards.'

'Don't be pedantic,' Lord Pallot rebuked, 'democracy takes precedence.'

'In which case,' said Baron Salmon, 'we're going to need maps, uniforms, and something for the diversions.'

'What about wooden hurdles from the athletics hut?'

'And the outfits they used for that production of *The Dover Road*?'

For a gang of underslept, overfed, and deeply squiffy fops, the Hysteron Proteron moved with startling dispatch. One dashed off to the athletics' department, another to raid the A.D.C. costume stores, and a third smashed an antique street map from out of its frame.

After much debate, and several more bottles, the plan to divert Spode's journey to the Union was finalised. Lord Pallot knocked on the table to bring the room to order, and raised his glass in a toast.

'Gentlemen! Time for some traffic problems on Jesus Lane.'

I left the Pitt in the affable company of Baron Salmon, who, like me, was in urgent need of fresh, uncigaretted air. We were tooling down Sidney Street (discussing whether 'have your cake and eat it' was Histrionically Proteroid) when I spotted in the middle distance a knot of Black-Shorted goons.

'Ugh!' I cried. 'What are they doing here?'

'Recruiting,' said Baron Salmon, bitterly. 'They've been at it all week.'

We crept a little closer and took cover in the doorway of a pet shop.

Strutting about on the pavement outside Holy Trinity were a dozen or so Saviours of Britain — several of whom were brandishing bright red banners with a lightning-bolt insignia.

'What's that ghastly flag?' I asked.

'They call it the Flash and Circle. They want it to replace the Union Jack.'

Those who were not waving these treasonous dusters were thrusting Black Short pamphlets into the hands of bemused passers-by. Most, very sensibly, declined such noxious *malles-lettres*, and many flung them to the ground, but once in a while some poor sap showed a flicker of weakness and was frog-marched to a trestle-table to be signed up by a trio of officers.

I recognised all three.

To the left was Lancelot Pinke, who had bedecked his uniform with a ludicrous tricorn hat; to the right was Evadne Pinke's appalling chiropodist; and in the centre – the *prima ballerina* of this gruesome *corps de ballet* – was Roderick Spode, deep in clandestine conversation with someone I couldn't quite make out. And then, as the crowd shifted, I spun on my heel and affected to study the pet shop's extensive selection of hedgehogs.

'Salmon,' I murmured over my shoulder, 'd'you see that chap talking to Lord Sidcup? Red hair, moist face, a whiff of the zoological gardens.'

'Oh, yes. Got 'em.'

'What are they doing?'

'Talking.'

'About what?'

'How would I know? I don't read lips!'

'Well, how scheming do they look?'

'By what measure?'

'Does it matter? *Any* measure!'

'In which case … I'd say … five to six.'

'Out of ten?'

'Twelve. I'm using the Rossi–Forel scale. Five is a Moderate Tremor, which disturbs furniture and rings clock bells; Six is a Strong Tremor, which stops clocks and awakens the sleeping.'

'Is that supposed to mean anything?'

'Probably helps if you're reading geology.'

Earthquake or not, it was something of a jolt to see such broad-daylight corroboration of Iona's suspicions: Whipplesnaith was indeed mixed up with the Black Shorts.

Deciding it would be safer if I *nunc*'d the old *dimittis* before they spotted me, I bade farewell to my faithful lookout and retraced the discreet long way back to my hotel.

*   *   *

'News!' I announced, striding into the Perseus Suite and unfettering my bow-tie.

Jeeves glanced nervously about the room. 'Belonging to Mr Fink-Nottle, sir?'

'*News*. Pages of it. You might use me to wrap fish 'n' chips.'

'Very good, sir.'

'Since we last met,' I counted off on my fingers, 'I've been threatened with ruin if I don't marry Madeline; arrested for trespass and banged up in a cell; then tried and acquitted by the maddest of beaks.'

'Might a brandy and soda be congenial, sir? Or one of my specials?'

'For once, Jeeves – and brace yourself – no. I've only just survived a Hysterically Proteinaceous breakfast. What would be congenial is coffee, as strong and black as the beans can jump.'

'Very good, sir.'

'And, as if all that wasn't enough, I've just witnessed Whipplesnaith hob-nobbing with the Black Shorts.'

Jeeves looked surprised. 'Indeed, sir?'

'They're recruiting in front of Holy Trinity Church. He was deep in collusion with Spode.'

'Most interesting, sir. I shall pass on your observations to Lord MacAuslan.'

'Oh! And have you heard the latest about Spode himself?'

'Do you refer, sir, to Lord Sidcup's non-payment of club dues; the defamation suit he has launched against his nanny; or his debate tonight at the Cambridge Union?'

How Jeeves accomplishes his effortless omniscience is one of those eternal, unfathomable mysteries, like the Hanging Gardens of Babylon, or Percy Gorringe's side-whiskers – which, now I picture them, also hang pretty Babylonically.

'I refer to tonight's debate: "This House says Hurrah for the Black Shorts!" or some such trumpery. Fortunately, the Hysteron Proteron has a plan to foil Spode rotten.'

'I'm heartened to hear so, sir.'

I outlined the scheme we'd thrashed out over breakfast, but was met with a cloud-bank of doubt.

'Do I sense dissent in the ranks?'

'While I admire the stratagem's byzantine complexity and laborious ambition, sir, it does place considerable weight upon one not insignificant imponderable.'

'Eh?'

'Specifically, sir, whether Lord Sidcup drives to the Union.'

'Drives? *That's* your imponderable? Of course he'll drive! Have you seen the man's heft? Added to which, the forecast is for heavy rain, and Spode melts in the rain like soap-flakes.'

'I hate to press the point, sir, but were his lordship to *walk* to the Union, would that not render the Pitt's labyrinthine vehicular diversion void?'

'Oh, he'll drive. Have no fear. We've even booked a taxi to be waiting outside his hotel.'

'Very good, sir.' Jeeves paused, and shifted his weight diffidently. 'Incidentally, sir, I feel I owe you an apology for the events of yesterday morning.'

'For allowing Monty to scoff my breakfast?'

'No, sir.'

'For dressing me up as a clairvoyante?'

'No, sir.'

'There was something else?'

'Yes, sir. It concerns a Miss Chitt.'

'What's *amischit*? The solution to Nineteen Across?'

'Miss Mabel Chitt, sir. The room-service waitress.'

'Ahh! Nervous girl. Spilled things. Fled the scene.'

He nodded.

'Come now, Jeeves, you don't have to apologise for the hotel staff. They are hardly within your purview, if purview is the *mot juste*.'

'Purview is most *apropos*, sir.' He paused. 'May I take it, sir, that you did not recognise Miss Chitt?'

'Should I have?'

184

'Possibly, sir. She was previously employed at an informal dining establishment near the Ritz hotel, during which time she formed a romantic understanding with—'

'Bingo Little!'

'Indeed, sir.'

'Well I never! Bingo's Bun Shop Mabel. It's all flooding back— But, *hangondo* a *secondo* – didn't Mabel of the Muffins *also* form a romantic understanding with ... '

Jeeves went ever so slightly pink about the gills.

'Yes, sir. A very *brief* understanding.'

'That explains why Mabel kept ogling you with spooning eyes while hurling things to the floor. Memories of love's labour's lost, eh?'

'Possibly, sir. For which I would like to apologise. I have spoken with Mabel, and I am confident the situation will not again arise.'

'The apology is accepted but, I assure you, unnecessary. Your romantic past is none of my beeswax. And anyway, this may all be moot judging by how comprehensively Mabel and Spode were clicking last night.'

Jeeves's eyebrows leapt to the ceiling, and he unleashed the italics.

'*Sir?*'

I dispensed a brief account of my supper *chez* Pinke, tactfully sidestepping Gussie's inebriation and my Evadne encounter, but spelling out in vivid technicolour Spode's threats concerning Madeline, and his porcine infatuation with Mabel.

Jeeves's brow furrowed. 'I hesitate, sir, to burden you with matters of a personal nature.' I bade him continue. 'But I would not wish Miss Chitt's affections to be trifled with.'

'No woman deserves a trifling from Lord Sidcup – excepting those named Madeline, of course. But I don't see what's to be done: Spode is a toad with no code.'

Jeeves stood for a moment, deep in thought, and I was on the brink of offering *him* a brandy and soda when he snapped out of his trance.

'Forgive me, sir,' he handed me the *Daily Sketch*, 'but you may wish to glance at today's "Iceberg" column.'

DRONES NAGS FOR BONES

Not content with being fingered in the Mount Street Diamond Heist (see pages 1, 3–7, 9, 11–14, 17, 20), the Drones is going to the dogs, by way of the nags. Senior members of this notorious Mayfair establishment have staked their polka-dotted cummerbunds on a 200/1 five-horse accumulator with William Edward 'Leviathan' Davies. A little bird informs Iceberg that the club is in a spot of financial bother. Good luck, chaps!

'Gah!' I hurled the paper across the room. 'Is Monty so pinched for copy that he's willing to snitch on his pals?'

'So it would appear, sir.'

'*Notorious Mayfair establishment!* What neck! What cheek! What ... '

I gestured for help.

'Nerve, sir? Or gall, assuming you are warming to a physio-logical theme? Though "brazen effrontery" has a certain sermonic force.'

'I note our brazenly fronted Iceberg neglects to mention the time *he* was caught impersonating a zookeeper.'

'No, sir.'

'Or when he hurled that guava at the Lord Mayor.'

'Indeed not, sir.'

'Montague Montgomery is well on his way to getting kicked out of the Drones altogether.'

'Rule Nine, sir?'

'Yup. I grant you that "bringing the club into disrepute" is a high bar for any Dronesman, but Monty looks to have cleared it with air to spare.'

I lit a restorative stinker and pondered who might have betrayed the club's secrets. The investment committee could probably be ruled out – even Stilton wouldn't grease it to Grub Street – but who else knew? I had mentioned the accumulator to Gussie, in the strictest confids, but surely *he* could be trusted? Well, Sober Gussie could; who knew of what outrages Sozzled Gussie was capable?

By this time Jeeves had reassembled the far-flung pages of my *Daily Sketch* and was dispensing the freshly delivered coffee.

'Might I suggest, sir, it may soon be convenient to change? I have laid out a set of athletic flannels in your bedroom.'

'You brought *whites*? How ever did you know I'd need them?'

'When packing for the country, sir, it is well to anticipate all vestimentary contingencies.'

'Jeeves, you never fail to amaze!' I sprang from my chair with a surge of pep. 'Coming to spectate the match? It should at least be amusing, if we manage to beat the rain.'

'Thank you, sir, but on this subject I am of the same mind as Mr Mark Twain.'

'He wasn't a fan?'

'No, sir. He described the game of croquet as "ineffably insipid".'

'Well, snubs to Mark Twain.'

'Very good, sir.'

*   *   *

A short while later, swinging the wooden mallet Jeeves had some-how contrived to locate, I was crunching down the gravel path that leads to Finella Gardens, when I spotted two burly men grappling in the centre of a huge expanse of lawn.

'What-ho!' I what-ho'd, once in what-ho'ing range.

They sprang apart and straightened their attire.

'Reverend Wooster!' The Master adjusted his eye-patch.

'Have I come at a bad time?'

'Not at all. We were just concluding our calisthenics.'

'Very wise. Important to stay spry. I myself do a "daily dozen" stretches every couple of weeks.'

'Are you alone?' enquired the Bursar, peering sarcastically around the garden like a sailor in search of land. 'No partner?'

'Not yet.'

'How *very* unlike a woman,' the Master smirked. 'If she's not here very soon, you forfeit our little wager!'

As a distant bell tolled the half-hour, Iona sashayed onto the lawn, her dazzling whites offset by a silk belt of red and green.

'Oh!' exclaimed the Bursar, bewitched by the approaching brunette. 'And *who* do we have here?'

'Helen Marion,' Iona lied. 'How d'you do?'

'At Girton, I see from your colours. And reading?'

'Philosophy.'

'How *terribly* clever. You know, I've always thought—'

'Can we crack on?' said the Master, irked by his partner's hapless fawning. 'The forecast's for rain, and I'd like to get this won.'

We lost the toss, and the Master elected to play red and yellow – allowing us the opening shot.

Iona positioned her blue in line with the first hoop, a mallet's length from the boundary rope, but instead of aiming dead ahead (as I, and countless generations, have always played), she rotated to the right and hit the ball briskly off the lawn.

'Have you gone loco?' I whispered. 'Why didn't you try for the hoop?'

'It's called a *tice*, Bertie. To *entice* them to hit me.'

The Master placed his red in the same starting position and, in a mirror image of Iona's shot, struck it briskly off the lawn to the left.

I, as black, played next.

'Do I go for him?' I asked Iona. 'Or the hoop?'

'Aim for me,' she coached, 'and don't worry if you go off.'

I hit and missed, rolling over the rope a foot from Iona's blue.

The Bursar followed suit, missing the Master's red by a yard.

So there we were: blue and black along the east boundary, red and yellow along the west, and me utterly at a loss.

'Shall we?' said Iona, striding confidently towards her ball.

It soon became clear that the croquet being waged was *not* the croquet of my youth. Rather than simply going it alone – hitting and hoping at every hoop – one attempted to ping and pivot around the course, using the other three balls as slingshots. Thus played, in theory at least, the game was uncannily reminiscent of chess crossed with conkers.

The Master was annoyingly good. Bold in his tactics and precise in his aim, he would have been a joy to watch had we not been at the tap-end of his malice. Added to which, he favoured a 'talking game' that involved muttering to himself, berating his partner, and disputing every other shot in an endless flood of complaint.

Mercifully, he was heavily handicapped by the Bursar, who, having fallen base-over-apex for my partner, was torn between clumsy flirtation and clumsier cheating. I'd not have thought it possible to make eyes at a girl while kicking her ball out of position – but the old boy gave it a valiant go on numerous occasions.

Iona, needless to say, was magnificent: at least as good as the Master technically, but significantly subtler in strategy and more composed in manner. She batted not an eyelid at the Bursar's philandering, or the Master's suspiciously timed sneezes, and she played with a graceful ease that put one in mind of a drifting swan, albeit a swan armed with a mallet.

B. W. Wooster was perilously out of his depth, and in need of patient schooling at every turn. I knew, of course, the rudiments of roquets, croquets, and running hoops, but I struggled to make the shots I attempted, or to 'see the whole lawn' as Iona advised.

In my defence, I might note that a full-sized croquet lawn is a sight to behold – both in terms of scale (vast) and smoothness (velvety). If you want an inkling of the challenge I faced merely connecting Ball A to Ball B, imagine shooting marbles on a sheet of glass the size of Wales.

None of this affected Iona or the Master, or course. But I took comfort in the Bursar's frustration, for he, like me, was used to more homespun conditions – like the pint-size croquet lawn at Totleigh Towers where it's a toss-up between snapping your ankle on an ancient molehill or concussion from a low-hanging branch.

The Bursar's solution to being outclassed was to play a doggedly 'Aunt Emma' game – i.e. joylessly disrupting the opposition at every turn. He attempted this with a succession of blatantly illegal push-shots and double-taps, which he failed to conceal behind his capacious Oxford-bag trousers. (Victorian men, Iona confided, knew such cheating as 'crinoline croquet' and refused to play against women in floor-length dresses.)

Rising above such cheap tricks, I opted for a gentlemanly approach – though not always with complete success. At one stage I managed to miss a swing completely and, tripping over my feet, fall onto my ball.

'Hard cheese,' called the Master from the rope. 'Take a bisque.'

('What's a bisque?' I asked Iona. 'Some kind of soup?'

'An extra shot you give to lesser players,' she explained.

'Damned cheek.'

'Quite.')

'Thank you, Master,' I called back across the lawn, 'but we'll play the balls as they lie.'

A short while later, the Bursar tripped similarly toe-over-kettle while attempting to play through a hoop backwards.

'Hard cheese,' I said, ironically. 'Take a bisque.'

'Don't mind if I do,' he replied, tapping his ball into position.

Pretty soon we became aware of a trickle of spectators strolling into the garden – suggesting that word of our wager had spread. Slowly but steadily, in twos and threes, they gathered along the boundary, until almost a hundred had amassed – including, I noticed, Lord MacAuslan, who leaned on an umbrella fashioned in the same deafening tartan as his suit.

Splendidly, these bystanders proved to be far from innocent: every shot Iona played was applauded with gusto, while every shot our oppos made was met with low rumbles of contempt. (My shots were generally ignored, the crowd having tacitly agreed not to intrude upon private grief.)

This vocal favouritism served further to nettle the Master, who became steadily more caustic in tone and aggressive in play until, about halfway through the match, he snapped. Having made contact with Iona's ball, he picked up his red and nestled it against her blue for the croquet shot – but then, with a villainous smirk, he turned side-on to the shot and placed a foot on his ball.

At this point, a word or two of explanation may be required. The traditional method of hitting a croquet shot involves swinging the mallet between one's legs, like a pendulum. One *can* stand side-on, and players do, for example when attempting tricky 'roll shots'. What one *cannot* do is place a foot on one's back ball to blast the enemy's front ball into the hollyhocks. This is known as 'tight croquet', and it's been outlawed for decades – as the jeering crowd knew only too well.

'That's the ticket,' shouted the Bursar, whose lust for victory had surmounted any other options. '*Send her back to school! Send her to Timbuktu!*'

For her part, Iona was merely puzzled.

'Master,' she called out across the lawn, 'I fear such shots are disallowed.'

'Nonsense, young lady.' He hacked his heel into the turf to secure a firmer foothold. 'This is how the *men* play.'

Then, like a golfer at the first tee, the Master raised his mallet high above his shoulder, paused for a moment to bask in the crowd's hostility, and slammed it down with pulverising force.

The screams could be heard for miles.

At some stage during his elaborate backswing, the Master must have misjudged his grip, for instead of making crushing contact with the red ball – thereby sending Iona's blue to Timbuktu – he made crushing contact with his shoe – thereby shattering the meta-whatsits of his right foot.

As the crowd reflexively flinched in horror, the Master fell to the ground.

'Are you all right, Dodo?' The Bursar waddled over to assist.

'Take your hands off me, you funny little man,' the Master shouted, white with pain. 'I'm perfectly fine.'

'If you're injured,' Iona suggested, softly, 'and since the sky is threatening, we could shake on a sporting draw?'

'*Shake on a sporting draw!*' the Master screeched, heaving himself up off the lawn with the aid of his mallet. '*Shake on a sporting draw!* What an idiotically *female* idea.'

You know that moment in every whodunnit when the killer makes his One Fatal Error?

Up until that point Iona had personified patience on a monument, smiling with forbearance at the infantile combination of chicanery and seduction. But now, as they say, the gauntlet was down, the gloves were off, and the knuckles were bare.

'Very well, Master. But since you caused your red to move, it's black to play.'

'Does it have to be?' I murmured.

'It does. I'll show you what to do.'

I don't pretend to understand what happened next.

I played my turn as instructed – so well, in fact, that the crowd lent me some of Iona's applause – but it was to be the last time I swung a mallet. As soon as the Bursar had missed his next shot, Iona, like a jockey who decides to push for the finish, kicked in her spurs and took the match by its scruff.

Ignoring the fortunes of my black and the Bursar's yellow, she focused her attentions on the Master, deftly deploying all four balls to knock his red through hoop after hoop.

The boundary-rope chatter was of 'dolly rushes', 'jump shots', and 'sextuple peels' – much of which was Greek to me – but in short order, Iona had guided the Master's red through the final six hoops, and was lining it up for the peg.

'Wait!' shouted the Master, who, nursing his fracture, had just twigged his fate. '*What* are you doing?'

'Pegging you out.'

'You can't do that!'

The crowd, as one, confirmed she jolly well could.

'But Harold can't play alone! The man's a complete buffoon.'

'Steady on!' puffed the Bursar. '*Pas devant les filles.*'

'Perhaps next time,' Iona smiled, 'you'll partner with a lassie.'

And then, very calmly, she croqueted the red against the peg, picked it up, strode to the boundary, and presented it to the Master with a curtsey.

Outplayed and outmanoeuvred, the Master was now out of the game. Given Iona's skill and the Bursar's ineptitude, the bet was as good as lost – but he had one final card up his sleeve.

Forcing a gummy leer to his face, he extended a limp hand. 'Miss Marion – *dear lady* – shall we shake on a sporting draw?'

Iona's answer was almost engulfed by the crowd's derisive hoots. 'What a generously *male* proposal, Master. But I think we'll take the claret – the *good* claret, that is.'

And then, with timing so impeccable I assumed Jeeves was somehow involved, a whip-crack of thunder heralded the long-threatened downpour of rain, and the spectating masses sprinted for cover.

Iona and I stood alone on the lawn, becoming rapidly water-logged in the deluge.

'Well played!' I said, extending my hand – just as she leaned in to kiss me.

'Sorry,' she said, extending her hand – just as I leaned in to kiss her.

We repeated this cuckoo-clocking misconnection several more times before Lord MacAuslan appeared under the canopy of his tartan umbrella.

'Come away now, you two!' he beckoned, his brogue thickening in solidarity with the weather. 'You'll be catching your deaths in this *spleeter*.'

Iona smiled, her face as drenched as mine.

'Is it still *spleetering*? I hadn't noticed.'

*   *   *

It was rather crestfalling to discover that both Iona and her uncle had engagements elsewhere, and so, having made plans to meet his lordship later for supper, I bade them (and their umbrella) cheerioski and set out into the rain alone.

I was hoofing back to the University Arms, dreaming of a long steam in a hot bath, when on the corner of Silver Street and Trumpington Street I came across a remarkable sight: some two hundred students sitting in the middle of the road, getting soaked to the skin as they played cards, juggled fruit, declaimed poetry, and sang.

I was taking cover under the awning of a tea shop to make sense of the scene, when my name was called by a broad, West Country voice. Turning on my heel, I came face to face with a face from the past – but a face I couldn't quite place.

'This is *terribly* embarrassing,' I grimaced, 'but you're going to have to remind me.'

'Epworth, sir. From Magdalene.'

And d'you know what? He was right! Standing before me, bright of eye and bowler of hat, was my old college scout, E. J. P. Epworth – who, for many terms, was almost as efficient a man-servant as Jeeves.

'You're at the wrong blue, Eustace! Oxford is a hard ride west.'

'Very true, Mr Wooster. Except these days I'm the Head Porter at Trinity.'

'That must feel dashed peculiar. Like putting on another chap's boots.'

'At first, perhaps, sir. But one college is much like the next, underneath. It's all a question of keys.'

'Gonville and Caius?'

'Keys, sir. With a K.' He unclipped a monstrous metal ring and shook it like a tambourine. 'Nine-tenths of portering is checking locks that should be locked stays locked, and vicey-versa. The rest is mollycoddling drunken Fellows and drunkener students. How you lot finds time for academicals, I'll never know.'

'Speaking of,' I waved at the sedentary chaos before us, 'what's occurring here?'

'Something called the Pavement Club, sir. They meet once a week, rain or shine, to do the kind of things they're doing now.'

'To what end?'

'Beats me, sir. My wife thinks it's something they put in the water.'

'Never happened in my day.'

'Well, sir,' Eustace grinned, 'there was that time you "borrowed" the *chargé d'affaires* of El Salvador.'

'Oh! I'd forgotten all about Mr Reyes-Guerra.'

This happy jaunt down memory lane was interrupted by a symphony of boos and whistles emanating from the Pavement Club and directed at a rabble of Black-Shorted ruffians who'd made the mistake of turning right on exiting St Catharine's. These self-appointed Saviours of Britain took one look at the *actual* people of Britain, and opted to save themselves.

'Good riddance!' said Eustace, shaking his fist at the retreating mokes. 'If I were a younger man, I'd put that mallet of yours to good use.'

'Any time, Eustace. You have only to ask.'

*   *   *

'Odd month, October,' I called through the steam.

'Sir?'

'Rain and shine, hot and cold – one never knows what to expect.'

'Without wishing to truncate your ablutions, sir, the debate begins in just over an hour.'

'October is the year's Belgium.'

'If you say so, sir.'

'I do say so! I say so with all the conviction of a croquet champion. Or, rather, the partner of a croquet champion.' I spun the hot-water tap with my big toe. 'Which reminds me, what's the latest with Boko's acca?'

'Manicou won by a head at Kempton, sir, and The Rip by a length at Aintree.'

'Crivens! So we're all teed up for a nail-biter tomorrow?'

'Yes, sir. I shall arrange for a taxi to convey you to Newmarket.'

'Convey *us*, you mean? This is your fox, Jeeves, and you should be in at the kill.'

'That is most kind, sir.'

'I don't suppose you'll be joining me now, though, to see the Hysteron Proteron thwart Spode's journey to the Union?'

'Actually, sir, I will accompany you, if that would be convenient?'

*　　*　　*

Jeeves was right.

Spode didn't drive to the Union.

He walked.

Despite the rain.

Despite the taxi we'd sent to *tice* him.

In a grisly combination of white tie, black shorts, and paisley umbrella, he walked.

Out of the Bull Hotel ... past St Catharine's ... along King's Parade ... past King's ... past the Senate House ... past Caius ... up Green Street ... he walked.

I know all this, because Jeeves and I were a mashie-niblick ahead of him, concealed from view by a titanic black brolly.

At the top of Green Street, Spode turned left and walked to the corner of Jesus Lane, where the Hysteron Proteron had erected the first of their twenty-eight vehicular diversions. Here he greeted as an old friend Adrian Whipplesnaith, and the two of them stopped to exchange some comradely banter with Lord Pallot, who was inexpertly disguised as a road-mender.

'That's torn it,' I said to Jeeves, as we observed proceedings from the corner of All Saints' Passage.

'Not necessarily, sir.'

'Aha! Do I perceive a hidden rabbit in an unseen *chapeau*?'

'Possibly, sir. If you'd be so kind as to follow me.'

He whisked me at speed down Bridge Street, across the road, and into the courtyard of The Round Church, where, obscured by a silver birch, we had a concealed view of Spode's approach.

'What now? Skulking?'

'Indeed, sir.'

We didn't skulk for long, for Spode was now just a chip-shot behind us – striding down the pavement with Whipplesnaith poodled at his heel.

They were almost (and temptingly) in spitting distance when, out of the narrow alley that leads to the Union building, stepped two rain-drenched policemen.

'Am I am addressing Roderick Spode?' the senior copper enquired.

'That is correct, Officer.'

'Roderick *Ernald* Spode?'

'At your service.' He raised his umbrella and bowed.

'I am Inspector Whitsun, and this is Constable Dockery.'

'Here to protect me from hecklers?' Spode guffawed, turning to share the hilarity with Whipplesnaith. 'Or hunting for autographs?'

'I am arresting you on suspicion of receiving stolen goods, knowing them to be stolen.'

'*What?*'

'Relating to a burglarious assault on Tuesday last, at the Mount Street Hotel, London W.1.'

Spode puffed out his chest and uttered the words that would surely be carved on his tomb: 'Do you know who I am?'

The Inspector frowned. 'I thought we'd just established that, Mr Spode.'

'Lord Sidcup, if you please.'

'Fancy!' said the Inspector, sardonically. 'A lord.'

'Actually, I am the seventh Earl of Sidcup.'

'Oh, I see – so *not* Roderick Spode. Well, well, well.'

'No, Inspector, you misunderstand. I am both.'

'An alias, is it? Very good. Any other sobriquets you'd like to admit? I should warn you that anything—'

'Listen here, my good man.' Whipplesnaith stepped up to the crease. 'You have the honour to be addressing the seventh Earl of Sidcup. If I were you, I'd watch my tone.'

'Is that a threat, Mr ... ?'

'Whipplesnaith. Adrian Noël Whipplesnaith.'

'Make a note, Constable Dockery. We don't want to lose track.'

'I'm not standing here to be insulted,' Spode sneered, stepping forward to elbow past the blockade.

At this point, a number of things happened almost simultaneously:

[i] Inspector Whitsun seized Spode's arm – twisting it with more than reasonable force to snap on a pair of cuffs.

[ii] Whipplesnaith made a pitifully amateurish lunge for Constable Dockery's helmet – receiving a truncheon in the ribcage for his trouble.

[iii] A spirited lass in a Newnham scarf appeared out of nowhere and – with a cry of 'Have a jelly, my friend!' – thrust a plate of trifle into Spode's face.

[iv] From within the crowd of astonished spectators, Iona emerged – lifting her camera and freezing the tableau with a flash.

Dripping in custard, and adorned with cherries, Spode was incandescent.

'Arrest that woman!' he shouted at the fleeing *trifleur*.

'Woman?' Inspector Whitsun had abandoned any pretence of constabulary sobriety and was shamelessly playing to the gallery. 'I saw no woman.'

'There are witnesses!' Spode waved at the crowd. 'Ask them!'

This proved to be a strategic error, for the witnesses had taken an immediate and intense dislike to Lord Sidcup and they expressed their ill-feeling with satiric glee:

—*Woman? What woman?*
—*I saw no woman!*
—*I thought I saw a man, but not a woman . . .*
—*A woman? In Cambridge? How odd!*

Spode turned to his acolyte for moral support, but Whipplesnaith was nowhere to be seen. He was a cowardly goon, as goons go; and as goons go, he'd gone.

Unaccustomed to facing 'his people' without a phalanx of *heil*ing henchmen, Spode once again pulled rank.

'As a Peer of the Realm, I'm immune from arrest.'

'Peers may be immune from *civil* arrest,' mused Inspector Whitsun, 'genuine Peers, that is – but receiving stolen goods is a *criminal* charge.'

Spode struggled against his cuffs. 'You're meant to be on *our* side!' he whimpered.

'And which side might that be?'

'The Saviours of Britain!'

'Ah!' Inspector Whitsun nodded. 'That explains the nasty shorts and offensive armband.'

'It is *not* an offensive armband! The Flash and Circle is the official insignia of the Black Shorts.'

'Plenty of dressing-up where you're going, Sonny Jim.'

The idea that his armband and shorts were no more than 'dressing-up' prompted Spode to unleash a tirade of obscenity that did credit to his boarding school.

'Dear, oh dear.' Inspector Whitsun shook his head. 'I see we're adding drunk and disorderly to the charge-sheet.'

'Disorderly I may be,' Spode snapped, 'but I am *never* drunk!'

'Is that so? Then how come I can smell alcohol on your breath?'

For some reason this accusation of insobriety tipped Lord Sidcup over the cliff of reason. He drew himself up to his full, fat height before bellowing at ear-splitting volume: 'IT'S. SHERRY. TRIFLE.'

To be fair, I think even Spode recognised this hadn't been his finest oratorical hour, and so, as a Black Maria drew up to the kerb, he permitted himself to be manhandled inside with something approaching grace.

'Care to enlighten me?' I asked my man, as we tootled past St John's.

'Concerning Lord Sidcup's arrest, sir?'

'Yes, Jeeves, concerning *that*.'

'This may help elucidate matters, sir.'

He handed me a page from the *Daily Mail*:

MAYFAIR HEIST: WHO IS THE FIFTH MAN?

Police are seeking a fifth man in connection with Tuesday's diamond heist at the Mount Street Hotel. It is believed that a 'fence' may have masterminded the robbery on behalf of a syndicate of Italian dealers. Scotland Yard is appealing for information, and has released an artistic likeness of the man they wish to question.

In the centre of the article was a large and detailed sketch of—

'Spode!' I turned to Jeeves in shock. 'Roderick Spode is the Fifth Man!'

'No, sir.'

'*No?*' I pointed to the sketch, which captured Spode down to his greasy follicles. 'How do you explain this?'

'Lord Sidcup has no connection with the robbery, sir. Except for a striking similarity to one of the suspects.'

'I don't unders— *Wait!* You tipped off the cops anyway?'

'I did, sir.'

'Have you gone completely bugs?'

'No, sir. I considered it a useful precaution in the event—'

'—Spode *didn't* drive to the Union!'

'Indeed, sir.'

'Gracious, Jeeves, I'm glad you're on our side.'

'Thank you, sir.'

'But why were you so adamant he'd walk? After all, he's fat and lazy, and it is still raining.'

'In situations such as this, sir, it is profitable to consider the psychology of the individual.'

'Here we go!'

'Since Lord Sidcup hoped to persuade a chamber of under- graduates to the cause of Fascism, it seemed likely he would attempt, at least superficially, *transitio ad plebem.*'

'Do you do this deliberately, Jeeves?'

'My apologies, sir. I meant only that he would seek to present himself as a "man of the people" by walking to the Union, rather than being chauffeured.'

'And that's *transitio ad whatsit*?'

'Approximately speaking, sir, yes. It also explains Lord Sidcup's desire to disengage himself from Miss Bassett and acquire a less, might one say, idiosyncratic wife.'

We strolled a little further.

'Lucky that custard-chucker was about.'

Jeeves cocked an eyebrow.

'Lucky Iona was there to capture the moment.'

Jeeves cocked the other eyebrow.

'Great snakes!'

'I endeavour to give satisfaction, sir.'

And then a wheeze struck me, the way they sometimes do.

'D'you know, Jeeves, what would utterly ice this cake?'

'Dispatching Miss MacAuslan's photographic film to the *Daily Sketch*, sir, for inclusion in Mr Montgomery's gossip column?'

I'm not ashamed to say that I actually tipped my hat to the man.

He is, as I may have mentioned, The Master.

*   *   *

We parted ways outside Great St Mary's, and I sauntered along Market Hill to supper with Lord MacAuslan.

'Have you heard the latest about Spode?' I asked as I sat.

'I know what plans Jeeves had in store for Lord Sidcup, but not yet how events unfolded.'

And so I gave him the ball-by-ball, placing particular emphasis on Whipplesnaith's cowardly vanishing act, and the cherry-topping slapstick of custard's last stand.

'That sounds *very* satisfactory,' Lord MacAuslan smiled, 'and I'll be sure to pass on your kind words to Thomasina.'

'Who's she?'

'The girl with the sherry trifle. Yet another MacAuslan niece, I'm afraid.'

'Iona's not the only one?'

'Oh, no – I seem to collect nieces like you collect aunts. Thomasina is my brother Abernathy's youngest. She's reading mathematics at Newnham.'

'Tell her from me she should take up the javelin.'

'I will, of course, though she fences épée with terrifying vigour.'

'That explains her penetrating aim. So what happens now to Spode?'

'I imagine the police will make their enquiries before releasing him later tonight with profuse apologies. Such mistakes occur from time to time.'

'Especially when Jeeves is about.'

'Well, yes. I'm always rather relieved he's on our side.'

'I said the exact same thing not fifteen minutes ago!'

We got down to brass tacks over dessert.

'So, tonight's the night the teddy bears have their pillage?'

'Actually, Mr Wooster, it's not. I did think we'd fire the starting gun today, but new information has emerged and we're postponing things until tomorrow.'

'Of course! Saturday night, so Whipplesnaith will be out and the coast will be clear. I assume one of your tame porters can slip me a key to his rooms?'

'They could,' Lord MacAuslan smiled, 'but this burglary needs to *look* like a burglary, not an "inside job". So we'd like you to enter by breaking a window.'

'An easily accessible ground-floor window?'

'An easily accessible *second*-floor window.'

'You jest, of course.'

'Come now, Mr Wooster, this should prove no great *struissle* to a man who night-climbed so enthusiastically at Oxford.'

I put down my glass. 'How ever d'you know that? I was never caught!'

'Little can be kept from a college scout.'

'Eustace Epworth! Funnily enough, I bumped into him just ... *ahh*, so he's one of us.'

'Mr Epworth is a "bob-a-nob", only loosely associated with the Ganymede, but nonetheless useful.'

'What else did Eustace blab-a-jab about my salad days? No, on second thoughts, I'd rather not lift up that rock.'

Lord MacAuslan smiled knowingly and took from his pocket a hand-drawn map of Trinity College. 'Now, Mr Wooster, regarding the plan for tomorrow night—'

We were distracted by a cheerful commotion at the restaurant's front door and the appearance of Leviathan, who, flanked by his crew of runners and touts, had evidently arrived to don the nosebag before a big day at Newmarket. At first, he affected not to know me, but as he rolled past our table he raised his hands to his face and wiggled his fingers like a man tickling an octopus.

'A friend?' asked Lord MacAuslan, amused.

'A friend's accountant,' I said, judging it wise to gloss over the prefix 'turf'.

*   *   *

After a long and unexpectedly arresting day, I was more than ready to return to Caius and climb the wooden hill. But I did rather feel I owed it to the Hysteron Proteron to see how they were bearing the blow. And so, having escorted Lord MacAuslan back to Trinity, I buzzed across to the Pitt and made my way up to the bar.

The sea of gloomy faces I'd expected was, in fact, quite otherwise – for there they all were, in the highest spirits and the loudest pyjamas.

'Wooster!' hailed Lord Pallot, whose jim-jams were cross-hatched in the colours of Balliol. 'Perfect timing!'

I was alarmed by the glint in his eye. 'For what?'

The answer arrived in the form of a double-handled, copper-bottomed Loving Cup, effervescing at the brim with three gallons of Black Velvet.

For those who've never taken part in a Loving Cup ceremony, it operates much like the parlour game 'Bunnies'. Of course, as I write this, it occurs that not everyone will be *au fait* with 'Bunnies', so ...

Picture yourself at a table, surrounded by chums, and, for the sake of this sermon, imagine yourself to be X:

T · U · V · W · <u>X</u> · Y · Z · A · B · C

X is presented with the Loving Cup, but is afraid to drink from it with both hands (the only possible way, given its heft) thereby leaving his left and right flanks undefended from a sneak attack (this is a medieval tradition, so pay attention). X takes the Cup and turns to face Y; X bows to Y, and Y bows in return before turning his back on X to defend X against Z. Then X turns to face W; X bows to W, and W bows in return before turning his back on X to defend X from V. Thus protected on either side, X faces forward, lifts the Cup, and drinks his fill. Since Loving Cups pass to the left, like port, it's now W's turn to drink – but only once protected from Y by X, and from U by V.

This rigmarole (easier executed than explained) is repeated until the entire alphabet of drinkers has drunk, is drunk, or both. And, as you'd expect from such an alcoholic toffee-scramble, additional fines of champagne are imposed on any who stand when they should be sitting, or vice versa.

Since I was seated to the left of Lord Pallot (the W to his X), I was the second person to partake, and I drank my fill without

any complications – allowing me to spectate the ensuing pande-
monium. Once the Cup had eventually made its rounds, Baron
Salmon (Y) handed it back to Lord Pallot, who, bowing to the
table, turned it upside down. To my amazement, and to exuberant hurrahs, not a drop was left.

'Supernacular!' cried Lord Pallot. 'Time for round two!'

'You can't be serious,' I protested.

'It's Hysteron Proteron Day. The cup must pass *twice* in *each*
direction.'

'Is it just me,' I asked as we waited for the first refill, 'or is this
Black Velvet uncommonly strong? I feel oddly light-headed.'

Lord Pallot glanced about feloniously. 'There are few rays of
joy in the dusty study of chemistry, but one of them is this.' He
handed me a small glass vial labelled, *Benzyl-methyl-carbinamine-
carbonate*. 'It's experimental. Very peppy. And if anyone asks, it's
for hay-fever.'

6.

SATURDAY

'Jeeves!'

'Jeeeeves!'

'Jeeeeeeves!'

It was futile.

Howl as I might, my cries of woe would never carry from Caius to the University Arms – a distance, as the crow flies, of two stiffish par fours.

I don't often exceed the recommended dose, being a man of modest self-control, but when I have taken a drop or two over the eight, it's a godsend to know that my man is on hand with his patent-pending (accept no imitations) morning-after elixir. Less 'hair of the dog' than 'Ride of the Valkyries', this life-saving panacea makes quick work of the heebie-jeebies, pink spiders, and *delirium tremens* that, once in a while, plague us socialising sorts.

But now I was Jeevesless, with the room spinning, the wallpaper galloping, and my wristwatch crashing out the seconds like an orchestra of cymbals. Lord Pallot's *Benzyl-methyl-carbo-doodah* may have been experimental, but its effects were as old as time.

I rolled out of bed, struggled onto all fours, and commenced crawling out to the study – whereupon I heard a key in the lock.

'Jeeves!'

'*Thieves?* No thieves here, dearie. They wouldn't bloomin' dare!'

And in bustled the bedder, Christine.

I fell to the floor with a whimper.

'You all right, petal? You're awful green.'

'How kind of you to notice.'

'You look like the "before" photo in one of those "before and after" advertisements for Buck-U-Uppo.'

'It's possible I was over-served last night.'

'Just like my George, may he rest in peace. Most nights, George was as over-served as a newt.'

Absent of anything to add to this dialogue, I closed my eyes and wailed.

'Don't fret, ducks, I've just the thing. You stay there, nice and still, and I'll be back in two shakes.'

I must have momentarily nodded off, because the next thing I remember was being prodded awake and handed a glass of something that smelled as evil as it looked – green, oily, and noticeably lacking in tomato juice, egg yolks, or Lea & Perrins.

'Down in one,' Christine encouraged, 'just like an oyster. Don't let it touch the sides.'

Any doubts I might have entertained about accepting hemlock from a deranged bedder were submerged by waves of vertigo buffeting the void of my skull.

And so I closed my eyes and drank.

The immediate sensation was of burning – strangely evocative of chewing stinging nettles – and the feeling that, were I to exhale, flames would emerge as if from a dragon's maw. Fortunately, breathing was not an option, indeed it was all I could do to remain flat on the ground and keep my hair attached to my scalp. Gradually the burning evolved into a pulsating sort of thrumming that originated at the knees before crawling up the spine until it reached the chest, where it competed for attention with the lungs. I attempted to speak, but managed only a guttural hacking noise, rather like a crow with the early indications of black lung.

In time, the burning and hacking abated, taking with them the nausea, dizziness, and clammy perspiration, until all that remained was an uncontrollable flutter in my left eye.

'That's the only side-effect,' said Christine cheerfully. 'It'll pass in a couple of months.'

I gingerly rose to the semi-recumbent and sleeved the tears from my cheek.

'I say! Does this magical potion have a name?'

'The Two-Quid Cure.'

'What a bizarre— *Oh!* Yes, of course. Let me find my wallet.'

'That's all right, ducks. No charge for the clergy. Wouldn't be right.'

'I won't ask what's in it – honestly, I'm fearful to know – but how ever did you concoct it out of thin air? Or do you carry a cauldron, just in case?'

Christine laughed. 'Professor Fitzsimons, two floors down, has all the doings. He's away right now, but I'm sure he'd not begrudge a thirsty priest. He's something of an expert on thirst!'

'Well, it's a miracle you were passing. Is Diane not with you?'

'Not today, petal. We don't do rooms on weekends, just stairs, gyp-rooms, and necessaries.' She looked at her watch. 'In fact, I must be finishing off.'

'What *is* the o'clock?'

'Just gone nine.'

Splendid: I had precisely zero minutes to wash, shave, dress, and appear in Aunt Agatha's suite at the University Arms for breakfast with my anonymous bride.

*   *   *

'What time do you call this?'

In idle moments I've often pondered writing some sort of *Field Guide to the Aunts of England* – and 'What Time Do You Call This?' would be the title of Chapter One.

It's not that aunts are always early – (though they usually are) (and they're unfailingly earlier than nephews) – it's that aunts exist in their own unique time-zones, like the royal estates which defy G.M.T. to prolong the hours of the shoot.

'Belgravia Aunt Time' is forever set in the amber glow of the Edwardian Age – when Standards were kept, and Stations were known, when the sun never set on a picnic (let alone the Empire), and before 'all that nonsense in the Balkans' made finding good staff such a trial. For aunts of Aunt Agatha's stamp, it was an age of tugged forelocks and doffed caps, averted eyes and unseen service, ironed papers and starched linen, capable nannies and silent children – an age, in other words, of deference, grace, and favour.

So, the next time an aunt rebukes your slouching posture / indolent spirit / slack manners / moral blankness / intellectual vapidity / lack of gainful employment / wilful failure to marry [tick all that apply], remember: deep below the Plimsoll line of her Prussian-blue tea-gown, the poor old B.A.T.'s just pining for the days of her youth.

'G'morning, g'morning, g'morning!' I trilled, adopting an unfelt mirth. 'Sorry I'm a molecule tardy – but so, I see, is my bride-to-be.'

'*She* has that prerogative, Bertram. *You* have no excuse.'

'I was stocking up on beauty sleep.'

'Something not even death could accomplish.'

(This was my second cold bath of the morning, but I pocketed the insult and pressed on.)

'What a charming suite of rooms this is.'

'Are you blind as well as imbecilic? This is the nastiest, pokiest room I've ever been offered. I usually take the Perseus Suite, but apparently it is "closed for renovations" – not that I believe a single word anyone here says.'

Given that her sitting-room was indeed smaller than the smallest room of my suite, I decided it safest to hurl myself under the horses.

'So, are we any closer to ascertaining the name of my affianced? On the off-chance it comes up.'

'Well—'

Her answer was pre-empted by a knock at the door and the appearance of Gussie Fink-Nottle, dressed as room-service waiter.

In any other circumstances I'd have predicted an explosion of animosity, for the last time these two had met, dogs had been kicked. Thankfully, like most aunts, Aunt Agatha is snow-blind to the servant class, and it didn't cross her mind for a moment that the flunky before us might be her son's tutor, my old chum or, indeed, both.

'Excuse me, Mrs Gregson,' Gussie bowed, 'but there is a call for Mr Wooster.'

Aunt Agatha stared at the telephone. 'I heard no ring.'

Gussie had evidently not expected his ruse to be so easily tumbled.

'A call ... ' he blustered, ' ... on the other line ... which can't be connected because of ... reasons.'

One of the odder features of Aunt Agatha's insistence that the world is awash with blithering idiots emerges when she encounters the clean potato. Then, rather than reacting with redoubled fury, as one might expect, she softens considerably, mollified by the knowledge she's been right all along.

'You'd better see who it is, Bertram. But *don't* dally. Our guest will be here presently.'

At this point, McIntosh, who had hitherto been snoozing under the table, abruptly awoke and – sniffing a foe with whom there was unfinished business – launched himself in a frenzy at Gussie's ankles.

'Did the silly man wake you up?' Aunt Agatha addressed her hound in nursery tones. 'Is he a *very silly* man?'

'Madam,' Gussie quivered in pain, 'might you control your dog?'

'If you didn't want to play with him,' Aunt Agatha snapped, 'you shouldn't have soaked your trousers in aniseed!'

'Aniseed?' Gussie was mystified. 'Why would I soak my trousers in aniseed?'

'That is a question, young man, only *you* can answer.'

Ever the peacemaker, I unlaced a shoe and waved it aloft, making canine-friendly clicking sounds. Almost immediately, McIntosh ceased his assault, pinned back his ears, and turned towards me. Having thus secured the beast's attention, I coaxed him away from his breakfast and into the bathroom, whereupon I slammed shut the door to a barrage of frustrated yips.

'Shan't be long,' I said cheerily, scooting out into the corridor.

'It's Mabel,' blurted Gussie, once we'd found a quiet corner.

'The waitress?'

'The love of my life!'

'Very soon, you realise, we're going to need some sort of numbering system.'

'They're going to sack her!' His voice was as full of emotion as his breath was heavy with gin.

'What? Who? Also, why?'

'They ... the hotel management ... found in Mabel's room ...' he struggled to get the words out, '... in her room ... in the servants' quarters ... they found ...'

'Yes?'

Gussie began gently to weep. 'She's been hiding in her room ...'

'What?'

'In Mabel's room ... they found ... '

'What?'

'In her room ... '

The tension was unbearable. What could *they* possibly have found in Mabel's room to cause Gussie such distress? A corpse? Two corpses? A polo team of corpses?

'Spit it out, old man. It can't be all *that* bad.'

'Bad?' His gulping tears spluttered into laughter. 'It's the most wonderful thing in the world!'

'For heaven's sake, Gussie, *what* has Mabel been hiding in her room?'

'Newts!'

I could have strangled him. 'And this concerns me how?'

'I want you to ask her to marry me.'

'Right, well, that's not going to happen. First, because you're clearly drunk. And second, because – thanks to untold toil and trouble on my part – you're engaged to Miss Pinke.'

'That's the other thing.'

'Amuse me.'

'I want you to tell Vonka the engagement's off.'

It took me surprisingly few words to inform Gussie Fink-Nottle that I washed my hands of his romantic entanglements, now and in perpetuity. However, as I retraced my steps to Aunt Agatha's lair, who should I encounter but one of the entanglements in question.

'Bertie!' she cried, seizing my elbow and hauling me along at her heel.

'Hi-ho, Vonka! Wandering—'

'The halls? Yes. I'm looking for the Medusa Suite, and you can help. Really, these room names are too bad.' She pointed to the doors as we galloped past. 'Phorcys, Tethys, Echidna – I mean, who can even pronounce them?'

I prayed I might be going deaf. 'Sorry, but did you say—'

'The Medusa Suite? That's right. I'm breakfasting with a new friend of Mama's called Mrs Gregson.'

My blood ran cold, and I would have halted in my tracks had I not been manacled to a speeding hyena.

Could Veronica Pinke – *Vonka!* – really be the 'Dottie' or 'Lottie' that Aunt Agatha intended I marry? The idea was so thoroughly repellent, it made even Madeline Bassett look like the pick of the litter.

'But what are *you* doing here?' Vonka asked.

'Mrs Gregson,' I confessed, 'is my aunt.'

Vonka was delighted. 'So you'll be breakfasting too? What fun! Oh, look, here's her room.'

And before I could even think of stopping her, she'd knocked on the door to Pandora's Box and recklessly opened the lid.

'There you are,' Aunt Agatha huffed, gesturing for us to sit. 'I feared you might be lost.'

'I was rather,' Vonka smiled, 'but then I bumped into Bertie.'

'*Bertie?*' Aunt Agatha was disconcerted by such casual famil-iarity. 'Do I take it you *know* my nephew?'

'I should say so! I'm engaged to his best friend.'

The emotions that swept across Aunt Agatha's face – shock, bafflement, fury, doubt – wove a Bayeux Tapestry of indignation.

'*Engaged?*'

'That's right, Mrs Gregson. Augustus and I are planning a Christmas wedding.'

The trick with aunts is: show no mercy – kick 'em when they're down.

'This is too killing!' I confected a careless laugh. 'You see, Aunt Agatha had high hopes for *our* engagement.'

'Really?' Vonka thought this hysterical.

'Oh, yes – she's planned it all for this very breakfast. Is that not so, aged relation?'

Aunt Agatha was on the back foot, a position she did not find at all commodious. 'It appears I may have misapprehended the situation.'

'I should coco,' I pointed to the ring-box on the table. 'She's even come armed with a diamond.'

'This contains ... pills,' Aunt Agatha improvised, sliding the box out of reach. 'I take two for my heart each morning.'

(As if she had a heart!)

'Also, get this: she doesn't even remember your name.'

'What nonsense you talk, Bertram. I am fully aware of ... this young lady's name.'

I was about to deliver the *coup de grace* by putting her to the test, when there came a timorous knock at the door.

'Enter!' cried Aunt Agatha, delighted by the distraction, and in came Bun Shop Mabel with breakfast to feed a battalion.

'Good-o!' I rubbed my hands with greed. 'Provisions!'

As Mabel wheeled the trolley into reach, I became aware of a crescendoing stampede in the corridor, as if hippos had taken to the tango. Then, violently and without warning, the door flew open and a colossal, red-faced man burst into the room.

Oblivious to his surroundings, he flung himself to his knees and roared: 'I LOVE YOU, MABEL! MARRY ME!'

I really can't say who was more dismayed – though Aunt Agatha was the first to find her voice.

'Lord Sidcup!' she remonstrated. 'What *do* you think you're doing?'

Spode was mortified to discover he had company.

'Mrs Gregson ... Miss Pinke ... Wooster ... '

'Hullo, Spode. I thought you were in prison.'

'Well, er ... '

'Fancy a sausage?'

'Forgive me ... I ... I ... I was just—'

'JUST WHAT?' shrieked a voice from the doorway.

Spode spun on his knees, as if plugged into a socket, to see stalking towards him on a high horse of wounded virtue, Madeline Bassett.

'Oh, look,' I pointed, unhelpfully, 'it's your fiancée.'

'Darling!' cried Spode, attempting to rise from his genuflection.

'Don't you *dare* "darling" me!' Madeline snapped, abandoning a lifetime of baby-talk in her jealous rage. 'And stay on your knees, like the snake you are!'

'Do snakes have knees?' I mused, helping myself to a poached egg.

'Shut *up*, Wooster!' Spode growled out of one side of his mouth, while attempting a smile on the other. 'Madeline, my precious, what a delightful surprise!'

'Surprise?' she hissed. 'That's rich from the man who *begged* me to come.'

'Begged?' Spode quavered.

'Begged!' confirmed Madeline, unfolding a telegram. '"BIG DOG MISSES FRUITY BASSETT. SCAMPER TO CAMBRIDGE UNION DEBATE TONIGHT. WOOFETY BARK." Not that you *were* at the Union last night. Instead I find you here, on your knees!'

'But, darling – I mean, *Madeline* – I didn't send that telegram.'

'Ha! Who else knows our nicknames?'

'Advantage, Miss Bassett,' I scored from the sidelines. 'Sidcup to serve.'

'SHUT UP, Wooster!' Spode shouted. 'This doesn't concern you.'

'Doesn't it?' asked Madeline, archly. 'Maybe it should.'

Just as I was beginning to regret tweaking this particular tiger's tail, there was a knock at the door and Gussie Fink-Nottle stepped into the lion's den.

'My apologies, Mrs Gregson, but Mr Wooster is—'

'AUGUSTUS?' cried Vonka and Madeline, as one.

Poor old Gussie was in a bit of a spot – faced, as he was, by his current fiancée (Vonka), his coveted fiancée (Mabel), his ex-fiancée (Madeline), and his ex-fiancée's current fiancé (Spode). Added to which he was [i] dressed as a waiter, [ii] carrying a carpet-beater, and [iii] drunk.

The exquisite agony of the silence that followed was terminated by Aunt Agatha.

'I have it!' she eureka'd, thrusting a bony digit in Gussie's direction. 'That man is *pretending* to deliver room service, but *really* he's my idiot son's idiot tutor, Think-Rottle.'

'FINK-NOTTLE!' shouted Spode, still on his knees. 'His name is Fink-Nottle, and he is a worm!'

'You mind your tongue!' snapped Mabel, abandoning all deference to enter the fray. 'I don't care if you are a lord, m'lord. My Gussie is the kindest, sweetest—'

'*Your* Gussie?' Vonka sneered. 'Since when does a waitress set her cap at a gentleman?'

'Pah!' snorted Spode. 'Fink-Nottle's no gentleman!'

'He's more of a gentleman than *you'll* ever be,' snapped Madeline, keen to re-establish her pre-eminence in this increasingly lopsided love rhombus.

'Thank you, Madeline,' Gussie bowed, before turning to Spode. 'Is it too much to ask, Lord Sidcup, why you are on your knees before the woman I love?'

'*The woman you love?*' Vonka's eyes darted between Gussie and Mabel. 'I don't understand.'

'Neither do I,' said Aunt Agatha.

'That makes three of us,' said Madeline. 'Explain yourself, Roderick.'

I tapped my spoon against the teapot to bring the room to order.

'Can I just say, boys and girls, I don't think I've ever enjoyed breakfast more.'

I was saved from an if-looks-could-kill firing squad by a knock at the door and the entrance of Jeeves, who took in the riotous assembly with an unflappable glance.

'Excuse me, Mrs Gregson, my lord, ladies, and gentlemen – but two representatives of the Cambridgeshire Constabulary are desirous of a short interview.'

And into the ring stepped Inspector Whitsun and Constable Dockery.

There's something unsettling about policemen in a hotel room – like finding a horse in a swimming pool, it does rather indicate foul play.

Aunt Agatha stiffened in reflexive chagrin; Gussie shrank back against the panelling; Madeline stood haughtily defiant, as befitted a magistrate's daughter; Mabel began trembling (presumably terrified that concealment of newts was a capital crime); Vonka looked mildly entertained; and Spode was as indignant as a seventh Earl could be while kneeling at the breakfast trolley of infidelity.

Despite Constable Dockery staring daggers at me from across the room (coppers *never* forget an acquittal), I was having a whale of a time. For once I could think of nothing I'd done that might attract the attention of the boys in blue, and the prospect of Aunt Agatha, Spode, or Madeline being arrested filled me with nothing but *joie de vivre*.

'Forgive our intrusion at this early hour,' said Inspector Whitsun with dry formality, 'but I have in my possession a warrant for the arrest of—'

Three voices interrupted in unison:

'—Is it about the newts?' squeaked Mabel.
'—If you arrest me again, I shall sue!' boomed Spode.
'—I promise I'll pay him back!' wailed Aunt Agatha.

Irritated that his denouement had been so heavily heckled, Inspector Whitsun paused, cleared his throat, and took it again from the top.

'Forgive our intrusion at this early hour, but I have in my possession a warrant for the arrest of—'

At which point young Thomas entered the already crowded room.

'Hooray!' I cheered. 'And then there were eleven.'

'Hullo, Mama! Hullo, Cousin Bertie! Hullo, Mr Fink-Nottle!'

'Thomas, dear,' Aunt Agatha spoke with a tenderness that could only be explained by the police presence, 'we're a *little* preoccupied at the moment.'

'Right-ho,' he replied, incuriously.

'McIntosh is shut in the bathroom – *don't* ask why, darling, just pop and fetch him, and take him for a nice long walk. A really nice *long* walk.'

By some instinctive agreement, none of the assembled cast moved a muscle nor said a word as Thos. collected McIntosh's lead from the sofa, walked to the bathroom, collared the beast, and dragged him yelping from the room.

'As I was saying,' said Inspector Whitsun, once the door had clicked shut, 'I have in my possession a warrant for the arrest of—'

And then the telephone rang.

And rang.

And rang.

Although it was Aunt Agatha's suite, the lady of the manor showed no intention of stirring from her chair, and everyone else considered themselves too elevated to stoop, or inferior to climb, to the task.

Eventually, Jeeves swam over to answer the call.

'It's for you, Inspector.'

Inspector Whitsun clenched his jaw in frustrated rage; these sorts of things did *not* occur in the detective stories he devoured.

'Can you take a message?' he asked, muttering under his breath, 'Here I am, in the middle of a delicate—'

'My apologies, Inspector,' Jeeves interrupted, 'but Chief Superintendent Larkin wishes to know if you've made the arrest?'

I stifled my giggles with a slice of fried bread.

'Tell. Him. I'm. Doing. It.'

'Very good, sir.'

Jeeves murmured briefly into the receiver, before drifting back to the periphery.

Now beyond furious that his well-rehearsed thunder had been stolen, Inspector Whitsun abandoned all propriety and retreated into the demotic.

'Veronica Pinke – you're nicked.'

'We have a winner,' I cried, forking myself a kipper. 'What's the charge, Officer?'

Inspector Whitsun consulted his paperwork. 'Theft of, and criminal damage to, rare books and manuscripts.'

'Naughty, naughty, naughty,' I wagged my finger. 'And you a librarian.'

In contrast to Spode's vitriolic fury the night before, Vonka appeared serenely unmoved by the accusation. 'Perhaps someone might telephone my father,' she said, as Constable Dockery snapped on the cuffs. 'I shall need to speak to a solicitor.'

And then, just as I thought things couldn't get any more delicious, Inspector Whitsun approached the table and leaned down next to Aunt Agatha.

'I wonder, madam,' he said discreetly, 'if you have a receipt for whatever's in that?'

'In *what*?' Aunt Agatha squawked, horrified to be in such close proximity to a uniform.

The Inspector pointed to the ring-box by her plate. 'You see, madam, we've been asked to keep an eye out for all suspicious Lambert Lyall jewels.'

There were several reasons why I might have lingered after Vonka had been clapped in irons: to see how Gussie might woo Mabel;

to discover if Spode would rise from his knees; to chide Aunt Agatha for proposing me to a book thief; to ascertain if our engagement ring was hot property; and to finish off my barely begun kipper.

Sadly, the longer I remained at the table, the greater was my risk of being snared by Madeline, who was glaring down at her affianced with barely concealed loathing.

And so, taking advantage of the general confusion, I executed the most Gallic of French Exits, and slipped through the door unobserved.

I was speeding down the corridor towards the safety of the backstairs, when a hand emerged from the panelling, seized my elbow, dragged me into an ink-black cupboard, and thrust me up against a stack of mops.

'My husband doesn't understand me,' a voice slurred into my ear.

I sighed.

'We established that on Thursday, Mrs Pinke.'

'Not like *you* understand me.'

'Ditto.'

'We *must* be preordained, Mr Wooster. When is your birthday?'

'Oh, no. I'm not tripping down that rabbit hole.'

She stamped her foot like a petulant child. 'But I *need* to know!'

'No, you don't.'

'Why don't you tell *my* fortune, like you told Veronica's?'

I was staggered. Could she *still* believe what 'Madame Sosostris' had 'foretold', even knowing I was an imposter? I put the question to her.

'You may have *thought* you were an imposter, Mr Wooster, but the Spirits still moved through you. The Gift is yours, even if you deny it—'

'Hang on—'

'*Especially* if you deny it.'

There was no escaping the circularity of this lunacy, as many accused of witchcraft knew only too well, and so I bowed to the unpalatable.

'If you insist, Mrs Pinke, I shall tell your fortune.'

'Yippee!'

'But you may not like what you hear.'

'The Spirits have never let me down.' She switched on the light. 'Now, where are your cards?'

'Hard as this may be to believe, but I rarely go equipped for prognostication.'

'Pity.' She glanced about. 'We'd need a book for bibliomancy . . . a candle for lychnomancy . . . or entrails for hieromancy.'

'We're in a broom cupboard, Mrs Pinke. Do the Spirits ever move through brooms?'

'Well, abacomancy uses dust, but—' She held up a hand, and pressed her ear to the keyhole. 'D'you hear that?'

'No.'

'Shhh!'

We waited in silence for a second or two, and then Mrs Pinke leapt out of the cupboard, grabbed something from a passing waiter and, with a cheery 'Thank you!', slammed the door shut.

I stared down at her tray of dirty crockery. 'Does this count as entrails?'

'Tasseomancy!'

She selected a teacup, swirled it three times counterclockwise, and upended it on a saucer.

'Which way is south?' she asked.

'I've no idea.'

'It probably doesn't matter: this isn't even my tea.' She handed me the cup. 'Tell me, Madame Sosostris, what do you see?'

I couldn't help myself. 'Don't you have to cross my palm with silver?'

'I'll put a cheque in the post. Now, what do you see?'

I peered at the pile of damp foliage.

'Look, I know you don't want me to say "tea leaves", but ... '

'What *pattern* do they form? What *shapes* do you perceive?'

I peered a little closer.

The honest answer would have been 'no pattern whatsoever' – but then I was hit by a Jeevesian flash of cunning.

'I *do* see a pattern, Mrs Pinke ... it's faint, but distinct.'

'Is it you and I?'

'No.'

'Are we in love?'

'No. Absolutely not. Quite assuredly not. Not in the slightest not.'

'Oh.'

'But I do see *you* ... '

'Oh!'

'With a tall, dark stranger ... '

'My absolute favourite!'

'A man of power and position ... '

'Tell me more.'

'A man of considerable heft ... '

'Gosh!'

'Really ... very, *very* hefty ... '

'Coo!'

'He's wearing ... can it be ... ?'

'It can! It can! ... *What?*'

'Black ... black something ... black ... shorts?'

Mrs Pinke seized my arm. 'RODERICK SPODE!'

I feigned ignorance. 'Who?'

'Lord Sidcup! The Saviour of Britain!'

I consulted the tea leaves. 'Oh yes, that's the chap.'

Mrs Pinke swooned a little. '*Roderick Spode!*'

'And shall I let you into a little secret, Evadne?'

'Do!'

'He's staying at this very hotel.'

'No!'

'Yes!'

'Where?'

'Let me check.' I peered into the cup. 'The Medusa Suite. Turn left down the hall, and it's third on your right.'

*   *   *

'Devious!' I declared, as we taxied along the Newmarket Road. 'And splendidly underhand.'

'Sir?'

'Of course, the harshest critics might quibble at the repeat of your "mistaken identity" gag so soon after Spode's arrest – but I say, if you've got a gag that wows the crowd, give 'em what they eat!'

'You have the advantage of me, sir.'

'Getting the cops to collar Vonka!'

Jeeves shook his head. 'Regrettably, sir, I played no part in Miss Pinke's arrest.'

'You mean, she's *actually* a book thief?'

'So it would appear, sir.'

He handed me a cutting from the *Cambridge Daily News*.

'I say, do you Jekyll and Hyde as a clipping agency?'

'No, sir. I have merely a passing interest in matters bibliothetic.'

RARE PRINTS RAZORED FROM U.L.

The wave of thefts plaguing the Cambridge University Library shows no sign of abating, after it was discovered yesterday that thirteen oversized illustrations had been razor-bladed from a priceless copy of John James Audubon's 1838 *Birds of America*. This brings to thirty-five the number of rare volumes known to have been stolen or ransacked for illustrations in recent months. Chief Superintendent Larkin said: 'We will leave no stone deterred in the hunt for this thief. We have our best men on the job.'

'Well!' I said, returning the cutting to Jeeves for his files. 'Yet another close shave with "The Wedding March".'

'Indeed, sir.'

'Any closer, and Aunt Agatha would've drawn blood.'

'Possibly, sir. Though I am confident we might have frustrated Mrs Gregson's matrimonial proposals even without constabulary assistance.'

'That's reassuring. But the threat of Madeline still hangs in the air, stinking up the joint like Stilton Cheesewright's hair-oil. I mean, what *is* she doing here? By the look of aghast on Spode's face, I think we can agree *he* didn't send the telegram. So who did?'

Jeeves examined his cuff in a meaningful manner.

'You sly old squid! I take it you didn't just *guess* their nicknames?'

'Big Dog, sir, and Fruity Bassett are common currency in the Junior Ganymede smoking-room. Lord Sidcup's valet tends to loose-lipped garrulity when intoxicated, which, as one might imagine, is a not infrequent occurrence.'

'That's the *how*. But what of the *why*?'

'Sir?

'*Why* did you send that wire? I'd have thought the last thing we need is Madeline in town, snapping at my heels like the hell-hound she's become. Aren't you concerned she'll finally chuck Spode for me?'

Jeeves was not concerned. Quite the contrary. In his estima-tion, Madeline was a twenty-four-carat social climber who 'prized as a ladder to the stars' the title of Lady Sidcup. Her overtures to me, he suggested, were no more than crude attempts to make Spode green. This apparently explained not only the hideous item of jewellery she'd commissioned, but also her choice of jeweller.

'Women of Miss Bassett's ambition do little without an ulterior motive, sir. They assuredly do not confide in tradesmen.'

'She *wanted* Lambert Lyall to blab to me?'

'Yes, sir. And her mistrust was not misplaced.'

'That doesn't explain why she was so very coquettish at Fortnum's.'

'I have little doubt, sir, that Miss Bassett considers you a tolerable last resort—'

'Charming!'

'But does it not seem curious that she would petition *you* to intercede with her fiancé, knowing of the deep and mutual antipathy that exists?'

'I thought she was just being dopey.'

'The greater threat, if I may so characterise it, sir, is presented by Lord Sidcup. Although romantic novelists traditionally suggest that "absence makes the heart grow fonder", a more apposite cliché would be "out of sight, out of mind".'

'You're not wrong, Jeeves. Out of Madeline's sight for a second, and Spode went out of his mind. You should have seen his marriage proposal to Mabel: I thought he'd bring the ceiling down.'

'Miss Bassett is a most tenacious suitor, sir, but tenacity does rather depend on proximity.'

'And if the mountain won't come to Madeline ... '

235

'Precisely, sir. I thought it only kind to reunite them – for their sake, and yours.'

It was, as ever, hard to knock holes in the man's logic, and so I lit a meditative cheroot and stared out at the dull, waterlogged fields, wondering how anyone could tolerate the country in autumn for longer than a long weekend.

After a while, Jeeves spoke.

'I wonder, sir, if you might permit me to raise an unrelated and possibly trivial matter?' I begged him continue. 'Splendacious, sir, is a word.'

'Eh?'

'Earlier this week, on Thursday morning to be precise, you advanced to Mr Fink-Nottle the theory that splendacious was not a word.'

'Did I?'

'Yes, sir. With some force. Whereas the word is, in fact, in use – albeit rarely.'

'I see.'

'Mr William Makepeace Thackeray, for example, employed splendacious to describe some silver dish-covers.'

'And you've been fretting about this for two whole days?'

'I did not wish to contradict you at the time, sir, in the presence of others. But I was concerned you were labouring under a misapprehension that might hamper your new-found interest in crosswords.'

'Ha! On which subject, I've been stuck for an age on today's Ten Across: *Encountered after choice fruit fall*. Seven letters, and I can't get any of them.'

'May I be of assistance, sir?'

'I've a hunch it involves bananas. Would you say I was hot, or cold?'

'Cold, sir. Very cold. Ice-cold. Frostily cold. Frigidly cold. Glacially cold. Hyperboreanly cold—'

Luckily, our taxi turned into Newmarket racecourse, and I managed to close the covers of Reginald's Thesaurus.

*   *   *

No sooner had we entered the grandstand bar than Boko descended.

'You're here!' he gasped, in a flurry of distress. 'What kept you?'

'Kept me? I'm an hour early, and as hungry as the steeds in yonder paddock.'

'The race starts in ten minutes!'

'So, *not* the 5:45?'

'The 4:45!'

I glanced at Jeeves, whose silence trumpeted 'I told you so' loudly enough to drown out even Boko's blazer.

'Right, well, we're here now. From where are we watching? This place is swarming.'

'I've taken a box on the second floor.' He beckoned to the committee. 'This way.'

'So,' I asked as we climbed the stairs, 'how does Inch Arran look?'

'Strong and sure-footed – I'd be tempted to say I was quietly confident, if I didn't want to jinx it.'

At the second landing we turned right into a long, musty corridor at the far end of which I heard, and then saw, a gang of loudly dressed chaps barrelling towards us.

'Speaking of jinxes,' I pointed, 'ain't that Leviathan?'

It was, and Boko, fearing the silver-tongued rogue would somehow bilk us of our bet, seized the handle of the nearest door.

'In here, quick! Before he sees us.'

As he propelled us inside, it quickly became clear that this wasn't a private box, so much as a caretaker's cupboard – reminiscent, to me at least, of the cupboards haunted by Evadne Pinke.

'This is outrageous,' boomed Stilton, a stranger as ever to subtlety. 'I'm not cowering from a bookie in a lumber room.'

'Hush!' shushed Boko, peeking through a chink. 'He's coming.'

The volley of voices was indeed getting closer, and I'm pretty sure I heard the word 'accumulator' bandied about in the hubbub. As they approached our covert, Boko clicked shut the door, and we held our collective breaths.

'I don't much care about the race any more,' whispered Bimbash after a while. 'I require a swizzle.'

'I've never needed a snifter more,' said Barmy.

'I'm pretty parched myself,' I chipped in.

'Will you all please shut up?' said Boko. 'I know what I'm doing.'

This evinced a general chuckle.

'Come on, Fittles, they'll be miles away by now.'

Sensing the truth of this, Boko turned the handle. 'It's locked!'

'What do you mean, it's locked?' said Stilton.

'I don't know how else to explain – it's not *un*locked?'

'Is there a key?'

'As usual, Bimbash, you pose the vital question. Of course there's no key – least not one I can see.'

'Let me try.' Stilton barged his way through. 'No, he's right, it's locked.'

'Well, let's bang and holler till we're released.'

'And risk alerting Leviathan?'

'Good point.'

'They'll be off any minute,' said Bimbash, tapping his watch.

And then Jeeves reminded us all of his presence.

'If you will forgive the interjection, gentlemen, the grandstand's architecture suggests there may be a partial view of the course from that window.' He pointed to a narrow slit of glass just below the ceiling.

'Well spotted, Jeeves,' said Bimbash. 'Someone give me a leg.'

He jostled into place and, with Stilton's assistance, scrambled up the wall to report that there was, indeed, a pretty workable vista of the Rowley Mile.

'Splendid, you can give us a commentary.'

'But I don't know one horse from the next! Who can remember all those colours?'

Jeeves cleared his throat.

'*You* know the silks?'

'Yes, sir.'

'*All* of them?'

'All those, sir, with a greater than marginal chance of finishing in a competitive position.'

'Well then, tarry not. Squeeze through, and climb upon Stilton's shoulders.'

'*My* shoulders?'

'You're the tallest and the thickest.'

'How dare—'

'I mean, the *strongest*.'

'He can borrow my bins,' said Barmy, handing Jeeves the largest pair of field-glasses I've ever seen. 'Thirty times mag. You can see the Hook of Holland.'

Picture the scene, as we narrators say: six men crushed into a damp cupboard that could uncomfortably hold three, with my gentleman's personal gentleman balanced on the shoulders of an irate Cheesewright, peering at the runners and riders through a tiny sliver of glass. Jolly boating weather, this wasn't.

'They're under starter's orders, sir. Would it be convenient for me to expound upon events as they unfold?'

'Yes, Jeeves, it would. And keep your eyes on Inch Arran. Much depends on Inch Arran.'

'Very good, sir ... and they're off ... a slow start, understandable, perhaps, given the soft conditions ... but a very level break ... and the field is moving well ... Chaou II is the first to show, sir ... but Inch Arran and Laffy are challenging at a good clip ... Escalus looks to be flagging slightly ... and Gay Record is seeking a way through, running in snatches ... as they come to the first

furlong, sir, Chaou II is leading the pace ... with Inch Arran tight
in ... '

'Where's Gawking Girl?' asked Boko, referring to the nag
Jeeves had nixed.

'Off to one side, sir, eating grass ... and here comes M'as-
Tu-Vu, sir, finding a way through the pack of twenty-six ...
which is rapidly losing shape ... Inch Arran is moving well ... as
are Makaldar and Laffy ... and Escalus seems to have found his
footing ... as they pass the halfway point, sir, it looks like Chaou
II committed too soon ... with Makaldar, Laffy, and Escalus
finding daylight ... Inch Arran, sir, is working hard to maintain
his new-found lead ... '

By now the blue veins in Stilton's whey-faced features were
beginning to pulsate, and beads of sweat were running down the
slope of his nose.

'How long is this damn race?' he wheezed, bracing himself
against the wall.

'Two miles, two furlongs,' said Boko, 'or, if you prefer, three
thousand nine hundred and sixty yards.'

'I mean, how long *in time*? Butlers weigh a ton.'

'Oh, I see. About four minutes.'

' ... and it's very much a four-horse race, sir ... as Laffy,
Escalus, Inch Arran, and Makaldar are fighting for position ...
Inch Arran looks to be breaking ahead ... yes, there's daylight
now ... Inch Arran has found a good foot ... and it's very
much Inch Arran as they come to the final mile ... but, no, a
slight stumble there from Inch Arran, sir ... possibly spooked
by the crowd ... quickly righted, but he's lost ground ... Laffy,

Makaldar, and Escalus have closed the gap, sir ... and now there is little daylight between the final four ... as they approach the finish, sir, the frame looks set ... but not the order ... '

Jeeves stopped, and the crowd's frantic roar took over.

'Well?' Boko was translucent with fear. 'Who won?'

'It is unclear, sir.'

'WHAT?'

'I am very sorry, sir. My line of sight was somewhat hampered by the window's frame, and the distance between the finishing horses was negligible. If it is of any consolation, sir, the Tic-Tac men seem equally uncertain of the outcome.'

As I helped Jeeves down from Stilton's shoulders, Boko began pounding on the door.

'HELP!' he hollered. 'LET US OUT!'

After many minutes of this, a voice finally permeated the woodwork.

'Who's in there?'

'WE ARE!' bellowed five voices in unison. (Jeeves never bellows.)

'Hang on.'

The door was unlocked and a caretaker appeared. 'Coo! What you doing in my cupboard?'

'WHO WON?' shouted Boko, allowing the urgency of his mission temporarily to conquer his manners.

'The last race?'

'OF COURSE THE LAST RACE!'

'It was a dead heat. Well, as a matter of fact, a triple.'

'A *triple*?' Boko clutched his head, and fainted into Stilton's arms.

I don't know if you follow the gee-gees as doggedly as we at the Drones, but dead heats are pretty infrequent, and triple dead heats the stuff of hen's teeth. They're also profoundly unpopular with the betting public, since winning tickets are evenly split, and most accumulators (including ours) are forfeited altogether. This explained Boko's dramatic collapse at seeing his five-horse acca unravel at the final nose.

By this time I was aware of a commotion in the corridor and the sound of running feet. I popped my head out of the door and flagged down a sprinting tout.

'What's the brouhaha? Is there going to be a run-off?'

'Don't think so,' he panted. 'Something's up. There's a Stewards Enquiry.'

I sensed Jeeves at my elbow, and turned. 'Triple dead heat, eh?'

'Most unusual, sir. I think the last such occurrence in this race was in 1857. I wonder, sir, if I might be excused to make further enquiries?'

'What? Oh, yes. Enquire away.'

We succeeded in raising Boko from the dead in the usual fashion (blowing cigar smoke into his jug-handled ears), and carried him to the Committee Room, which was quickly filling with irate gamblers and agitated members of the pencilling fraternity.

After a brief hiatus, a prim little chap stepped through the door and called for order.

'Ladies and gentlemen. Certain irregularities concerning the last race have been raised with the judges, and there is at present a Stewards Enquiry. We expect the Chief Steward's adjudication—'

'Right now!' said a stentorian voice, and into the room rolled Lord Sidcup.

Spode was Chief Steward! Was there no escaping this swinish ape?

Heaving himself onto the rostrum, he surveyed the room like a grudge in search of a fight. 'I won't beat about the bush, ladies and gentlemen. According to the official judge, three horses tied the last race: Makaldar, Laffy, and Escalus. But the Stewards are not content with this result. Not content at all. So: Makaldar is disqualified for failing to supply a veterinary certificate—'

'That's a lie!' shouted a man whose anger and demeanour indicated he was likely the owner. 'I have it here!'

'And,' Spode continued, savouring every ounce of his tin-pot power, 'Escalus is disqualified for carrying the wrong weight.'

'You're havin' a giggle!' cried a chap whose stature and clothing indicated he was likely the jockey. 'Weigh it again!'

'The winner, therefore, would seem to be Laffy—' Spode held up his hands to quell the noise. 'But there was clear evidence of bumping *and* boring, and so under the Rules of Racing we have no option but to disqualify Laffy, and award the race to Inch Arran.'

The stunned incredulity that followed this adjudication was punctured by whoops of delight from the investment committee, who could scarcely believe their luck. Spode glared in horror at this unexpectedly gleeful reaction – but before he might speak, the room exploded into confusion and the crowd surged forward to engulf him.

'We've only gone and done it,' cried Boko, now fully recovered from his fit of the vapours. 'We've only gone and saved the jolly Drones!'

'Perhaps,' I cold-watered. 'First let's see the green of his lettuce.'

We located Leviathan against the back wall, occupying three chairs in his double-breasted bulk and looking remarkably jovial for a man who'd just parted company with his shirt.

'Mr Fittleworth!' he flashed his pearly whites. 'Welcome to Newmarket, and congratulations.'

'Thank you,' said Boko cautiously. 'I don't *quite* understand what happened, but we're certainly not complaining.'

'That's the ponies for you, always an upset. Now, concerning our little wager: I have about twenty on hand, and the other eighty can be settled on Monday when the banks open?'

'We'll take a cheque,' said Boko, fearing a trick even in triumph.

'Of course! *Unless* ... ' Leviathan was struck by bogus inspiration, 'unless you'd like to parlay this fine piece of fortune, and open a private account?'

Boko shook his head, not trusting himself to speak.

'Fair enough.' He took out a Trollope & Sons chequebook. 'Made payable to?'

'His Majesty's Commissioners of Inland Revenue.'

Leviathan laughed and looked round to share the joke – but the melancholy eyes of the investment committee indicated we were, tragically, in earnest.

'The tax man, eh? Ain't that a mouse in the cheese!'

Leviathan took his time with the paperwork, relishing the t-crossing and i-dotting of such a munificent civic donation.

'I say,' I said, 'you seem deuced chipper for someone who's just lost a hundred grand.'

'Blimey,' he peered about the room, 'did someone lose a hundred grand?'

I pointed to the cheque he was writing.

Leviathan stared at me in disbelief. 'Do you have *any* idea how bookmaking works?'

'Well ... '

'You think I makes one single, solitary bet and walks away?'

'Er ... '

'I *hedges*. I *covers*. I *lays off*. See, I knew something was up when Mr Fittleworth chucked Gawking Girl for Inch Arran. That struck me as either very, very foolish, or very, very sharp. So I had my boys do some digging, and your tip turned up diamonds – for both of us.'

He signed the cheque with a flourish, blew the ink dry, and held it up for collection. But just as Boko leaned in to take it, Leviathan flicked it away.

'Whoa there, hasty! I do need *one* more little tickle from your pal here with the voice.'

'Of course!' said Boko, his eyes glued to our salvation. 'Bertie is yours to command.'

'I'm jolly well not!'

Leviathan smiled. 'Just a phone call. Like before.'

'Right this minute?'

'Monday morning. My office. It's one of those newly wedded punters who needs to be nobbled at work – him having a wife who doesn't fully appreciate the Sport of Kings.'

'He'll be there!' Boko pledged. 'Bright and early. You have my word.'

'Very well,' I surrendered. 'But in return, Mr Leviathan, you promised to tell me who I tickled on Wednesday morning.'

Leviathan looked blank. 'Oh, yes! Let's have a look.' He flicked through the pages of a ledger. 'Gallagher, Gibson, Glazebrook, Goodman ... here we are. She's been a regular for years. Very loyal, but *very* unlucky. In fact, between ourselves, the old girl owes me a good few thousand. Gregson's the name – Mrs Agatha Gregson.'

To discover, after a lifetime of vituperous scolding and vicious complaint, that Aunt Agatha – the Pest of Pont Street, no less – was no better than a turf-addled betting lush ... well, you could have k. me d. with a f.

Indeed, I was still a little giddy from the disclosure when I heard Boko enquire if Leviathan had any more bird prints for sale.

'Not so loud!' he snarled. 'But I might do. And I *might* be getting a Shakespeare First Folio.'

This jolted me back to my senses.

'You know, I think *that* little tickle might be over.'

Leviathan shot me a uneasy glance. 'Says who?'

'Do the initials V. P. mean anything to you?'

'They ... might.'

'Well, let's just say V. P. is, as of a few hours ago, N. I. C. K. E—'

I've never seen so large a man move with such dispatch. Before I knew it, he'd seized his belongings and was blurring through the door, leaving in his wake a cloud of gardenia petals and a Trollope & Sons cheque, which spun to the floor like a sycamore seed.

I picked it up.

'Boko, old man, this cheque is made out for a hundred grand and a hundred pounds.'

'Naturally. Ninety-nine thousand six hundred, plus our original five hundred stake.'

'So we're a hundred quid over?'

'And we'll claim it as a refund.'

'Excellent. I'll have *my* hundred back.'

'Now, look here, Bertie, the committee was planning to split that hundred five ways.'

I did some finger arith. 'So, I'm giving the Drones eighty quid because you lot defrauded the Revenue?'

'That's a little strong!'

'But not actually wrong?'

'Well, no.' And then *he* was struck by bogus inspiration. 'I say, why don't we invest the extra hundred on a three-horse—'

'I will take coin of the realm, Boko, whenever it's convenient.'

*   *   *

'That was a shilling shocker!' I said to Jeeves, as we taxied back to town. 'Snatching victory from the Spode of defeat.'

'Yes, sir. And also, no.'

'This is worse than Ten Across! If you've a cat, Jeeves, kindly unbag him.'

'My apologies, sir. I meant only that Lord Sidcup's adjudication may have been swayed by what they call in the trade "a whisper at the post".'

'A whisper *you* supplied?'

'Very possibly, sir.'

Jeeves explained that, after he'd left us to make his enquiries, he happened to spot Lord Sidcup entering one of the refreshment tents. Contriving to stand close behind him, he engaged the barman in a 'somewhat amplified conversation', during which he let slip that his master, and his master's friends, had 'gone a bundle' on the last race, and anxiously awaited the Stewards Enquiry.

It took me a couple of miles to jigsaw this together.

'You mean to tell me, Spode chucked a Newmarket race simply to punish me?'

'Yes, sir.'

'*Sacré bleu!* He *must* be ball-and-chained back to Madeline.'

'I gather that is indeed the case, sir.'

'But why disqualify all three horses?'

'By keeping my statements deliberately vague, sir, I calculated that Lord Sidcup could not be certain *which* horse you had backed, and would be forced to exclude the winning trio.'

'Leaving us with Inch Arran, your original pick.'

Jeeves nodded.

'Much as I hate to quote Gussie Fink-Nottle, that was decidedly A.B.C.D.'

'Thank you, sir. I have much affection for the Drones Club, and little enthusiasm to relocate south of the Thames.'

'I'll bet. But how did you know Spode was the Chief Steward?'

'I assumed his appointment was common knowledge, sir.'

In time we arrived back at the University Arms.

Reassured by Jeeves that Aunt Agatha had flown the coop promptly after breakfast, I risked a maiden voyage through the hotel's front doors, whereupon the receptionist handed me a telegram:

BANG 11:10

'Well, Jeeves, either *The Times* has begun wiring crossword clues to each of its readers individually, or Lord MacAuslan has finally fired his starting gun.'

'I would suggest the latter, sir.'

'Makes sense. What's the o'clock?'

'Eight thirty, sir.'

'Time enough to nap, change, and summon an omelette before sneaking out as Burglar Bill.'

'Very good, sir. I shall collect the omelette from the kitchens myself.'

'Whatever for?'

'In case, sir, Mr Fink-Nottle or Miss Chitt are still on duty.'

'Ah, yes. Good thinking.'

*   *   *

I gumshoed stealthily down Trinity Lane until – just yards from where my collar had been felt on Thursday night – I arrived at an unremarkable wooden portal that, by the look of the lock, hadn't been used for years. I tapped softly at the door-within-a-door, which was eased silently open by Eustace Epworth.

'This way, sir. Quick as you like.'

Following him into Great Court, we turned left, and left again, to enter a dimly lit passage where Lord MacAuslan was waiting.

'Good evening, Mr Wooster, and welcome once again to Trinity.' He regarded my all-black ensemble with approval. 'I see you've relinquished the clerical.'

'Not even Jeeves demands best bib and tucker for burglary.'

'Well, we've been over the plan, so all that remains is to give you this.'

He handed me a Dunlop Dimple.

'For a quick nine holes?'

'For breaking and entering.'

'I was rather expecting a hammer.'

'But what could be more innocent, or easier to jettison, than a golf ball?'

(Clearly he'd never seen my bunker shots.)

Lord MacAuslan took out his fob-watch. 'Eleven fifteen. I think conditions are as good as we're likely to get.'

'I just wish it were darker.'

'It is indeed a *braw, bricht, moonlicht nicht*.' He grinned. 'But at least it's not *spleetering* or *cauld*.'

'That's October for you – the year's Belgium.'

'I see. Well, I'm away to establish an alibi, so let me wish you the very best of luck.'

Keeping close to the brickwork's shadow, I stole silently into New Court and turned immediately right to approach my first vertical challenge: a single-storey edifice topped with ugly, oversized battlements. Running down the centre of this structure, per Lord MacAuslan's sketch, was a sturdy iron drainpipe which, jutting proudly from the stone, might have been installed with theft in mind. It was simplicity itself to curl my fingers around this pipework and monkey up, hand over hand, using my rubber-soled gym shoes for grip. Once at the top, I slipped between a wide crenellation and onto the parapet roof, bang in front of Whipplesnaith's study.

Unlike some in the Drones (no names, no pack-drill, Bimbash Kidd), I've never thrilled to the sound of breaking glass, nor have I terrorised the restaurateurs of Mayfair with games of 'smash and dash'. I'll admit that, over the years, golf balls under my command have shattered any number of clubhouse windows and greenhouse glazings – but always by accident, and only ever in the noble pursuit of par. So it was rather alarming to discover how much I relished hurling my Dunlop Dimple through Whipplesnaith's window.

I reached through the shards, unhooked the latch, and climbed in.

Stealing the incriminating negative of Fabrizio Orsini was as simple as Lord MacAuslan had promised ('It's hidden in an anthology of poems called *Weasel Words*, easily spotted as the only book not about football'), and I was almost out of the blackmailer's window when a shaft of light clicked on from under the bedroom door.

'Who's there?' shouted a thuggish and all-too-familiar voice.

So much for Whipplesnaith being out, I silently cursed, climbing free of the sill and dashing across the parapet roof.

I was on the brink of beanstalking back to safety when the sound of boots crunching on gravel prompted me to peer down between the battlements and spy the flash of a porter's torch. Sensing that Whipplesnaith might be coming to get me ('I'm coming to get you!' he hissed), I abandoned Lord MacAuslan's best-laid schemes and hauled myself up a second iron drainpipe to the roof.

Here, I discovered an enchantingly colonnaded vista of Nevile's Court and, more enchanting still, Christopher Wren's library – which beckoned me as it would beckon any night climber with a pulse.

Crouching low, I sped along the cold, smooth leading until I came to a cumbersome 'dip' where the rooflines of various architectural styles intersected chaotically. Under-gripping a mantlepiece to stretch across a narrow gap, I heaved myself onto a mossy ledge, and paused to take stock of my pursuit.

For a while all was still, but soon I spotted Whipplesnaith's pyjama'd outline on the roof above his rooms, scanning the horizon like a castaway. After a minute's indecision, he made the wrong decision and struck east in the direction of Great Court. With a sigh of thanks, I scrambled up a slope of tiles, and tipped myself over the stone balustrades that encircle Wren's timeless design.

My cat-like progress along the library's front parapet was soon impeded by the curious obstacle of a wild-eyed chap reclining in a deckchair, whistling softly, and bobbing a balloon.

Curiouser still, I recognised him.

'Dr Wittgenstein, I presume?'

'In order to know an object,' he frowned, 'I must know not its external but all its internal qualities.'

'Jolly good. Look, what's the quickest way out of here?'

'Everything we see could also be otherwise. Everything we can describe at all could also be otherwise.'

'So, left or right?'

'A right-hand glove could be put on a left hand if it could be turned round in four-dimensional space.'

'Might you be able to point?'

'What *can* be shown *cannot* be said.'

'Ludwig, old cock, you're not being terribly helpful.'

'My propositions are elucidatory in this way: he who understands me finally recognises them as senseless, when he has climbed out through them, on them, over them. (He must so to speak throw away the ladder, after he has climbed up on it.)'

Thinking a ladder would indeed be handy, I left the philosopher to his balloon juice and, climbing round him, continued along the parapet.

By now I'd rather assumed Whipplesnaith had given up the ghost, but as I lowered myself carefully onto the roof of the North Cloister, I heard his tell-tale cry of, 'Hey, you, wait!'

Clearly the time had come to return to earth, and so I located a drainpipe in the corner channel where library meets cloister, and began a rapid descent. I had just climbed clear of the third-floor windows when the section of ironwork to which I was clinging began slowly to hinge from the wall. Flailing around as best I could, I managed to shuffle sideways onto a narrow ledge, which immediately proved itself more decorative than supportive.

As Whipplesnaith thundered about on the roof above me, my grip on the stone began to fail, and I realised my only option was to break back *into* college. True, this would likely involve a second appearance before Sir Godfrey Winthrop-Young, but living to fight another day has always been high on the Wooster to-do list – especially when thirty feet above ground. Since the nearest window appeared slightly ajar, I shimmied along the crumbling ledge, hooked a leg round the open frame, and folded myself inside.

'Who the devil are you?' barked a silver-haired man, leaping from his armchair and grabbing a poker from the fire. 'And why the devil are you in my rooms?'

'Well ... '

'Don't move a muscle, you thieving rascal. I'm armed, and I'm calling the police.'

'Wait a second, Harold.' His plump companion put down his Bible and peered at me. 'I know this man.'

'Are you *sure*, Dean?'

'Yes, we met on Wednesday. He's from the Ordnance Survey.'

'*What?*'

'They're gathering preliminary mapping coordinates for a proposed retriangulation.'

'On the second floor? In the middle of the night?' Mr Poker was unconvinced, to say the least. 'And anyway, where's his theodolite?'

'In the motor,' I lied, silently thanking Jeeves as I sprang for the door. 'I'll be back in a blink, Dean, don't move a muscle.'

I launched myself down the stairs three at a time, and took refuge in the dark colonnade to catch my breath.

'*Psssst!*'

Swinging to my right, I saw a bowler-hatted shadow unlocking a gate that led out to the river.

'I told you it was all about keys, Mr Wooster.'

Following Epworth's whispered instructions, I dashed across the grass to a waiting punt, grabbed the pole, and pushed off with a mighty heave in the direction of King's.

Bah-humbuggish as it may be to confess, I abominate punting.

Unlike most of my pals, I've never had the desire, nor acquired the knack, and consider transporting oneself on a flat wooden barge with a wet wooden pole an undignified squander of calories. It's possible I was put off the sport when, as a child, I was catapulted into the brackish shallows of the Cherwell and left to swim to the bank. Since then, punting has always seemed like the kind of sweat best observed from a safe distance – like accountancy.

Of course, up until that moment, I'd never punted by way of fleeing a pyjama'd baboon, but while this frisson of terror certainly added salt to the gruel – gruelling the business remained.

As I propelled myself under Garret Hostel Bridge, I heard the nearby sounds of splashing and was alarmed to spy Whipplesnaith aboard his own punt, closing in. (How he'd managed to escape Trinity was a mystery, and I only hoped the brute hadn't overpowered poor Eustace.) Redoubling my efforts, I approached Clare at a flood and, glancing up to the bridge where Jeeves and

I had Pooh'd our sticks a few days earlier, spotted an aquiline figure staring intently at my pursuer.

Punting beneath him, I steered across to the bank of King's and scrambled ashore. Whipplesnaith was approaching at speed, but as he passed under Clare Bridge the aquiline figure leaned over the balustrade and deftly snatched away his pole.

'Hey, you!' Whipplesnaith cried, before losing his footing and toppling sideways into the Cam.

Abandoning 'Alfonso' (for that was my punt's painted name) to float merrily down the stream, I dashed along the herbaceous border until I reached King's Chapel. Here, following Eustace's instructions, I turned left towards Clare and made for the gate he assured me would be unlocked ... except, like Boko's Newmarket cupboard, it wasn't.

As I stepped closer to give the mechanism a couple of futile jiggles, I found myself eyeball to eyeball through the gate's iron bars with another black-camouflaged climber. It was Cousin Thos.

'...'

'...'

Much was said in those silent seconds – for while his guilt was undeniable, so was mine, and though I could, in theory, simply shop him to his mother, Aunt Agatha has an unerring ability to pin on others the blame for her son's myriad failings (putting the *loco*, as Jeeves once said, into *in loco parentis*).

And then I spotted his chamber pot.

There are two species of night climbers: those (like me) who aspire to leave no trace; and those (like Lord Byron, in his day) who aspire to advertise. Clearly, Cousin Thos. fancied himself of the Byronic school and was planning to hang his po, like a polar explorer, somewhere provocatively inaccessible. (Adding insult to idiocy, he'd painted the indecent object in the stripes of the French flag.)

I was calculating how best to mime a stern rebuke through the bars – since this is *precisely* the kind of oompus-boompus that gets innocent night climbers expelled – when I heard yet another cry of 'Hey, you, wait!' and saw a distant shadow lumbering out of the drink.

Unexpectedly sensitive to my plight, Thomas beckoned me along the railings until they became engulfed by an overgrown, evergreen shrub. I followed him into this bushy entanglement to the point where some resourceful student had bent back a narrow section of bars. After helping me to slip out to freedom, Thomas snuck past me into King's and vanished into the shadows without a word.

Now safely back on the public highway, I headed for home at a cautious pace, turning into Senate House Passage with every intention of rousing the Night Porter, regardless of his ire. But as I snuck past the University Library, I spotted Constable Dockery, leaning against a lamp-post, smoking a cigarette, and humming snatches from *The Pirates of Penzance*.

I was trapped: ahead of me a copper with a grudge, behind me a dripping-wet thug, to my left the brick walls of Caius, and to my right the spiked railings of the Senate House.

'*Pssssst!*'

I whirled clockwise to see a half-illuminated bowler hat, unlocking a gate in these railings.

'Eustace,' I whispered in awe, 'do you have a twin?'

'No, sir. A bicycle.'

'What now?'

He pointed to the looming white-stone edifice of the Senate House, one side of which was encased in a maze of scaffolding.

'Up there, sir.'

'Are you sure?'

'Oh yes, sir. Quick as you like.'

After the nerve- (and trouser-) shredding agony of sharp bricks and loose tiles, swarming up a five-story ziggurat of ladders was really rather a pleasure – even if 'going to the scaffold' felt a little on the nose.

I made quick work of the ascent, but once at the summit discovered that the body of the roof had been fenced off with tarpaulins. This meant my options were to turn right and sneak along the front of the Senate House (in full view of anyone on King's Parade), or turn left and sneak parallel to Caius (in partial view of anyone in the Senate House Passage). Any thoughts of climbing back down were perished by Whipplesnaithian emanations from below.

I turned left and, as I inched along the parapet, took in a bird's-eye view of my newly adopted college. Although most of the rooms were shuttered against the night, one set of windows shone out like a lighthouse. Inching closer, I saw they were my windows and, inching closer still, I saw the aquiline profile of Jeeves – who pulled up a sash, and popped out his head.

'Good evening, sir,'

'Good evening, Jeeves. And also: *help*!'

'May I take it, sir, that you are being pursued?'

'You think I'm up here for my health?'

'Of course, sir. My apologies. Two courses of action suggest themselves.'

'In your own time. Don't mind me.'

'The first, sir, is to jump from where you are standing across to this window.'

'Really, Jeeves? The famed and likely fatal Senate House Leap? Humour me with your second course of action.'

'That, sir, would be to continue your clockwise circumnavigation of the roof, and hope that Mr Whipplesnaith does not make his approach counterclockwise.'

'And if he does?'

'I imagine, sir, a scuffle will ensue.'

'A *scuffle*?'

'Yes, sir. Or fisticuffs, if you prefer—'

'Not really.'

'Either is likely to prove disagreeable, given the elevation, unless you continue to encircle one another without ever meeting.'

The sound of leaden feet on creaking boards suggested this chinwag would soon advance from the theoretical to the threatening.

Jeeves tilted his head. 'It's funny, sir.'

'Funny, Jeeves? Funny how? Like a clown? It amuses you?'

'Funny *peculiar*, sir. One is reminded of Winnie-the-Pooh's attempts to catch a woozle.'

'A woozle?'

'In the snow, sir. With Piglet. Round a tree in the Hundred Acre Wood. Except, of course, in this instance the woozle exists.'

I began to formulate a reply, but thought better of it. There are times, are there not, when silence is golden.

Whipplesnaith disagreed. 'I know you're up here,' he half shouted from the darkness. 'Why don't you hand over the negative like a sensible chap, and we'll say no more about it?'

I remained as still as stone, and cocked an ear to the echo.

'It's only sporting to warn you,' he continued, 'I have a gun.'

I swung back to Jeeves. 'About this leap.'

'Sir?'

'Is it safe?'

'No, sir.'

'How far do you think it is, across?'

'Just under seven feet, sir.'

'And down?'

'Eighty-five feet, sir.'

'That pavement looks dashed unforgiving.'

'Indeed, sir.'

'And even from here those railings seem fearfully pointed.'

'They do conclude at a penetrating apex, sir.'

'So, all in all, you wouldn't risk it?'

'Well, sir, not being in your shoes, literally or metaphorically—'

'Is this really the time for metaphors?'

My question was answered by the Caius Chapel clock, which, in striking midnight, provided the kind of heavy-handed symbolism I could frankly have done without.

Sensing Whipplesnaith's shadow in the old peripheral vision, I crouched low like a sprinter on his mark, took a long deep breath, and, trusting all to fate, leapt up and out and into the void.

Jeeves is forever saying, 'When you gaze long into the abyss, the abyss gazes back' – and let me tell you, he's not wrong.

It wasn't that my life flashed before my eyes, or anything quite so nautical, but as I sailed through the air above the Senate House Passage, I did find myself questioning a few of my recent decisions, not least how I'd fallen for this preposterous Ganymede encounter when my happier habitat was sipping something fruity in—

And then, much to my astonishment, the crossword sprang to mind ...

Ten Across ...

Encountered after choice fruit fall ...

Seven letters ...

If *encountered* was MET ...

And *choice fruit* was PLUM ...

Then . . .

Suddenly, my foot made crashing contact with the stone ledge, and all flights of fancy were grounded.

With characteristic foresight, Jeeves had partly opened both halves of the sash window, allowing me to fling my arm through the gap at the top, and cling on like a fearful koala.

'PLUMMET!' I gasped.

'Really, sir? I would have said quite the opposite was—'

'*Not me!* Today's Ten Across.'

'Indeed so, sir. Well solved – and furthermore, *well leapt!*'

The admiration in Jeeves's usually poker-faced voice drove home how lucky I'd been to make it across alive, and so I savoured my victory against gravity for a breath or two, before telescoping myself through the lower sash and falling to the floor.

Springing back up to the window, I saw Whipplesnaith crouching where I'd just crouched, preparing himself to jump.

'It's a long way down, old bean,' I said, leaning casually out of the window. 'And not an easy landing. Especially in sopping wet jim-jams and slippers.'

'How hard can it be,' Whipplesnaith sneered, 'if *you* can do it?'

And then something clicked, or, rather, failed to click.

'Hold up! Where's your gun?'

Whipplesnaith grinned.

'You *haven't* got a gun?'

He shook his head with slow malice.

The realisation that I'd diced with death *not* as the last resort against an armed yahoo, but as some kind of recreational folly, filled me with terror afresh. But before I might unpick the deeper signif. of this paradox, I felt a tap on my shoulder and turned to see Jeeves brandishing a white china jug.

'Excuse me, sir,' he murmured, stepping up to the window and carefully zig-zagging the jug's pungent contents over the stone sill.

Whipplesnaith stared at him in disgust.

'What the hell is *that*?'

'Goose fat, sir.'

'*Goose* fat?'

'Yes, sir.'

'I don't call that very sporting!'

'Neither, I expect, sir, did the goose.'

This unlikely exchange was interrupted by the sliding open of a nearby sash window, and the shriek of a voice that sounded rather like my bedder's assistant, Diane.

'SAY PRUNES, DUCKY!'

As Whipplesnaith spun to his right, a dazzling pop of flash exploded the darkness.

'Ooh, *what* a picture!' cackled the voice I was now certain belonged to Iona. 'Shocking proof of night climbing, I'd say, ducks. The kind of proof that gets a promising young student sent down.'

Whipplesnaith turned to me with a scowl. 'I'll get you!'

'Not from over there, old fruit. You should have brought that gun.'

'Wait a sec – I *know* you! You're that cad from the train. You owe me a pipe!'

'It was a no-smoker, old boy. All the signs were there.'

'You haven't heard the end of thi—'

I slammed down the sash and drew shut the curtains, just as Iona entered the room.

'You made it, Bertie – the Senate House Leap!'

'Oh,' I said carelessly, not at all displeased she'd witnessed my derring-deed, 'you saw that?'

'I had the perfect view. I'm only sorry I couldn't capture it for posterity, but the flash would have rather given things away.'

'I'm a little confused as to why you were there, primed and ready to shoot. How did you know where I'd end up?'

'Just a hunch,' she smiled. 'You must have noticed we did what we could to guide your escape.'

'All the way to the edge of the world! What made you so certain I wouldn't Reichenbach to my doom?'

This time Jeeves answered. 'I chanced to observe, sir, your performance at the Drones Club summer fête—'

'When I simply slayed in the sack-race-egg-and-spoon?'

'Indeed, sir. However, it was your victory in the three-legged-blindfold-long-jump which suggested that the Senate House Leap was well within your capabilities.'

'That *was* a pippin! Shame young Clifford broke his leg in the process. By the way, Jeeves, your jugful-o'-grease gimmick was inspired.'

'Thank you, sir. For various reasons I have become interested in the physics of friction, lubrifaction, and polish.'

'Right, well, every man needs a hobby. But wherever did you find the goose fat?'

He gave me a look. 'The kitchens, sir.'

'Before we forget,' said Iona, tactfully changing the subject, 'I take it you managed to pinch the negative of Orsini?'

'*Bien sûr!*' I beamed, patting every pocket with increasing panic, until I found it in the first pocket I'd patted. 'Of course, now you've snapped Adrian Whipplesnaith in the act of night climbing, we can turn the tables and get *him* sent down.'

'We could,' said Iona cautiously.

'Why would we not? Surely, expelling Whipplesnaith would cherry the chocolate sundae.'

She glanced briefly at Jeeves. 'Let's just say our plans for Adrian have developed.'

A keener spy would, I suppose, have demanded to know more – but I was less in need of enlightenment than a nerve-steadying cigarette, and so I relinquished my stolen treasure and suggested we pop outside for a gasper.

'Just what the doctor ordered,' said Iona, slipping the negative into her jacket. 'But we shouldn't go down quite yet. Best to let the coast clear. I wonder, Jeeves, might you lend me a key to the roof?'

Clambering out onto the tiles, we located a comfortable slope next to the flagpole, which afforded us the kind of moonlit silhouette that might profitably be printed on tea-towels.

Iona lit two Gauloises, passed one to me, and we basked in the companionable silence of an enemy vanquished, watching our blue smoke loop and curl in the unseasonably warm air.

Time passed.

I can't be certain if the aroma of autumnal bonfires hung o'er us like a fragrant cloak; let's agree it probably did.

Time continued to pass.

Then – slowly, softly, and almost completely by chance – our hands brushed together.

Still not a word had been spoken, and our eyes remained decorously glued to the spiritually sobering profile of King's College Chapel.

Very tentatively, though, our fingers entwined, and my heart mislaid its beat.

I was still struggling to regain control of the old ticker, when I observed that Iona's pinkie was tucked in neatly between my middle and index fingers. This was all rather curious – and it immediately brought to mind the 'overlapping grip' made famous by Harry Vardon in *The Gist of Golf*.

'Play often?' I asked, noticing she'd noticed I'd noticed.

'When I can. Sometimes just a front nine.'

'Any good?'

'Oh, well,' she shrugged, 'you know.'

This was suspiciously casual.

'What do you play off?'

'Somewhere around three.'

Three?

Three!

Somewhere around three!

Look: if a golf course has a par of seventy-two, then a player with Iona's handicap can expect to zip round in seventy-five – which means only three (!) opportunities to hook a drive, top a chip, or duff a putt during the entire eighteen holes. For golfers of my persuasion – the kind that hit six, lose two, and shout 'fore' – a handicap in single digits is the stuff of myth and legend, to be spoken of in the same hushed tones as Arcadia, Elysium, or Tuppy Glossop's overdraft.

Furthermore, it struck me as the filbert reeled, Iona would have honed her game on the wild and unforgiving links of the Highlands, where the blast of the coastal wind is matched only by the depth of the pot bunkers. To the average Englishman, Hadrian's Wall is as naught to the challenge of finding the fairway on a Scottish par five.

A handicap of three up in Scotland might easily translate to two down South ... or one ... or *scratch*! (Whereas mine, dear reader, refuses to sink below sixteen.)

I was about to deploy the pretext of lighting another cigarette to disencumber our hands – for surely this lassie was out of my league? – when the Caius Chapel clock struck one, and Iona leapt to her feet.

'*Jings!* Where does the time go? I'm going to be late.'

'At this hour! Late for what?'

'For whom,' she said bashfully, making for the stairs. 'I'm meeting Adrian Whipplesnaith.'

7.

SUNDAY

I rose in time to avoid another awkward encounter with Christine the bedder, and was sneaking to freedom through the porter's lodge when my escape was halted by a white-bearded clergyman.

'Who are you?' he demanded. 'And why are you dressed like that?'

'I'm Reverend Wooster, and I'm Reverend Wooster.'

'I assume, then, you're on your way to Chapel?'

'Er—'

'Splendid. I have a job for you.'

My bones turned to water. 'You mean ... take the service?'

'Are you *quite* out of your mind? I mean, conduct the choir.'

I couldn't tell if this was any better.

'You've conducted choirs before, I assume?'

'Well—'

'Of *course* you have. Goes with the collar.'

He seized my arm in an almost friendly grip, guided me back out of the lodge, and dragooned me across Tree Court.

'Nothing too tricky hymn-wise this morning: "Pilgrim", followed by "Eternal Father", and then "All Things Bright". I like to kick off a new term with the hits.'

As he marched us through the Gate of Virtue and into Caius Court, we were met by a flock of black-suited porters, one of whom was taking aim at the Chapel roof with a twelve-bore.

'Stop!' cried my captor. 'What *are* you doing with that gun?'

'Morning, Dean,' said a senior porter, striding over to greet us. 'Chapel's postponed for an hour.'

'I *beg* your pardon?'

'Orders of the Master, sir. Can't have prayers going on with *that* indecent article defiling the college.'

He pointed to the Chapel clock, from the hour hand of which dangled a chamber pot cheerfully painted in the colours of the French flag.

'You can't open fire on the Chapel!' the Dean protested. 'It dates to 1390.'

'No other way to get it down, sir. We haven't a ladder long enough.'

'Can't someone just climb out of that upper window?'

'Too perilous, sir. The only folk who'd risk it are the vandals who hung it there last night.'

'*Perilous?* What tommyrot! It's a simple under-grip from that overhang.'

'Well,' I said, attempting nonchalance, 'I just might pop along and get some coffee.'

'Of course, dear boy,' said the Dean, who was staring up at Cousin Thomas's handiwork with the admiration of one who'd clearly night-climbed vigorously in his youth. 'But I shall expect you back in the hour.'

'Absolutely,' I lied. 'You can put your faith in me, Dean.'

* * *

I trod the now well-worn path to the Perseus Suite, and found within a quartet of faces: Lord MacAuslan, Iona, Jeeves, and ... Christine the bedder.

'Good morning,' she drawled in disarmingly Chelsea tones. 'That's right, Mr Wooster, this is that moment where Miss Marple explains the crime and unmasks the killer.'

'Good morning— *Sorry*, do I call you Christine?'

'Lady Chatterton, if you care about such baubles. Can't say I do.'

'And— Sorry, *are* you a bedmaker?'

'Now and then.'

Lord MacAuslan took over. 'Lady Chatterton is the Junior Ganymede's Cambridge liaison. From time to time she takes on any number of casual roles – maid, typist, waitress, bedder – allowing her to observe everyone, and overhear everything.'

She could see I was still perplexed. 'Many moons ago I was a secretary in the Cabinet Office, where I met Lord MacAuslan – and my husband, Sir George. When George popped his clogs, I escaped to Cambridge to garden and paint – but soon got sick of both. Then one day, Torquil turns up to offer me a job, and I nearly bite the poor man's hand off.'

'So you were simply teasing me on Thursday morning?'

'Frightfully sorry,' she smiled, before slipping back into character, 'though I 'ave done some terrible things, ain't that right, Diane?'

'That's right, ma'am,' Iona nodded, 'terrible things.'

'And I did save your life with George's Two-Quid Cure!'

I turned to Lord MacAuslan. 'Is it too much to ask what's going on?'

'What do you know – or think you know?'

'In truth, I haven't the foggiest. I *thought* I was helping to foil Whipplesnaith. In fact, I'm pretty certain I *did* help to foil Whipplesnaith.'

'You did indeed, Mr Wooster. We've your stolen negative to prove it.'

'But when I suggested getting Whipplesnaith sent down, using the photo of him on the roof, Iona said your plans had "developed". And half an hour later, in the dead of night, she dashes off to meet the thug. So, I suppose my question is: who is Whipplesnaith, and what is he to you?'

'He's my new source,' said Iona.

I was gasted by the flabber. 'You've *recruited* Whipplesnaith into the British Secret Service?'

'The Italian Secret Service.'

'Eh?'

'Look,' said Christine, leaning back and lighting a cigarette, 'the chump thinks he's a Fascist, he was dying to be recruited by the Fascists, and it's possible that even the Fascists might have relented – causing us no end of irritation.' She took a leisurely drag. 'The original plan was simply to secure Orsini's future by stealing the blackmailing negative. But when we saw Whipplesnaith was mixed up with the Black Shorts, and becoming increasingly chummy with Lord Sidcup, we had a better idea: rather than rid ourselves of this troublesome beast, why not recruit him – *pretending* to be the Italians?'

'The navy boys call it "flying a false flag",' said Lord MacAuslan. 'It's a pretty shabby trick, but it worked a treat with Mr Whipplesnaith.'

'So Whipplesnaith thinks Iona's an Italian spy?'

'Yes – in her guise as Helen Marion.'

'And I was simply a stooge?'

'Not at all, Mr Wooster. You were the face of British Intelligence.'

'The bungling face?'

'The *brave* face,' reassured Iona. 'You made the Senate House Leap!'

Well, I did. There was no denying it. Though I shivered at the memory, and doubted very much whether I could repeat the performance between two chalked lines on *terra firma* – let alone four dizzying floors above.

And then I had a thought. 'Could you not simply have *asked* Whipplesnaith for his negative, now you're in league?'

'How would we, the Italians, know the negative existed?'

'True. Come to think of it, how did you, the British, know the negative existed?'

'Mr Orsini, when drunk one night, confided in the barman at the Pitt—'

'Who's a Ganymede ear! Of course. But why did you need me? Why not sneak a bedder into Trinity to nab the negative on her morning rounds?'

'That's just how we found where the negative was hidden,' said Christine. 'But bedders, like chambermaids, are always the first to be accused when "Madame's pearls" go missing. It would have jeopardised my cover and put ugly Adrian on his guard to steal it surreptitiously. Much better for him to know for certain it was you.'

'*He knows who I am?*'

'Not your actual identity,' reassured Lord MacAuslan, 'but Iona has told him you're with British Intelligence, which makes him all the more eager to help the Italians – us, that is – foil the British – also us.'

'He's terribly excited to be of interest to you,' smiled Christine. 'I imagine he's seldom of interest to anyone.'

'Hang on! I thought we moved the burglary from Friday to Saturday night because you specifically wanted Whipplesnaith to be out?'

Lord MacAuslan looked contrite. 'I'm sorry about that deception, Mr Wooster. We were, in fact, keen for him to see his antagonist.'

'You *wanted* him to see me? Why?'

'Two reasons. First, so he'd be lulled into a false sense of security when you left. And second, so you might lure him to the Senate House roof to be photographed. This is where the resourceful Eustace Epworth came in – he permitted himself to be "overpowered" very convincingly.'

'But if you've recruited Whipplesnaith, why bother taking snaps of him night-climbing?'

'Insurance,' said Lord MacAuslan. 'In case he discovers the truth, double-crosses us, or simply wakes up in a bad mood. We see great potential in Fabrizio Orsini and can't risk it on the caprice of a delinquent like Mr Whipplesnaith.'

'And,' said Christine, 'to keep Adrian's Fascist little fingers busy, we've instructed him to hunt for the British informer inside the Saviours of Britain.'

'There's a British spy inside the Black Shorts?'

'There is now.'

'You've lost me.'

'Whipplesnaith's the spy.'

'He's ... hunting for himself?'

'And reporting back to us,' Lord MacAuslan smiled. 'That little wrinkle was Jeeves's idea.'

'I thought I detected a hidden hand.' (Jeeves acknowledged the compliment as he poured more coffee.) 'So what now for Orsini? I saw him across a crowded Pitt, but never actually met the feller.'

'And you likely never will. Mr Orsini is a sound man, if a little slow-witted, who will be welcomed to the Foreign Office with open arms, despite the third-class degree he's almost certain to scrape. Smooth sailing now Whipplesnaith's under control.'

'And we're *sure* he's under control?'

'Under control, and in love,' said Iona. 'Only partly with me, I hasten to add – and when I say me, I mean Helen Marion. No, Adrian has fallen more deeply in love with this.'

She handed me a membership card for something called the P.N.F.

'It's like a crossword clue! P.N.F. stands for ... *Pretty Nice Friends*?'

'*Partito Nazionale Fascista.*'

I held it up to the light. 'Freshly forged by the Ganymede's paper-hangers?'

'A rush job on Friday, allowing me to recruit him late last night.'

The meeting concluded soon after.

Lord MacAuslan was anxious I quit Cambridge at the earliest opportunity to avoid encountering Whipplesnaith; I felt much the same about Spode, Madeline, Gussie, Mabel, Constable Dockery, Inspector Whitsun, the Master of Trinity, the Bursar of Trinity, or *any* of the benighted Pinkes – especially Evadne.

After we'd said our goodbyes, I took Iona aside.

'I say ... '

'Yes?'

'About Whipplesnaith.'

'Yes?'

'You don't ... I mean ... you didn't ... or ... ?'

She took my hand. 'Really, Bertie. What do you think?'

*   *   *

As I crossed the threshold of Home Sweet Home my nostrils were struck by the acrid tang of fresh paint, instantly reminding me that Dicks & Rudge had been up to no good in my bedroom. And so, with a profound sense of regret, I plodded towards the scene of the crime, aware that a fleeting victory over my gentle-man's personal gentleman would condemn me to countless morning migraines of a rustic hue.

Was this, I wondered, what Jeeves calls a 'Pyrrhic victory'?

I closed my eyes as I opened the door, bracing myself for an onslaught of *Jollities*.

I opened my left eye . . .

And then my right . . .

To see row upon row of utterly charming – if distinctly mutinous – *Chevrons*.

'JEEVES!'

The ensuing echo reminded me that the turncoat was off consulting Crawshaw about our Aunt Agatha dilemma. And so, concluding that anger keeps better than hunger, I stalked my way back to the kitchen.

The pantry was pretty depleted after our five-day absence, but, as Sherlock Holmes once observed, when you've excluded the inedible, whatever remains, however unpalatable, must be lunch.

Some hours later, I was putting for par down the long, carpeted corridor (with an overturned egg-cup for aim) when I heard a key in the front-door lock. Anxious not to be discovered in such a subordinate state, I dashed to the sitting-room and draped myself along the mantlepiece before summoning my man with the bell.

In he flowed, like a silver fog.

'You rang, sir?'

'I'm speechless, Jeeves.'

'I am sorry to hear that, sir.'

'Struck dumb!'

'Sir?'

'Not literally.'

'Sir.'

'But the other one.'

'Very good, sir.'

'I mean to say!' I gestured towards my bedroom.

'Indeed, sir.'

'Words fail me.'

'So I gather, sir.'

'I assume you've an explanation?'

You've got to hand it to him – he did, and it was a lulu.

He cast my mind back to Wednesday pip emma when, on entering my bedroom at Gonville & Caius, I first encountered its hunting-scene wallpaper. He had, so he said, 'chanced to observe a look of anguish' cast a shadow across my 'customarily carefree features'. From this shadow of anguish, he somehow deduced that I'd secretly changed the wallpaper order and, notwithstanding my protestations of delight, regretted my decision. Then, being the sort of feller who never lets 'I dare not' wait upon 'I would', he seized the horn to Dicks & Rudge and restored the *status quo ante*.

'So,' I clarified, 'you countermanded my countermanding of your countermanding of my original manding?'

'Yes, sir. If I follow you correctly.'

'I bet Fred and Charlie were waxy.'

'I would describe their reaction, sir, as apathetic.'

'So, there it is.'

'Yes, sir.'

'And here we are.'

'Indeed, sir.'

There was a moment of silence.

'Shall I prepare, sir, a whisky and soda?'

'Do that, Jeeves. And don't let the soda win.'

The w. and s. was slipping down nicely, smoothing the edges of whatever wallpaper vexation still lingered, when I came a cropper with Twenty-six Down.

'I say, Jeeves, d'you know much about knitting?'

'A modicum, sir.'

'This clue: *He said, she said – get knotted.* It's a bit of a puzzler, since it's four short words – one, two, one, two – and I thought it might have something to do with knitting patterns. Knit one, purl one, that sort of gas.'

'It *might*, sir.' Jeeves imbued the word with an empire of doubt. 'Though I suggest that, in this instance, the knot is not knitted, but tied.'

'Like a noose?'

'Some have made that association, sir, though usually in a jocular fashion.'

'Heavens, Jeeves, solving *you* is harder than these clues. All right, *pax*, throw off the mask!'

'I DO I DO, sir.'

It took me a moment.

'Ah! *Get knotted* … tie the knot … get married … *he said*, I DO … and *she said*, I DO. Ker-levver!'

'Naturally, sir, Twenty-six Down then assists with Sixteen Across.'

I consulted the paper. *Polygamist agreeing with* 26 (2,2,1).

'Does it?'

'Yes, sir. I would say Sixteen Across is of the essence.'

'Really?'

I stared down at the grid, more bemused than before, but further deciphering was abbrev'd by the doorbell, which Jeeves treacled out to attend.

'Tell me it's not Aunt Agatha already,' I pleaded on his return. 'Even for her this would be unforgivably early.'

'No, sir. It is Mr Fink-Nottle—'

I growled.

'And Miss Chitt.'

'Who?'

'Miss Mabel Chitt, sir. The waitress.'

'Love's young scream. Send 'em in.'

Seconds later Gussie appeared, bearing before him, like the priest of a new religion, a large glass box – except rather than gold dust or peacock feathers, his sacred offering was teeming with newts.

'Afternoon, Bertie!'

'Ugh! What *do* you see in those slimy things?'

'Do you refer, in your ignorance, to *Taricha granulosa* – the famously *rough-skinned* newts of North America?'

It was going to be one of those afternoons, I could tell. Sundays are always a trial.

'Bung 'em somewhere out of sight, and I will summon a swizzle.'

'Squash for me, please, orange or lemon.' He clocked my look of surprise. 'I am re-wagoned, thanks to the marvellous Miss Mabel.'

'Speaking of, I thought she was with you?'

'She's in the kitchen, with Jeeves.'

'Now look here, Gussie, just because the girl's a waitress, she doesn't need to hide below stairs. This isn't *The Forsyte Saga*.'

'No, no, it's nothing like that. Apparently Jeeves and Mabel are old chums.'

I briefly considered disclosing just how chummy they'd once been, but thought better of rocking the romantic boat. Meanwhile, Gussie had crept over to the door and eased it shut.

'While we're alone, Bertie, I've a favour to ask.'

'Imagine my surprise.'

'Might I borrow your car?'

'For what purpose?'

'We're eloping,' he beamed, 'to Gretna Green!'

'Not in my Widgeon Seven, old bird.'

'Why ever not?'

'First, because it'll take you three months to drive there. Second, because your rough-skinned newts will befoul my coachwork. And third, because elopement's a bankrupting idea. What about your quarterly allowance?'

Gussie adopted a pose of martyred self-regard. 'Mabel and I have vowed to live unshackled by the chains of wealth.'

'I see.'

'Assuming you can lend me a tenner?'

'Nope.'

'For the train, and sundry wedding expenses.'

'Nothing doing.'

'That's pretty cheap, if I may say.'

'Cheap?' I scoffed. 'Not half as cheap as you betraying the Drones.'

He had the wit, at least, to feign confusion. '*Betray* the Drones? How so?'

'By telling Monty what I told you – in confidence – about our accumulator and the club's tax hole.'

'I did no such thing! A secret shared with Gussie Fink-Nottle is a secret taken to the grave.'

I gave a low, sarcastic laugh and reminded him of his slanderous performance at supper *chez* Pinke.

'No, Bertie. I'm deadly serious. Soberly serious.'

'Swear it!'

He raised his hand. 'By these five bones. Scout's honour.'

Gussie may never have been a Scout, but he was approximately a man of honour – and so I reluctantly withdrew the charge.

'Boko's to blame,' he said. 'Perhaps *I* should stand for chairman of the investment committee.'

'Aren't you living "unshackled by the chains of wealth"?'

'There are limits, obviously.'

'Half a tick, how can you elope in the middle of term?'

'That's the other thing. Mabel and I have thrown off the yoke of bourgeois employment.'

'You've both been sacked?'

'It amounts to the same thing. I could hardly continue toiling for Vonka's father after, well, everything. And the hotel's policy concerning newts was positively inhumane.'

I was spared further exploration of man's inhumanity to salamanders by the mantlepiece clock, which, like a pal, struck five.

'Listen, Gussie, I hate to play the scurvy host, but Aunt Agatha's blowing in for supper, and we've yet to hide the sharp objects.'

'Then Mabel and I shall detain you no further.' He held out his hand like a bouncer soliciting a bribe.

'Very well,' I went for my wallet, 'but don't spend it *all* on confetti.'

Just moments after I'd seen them off the premises, the doorbell rang again.

Assuming they'd mislaid a newt, or remembered another favour, I tiptoed back to the sitting-room.

'Tell them I'm dead,' I whispered.

I heard the strains of a murmured transaction and, before long, Jeeves appeared.

'A delivery, sir.'

284

He handed me a long, pencil-thin box, which I tore open with Christmas-morning glee.

'It's ... a walking stick? Yes, an antique walking stick. How very irregular. Is there a card?'

Jeeves inspected the shreds. 'It appears not, sir.'

'Why would anyone send me a walking stick? Am I developing an, as yet unperceived, limp?'

'Actually, sir, I believe it to be a Sabbath Stick.'

'A what?'

A Sabbath Stick (or Sunday Stick, depending on the Highland glen you haunt) is, so Jeeves informed me, a devilish invention designed to circumvent the Church of Scotland's prohibition of God's Day golf. At first glance, to the casual observer, it resembles nothing more than a common or garden walking stick, but the handle (which, when walking, is concealed in the palm) is actually a brass-faced club-head. Such devices allow the Scottish links-fanatic to stroll innocently round his common or garden and, when out of sight of praying eyes, drop a ball from his pocket and buff up his short game.

I gave the stick a few exploratory whangs – narrowly missing, I'm sorry to say, the repulsive portrait of McIntosh presented to me by Aunt Agatha, and hung by Jeeves in a prominent place whenever she threatens to visit.

'Are you sure there's no card?'

'Yes, sir. Though I am confident the inscription on the club's heel may furnish an indication of provenance.'

'Inscription?' I upended the stick to discover Jeeves was right, for discreetly engraved into the brass were the letters ...

'K-C!'

'Indeed, sir.'

'D'you know she plays off *three*?'

'How very dispiriting, sir.'

'You said it. Well, seeing as it's Sunday, I think I'll take my Sabbath Stick to Green Park and ruin a good walk. Are you and Crawshaw ready for Aunt Agatha's landfall?'

'Yes, sir. Everything is in hand.'

*   *   *

Having clambered out of my golfing plus-fours and into the supper-time soup-and-fish, I pushed through the green-baize door to find Jeeves and Crawshaw scheming over a pot of tea.

'So, gentlemen, how does this intrigue work? It's almost six thirty and, from the pricking of my thumbs, Aunt Agatha broomsticks ever closer.'

'If you will permit me, sir,' Jeeves replied, 'I would rather not say. Much of the scheme's effect will derive from the ingenuousness of your response.'

'You mean, I've got to wing it?'

'Precisely, sir.'

'D'you agree, Crawshaw?'

'Yes, sir. I only hope you don't take my words or deeds too much to heart.'

This sounded pretty sinister, but before the matter might be discussed any further, a Wagnerian thumb on the doorbell indicated either that Aunt Agatha was upon us, or that the Royal Bavarian Flying Corps had popped by to read the meter.

Crawshaw rose to answer the call and, with an uncertain glance at Jeeves, who had turned his attention to the crossword, I followed.

'*Who* are *you*?' Aunt Agatha demanded, striding into the hall and discarding her hat, coat, gloves, and brolly.

'This, dear Aunt, is Jeeves's replacement – Crawshaw.'

She gave him a slow, skeptical up-and-down, and was peeved to find nothing amiss.

'Good evening, Crawshaw,' she conceded.

'Good evening, Mrs Gregson. Or shall I call you Aggy?'

It was obvious that Aunt Agatha hadn't heard this remark, because Crawshaw remained upright and breathing, rather than dead on the carpet in a pool of his own blood.

Anxious to exploit this momentary blip of deafness, I led Aunt Agatha swiftly to the sitting-room, where the drinks trolley shimmered like an oasis.

'Now, what can I fix you? Absinthe rickey? Absinthe Suisse? Absinthe *frappé*?'

'I will take a glass of milk.'

'Are you sure? We've a lake of absinthe to swim through.'

'It is good for the digestion to drink a glass of milk before eating so *very* late at night, Bertram. You should try it.'

For all Jeeves's professional foresight there was no milk to hand, and so I deployed the bell. Almost instantly Crawshaw appeared – so instantly, in fact, it was obvious he'd been earwigging at the keyhole.

'You rang, sir?'

'Mrs Gregson will take a glass of milk.'

'With pleasure, sir. Cow's milk, sheep's milk, goat's milk, or pigeon's milk?'

'*Milk* milk, Crawshaw.'

'Milk *milk*, sir?'

'*Milk* milk.'

'Will everyone *please* stop saying milk!' Aunt Agatha cried.

'Very good, madam,' Crawshaw bowed, mooing loudly as he left the room.

Aunt Agatha looked like she'd been punched.

'Did that man just moo?'

'How now?'

'Like a cow.'

And then she did something I'd never have believed had I not heard it with my own incredulous ears: she mooed – like a cow – a long, luxurious, velvety, bovine moo.

'MOOOOOOOOOOOOOooooooooooooooo.'

There was a pause.

'I don't *think* so,' I said. 'And I *suspect* I would have remembered.'

The milk was delivered, in silence, and Aunt Agatha began her customary tour of inspection: testing horizontal surfaces for dust, straightening bibelots and knick-knacks, and ensuring her hideous portrait of McIntosh had pride of place.

On several occasions I attempted to broach the subject of Vonka Pinke (our asinine engagement, her shaming arrest, my triumphant vindication), but Aunt Agatha, like a mosquito under the netting, never stayed still enough to be swatted. Every time I plucked up the courage to speak, she opened a withering new front of domestic complaint until finally, my head spinning, I admitted defeat. Whether I liked it or not, a line had been drawn, and my Vonka victory was to be as fleeting as it had been fabulous.

(You may be wondering why I didn't detonate Leviathan's bombshell concerning Aunt Agatha's secret life as a gambling fiend. Let me assure you that I very much wanted to, and had already envisaged the look on her dial as I casually let slip the name 'Arbuthnot Scratch'. Sadly, Jeeves's cooler counsel had prevailed. Repeating his grand-masterly advice about queens and endgames, he advised me to keep this particular keg of gunpowder dry for the next time I was under siege – and there was *bound* to be a next time, for, as he said, *Aunts longa, vita brevis.*)

I rang the bell for supper and led her to the dining-room.

The table had been set for three.

'Is someone joining us?' Aunt Agatha sniffed.

'I don't think so. Why is there an extra place, Crawshaw?'

'Well, sir, it being my first day, I naturally assumed ... No? ... Oh well, please yourself.' He cleared away the superfluous setting with a belligerent clatter. 'I suppose you'll be wanting wine?'

'That's right.'

'The good stuff,' he stage-whispered, 'or the cheap?'

'What?'

'Just a joke!' He ruffled my hair. 'Back in a jiff.'

Aunt Agatha stared at his departure with stunned incredulity, overwhelmed by her options for grievance. But before she could marshal her arsenal of outrage, Crawshaw was back with a bottle of Chablis, from which he dispensed three full-to-the-brim measures.

With a hearty 'Bung-ho!' he drained his glass, clicked his heels, wiped his mouth on the edge of the tablecloth, and left.

'Where,' Aunt Agatha vibrated with consternation, 'did you find that man?'

'It wasn't easy, I can tell you. Not many chaps free at the moment. And he's the very best the agency had.'

'If that is true, Bertram, I despair for this once proud nation.'

Seconds later, Crawshaw kicked open the door juggling two scalding bowls of tepid cock-a-leekie, much of which he slopped on the floor.

'Salt, madam? Pepper?' He nudged her with his elbow. '*Gentleman's Relish?*'

'A spoon is traditional,' Aunt Agatha observed.

'Oops-a-daisy. I'll nab one from the pantry.'

He returned with a battered and heavily soiled ladle which he held up to the light, spat upon, and then polished with the fat end of his tie.

'*Bon appétit.*'

Aunt Agatha stared at the utensil as if at a putrid rat.

'Tell me, Crawshaw, where was your previous position?'

'You won't credit it, madam, but I've been on my heels for a spell.'

Aunt Agatha indicated she found the idea remarkably easy to credit.

'Before that, though, I was with the Duke of Strathearn.'

Her lips puckered into a disbelieving *moue*. 'A duke?'

'Yup. Me and Charlie-boy were together a good few years.'

'And you left the duke's service why?'

'This 'n' that!' He gave her a saucy seaside wink. 'And a bit of *the other*. I would have been on easy street, 'cept it ended up being twins.'

'Twins?' I gasped, fearing he'd gone far too far.

'Boy and a girl. Luckily, they're the spit of the guv'nor, so where's the harm, eh?'

Before the full implication of Crawshaw's confession could surmount Aunt Agatha's besieged sense of propriety, he'd whistled his way out of the room.

We ate our soup in silence – Aunt Agatha using my spoon, I using a fork.

This agonising culinary standoff was interrupted by the doorbell, closely followed by raised voices, a scuffle, some honest-to-goodness shouting, and then the smashing of what sounded like my porcelain bust of W. G. Grace.

Aunt Agatha glared at me through hooded eyes – the face that drowned a thousand kittens.

In time, the shouting stopped, the front door slammed, and Crawshaw appeared, flushed and perspiring, to collect our bowls.

'Who was at the door, Crawshaw?'

'Door, sir?'

'We heard the doorbell *most* distinctly,' said Aunt Agatha.

'I don't think so, madam. You should get your lugholes checked.'

The entrée arrived under a vast silver cloche, which Crawshaw swept away with pantomimic ceremony – including his impression of a trumpet fanfare – to expose a wobbling mass of mud-green sludge.

'And what do we have here?'

'*Anguille grillée en gelée*, sir.'

'Eh?'

'Grilled eels in aspic.'

Aunt Agatha gripped the table and gagged quietly in disgust. I peered closer at the dish. 'I don't *see* any eels, Crawshaw.'

'Awfully hard to come by, eels – especially on a Sunday.'

'So, this is ... just aspic?'

'Not *just* aspic, sir! *Delicious* aspic.'

He stepped forward. 'Can I ask you a question, madam?'

'You *may* ask me a question,' she corrected, as aunts are contractually obliged.

'Do you believe in God?'

I don't think I've ever seen the blood drain so fast from any-one's face; it was like an avalanche at an abattoir.

'I *beg* your pardon?'

'God, madam. Are you a fan?'

'A *fan*? ... Of the Lord Almighty? ... How *dare* you?'

I began now to fear for my safety, as well as his.

'Stone the crows! Just a bit of chit-chat. No need to get aerated!'

He blew a cheerful raspberry, and left.

'He has to go.'

'He's only just arrived!'

'*He has to go.*'

'And valets don't grow on trees.'

'He. Has. To. Go.'

'Leaving me with no one?'

There was a dark, Macbethian silence during which one ghostly name hung unspoken between us.

Eventually, and historically, Aunt Agatha blinked.

'I wonder,' she mused, aiming for indifference and missing by a mile, 'if Jeeves has found another position?'

I mentally applauded Mayfair's Moriarty, who had, yet again, picked the pocket of auntly psychology.

'I expect so. I've lost count of the attempts to poach him.'

'You know, Bertram, I think you were rather too hasty in dis-missing Jeeves.'

'I see that now.'

'One has a duty towards servants.'

'Absolutely.'

'A loyalty.'

'Of course.'

'*Noblesse oblige.*'

'How very well put.'

'Perhaps, if you offered Jeeves a fulsome apology, he might return?'

'I will telephone him first thing in the morning.'

'Do that, Bertram. And let this be a lesson to you.'

'Champagne!' I hollered, flying back through the green-baize door.

Jeeves popped the magnum that was already in his hands. 'Very good, sir.'

'You're a brave man, Crawshaw.'

'Thank you, sir.'

'Recklessly so. Do you have *any* idea how close you came?'

'I've encountered several ladies like Mrs Gregson, sir, and their bark is generally worse than their bite.'

'Tell that to her hospitalised milkman. But how ever did you conjure such a gruesome bruiser?'

'He owes much to a butler I knew at Llanabba Castle who had, if you'll forgive the expression, sir, gone completely john-john.'

'Well, it was a striking performance. Miss MacAuslan is fortunate to have secured your services.'

'Thank you, sir. I look forward to starting in her employ. Incidentally, sir, I'm sorry about the china bust in the hall. Things got a little out of hand.'

'Think nothing off it, Crawshaw – it's a negligible price to pay, given the alternative. And now it is my happy duty to fire you.'

'Thank you, sir.'

'And you, Jeeves, are rehired.'

'Thank you, sir.'

I raised my glass in a toast: 'To *Anguille grillée en gelée*, and all who sail in her.'

(Only a little while later did it occur to me that Jeeves had never much liked my bust of W. G. Grace.)

*　　*　　*

'Has it started?' I gasped, sprinting into the lobby and javelining my umbrella into the elephant's foot.

'You've time, Mr Wooster,' said Bashford, serenely. 'They postponed kick-off on account of Mr Glossop not having remembered the barrel.'

'Typical Tuppy. It's his only job, and every year he forgets.'

The Drones social calendar has many highlights – from the Fat Uncle Sweepstake of early spring, to beetle-racing in the weeks before Christmas – but there are few events that the Crumpets of the club take more seriously than Boot-Finding.

Originating in the taverns around Spitalfields Market, the sport was introduced to the Drones by Lord Benton-March, who, while sitting as a beak in the East End, gleaned its rules from the procession of costermongers hauled before him for breach of the peace.

I've not taken part for many a moon – Boot-Finding is strictly a young man's game – but I make a point of scrutinising each year's line-up and, if I spot a usefully sharp-elbowed contestant, bung on a quid or two with whoever is running the book.

This year, the fast money was clustering round Phineas 'Piebald' Bullivant, who had just joined the Drones via Rule Two (g), being as he was Freddie's younger brother. A rugger Blue at Cambridge, Piebald was a fearless fly-half, well used to having a crack when the ball comes loose from the scrum. Add to this his fitness and youth, and you could see why he was so heavily backed.

I, however, was not so sure. An inevitable aura of juvenile confidence clung to Bullivant Jr. and, though similarities exist, it's a schoolboy error to think Boot-Finding is analogous to rugby union, or even rugby league.

No – my pound notes were pinned to a junior cellarman called Osbert Finlay, who was cunning, wiry, formidably strong, and carried odds of 18/1.

A thunder of voices guided me towards the dining-room, which, as per, had been denuded of chairs, tables, paintings, rugs, and anything vaguely of value. Picking my way through the madding crowd (almost every member, and member of staff, was present), I climbed up onto my reserved, dress-circle window sill.

'You're cutting it a bit fine,' said Oofy Prosser, as I edged in beside him.

'Travails with my aunt,' I explained.

The ringing of a hand-bell indicated that the game was afoot and, to a cacophony of yips and yodels, the four official 'Boot-Finding Generals' marched into the room: Landlord (Freddie Widgeon), Chalker (Ginger Winship), Barrel Man (Tuppy Glossop), and Sawbones (Dr Rossor, a game local G.P. armed with bandages, morphine, and ice).

'Time, gentlemen, please,' proclaimed the Landlord. 'Let all those with business before the bar make themselves known.'

Some fourteen chaps in white tie and tails stepped out of the throng and formed a ragged line.

'I see you are suited, Finders, but are you *booted*?'

'BOOTS! BOOTS! BOOTS!' they chanted, stamping their feet in time.

'Chalker – you have the chalk?'

'Landlord, I do,' said Ginger, holding up a stick of yellow.

'Barrel Man – you have the barrel?'

'Landlord, I do,' said Tuppy, and McGarry rolled into the room an ancient herring barrel.

'OFF WITH 'EM!'

The Finders scrambled to the floor and set about removing their boots, thereby exposing which socks they'd selected for the occasion. As each sartorial choice was unveiled, the spectators cheered in approval or jeered in scorn; poor old Osbert Finlay got an especially rough reception for not wearing any socks at all.

When all were unshod, the Landlord shouted 'MARK 'EM,' and Ginger Winship sprang into action – chalking a large yellow number on each player's back and on the soles of both of their boots. As the Chalker worked his way down the line, the spectators chanted each new number with increasing vigour until by number fourteen, Bimbash Kidd, the chandeliers were tinkling in protest.

The Landlord then barked a sequence of familiar commands:

'PITCH 'EM' – each man threw his boots into the barrel.

'FIX 'EM' – the barrel was secured with a lid.

'ROLL 'EM' – the barrel was rolled down to the room's far end.

'MIX 'EM' – the barrel was spun, shaken, and jostled.

'TIP 'EM' – the barrel was upended, strewing a confusion of boots across the floor.

The crowd fell reverently silent.

'Right, Finders, I think you all know the rules pretty well: no biting, no kicking, and nothing below the cummerbund—'

(At this the crowd erupted, pointing to those Dronesmen sporting the now criminally implicated Crimson Polka.)

'—and the first man with his own boots on, wins. On my mark ... GO!'

The ensuing chaos might best be headlined: PENGUIN POOL PIRANHA ATTACK.

An uproar of exhortation accompanied a frenzy of action as each white-tied Finder sprinted towards the barrel and dived into the mêlée of leather.

Of course, Boot-Finding isn't simply a question of *finding* your boots – though this is harder than you'd think. The real skill is jamming them on and lacing them up without rival Finders slapping them out of your hands, or hurling them into the crowd.

Ordinarily, the tumultuous blur of arms, legs, elbows, and fists makes gauging advantage all but impossible, but this year one player stood firm in the turmoil of jostling: Finlay the junior cellarman.

From my elevated position it was clear to see why Finlay held his ground with such aplomb, while the rest of the field (notably Bullivant Jr.) skidded and banjoed across the freshly waxed parquet. His advantage was socks – or, rather, the absence thereof.

Having swiftly located his boots, while fending off an octopus of elbows, Finlay made nimble work of inserting his feet, and, deftly evading a fusillade of trips, he jinked his way across the room to stand panting before the committee.

The Chalker compared the number on Finlay's back with the numbers on his soles before declaring 'BOOTS FOUND' – to the huzzahs of the few (like me) who'd backed him, and the heckles of the many (like Oofy) who'd not.

As Dr Rossor set about tending to the fallen, I collected my winnings from a disconsolate Boko and hacked through the mob to hail the conquering hero.

'Congratters, Finlay. Well booted!'

'Thank you, Mr Wooster.'

'Barefooting was a master-stroke. I imagine everyone will be at it next year.'

'Actually, sir, it was your man's idea.'

'Jeeves? How so?'

'I happened to mention Boot-Finding when he came to collect your absinthe, and the next day he sent me a note which said "friction is greatest between rough surfaces, and diminished by polishing".'

'That does sound like him.'

'Which apparently means: boots and no socks.'

'Very Hysteron Proteron, what?'

'If you say so, sir.'

Although gratuities at the Drones are strictly *verboten* (members bung into a Christmas Fund that is divvied out just before the Grand National), I've always considered sporting events to be 'off the books' – especially when, as with Boot-Finding, members and staff compete on equal terms. And so, having made a tidy sum from Finlay's feet, it was the least I could do to fold a fiver into his hand, before edging my way along the panelling to my appointment with Iona MacAuslan.

I was almost out of the front door when Bashford called me back.

'Sorry, Mr Wooster, but there was a telephone call for you during the match. A somewhat tearful lady,' he consulted his pad, 'by the name of Miss Madeline Bassett.'

'Hell and hounds! Did she leave a message?'

'No, sir. She merely enquired if you were in the club.'

'And was I?'

'You weren't, sir. In fact, I've not seen you here for years.'

*　　*　　*

Most of Mayfair's hot spots (including The Hot Spot itself) go dark on the Sabbath – doubtless to cosy up to the police, the pulpit, and their long-suffering neighbours. But since the Quarrelsome Crab is seldom free from legal hot water, its management takes a hung-for-a-sheep approach to the 1921 Licensing Act, and generally declines to close.

As a result, Sunday evening is a reliably up-tempo affair.

I parted the velvet curtains at a quarter to ten to find the joint jammed to the rafters and louder even than curry night at the Drones. I gave my name to the hostess, and was being guided through the throng to my table when a sozzled young whippersnapper barged straight into me.

'I say,' he sneered, 'why don't you watch— *Oh, lor!*'

Oh, lor indeed – for the bargee was none other than my loutish Cousin Thos. who, in an instant, turned as red-faced as he was red-handed.

'Ahoy there, Cousin Bertie!'

'Ahoy me no hoys, Thomas. Why aren't you at school?'

'End of term?' he attempted.

'*Beginning* of term, you oaf. Anyway, you're far too young to be drinking alone.'

'I'm not alone.' He pointed to a table of callow youths drunkenly attempting the egg-and-matchbox trick. 'I'm with the chaps.'

'They too are far too young.'

'I'd bet anything *you* haunted clubs like this at my age.'

He had a point. 'That's not the point.'

'Be a brick, Bertie! I'm already on the gridiron with Mama. She says if I flunk out of Pinke's, it's the navy.'

It was hard to fathom what the Admiralty might have done to deserve Able Seaman Gregson shivering his timbers about the deck – unless they planned to use him as a buoy, or fire him from a cannon. But, truth be told, I was far from torn. For although young Thos. has all the charm of an unlanced boil, we were cousins in arms against a terrible foe. And if *amicus meus* is indeed *inimicus inimici mei* (as Jeeves is fond of saying), then yah-boo-skoosh to Aunt Ag.

I was on the brink of dismissing the perisher with a scathing *nolle prosequi*, when I spotted at his midriff the Crimson Polka.

'Where, Thomas, did you get *that*?'

'This snazzy number?' He adjusted his cummerbund with pride. 'There's a stall on Berwick Street that knocks 'em out for next to nothing. All the blades are wearing them – they're really quite the thing.'

I was floored. 'Don't you read the papers?'

He gave me a pitying look. 'Nobody reads the papers, Cousin Bertie.'

Much as I would have applauded this juvenile palooka's arrest and imprisonment for theft, I knew he couldn't be trusted under interrogation with the secrets of my night-climbing mission. And so I found myself in the novel position of dispensing Thomas the *beau geste*.

'Very well. We will draw a veil over your presence tonight, provided you remove that cummerbund immediately.'

'But, Bertie—'

'Immediately!'

He rolled his eyes theatrically, but nonetheless complied.

'And leave the premises forthwith.'

'D'you mind if we finish the bottle?' He grinned. 'It's a crime to waste good fizz.'

Exhausted by this fleeting brush with parental responsibility, I strode to my table, seized the phone, and summoned from the bar their most muscular dry Martini. No sooner had I replaced the receiver than the instrument's red light flashed.

'Table Twelve: how may I direct your call?'

'Bertie?'

I glanced round the room, but saw no one in the twilight I knew. 'Speaking.'

'*It's-a-disaster-a-complete-disaster-I'm-being-sued-well—*'

'Whoa there, Monty!' Even down the line his fumes were unmistakable. 'Come join me.'

I soon spotted Montague Montgomery corkscrewing through the crowd, patently long in strong drink. But whereas he pitched and yawed like a skiff on the high seas, the cocktails he carried – two in each hand – remained as steady as the spirit levels they were.

He tabled his drinks with practised precision, before crashing into a chair like a sackful of spuds.

'*It's-a-disaster-Bertie-a-complete-disaster-I'm-being-sued-well-the-paper-is-being-sued-but-I'm-a-named-party—*'

'Steady on, old bean, you're making little to no sense.'

He took a deep breath, and a deeper swig.

'It's a disaster. We ran a piece in the column on Saturday about a trial in Cambridge where Alfred Duff Cooper, of all people, mysteriously went free after being nicked for night climbing.'

Ah.

'Except it wasn't Alfred Duff Cooper. It was either someone with the same name – and *what* are the odds? – or some dunderhead who chose as his criminal alias the Financial Secretary to the War Office.'

Ah.

'The *real* Alfred Duff Cooper was at his own book launch in London. His alibi is supported by half the Cabinet, and he's threatening to sue the paper, and me.'

'Who gave you the story?'

'An anonymous tip. But we double-checked, and it was confirmed by the clerk of the court.'

'Isn't that some kind of defence? Reporting official proceedings?'

'Who knows? We'll find out tomorrow morning when I meet the paper's lawyers.' He groaned. 'Oh God, the lawyers!'

Draining one glass, he began work on the next, and I thought it tactful to shift gears.

'It's a shame you missed Boot-Finding.'

'You're telling me! Mongering gossip is cramping my style, which I suppose passes as irony. I assume Piebald romped home?'

'Actually, no. Finlay took the laurels.'

'Good for Osbert! All that toil in the cellars paying off. Boko must be hopping mad at 18/1. I wonder if it makes a couple of pars for Tuesday's column?'

'I think *not*, Monty. The Drones is in a deep enough ditch, what with the Crimson Polka and your recent indiscretions about our finances.'

'Freedom of the press, old boy. My hands were tied.'

'I hope the general committee agrees. You have rather kicked the lid off Rule Nine.'

He laughed. 'Has that provision ever been used?'

'Not that I know of.'

'Tricky to prove the Drones has a repute to dis.'

'Speaking of, who tipped you off to our accumulator? I trust it wasn't Gussie, for he swore on his Scout's honour.'

Monty leaned closer. 'I shouldn't be telling you this, but since you're buying the drinks—'

'Hey!'

'—the word came from Leviathan himself. He's one of our regulars. The old rogue considers it free advertising.'

'So much for the sanctity of the turf.'

The telephone flashed, and I plucked the receiver.

'Table Twelve: all-night chemists.'

'Table Thirty-five here. Is that Iceberg?'

I was momentarily nonplussed, before remembering Monty's *nom de scandale*. 'That's right, caller, hold the line.'

Monty pressed the phone to his ear. 'This is Iceberg ... I see ... I see ... I see ... *Really?* ... How very interesting! Thank you.'

'Wrong number?'

'Very witty. Actually, it was a tip-off. It seems the cops have a line on the Mount Street diamond mob. Arrests are expected tonight.'

'Speaking of, I hope you're featuring the arrest of Roderick Spode?'

'Oh, yes – it's in tomorrow. That photo you sent me is a scream. Five more along those lines and you get your bottle of claret.'

'Assuming you're not in prison, of course.'

'Not even in jest, Bertie! But, look, if anything did happen, can I suggest you as my successor?'

'As a gossip columnist? I hardly think—'

'Don't say no. You've an eye for a story and a neat turn of phrase. Of course, it may never arise, if Duff Cooper comes to his senses. And now I'd better call it a night. I've got to be at the Inns of Court at the crack of dawn to see if I'm for the jump.'

He drained the third of his cocktail quartet, and slid the fourth over.

'What's in it?' I asked, examining the vibrant blue gloop.

'Haven't a clue.'

I was pondering the likelihood of being collared as a co-conspirator in Monty's Duff Cooper disaster, when who should appear in my eyeline but Lancelot Pinke – arm in arm with a woman most decidedly *not* Evadne.

We shared one of those quintessentially nightclub glances that starts with curiosity (Do I *know* him?), dallies with confusion (*How* do I know him?), and ends in crisis (Oh God, it's *him*!) – though in this instance, the crisis was all Pinke's, since the arm he was holding belonged to the appalling wife of *his* appalling wife's equally appalling chiropodist.

He attempted a conspiratorial wink as he shuffled past, which was almost as unpleasant as the evening we'd spent together; indeed, I was still recovering from the memory when, a few minutes later, Iona arrived.

'Sorry I'm late.' She kissed my cheek with autumnal lips. 'Trouble with a propeller. Was that your actor friend I narrowly avoided in the cloakroom?'

'Montague?'

'He looks like a piano fell on him.'

'He was always terribly musical. Now, what can I get you?'

She pointed to Monty's abandoned gloop. 'Whatever *that* isn't.'

I phoned the bar for fortifications, and enflamed her cigarette.

'So,' she puffed, 'how did things unfold at supper?'

'Like shelling peas! With Jeeves's guile and Crawshaw's greasepaint they make a formidable duo. Aunt Agatha didn't know what hit her – she very nearly apologised.'

'Gracious! So, you're in the clear?'

'For now. But I expect she'll lie low – in a dark, dank burrow – cooking up some suitably tepid revenge. You can't turn your back on aunts for a second.'

The telephone flashed, and I plucked the receiver.

'Table Twelve: palms read, fortunes told.'

'Wooster, it's Lancelot Pinke.'

'I thought it might be.'

'Look, I know how it must appear.'

'As do I.'

'But the thing is, my wife doesn't understand me—'

'Say no more.'

'What?'

'Your secret is safe.'

'Really? Just like that?' The relief in his voice was touching. 'Thank you!'

'On one condition. Should you happen to encounter tonight, for the sake of argument, my cousin and your student, Thomas Gregson, you will turn to him an eye as blind as the eye I'm turning to you.'

'Oh, yes, right. Of course. One hand washes the other, eh?'

'What a revolting idea, Pinke. Never speak of it again.'

I replaced the receiver.

'What was all *that* about?' asked Iona.

'Merely doing good by stealth and blushing to find it fame.'

'Alexander Pope?'

'*The Oxford Book of Jeeves.*'

And then the telephone flashed once more.

'Care to shimmy?' asked a muffled voice.

'Which of us are you inviting?'

'Either.'

'Not tonight, thank you.'

'It's all go,' Iona arched an eyebrow. 'No wonder this place keeps getting raided.'

'Last time they came in through the skylights. Jolly dramatic. Which reminds me, your Spode photo is running in tomorrow's *Sketch*. Monty was as pleased as Punch, not that I've yet seen it ... '

She took the hint and extracted from her handbag a manila envelope, from which she slid a glossy print.

In the centre of the frame stood Lord Sidcup, bespattered by rain, with his arms outstretched in quasi-religious torment. To his left was Inspector Whitsun, snapping on the cuffs; to his right, Constable Dockery, fending off an unseen assailant; and from below, Thomasina MacAuslan, hidden by her Newnham scarf, was mere moments from landing her trifle.

'This is quite the snap, Iona. Someone should paint it in oils!'

'Caravaggio got there first.'

'And please do congratulate your cousin for me.'

'You can probably congratulate her yourself. She's often here on a Sunday.'

'Hang on ... where's Whipplesnaith? He seems to have disappeared.'

'I had the paper-hangers airbrush him out. We don't want the *gouster* getting famous, now do we?'

'I suppose not.'

'But I do have a snap of our blackmailer on the roof. It's not nearly as artistic, but it gets the job done.'

She handed over a second print.

'His waterlogged pyjamas,' I observed, 'are an especially endearing detail.'

'And here,' she took out a third print, 'is something that may also be of interest.'

I examined it carefully. 'I'm confused.'

'You've got it upside down.'

I had, though it was so grainy I hoped I might be forgiven.

'Great Scott! Is this what I think it is?'

'I'm afraid so.'

'I didn't even know you were at Newmarket!'

'It's called the Secret Service—'

'—for a reason, yes, I remember. But how ever did you take it?'

'Blind luck. I was surreptitiously snapping Lord Sidcup for the files, documenting his very curious new role as Chief Steward, and only after the film was developed did I spot what I'd caught in the background. I'm sure I couldn't catch it again in a hundred years.'

This was dynamite. If Leviathan found proof – *photographic* proof – that the 4:45 had *not* been tied three ways, but won by a nostril by what looked like Laffy … well, actually, I wasn't sure. Could it change the result of Spode's mad adjudication? Who knew? But the risk was surely that Boko would never again play the bassoon.

'We must destroy this photo. And the negative. And possibly the camera which took it.'

I extracted my lighter and ignited a corner of the print, which curled and blackened into the latest design of ashtray: a quarrelsome crab nipping with ragged claws at the club's initials.

A fresh batch of snifters had just been delivered when Iona straightened herself in the manner of one about to Speak Seriously.

'May I ask you something, Bertie?'

'Fire at will.'

'I wonder if you've plans for the week ahead? Plans you can't escape.'

'You sound just like your uncle when there's a caper afoot.'

'Funny you should say that,' she twinkled. 'I'm returning to Le Touquet, and thought you might like to join me.'

'Back to your thirty-nine-cups assignment?'

She nodded.

'With your uncle and Jeeves in tow?'

She shook her head. 'Just us.'

I took a sip to calm my nerves, a little concerned my pulse was distracting the band.

'Will it be like last time? Me zipping to France only for you to pop up in Peru?'

'I think I can guarantee that won't happen.'

I clearly looked a little sceptical.

'We'd leave together. Tonight, in fact – I'm flying.'

'Gosh! Well!' The belfry whirled. 'I don't have any things.'

She handed me a cloakroom token inscribed K4.

'What's this?'

'Your things. I had Jeeves pack you a bag.'

'So you two are in cahoots!'

'*Cahoots?*' Iona laughed. 'Is that your best Scottish accent?'

I blushed and took another sip.

'I see you're uncertain.' She rose from her seat. 'I'll powder while you ponder.'

As she slinked through the crowd like the sleekest of otters, I brooded on how to proceed.

From time immemorial, the Code of the Woosters has incarnated the *ne plus ultra* of chivalry, gallantry, and assorted knight-errantry. We think nothing of stooping for dropped handkerchiefs, unbranching kittens from tall trees, or flinging our capes across mud-spattered streets. And surely the conventions of a *preux chevalier* dictate it *de rigueur* – to say nothing of *comme il faut* – that the chap makes all the running?

The trouble was, Iona laughed in the face of convention, and much else besides.

Was this a test, I wondered? And, if so, a test of what? Etiquette? Loyalty? Duty? Was it strictly Ganymede business? Partly Ganymede business? Or Ganymede business at all? What did it signify that Jeeves had packed my things? Did he approve? And, if so, of what? He rarely approves of the fairer sex, so what might have changed his mind? Iona? Le Touquet? Or were there other shoes yet to drop?

It was in this maelstrom of indecision that I decided to let fortune determine my fate. I plucked up Iona's cloakroom token, balanced it upright on the table, and flicked it like a spinning-top: Heads, I'd stay in London; tails, I'd fly to France.

The two sides blinked and blended like a nursery zoetrope.

QC ~ K4 ~ QCK ~ 4QC ~ K4Q ~ CK4Q ~ CK4QC ~ K4QC ~ K4QC ~

The token was still whirling as I snapped it to the table, my mind resolved to—

The telephone flashed.

'Table Twelve: wigs and haberdashery.'

'It's me,' said Iona, 'I'm at the bar.'

'Look, about Le Touquet—'

'Hush, Bertie, and listen! Don't make any sudden moves, but, very slowly, glance over your left shoulder.'

I rotated my head until I saw two shadowy figures huddled in an alcove.

'Now what?'

'Keep watching.'

I did as instructed, and then the bandleader's spotlight swung across the stage, briefly illuminating one of the faces.

'Oh, I see. How unpleasant.'

'Unpleasant! Is that all you can say?'

'Well, is there any reason why Roderick Spode *shouldn't* be here?'

'That's not the point! Look who Spode's with.'

I craned my neck as far as it crooked, rising out of my seat like a swan peering round a post box, when the spotlight swung back, illuminating the second face.

'*Mon Dieu!*' I gasped down the line.

'*Précisément!*'

'*Avec* Spode!'

'*En effet.*'

'I've run out of French.'

'You started it!' she laughed.

'But what are they doing together?'

'I've no idea.'

'It's pretty suspish!'

And it was – for standing in the shadows, engaging Spode in what Jeeves would call 'treason's secret knife', was none other than Algernon Crawshaw.

'Cahoots?'

'So it seems.'

'Conspiracy?'

'Who can say?'

And then, with a furtive glance, Spode slipped Crawshaw an envelope embossed with the Flash and Circle insignia, and Crawshaw slipped Spode a ring-box from Lambert Lyall.

Before I could begin to fathom what this perfidious transaction might mean – Treason? Theft? Extortion? Collusion? – the club was thrown into a tumult of breaking glass, female screams, and police whistles.

'This is a raid,' a copper's voice blared through a megaphone. 'Remain exactly where you are.'

Bored by such interruptions, the club's regulars drank on as if nothing had happened, and the band merely segued from 'Ain't Misbehavin'' to 'In the Jailhouse Now'.

Flouting police orders, I replaced the receiver and resumed my seat, baffled by what I'd just witnessed. Was Spode the diamond heist's 'Fifth Man' after all? Was Crawshaw a secret Black Short agent? Had I put Iona in danger by urging her to hire a traitor? Or was his employment part of a darker Ganymede plan?

I reached for the anaesthetic in a fog of bewilder – but in the slip 'twixt cup and lip, the telephone flashed once more.

Too dazed for pleasantries, I simply guided the instrument to my ear.

'*Bertie!*' The voice was frantic.

'Gussie? What the dickens are you doing here?'

'I've been hunting for you all over Mayfair.'

'You're meant to be speeding north on the night train to Gretna Green.'

'It's off!'

'The train?'

'The engagement.'

'Ding-ding-ding! A new Fink-Nottle record.'

'I didn't call it off!'

'*What?*'

'Mabel did.'

'Very well,' I sighed, 'what did you do?'

'Nothing, I swear! She's become engaged to someone else.'

It rather snapped the elastic of credulity to think that Mabel Chitt – in a few short hours on a wet Sunday night – had unearthed a fresh fiancé. And, frankly, given the gunpowder, treason, and plot unfolding around me, I wasn't all that sure I cared.

'Engaged? Since we last met? I simply don't believe it.'

'You'd better,' said Gussie, ominously.

And then suddenly the pieces fell into place: Mabel's last-minute disavowal … Spode's clandestine ring transaction … Madeline's tearful call to the Drones … together they could only mean one thing.

'Mabel's engaged to Spode! Will I never be free from the Mad Bat?'

'Oh no,' said Gussie, 'it's not Spode.'

'What?'

'It's *much* worse than Spode.'

'Worse than Spode? How is that possible? To whom is Mabel engaged?'

'Jeeves!'

NOTES ON THE TEXT

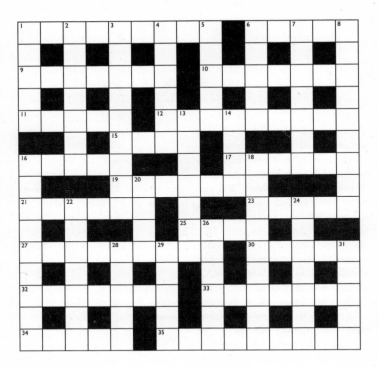

ACROSS

1 Upset ear doctor, one who changes rooms (9)
6 Finding a penny during repast gets an award (5)
9 Just past eight, you get squiffy! (3,4)
10 Encountered after choice fruit fall (7)
11 Soar out of prison almost (4)
12 Weirdly alert sons learn to draw etc. here (3,6)
15 Point out ineptitude, partially (4)
16 Polygamist agreeing with 26 (2,2,1)
17 Forecast front will come off wicker vessel (6)
19 After adjusting tie, can't blink (7)
21 In the distant past, silver article I must hide (3,3)
23 Exhaling very very loudly during exercise (5)
25 Place to convalesce, not quite (4)
27 Silly pater, nearly dead drunk (9)
30 Look to include uranium for fine fabric (5)
32 A pro putt almost acceptable (2,2,3)
33 One not grabbing snake, cornered (2,1,4)
34 Such a bore! (5)
35 Agitato's played. Why aloud? One needs to speak! (1,5,3)

DOWN

1 Medic with singular low hum (5)
2 Made over poetically in cricket club by editor (7)
3 Nasty vicar's lot drunk with gin (9)
4 Coat of black and yellowish-brown material (6)
5 Transplant for one who drinks up (5)
6 Just one of James's Madame's family in the shade? (5)
7 Death before a hundred is dry enough (4,3)
8 Classic exam, most recent containing one set of books (5,4)
13 Salesman put on hat, snakeskin? (7)
14 Spin tool for ill-gotten gains (4)
16 Trust fair to supply something juicy (9)
18 Disrupt urgent nap? Disgusting (9)
20 Some affection admitted for island (4)
22 Landed after expedition initially declared (7)
24 Fake father, I hear, is tactless in France (4,3)
26 He said, she said – get knotted (1,2,1,2)
28 Drive away dead skin (or most) (5)
29 Risk attempting Prufrock's peachy question? (4,1)
31 Short dash to attempt admission (5)

1. MONDAY

The crossword! · Plum was very fond of crosswords, and they appear throughout his work, perhaps most splendidly when George Mulliner proposes to his fellow cruciverbalist, Susan Blake: 'Will you be my wife, married woman, matron, spouse, help-meet, consort, partner or better half ?' And she responds: 'Yes, yea, ay, aye! Decidedly, unquestionably, indubitably, incontrovertibly, and past all dispute!' [P. G. Wodehouse, Meet Mr Mulliner (Herbert Jenkins, 1927), p. 37.]

The *Times* crosswords of the 1930s differ somewhat in style and format from contemporary versions – for example, clues in 1932 did not include enumerations, and setters would usually signpost anagrams with 'anag.', rather than with cryptic code-words such as 'upset' or 'spin'. The above grid is identical to that printed by *The Times* on 3 October 1932 (No. 829). In composing the clues I have attempted to steer a midcourse between ancient and modern styles and, in so doing, am indebted to Richard Rogan, Crossword Editor of *The Times*, for his invaluable assistance – though any errors or infelicities are mine alone.

Jorrocks's Jaunts & Jollities · The title of a series of comic stories by Robert Smith Surtees, first published in book form in 1838.

Right, said Fred · The cloth cap is doffed to Ted **Dicks** and Myles **Rudge**, as well as the great Bernard Cribbins.

Gussie, Gussie, Gussie · I imagine Bertie sang this to the tune of *Nicaea*, written by John Bacchus Dykes to accompany Reginald Heber's hymn 'Holy, Holy, Holy'.

Prize-day speech · See *Right Ho, Jeeves* (1934).

Parisian Blonde · ⅓ sweet cream, ⅓ curaçao, ⅓ Jamaica rum. Shake well, strain, garnish, and discard.

Cambridge won the Boat Race · The Light Blues were pretty unassailable on the Thames during the interwar years, winning 17 of the 20 races contested between 1920 and 1939.

A hundred grand · Valuing money, always tricky, is trickier still in Woostershire, not least because the canon's creation spanned so many decades. As Plum wrote to his publishers in 1973, albeit about the novel *Bachelors Anonymous*: 'This money business always worries me. I can't get used to the present inflation. Do you think it ought to be five pounds? It seems a terribly big sum.' [*P. G. Wodehouse: A Life in Letters*, ed. Sophie Ratcliffe (2011) (Arrow Books, 2013), p. 535.]

If you trust the Bank of England (and surely Bertie would), £1 in 1915 would have been worth c.£10 in 1974, and c.£100 now. Many of the sums mentioned herein (and in *Jeeves & The King of Clubs*) were chosen because they *felt* right, regardless of inflation. The £100,000 required to save the Drones is nowadays equivalent to c.£7 million – far less than the current price of a Mayfair clubhouse; far more than most sane bookies would stake.

Plucking the goose · Jean-Baptiste Colbert, Louis XIV's Minister of Finances, is commonly quoted as saying: 'The art of taxation consists in so plucking the goose as to obtain the largest possible amount of feathers with the smallest possible amount of hissing.'

2. TUESDAY

Twang of the banjolele · Jeeves, like all right-minded people, is unable to tolerate the banjo, as we learn in *Thank You, Jeeves*: 'If it is really your intention to continue playing that instrument, I have no option but to leave.'[1] According to one of Wodehouse's biographers, in 1905 Plum actually purchased a banjo with every intention of becoming proficient, but the instrument was pawned by his room-mate Herbert Westbrook (the model for Ukridge), who promptly lost the ticket.[2] [1. P. G. Wodehouse, *Thank You, Jeeves* (Little, Brown, 1934), p. 15.; 2. David Jasen, *P. G. Wodehouse: A Portrait of a Master* (Mason & Lipscomb, 1974), p. 34.]

Charles Pikelet · This turf-accountant won £10 off Bingo Little by having the uglier baby; see *Eggs, Beans and Crumpets* (1940).

Leviathan · William Edmund 'Leviathan' Davies (1819–79) was the most famous bookmaker of his day. His career began when, while working as a carpenter in Newmarket, he overheard information about upcoming races and realised he was in the wrong trade. Early success in half-crown betting prompted him to establish offices in Covent Garden, and soon his reputation for honest dealing meant that punters exchanged his winning tickets like banknotes. Leviathan's reputation was secured in 1848 when he accepted the Earl of Stratford's £1,000 stake at 12/1 on The Cur in the Cesarewitch Handicap, and paid up the next day. In 1853 (four years before he retired) he had £130,000 in the bank, some £16.6 million in today's money. Although my Leviathan is a well-upholstered chap, Davies earned his nickname not from his physical heft, but from the size of the bets he accepted. [See *The Dictionary of National Biography*, vol. XIV (Smith, Elder, & Co., 1888), p. 162.]

A2 · This was the Albany set occupied by, among others, Lord Byron – who was pleased it had 'room for my books and sabres'. [Roy Porter, *London, a Social History* (Harvard University Press, 1995), p. 109. For more on Albany, see, for example, Harry Furniss, *Paradise in Piccadilly: The Story of Albany* (John Lane, 1925).]

Theology · What Bertie studied at Oxford, and whether he obtained a degree, are discussed at length in a series of essays in John H. C. Morris's *Thank You, Wodehouse* (Weidenfeld & Nicholson, 1981), pp. 21–30.

Cohen Bros. · The Cohen Brothers (Isadore, Lou, and Irving) feature in several of Plum's works, and are clearly modelled on the Covent Garden clothing firm Moss Bros.

'But the Brothers Cohen, though their main stock-in-trade is garments which have been rejected by their owners for one reason or another, do not confine their dealings to Gents' Wear. The place is a museum of derelict goods of every description. You can get a second-hand revolver there, or a second-hand sword, or a second-hand umbrella. You can do a cheap deal in field-glasses, trunks, dog collars, canes, photograph frames, attaché cases, and bowls for goldfish.' [P. G. Wodehouse, *The Heart of a Goof* (Herbert Jenkins, 1926), p. 156.]

Screever · Literature's most famous screever is surely Herbert 'Bert' Alfred who was created by P. L. Travers in *Mary Poppins* (1934), and immortalised by Dick Van Dyke in the 1964 film.

Fenchurch-Smythe · Monty may be alluding to Adam Fenwick-Symes, who was 'Mr Chatterbox' for the *Daily Excess*. [See Evelyn Waugh, *Vile Bodies* (Chapman & Hall, 1930).]

Playboy of the West End World · Monty is punning on J. M. Synge's 1907 play *The Playboy of the Western World*. Later this nickname would be bestowed upon a host of characters, including Kenneth Tynan, Brendan Behan, Oscar Wilde, Michael Ball, Aneurin Bevan, Paul Raymond, and, most famously, Noël Coward.

Twenty-two near-Mrs · The precise number of Bertie's engagements is hotly debated by Wodehouse scholars, and opinions differ. I have relied upon the heroic analysis of Mr Bengt Malmberg, who has generously consented for me to reproduce his chronology of Bertie's engagements:

1. **Florence Craye** (1916, 'Jeeves Takes Charge'); 2. **Cynthia Wickhammersley** (1922, 'The Great Sermon Handicap'); 3. **Honoria Glossop** (1922, 'The Hero's Reward'); 4. **Aline Hemmingway** (1923, 'Pearls Mean Tears'); 5. **Heloise Pringle** (1925, 'Without the Option'); 6. **Roberta Wickham** (1927, 'Jeeves and the Yule-tide Spirit'); 7. **Gwladys Pendlebury** (1930, 'Jeeves and the Spot of Art'); 8. **Madeline Bassett** (1934, *Right Ho, Jeeves*); 9. **Angela Travers** (1934, *Right Ho, Jeeves*); 10. **Pauline Stoker** (1934, *Thank You, Jeeves*); 11. **Stephanie 'Stiffy' Byng** (1938, *The Code of the Woosters*); 12. **Madeline Bassett** (1938, *The Code of the Woosters*); 13. **Florence Craye** (1946, *Joy in the Morning*); 14. **Cora Potter-Pirbright** (1949, *The Mating Season*); 15. **Florence Craye** (1954, *Jeeves and the Feudal Spirit*); 16. **Roberta Wickham** (1960, *Jeeves in the Offing*); 17. **Madeline Bassett** (1963, *Stiff Upper Lip, Jeeves*); 18. **Honoria Glossop** (1965, 'Jeeves and the Greasy Bird'); 19. **Trixie Waterbury** (1965, 'Jeeves and the Greasy Bird'); 20. **Madeline Bassett** (1971, *Much*

322

Obliged, Jeeves); 21. **Florence Craye** (1971, *Much Obliged, Jeeves*); 22. **Vanessa Cook** (1974, *Aunt's Aren't Gentlemen*).

Mr Malmberg notes: this list is 'complete to 98%'; it omits the various uncanonical works; and it excludes engagements that are merely discussed, including those between Bertie and: Zenobia 'Nobby' Hopwood, Daphne Braithwaite, Muriel Singer, Beatrice Slingsby, Phyllis Mills, Angelica Briscoe, and Heloise Pringle.

Either that bedroom wallpaper · Presumably Jeeves is alluding to the supposed last words of Oscar Wilde: 'My wallpaper and I are fighting a duel to the death. One or the other of us has to go.'

Bright raven · Jeeves is, naturally, correct. See, for example, Charlotte Mary Yonge, *History of Christian Names*, vol. 1, (Parker, Son, & Bourne, 1863), p. 415.

Gentleman's Third · There were four traditional sizes of visiting cards: *Smalls* (3⅝" × 2⅜") for ladies and couples; *Reduced Smalls* (3½" × 2⅛") for ladies; and *Extra Thirds* (3 × 1¾) or *Thirds* (3 × 1½) for gentlemen. Certain ladies of dubious repute would have their cards made up in *Thirds* or *Extra Thirds*, in case one of their married 'friends' chanced to take out his wallet in front of his wife. [See, for example, Ben Schott, *Schott's Quintessential Miscellany* (Bloomsbury, 2011), p. 83.]

Rachele and Benito · Rachele Guidi married Benito Mussolini in 1915.

Budd · This fine bespoke shirtmakers has been a fixture of Piccadilly Arcade since it was established by Harold Budd in 1910.

Empress Eugénie · A style of hat originally made famous by Eugénie de Montijo, the wife of Napoleon III; subsequently revivified by Greta Garbo in her 1930 film *Romance*.

Aage Thaarup · The celebrated Danish milliner who in 1932 opened his first London shop just off Berkeley Square.

Quarrelsome Crab · Although the Q.C. is a club of my own invention, much of the 'schizophrenic metamorphosis' of its lineage comes from *Jeeves and the Feudal Spirit* (1954).

Table telephones · Although a few London nightclubs of the period did feature such phones (including the Florida Club in South Bruton Mews), the elaborate scale of the Quarrelsome Crab owes much to the Berlin nightclubs Femina (which had some 200 *Tischtelefonen*) and Resi (which also featured a network of pneumatic tubes). [See, for example, Helen Josephy & Mary Margaret McBride, *Beer and Skittles: A Friendly Guide to Modern Germany* (G. P. Putnam's Sons, 1932).]

C Division · The Metropolitan Police division that covered Soho and Mayfair; it was served by Vine Street and Great Marlborough Street police stations.

Diamond Heist · The 'Mount Street Hotel Heist' was inspired by the 1937 'Hyde Park Hotel Robbery', during which the manager of Cartier's Bond Street store, Etienne Bellenger, was

lured to Room 305 by four public-school 'Mayfair playboys', before
being robbed of nine diamond rings
worth £16,000. I am indebted to Angus
McLaren's fascinating exploration of
this largely forgotten *cause célèbre* –
although many of the details, not least
the cigars and cummerbunds, are
mine. [See Angus McLaren, *Playboys
and Mayfair Men* (Johns Hopkins
University Press, 2017).]

Crimson Polka · Although the Drones
Club cummerbund is my invention, the
debate about the club's necktie is not:
'there was talk at one time of having it
crimson with white spots, but the sup-
porters of that view were outvoted.' [P.
G. Wodehouse, *Aunts Aren't Gentlemen*
(1974) (Arrow Books, 2008), p. 170.]

Remarkably · Erich Maria Remarque's
1928–9 novel, *Im Westen nichts Neues*,
was translated by Arthur Wesley
Wheen in 1929, and retitled *All Quiet
on the Western Front*.

Threats of pain and ruin to despise ·
Thomas Gray, *Elegy Written in a
Country Churchyard*, 1750–1.

Cool side of the pillow · In German:
Kissenkühlelabsal.

3. WEDNESDAY

200/1 · It seems only fair to quote the
sportswriter 'Larry Lynx' of *The People*
who wrote in 1935: 'I dare say an owner
could win £25,000 on a horse if he laid
himself out for a coup, but I very much
doubt whether he could win £60,000,

while any such sum as £200,000 is a
dream that novelists can put up to their
readers, because those who know the
inner workings of the Turf condescend
to grant them "poet's licence".' [Arthur
J. Sarl, *Horses, Jockeys, and Crooks*
(Hutchinson, 1935), p. 232.]

Good as gold with this · All of the
horses mentioned in the book (save for
the fictional Gawking Girl) were
owned by Queen Elizabeth the Queen
Mother and trained by Peter Cazalet,
who, in 1932, married Plum's daughter,
Leonora. Racing aficionados will, I
hope, forgive any liberties I have taken
with the Sport of Kings.

Purveyor of fish and chips · This dubious establishment was inspired by a
notorious Southampton fish-and-chip
gambling front which, in the 1940s and
'50s, was known as 'the shop for a win
or a plaice'. [Mark Clapson, *A Bit of a
Flutter: Popular Gambling and English
Society, c.1823–1961* (Manchester University Press, 1992), p. 54.]

Masonic knock · This knock is variously
described, but the pattern Boko uses is
'Dorbie's Knock', which, in Morse code,
would be (· · – – – ·). [John Farmer &
William Henley, *Slang and Its Analogues
Past and Present*, vol. 2 (Printed for
Subscribers Only, 1891), p. 310.]

Double elephant · Although specifica-
tions vary, such sheets usually measured
around 27 by 40 inches.

Apple Scrumping · The scooter helmet
is tipped to Pete Townshend. Also for:
Eau de Cologning.

324

Punctual payment with a pleasant courtesy of words · This was, in fact, Leviathan Davis's actual motto, though it seems unlikely he ever had it needle-pointed. [Louis Henry Curzon, *A Mirror of The Turf* (Chapman & Hall, 1892), p. 232.]

Tricks of the trade · This classic railway con is neatly described by Charles George Gordon in *Crooks of the Underworld* (Geoffrey Bles, 1929), pp. 230–1.

The Nuer · Any similarities between Professor Evelyn Evan-Evans and Sir Edward Evan Evans-Pritchard are entirely coincidental.

Rooftop panorama · Younger readers may be wondering how Bertie could see the University Library from Gonville & Caius; the answer is that the current library on West Road (designed by Giles Gilbert Scott) only opened in 1934. Prior to that, the U.L. was housed in the Cockerell Building (now the Caius library), which can indeed by seen from N Staircase.

Anglepoise · The car designer George Carwardine invented the elegant and revolutionary Model 1208 prototype Anglepoise lamp in 1932.

Night Climbing · Much of the technical description of Cambridge roof climbing is drawn from two classic texts on the subject.

The first, *The Roof-Climber's Guide to Trinity*, was written anonymously 'as a May Week joke' in 1899 by Geoffrey **Winthrop Young** (1876–1958).[1] Winthrop Young was a good egg. An educationalist, author, humanitarian, and war hero (he lost his left leg in the 1917 Battle of Monte San Gabriele), his twin passions were mountain climbing and poetry – which he combined in elegiac works such as *A Rock Called Le Père Eternal*. The *Dictionary of National Biography* calls him 'one of the most famous British mountaineers before the First World War'.[2]

The second text, *The Night Climbers of Cambridge*, was written under the pseudonym '**Whipplesnaith**' in 1937, by Noël H. Symington (d.1970).[3] Symington was a bad egg. Born into a powdered-soup fortune (Robert Falcon Scott took 'Symington's Pea Flour' to the Antarctic), Noël studied at King's before becoming a gentleman-farmer and ungentlemanly follower of Oswald Mosley. In 1958, Symington launched his own pathetic squib of a Fascist party on the steps of Northampton Guild Hall, to an apathetic assembly of 'curious bystanders' and 'plain-clothes detectives'.[4]

One of the odder aspects of both these texts is their contemporary relevance: because most of the buildings they described were (and are) protected, many of the climbs have not changed significantly since publication.

[1. Geoffrey Winthrop Young, *The Roof-Climber's Guide to Trinity* (Omnibus Edition) (The Oleander Press, 2013); 2. See, for example, Alan Hankinson, *Geoffrey Winthrop Young: Poet, Educator, Mountaineer* (Hodder & Stoughton, 1995); 3. 'Whipplesnaith' (Noël H. Symington), *The Night Climbers of Cambridge* (1937) (Oleander Press, 2013); 4. 'Noël H. Symington', *The Times*, 21 October 1958, p. 11.]

Austrian accent · 'Witnesses differ about exactly how good Wittgenstein's spoken English was. No doubt it varied with date and circumstances. Occasionally, it is clear, a German idiom would betray him, but the accent is generally agreed to have been good. Those with whom he was most relaxed tend to say he had no foreign accent whatsoever.' [Brian McGuinness, *Wittgenstein, A Life: Young Ludwig, 1889–1921* (University of California Press, 1988), p. 65.]

Birthday cake · On 17 October 1934, Ludwig Wittgenstein wrote an impassioned letter to Trinity College's garden committee (complete with diagrams) complaining about the planting, layout, and upkeep of the Fellows' Garden: 'I believe the kidney shaped bed with the dahlias in it looks very bad because of the border of Veronica round the dahlias. This fringe makes it look like a gaudy birthday cake.' On the subject of paths through the rough grass, Wittgenstein felt that 'the garden is better without any such paths', though he suggests several layout improvements should paths 'be insisted upon'. [Ludwig Wittgenstein, 'Letter to the Garden Committee' (Trinity College, Cambridge, 1934).]

Blue notebook · For more on Wittgenstein's famous blue and brown books, see, for example, O. K. Bouwsma, 'The Blue Book', *The Journal of Philosophy*, vol. 58, no. 6 (16 March 1961), pp. 141–62.

Retriangulation · In 1935, the Ordnance Survey launched a 'Retriangulation of Great Britain' to create more accurate maps. It's more than likely that the

Junior Ganymede would have received advanced notification of such an undertaking. [See, for example, *The History of the Retriangulation of Great Britain, 1935–1962* (H.M. Stationery Office, 1967).]

Dr Wittgenstein · The Austrian-born philosopher and logician (1889–1951) spent much of his professional life at Trinity College, Cambridge; he was awarded a PhD in 1929, and a professorship in 1939 – hence Jeeves refers to him as 'Dr Wittgenstein'.

Der Struwwelpeter · The 1845 German children's classic by Heinrich Hoffmann, usually translated in English as *Shock-headed Peter*.

Wondered if there was a German word · There is: *Sofortkönner*.

Pevenhurst · A public school notorious for requiring its students to wear mortar boards with pink tassels; see *Very Good, Jeeves!* (1930).

Lungless salamanders · *Plethodontidae*.

It's not preordained · Gussie is *Potamogeton perfoliatus* – the clasping-leaf pondweed; Vonka is *Dionaea muscipula* – the Venus flytrap.

Blarney Stone · An awkward-to-access stone in the wall of Blarney Castle, north-west of Cork, Ireland, which, according to nineteenth-century myth, bestows the gift of persuasive eloquence on those who kiss it.

University Arms hotel · I have taken many liberties with the structure and

326

room-naming of Cambridge's oldest and most impressive hotel, which opened as a coaching inn in the 1840s, before being redeveloped in the 1930s and 1960s, and then extensively renovated and expanded in the 2010s by the classical architect John Simpson.

Perseus Suite · The only son of Zeus and Danaë, **Perseus** is one of Greek mythology's greatest heroes, renowned for slaying **Medusa**.

Hic ego aut omnino ... · 'I am confident that these things are either altogether false, or at any rate less serious than they are thought to be.' [William Windham Bradley, *Latin Exercises* (Longmans, 1855), pp. 148–9.]

Te Deum Patrem colimum · Bertie is struggling to remember the *Hymnus Eucharisticus*, which, for centuries, has been sung each May Day dawn from the tower of Magdalen College, Oxford. The first verse is: *Te Deum Patrem colimus / Te laudibus prosequimur / qui corpus cibo reficis / coelesti mentem gratia.*

One paraphrase runs: 'Thee, mighty Father, we adore / And praise thy Name for evermore; / Whose bounty feeds all Adam's race / And cheers the hungry soul with grace.' [William Jones, *The Works of the Right Reverend George Horne*, vol. 1 (H. M. Onderdonk, 1846), p. 89.]

The other Latin tags are loosely translated thus: **Ave atque vale** – *Hail and farewell*; **Timeo Danaos et dona ferentes** – *I fear the Greeks, even when they bear gifts*; **De gustibus non est disputandum** – *In matters of taste, there*

can be no dispute; **Ignorantia juris non excusat** – *Ignorance of the law is no excuse*; **Post hoc, ergo propter hoc** – *After this, therefore, because of this*; **Mens sana in corpore sano** – *A healthy mind in a healthy body*; **Cum grano salis** – *With a grain of salt*; **Panem et circenses** – *Bread and circuses*; **Vox populi, vox Dei** – *The voice of the people is the voice of God*; **Habemus papam** – *We have a pope*; **Apologia pro vita sua** – *A defence of one's life.*

Regent House · The governing body of Cambridge University, congregations of which are held in the Senate House.

Sent down immediately · Night climbing was actually prohibited in Trinity in 1901 after a Committee of Inquiry (onto which the real-life Geoffrey Winthrop Young was co-opted) tested many of the climbs in *The Roof-Climber's Guide* during the hours of daylight and found them, unsurprisingly, to be perilous. [See *The Roof-Climber's Guide to Trinity*, p. 77.]

Gating/Rustication · Defined respectively by the *Oxford English Dictionary* as: 'To confine (an undergraduate) to the precincts of the college, either entirely or after a certain hour'; and, 'Temporary dismissal from a university.'

Bishop of Norwich · It's unclear why, or when, 'Do you know the Bishop of Norwich?' became the accepted euphemism for dislodging a run-aground decanter of port. Various theories exist; none of them seems plausible (or amusing) enough to repeat.

Pitt Club · For more on this establishment, see, for example, Walter Morley Fletcher, *The University Pitt Club: 1835–1935* (Cambridge University Press, 1935).

Reciprocal from the Drones · The Pitt currently has a number of reciprocal arrangements; I have lent the Drones the reciprocity enjoyed by Buck's Club.

Hysteron Proteron · This bizarre club existed at Balliol College, Oxford, during the 1920s, and counted Graham Greene amongst its participants. As Evelyn Waugh wrote in his autobiography, 'members put themselves to great discomfort by living a day in reverse, getting up in evening dress, drinking whisky, smoking cigars and playing cards, then at ten o'clock dining backwards starting with savouries and ending with soup.' [Evelyn Waugh, *A Little Learning* (Methuen, 1983), p. 196.]

For more on the rhetorical trope (which Professor Hermann Menge decried as 'a blemish that should not be glossed over by calling it a figure of speech'), see Herbert C. Nutting, 'Hysteron Proteron', *The Classical Journal*, vol. 11, no. 5, 1916, pp. 298–301.

A nice usage of the term appears in Sir Roger L'Estrange's *A New Dialogue between Some Body and No Body, or The Observator Observed* (29 November 1681): 'Ay, Ay, all things are *arsa versa*, *topsie turvie*, *histeron*, *proteron* – The Chimes go backward, the World runs backward, the Age backslides, and all things turn backward.'

Helen Marion · Iona's alias is based on the celebrated philosopher and educationalist Helen Marion Wodehouse,

who, in addition to being Plum's cousin, was Mistress of Girton College, Cambridge, between 1931 and 1942.

4. THURSDAY

Repeated the phrase · The axe is tipped to Jack Torrance.

Madame Paladino · Eusapia Palladino (1854–1918) was an Italian 'séance medium' and gifted fraud. [See, for example, Hereward Carrington, *Eusapia Palladino and Her Phenomena* (B. W. Dodge & Co, 1909).]

Daredevil Bertie · See *The Code of the Woosters* (1938).

Madame Sosostris · Literature's most famous clairvoyante first appeared in Aldous Huxley's 1921 debut novel, *Crome Yellow* (in which Mr Scogan cross-dresses as 'Sesostris the Sorceress of Ecbatana'), but she achieved immortality in T. S. Eliot's 1922 epic, *The Waste Land*. [See, for example, Grover Smith, 'The Fortuneteller in Eliot's *Waste Land*', *American Literature*, vol. 25, no. 4 (January 1954), pp. 490–2.]

Cross my palm with silver · This fortune-telling catchphrase dates at least to the 1830s.

Knock once · The idea that 'spirits' might 'knock once for "Yes", and twice for "No"' dates back to at least the 1860s.

Alexander the Orbuculum Seer · The actual poster was for 'Alexander the

328

Crystal Seer', which promoted the American magician Claude Alexander Conlin (1880–1954).

Never seen such a Mount of Venus · Evadne Pinke's impressive chiromantical knowledge owes everything to William Brisbane Dick, *Dick's Mysteries of the Hand, Or, Palmistry Made Easy*, (Dick & Fitzgerald, 1884).

Band still attached · The kind of cad who'd smoke a cigar with its band still attached is very much the kind of cad who'd wear a trilby in town before Goodwood.

Punch elegantly satirised the cigar-wrapper issue: 'USEFUL ECONOMIES: A good device is carefully to preserve the paper bands – or "waistcoats" as a funny friend of mine insists on calling them – of really first-rate cigars and then transfer them to weeds of inferior calibre. My firm impression is that in these matters imagination goes a long way, and that if you give a man a two-penny Borneo wrapped in silver paper, with the waistcoat of an Absolute Flora, he will discover in it all the fine qualities of a half-crown cigar.' [*Punch*, 9 March 1904, p.178.]

Wagger-pagger-bagger · Oxford University slang for 'waste-paper basket '. According to the O.E.D., the tradition of facetiously suffixing words with '-er' originated at Rugby School and was introduced into Oxford in the Michaelmas term of 1875. Other examples include *footer* (football), *rugger* (rugby), *brekker* (breakfast), *lekker* (lecture), *ecker* (exercise), *Wagger* (warden), *Ugger* (the Union), *stragger* (stranger), *sensagger* (sensation) and, preposterously, *Pragger-Wagger* (the Prince of Wales).

Consommé royale à la Bowes-Lyon · Elizabeth Angela Marguerite Bowes-Lyon (The Queen Mother) was a keen fan of the aperitif Dubonnet, as one of her former equerries disclosed: 'She would have her first drink at noon, which would be a gin and Dubonnet – two parts Dubonnet to one part gin, a pretty potent mix. She rarely went a day without having at least one of these and getting the mix right was crucial. For official engagements, I would go ahead to the venue a few days before and instruct the waiting staff on the correct way to put the drink together. On occasion, I would have to take a bottle of Dubonnet along with me. It is not a standard drink these days.' [Major Colin Burgess, *Behind Palace Doors – My Service as the Queen Mother's Equerry* (Kings Road Publishing, 2007), eBook.]

I once stole a policeman's helmet · Spode committed this crime ('an uncontrollable impulse') while at Oxford. See *The Code of the Woosters* (1938).

Bertie Bassett · The corporate mascot of (and fabricated from) Bassett's Liquorice Allsorts was introduced in 1929. Folklore has it that the jumble of liquorice shapes originated when a salesman muddled his display tray in *c*.1899. [Kathy Martin, *Famous Brand Names and Their Origins* (Pen & Sword, 2016), p.43.]

Lord Sidcup is debating at the Cambridge Union · Sir Oswald Mosely, founder of the British Union of Fascists, on whom Sir Roderick Spode was clearly modelled, spoke at the Cambridge Union on 21 February 1933, debating against Clement Attlee on the motion: 'That this House prefers Fascism to Socialism'. According to *The Times*, Mosley 'said that Italian Fascism had little in common with British Fascism. It must not be thought that they took their orders from Rome, even if the Socialists took their orders from Moscow. He gave his personal word that Fascism had advanced more rapidly in Britain in the time at its disposal than any other Fascist movement in the world.' In opposing the motion, Atlee 'said that Fascism rejected democracy; it depended on the power of some "spellbinder" – Mussolini, Hitler, Mosley. If they hitched their wagon to such a star it should at least be a fixed star, not one that twinkled, sometimes red and sometimes blue, but always with an undercurrent of green.' Fascism lost the vote by 335 votes to 218. ['Cambridge Union', *The Times*, 22 February 1933, p. 12.]

Nasty in the woodshed · See Stella Gibbons, *Cold Comfort Farm* (Longman, 1932).

5. FRIDAY

Pheasant season · In England, between 1 October and 1 February.

Failing to abate a smoky chimney · One of Plum's favourite crimes, this contravention (I assume) of the 1853 Smoke Nuisance (Metropolis) Act appears in a slew of his stories.

Alfred Duff Cooper · Bertie borrows this pseudonym from Gussie Fink-Nottle, who supplied it to the police court after being nabbed for 'wading in the Trafalgar Square fountain at five ack emma'. It is (presumably) a reference to the first Viscount Norwich (1890–1954), who was a well-known politician, diplomat, writer, and diarist. [P. G. Wodehouse, *The Mating Season* (H. Jenkins, 1949), p. 35.]

23 Leinster Gardens · One of London's most famous 'fake' addresses, this Bayswater building (along with No. 24) is a merely a five-foot-deep brick frontage constructed in the 1860s to conceal a venting area of the Metropolitan Railway. [See, for example, *The Railway Gazette*, vol. 103, 1955, p. 531.]

Constable Dockery · The slouch-brimmed hat is tipped to Philip **Larkin**. See also, **Inspector Whitsun**.

Two Tars · Laurel and Hardy's 1928 silent short, produced by Hal Roach and directed by James Parrott.

The Dover Road · A 1921 three-act comedy written (coincidentally) by A. A. Milne.

A. D. C. · The theatre owned by the Cambridge University Amateur Dramatic Club.

Flash and Circle · The flag of Mosley's British Union of Fascists showed a white bolt of lightning in a blue circle, set against a red background. It 'represented the flash of action in the circle of unity ... it was similar to the Nazi emblem with the white flash substituted for the black swastika'. The anti-Fascists called it the 'flash in the pan'. [Robert Benewick, *Political Violence and Public Order: a Study of British Fascism* (Allen Lane, 1969), p. 139.]

Rossi–Forel · See, for example, William Herbert Hobbs, *Earthquakes: An Introduction to Seismic Geology* (D. Appleton, 1907), pp. 312–13.

Mabel Chitt · We are introduced to Mabel in *The Inimitable Jeeves* (1923), where both Bingo Little *and* Reginald Jeeves fall for her charms during a subscription dance in Camberwell. I have transferred Mabel's serving skills from 'one of those blighted tea-and-bun shops' located 'about fifty yards east of the Ritz' to the University Arms hotel, and given her the surname Chitt.

Daily dozen · Plum swore by an exercise regime called 'The Daily Dozen' devised by Walter Camp, which he saw in *Collier's* magazine in July 1920. 'I have been doing them for a month and they are simply terrific,' he wrote to a friend, 'they really are the most marvellous things. You get out of bed feeling a wreck, and you do these exercises and feel as if you were in training for the Olympic Games.' [*A Life in Letters*, p. 129.]

Aunt Emma · See Arthur Lillie, ed., *Croquet up to Date* (Longmans & Co., 1900).

Crinoline croquet · See Arthur Lillie, *Croquet: Its History, Rules, and Secrets* (Longmans, Green, & Co., 1897).

Tight croquet · For more on this engrossing topic, see 'Cavendish', 'The Science of Croquet', *The Gentleman's Magazine*, vol. 1 (Bradbury, Evans, & Co., 1868), p. 235.

Pavement Club · This bizarre Cambridge society did indeed exist, although about a decade before Bertie would have encountered it: 'With the laudable purpose of lending "verisimilitude to the rapidly disappearing illusion that university life is a life of leisure," undergraduates at Cambridge University have organised the "Pavement Club". The Club meets at noon every Saturday, if the weather is fair, upon any centrally situated pavement where the members sit in quiet conversation, perhaps reading newspapers aloud, playing marbles, doing a little knitting, or whiling away the hours by similar expedients which present themselves readily enough to the fertile undergraduate brain. So great was the rush to join the first meeting of the Club, held on King's Parade, Cambridge, that the "premises" of the Club had to be extended from the pavement to the road, and traffic diverted to another street.' [*The Living Age*, vol. 309, April–June 1921, p. 681.]

Mr Reyes-Guerra · Dr Antonio Reyes-Guerra was, during Bertie's time at Oxford, El Salvador's *chargé d'affaires* and consul general in London.

331

Ernald · Plum seems not to have given Spode a middle name, so I have lent him Oswald Mosley's.

Have a jelly · This attack is inspired by another of Oswald Mosley's visits to the Cambridge Union, when, on 24 April 1960, his speech to the Cambridge University Conservative Association was interrupted by a jelly-hurling undergraduate. [See *The Times*, 25 April 1960, p. 7.] The cry of 'Have a jelly, my friend!' was reported to me by a friend who witnessed the assault.

Peers may be immune from civil arrest · See, for example, Francis Beaufort Palmer, *Peerage Law in England* (Stevens & Sons, 1907).

As goons go · The toque is tipped to Saki's cook.

Black Maria · Originally American slang for a van used to transport prisoners, by the 1920s the term was in British usage.

Transitio ad plebem · *Transition to the people* · A (little-understood) legal process of Ancient Rome by which a patrician could become a plebeian. [See, for example, W. Jeffrey Tatum, *The Patrician Tribune* (University of North Carolina, 1999).]

Loving Cup · The choreography of this ceremony varies; the Hysteron Proteron uses the same sequence as the Shakespeare Society of Gonville & Caius. Of course, the *real* trick of the Loving Cup is to drink not a drop.

Black Velvet · Equal parts Guinness and champagne – poured in that order to avoid excessive effervescence.

Small glass vial · The 'hay-fever' medication Lord Pallot added to the Loving Cup is an amphetamine, the chemistry of which was just being developed at the time. [See, for example, Harry V. Byrne, 'The Use of Benzyl-Methyl-Carbinamine-Carbonate in the Treatment of Rhinitis', *New England Journal of Medicine*, 1933; 209:1048–51.]

On 25 November 1947, the socialite parliamentarian 'Chips' Channon wrote in his diaries: 'I "laced" the cocktails with Benzedrine, which I find always makes a party go.' [Henry Channon, *Chips: The Diaries of Sir Henry Channon* (Weidenfeld & Nicolson, 1967), p. 419.]

Possession of amphetamines was legal in Britain until the Drugs (Prevention of Misuse Act) 1964.

6. SATURDAY

Expert on thirst · See, for example, James T. Fitzsimons, *The Physiology of Thirst and Sodium Appetite* (Cambridge University Press, 1979).

Medusa Suite · In Greek mythology, **Medusa** was a snake-haired raven who turned to stone any who gazed upon her; **Phorcys** was a sea god; **Tethys** a goddess of fresh water; and **Echidna** a half-woman, half-snake monster.

Defy G.M.T. · King Edward VII introduced 'Sandringham Time' (G.M.T. +

332

30 minutes) to '[take] time by the fore-lock' and extend the daylight available for shooting at Sandringham House. The tradition seems to have died with George V. [See, for example, Marguerite Cunliffe-Owen, *Within Royal Palaces* (Enterprise Publishing Co., 1892), p. 150.]

Prussian-blue tea-gown · The ladies of Tilling thrilled to tea-gowns of crimson-lake and kingfisher-blue. [See E. F. Benson, *Miss Mapp* (Hutchinson & Co., 1922).]

Tea leaves · See Cicely Kent, *Telling Fortunes by Tea Leaves* (Dodd, Mead, & Co., 1922).

Newmarket racecourse · Readers familiar with this course will forgive the liberties I have taken with its topography. Readers familiar with racing will forgive the liberties I have taken with its rules.

Triple dead heat · This race is loosely based on the Cesarewitch Handicap, which has been an October fixture at Newmarket since 1839. Jeeves is correct in his recollection of a triple dead heat in 1857.

Reclining in a deckchair · Wittgenstein seems to have favoured deckchairs, as the philosopher Wolfe Mays recalled: 'During his lectures he sat by the stove in a deckchair, sometimes warming a hand near it ... There was a pile of deckchairs outside the room, and you took one in with you on entering, seating yourself a respectful distance from Wittgenstein'.

Incidentally, Sir Henry Desmond Lee recalled: '[Wittgenstein] read very little, or said he did. And what he did read was read largely for relaxation. I think he used to read detective stories: he certainly read P. G. Wodehouse, and I remember an argument about whether the Bishop who took Mulliner's Buck-U-Uppo painted the statue blue or green.' (It was actually painted pink.) [*Portraits of Wittgenstein: Abridged Edition*, ed. F. A. Flowers III & Ian Ground (Bloomsbury Academic, 2018), pp. 337, 179.]

Whistling softly · As J. R. Henderson recalled: 'Wittgenstein did not play a musical instrument, but he was a virtuoso whistler; [Roy] Fouracre recalls how he could whistle whole movements of symphonies, his show piece being the Brahms *St Anthony Variations*.' [*Portraits of Wittgenstein*, p. 356.]

Bobbing a balloon · For more on this, see Ian Lemco, 'Wittgenstein's Aeronautical Investigation', *Notes and Records of the Royal Society of London*, vol. 61, no. 1 (22 January 2007), pp. 39–51.

In order to know an object · All of Ludwig's dialogue in this scene is quoted verbatim from Ludwig Wittgenstein, *Tractatus Logico-Philosophicus* (Harcourt Brace, 1922).

Lord Byron · 'As an undergraduate [Lord Byron] not only accomplished the apparently impossible feat of climbing by night to the roof [of Trinity College Library] ... but abominably disfigured the statues upon it.' [Edward Conybeare, *Highways and Byways in Cambridge and Ely* (Macmillan, 1923), p. 90.]

Like a clown · The fedora is tipped to Joe Pesci, Nicholas Pileggi, and Martin Scorsese.

About this leap · Both the width of the gap between the Senate House and Gonville & Caius, and its height above ground, are disputed. The former (which varies depending on one's position and angle) I estimated myself. The latter is taken from an essay in the Caius alumni magazine, which explores the audacious 1958 prank when a dozen engineering students manoeuvred an Austin Seven car onto the Senate House roof. [*Once a Caian*, issue 2, September 2005, pp. 8–11.]

Gaze long into the abyss · Uncharacteristically, Jeeves is quoting Nietzsche. [*The Complete Works of Friedrich Nietzsche: Beyond Good and Evil*, trans. Helen Zimmern (T. N. Foulis, 1914), p. 97.]

Say prunes! · This forerunner of 'say cheese' was thought to give the photographic subject a dignified pout. [See *British Journal of Photography*, vol. 82, 1935, p. 384.] According to James Joyce: 'Say prunes and prisms forty times every morning, cure for fat lips.' [James Joyce, *Ulysses* (Shakespeare & Co., 1922), p. 354.]

Overlapping grip · 'I am told that I have acquired a reputation for laying down a kind of dogma, that nobody can hope to excel at golf unless he adopts the overlapping grip. I really do not deserve such distinction, because, while I am convinced that the grip mentioned is the best, it has never occurred to me to tell anybody that it is the only proper method.' [Harry Vardon, *The Gist of Golf* (George H. Doran, 1922), p.15.]

Below sixteen · Bertie's golfing handicap, mentioned in the 1930 short story 'Jeeves and the Kid Clementina', seems to reflect Plum's own, assuming we are to take seriously his 1926 quip: 'Playing to a handicap of sixteen ... I went through a field consisting of some of the fattest retired business-men in America like a devouring flame.' [*The Heart of a Goof*, viii.]

7. SUNDAY

And I'm Reverend Wooster · The hat is tipped to Dutch Gunderson and Frank Drebin, as well as David Zucker, Jim Abrahams, and Jerry Zucker.

Flying a false flag · 'Ruses are customarily allowed in sea warfare within the same limits as in land warfare, perfidy being excluded. As regards the use of a false flag, it is by most publicists considered perfectly lawful for a man-of-war to use a neutral's or the enemy's flag (1) when chasing an enemy vessel, (2) when trying to escape, and (3) for the purpose of drawing an enemy vessel into action. On the other hand, it is universally agreed that immediately before an attack a vessel must fly her national flag.' [Lassa Oppenheim, *International Law: A Treatise*, vol. 2 (Longmans, Green, & Co. 1921), pp. 291–2.]

Sabbath Stick · 'It is said, with what truth we know not, that at St Andrews on Sunday the good folk who have been to church in the forenoon walk out over the links in the afternoon with their walking-sticks in their hands, and when they have reached a remote corner of the links they pull surreptitious golf-balls out of their pockets, and indulge in a quiet game, out of sight and mind of the authorities'. ['Scotia', 'Golf', *Time*, vol. 4, 1886, p. 469.]

Llanabba · It's likely that Crawshaw is referring to Philbrick, the butler at Llanabba Castle. [See Evelyn Waugh, *Decline and Fall* (Chapman & Hall, 1928).]

Boot-Finding · This was indeed a tradition of London's Spitalfields Market; my description quotes details from the account in Arthur M. Binstead's *A Pink 'Un and a Pelican* (Bliss Sands & Co., 1898), pp. 243–4.

When the ball comes loose · In this regard, at least, Piebald has much in common with The Rt Hon Boris Johnson M.P.

Friction is greatest · Jeeves was presumably alluding to Charles-Augustin de Coulomb's work on impediments to motion. [See, for example, *First Principles of Physics*, Benjamin Silliman (H. C. Peck & T. Bliss, 1859), p. 148.]

Egg-and-matchbox trick · Cousin Thos. may be attempting the gag later made famous by man-of-letters Keith Waterhouse, and described in his obituary: 'It involved borrowing from the [pub] management a biscuit tin lid, a pint pot of water, the sleeve from a box of matches and a raw egg. When he had the full attention of the right gathering of like-minded drinkers, the tin lid would be placed on top of the glass of water, the matchbox sleeve on top of the lid and the egg in the open end of the matchbox. The trick was to strike the edge of the tin lid with a shoe. The lid would then fly away, having caught the matchbox on its edge, the matchbox would topple over and deposit the intact egg in the pint of water – sometimes. Other times, the premises would be coated with raw egg.' [Mike Molloy, 'Keith Waterhouse', *The Guardian*, 5 September 2009.]

Amicus meus ... inimicus inimici mei · Commonly translated as, 'My friend, the enemy of my enemy'.

Book launch in London · Alfred Duff Cooper's diaries lapsed between 1926 and 1933, so it's unclear exactly what he was up to on the night of Bertie's arrest. However, on 3 October 1932, his long-awaited biography *Tallyrand* was published, and so I've thrown him a book party. [*The Duff Cooper Diaries*, ed. John Julius Norwich (Phoenix, 2006), pp. 219–20.]

Wigs and haberdashery · The syrup is tipped to David Croft and Ronnie Hazlehurst.

Across:
DECORATOR, MEDAL, ONEOVER, PLUMMET, EXCEL, ARTLESSON, SODOI, ORACLE, NICTATE, AGEAGO, PFFFT, LIEU, FATHEADED, GAUZE, UPTOPAR, INASPOT, TIDAL, IGOTTASAY